A FORGED HEARTS NOVEL

TWISTED TIDES

L. RENÉE RICHARD

Cover Design by: Designs By Charly
https://www.designsbycharlyy.com/

Interior Formatting by: Designs By Charly
https://www.designsbycharlyy.com/

Editing by: Editing Done Write
https://www.editingdonewrite.com/

Evie's story-
He stole their past. They'll reclaim their future.

Twisted Tides
Book 2 of the Forged Hearts Novel
Three of the hardest things I have ever had to do:
Not being able to protect my family from Julian.
Breaking a promise to my sister.
Pretending I was dead.

The tides turned the day Julian took everything from us.

My only regret is that I wasn't able to save my parents. My sister thinks I died in that fire, but it was necessary to save her life.
My heart twisted, grieving at seeing her alone and at his mercy. I've been watching from afar, waiting and biding my time. All of the secrets and twisted lies will come to light.
The element of surprise will be his demise. But exacting revenge doesn't come without consequences. Now it's time to finish this war we've started.
Now, reunited with my sister and our families, how far will we go to win it all?

TWISTED TIDES
SPOTIFY PLAYLIST

https://open.spotify.com/
playlist/6ed0YlTvIf0q5Q6REVCy8l?si=c036f35f9cc246c5

CONTENT WARNING

This book, the conclusion of the Forged Hearts Series, contains dark themes and is intended for readers over eighteen. Profanity, assault, violence, and other topics may be triggering to sensitive readers. Please check my website, L. Renée Richard, for more details and a complete list of trigger warnings, further information, or updates if there are any concerns about your mental health. Your well-being is my utmost concern, so please proceed with caution.

PREVIOUSLY...

He saw me. He had me. But he won't break me.

What should have been the beginning of my life felt more like a death sentence–an all-encompassing blackness.

Evie, my twin sister and best friend, is no longer here. Now alone, I've become as dark as the man who tries to imprison me. Julian.

He thinks he is all I have left in this world.

His to toy with.

To manipulate.

To fear.

But that woman died along with her family that night, and a stronger woman rose from those battered waves, breathing in a newfound purpose– to take revenge and reclaim my life.

I am waiting on a black wave, biding my time, until a powerful wave rises in the aftermath of a storm, leaving unexpected casualties in its wake, ensuring once again that I will be free.

PROLOGUE

Emma sits tied to a chair. Her hands are restrained while Julian presides above her. A maniacal look in his eye shows the depravity residing in his soul, ready to unleash his fury at any further attempt to take his prized possession from him.

Emma thinks her time has run out, but I've been watching from afar, waiting and biding my time. My heart twisted, grieving at seeing her alone and at his mercy, unable to intervene all this time.

My sister thinks I died in that fire, but it was necessary to save her life. I was so close to her that night as I watched our life as we once knew it go up in flames. Julian had carried her away and placed her unconscious body into an SUV. Now, all of our family secrets and twisted lies will come to light.

Despite Emma hiding from Julian with the protection of our Uncle Andrés, Cousin Adrian, and Eduardo, Julian has managed to locate her. No amount of skillful planning could have prepared her for this exact situation.

Eduardo has been the best at keeping her safe until now, but it was always going to come to this. I hope that he doesn't blame himself, but it's obvious by the anguish on his face that he's waging an internal war, which excites Julian, who wears a sadistic smile. Eduardo's need to keep her safe, concurrent with feeling helpless and having no weapon to use against Julian, could be a recipe for disaster, but it was unavoidable, and now they all think it's over.

This moment is the pivotal point in our family's story. The defining moment when everything you hold dear is tested, and you can only hope to walk away with no more casualties—your body, mind, and soul intact.

I can sense her emotions. I have always been able to, and now, in this moment, it's increased exponentially. Emma feels if she is gone, she won't be a burden to anyone any longer. Eduardo might be sad for a while, but eventually, he will move on and have the chance to be happy.

She'd rather die than see him hurt, but doesn't she realize that there will be no getting over her? She is the light in our crazy darkness—our beacon of hope in a storm that wages destruction on our family.

We would do anything for her.

Who knew that it would be Cherry, that crazy bitch, to hand her over to Julian, thinking that once Emma was gone, they could be together. Julian has found her, and now it's over. She sits, restrained to a chair, entirely at his mercy, and Cherry lies dead on the cold cement floor.

Unfortunately, Julian has no merciful tendencies.

Emma spares a glance at Cherry. Her vacant stare is fixed on something she no longer sees. Blood speckles Cherry's face from her final breath. Now, her lifeless body, slowly growing cold, is lying in a pool of her own blood, showing how quickly we can be taken from this world.

A shudder runs through Emma as she tries to control her emotions and refrain from showing Julian weakness. I bet she wonders if she will have the same fate.

"I think this has gone on long enough, Emma, don't you? Why don't you tell Eduardo who you really love!" Julian bellows triumphantly, his voice echoing in the ample, empty space of the warehouse. He's delusional.

Eduardo makes a final attempt to get to Emma, but Julian already has his weapon pointed at my sister. He tsks as he kicks their firearms from their reach. Eduardo pales, shaking as he restrains himself from lunging toward Emma.

No, she is strong. I can't help but smile as she rolls her shoulders back, preparing to face her death head-on. She accepts her fate. She closes her eyes, and that's when I know this has gone on long enough.

This moment changes everything. I can't control much, but I can manage this.

I nod, willing this exchange to be over. Mateo catches on. His weapon is ready to fire at the right moment.

Mateo is by my side, as he has always been these days. I can't say that I don't have regrets in my life. Seeing her this way almost breaks the protective barriers around my heart, which have been carefully crafted into place throughout the years. I can never make amends for all the lives lost at our expense. I can see the same thoughts reflect on her face. However, I can try to punish those who hurt us and continue to be a threat to us.

Julian waits for her reply, getting angrier by the second at her continued silence. I narrow my eyes at his demand. She opens her jade-green eyes that match my own and stares at him sans emotion.

Emma juts her chin out at him in a last attempt at defiance. I smile, knowing she is still brave, despite the circumstances. Emma will make him wait a long time if he seriously thinks she will ever say those words to him.

She refocuses her gaze at Eduardo one last time. I bear witness to what she believes are her final words to him as she mouths, *'I love you always.'*

My smile widens. *Yes, that's my girl.* I internally fist pump the air. I can't help but be proud. A final 'FU' to the man who made her life miserable for months.

Julian's face contorts in rage as he lifts his gun and points it right at her. She can no longer look at Eduardo and see his sadness looking back at her with tears in his eyes. She finally closes her eyes one last time.

I see her smile and imagine she is thinking of all the time spent with our family in Mexico. All the times she spent with Eduardo under the stars. The time he gave her the necklace. When he proposed and worshiped her body.

And it's the exact moment she accepts her death.

"Good-bye, Emma," I hear Julian say.

Eduardo screams, "No!"

I hear the gun fire, and then...

CHAPTER ONE

EVIE

"BODIES" BY DROWNING POOL

A loud *'thud'* echoes through the open room. I step out of the shadows that have been my home, shielding me from the living. Upon hearing the noise, Emma opens her eyes to see Julian on the floor beside her. Her eyes widen in shock as Eduardo runs over to her, and Jameson, their friend, looks over at me with his mouth hanging open as if he is seeing a ghost. I stare back at him, gauging his intentions before shifting my vision to my sister.

"Oh, my Emma." Eduardo kisses her over and over. With a firm hold, he lifts her out of the chair and into his arms. Eduardo pushes her away from him to assess her for injuries as he rubs Emma's arms up and down, then he pulls her close against his body just as quickly, holding her tight as if she'll be abducted again.

I see her follow Jameson's line of sight, and if Eduardo wasn't holding on to her, she'd probably pass out. Jameson hasn't stopped staring at me, and I can feel him willing me to return his stare. Instead, I need to focus on what's important right now—my sister.

I walk over to her with a smile that matches hers. I can see her take in the physical changes to my appearance: my hair is cut short and slicked back, but it's still me—Evie, her twin sister.

"She's alive," Emma sobs, and Eduardo holds her up, equally as shocked.

"You're alive?" he asks somewhat rhetorically. He looks over and shakes his head. "You were always one for dramatics, Evie."

"Good to see you too, future brother-in-law." I chuckle and hug Eduardo, and then Emma grabs on to me, almost pulling me down with the unexpected sheer weight of her body as she clings to me as if I will suddenly disappear into thin air, like a ghost. She wouldn't be wrong. That's what I have been all this time.

"Sis, I've missed you so much." I hold on to her. She hugs me, and we begin to cry. I can't help the emotion that comes over me. I've held it in for so long that it now pours out against my will.

Her body shakes, wracked in sobs, but it sounds odd because we are also laughing.

"I suppose these are what you call tears of happiness." I laugh as we rock back and forth in a tight embrace.

"Yes," she laughs. "I swear, sometimes I don't understand us, Eves."

Eduardo shakes his head, leaving us to chat. He walks over to Jameson, who is staring at me. "Close your mouth, James. You're drooling on the floor. It's not a good look."

From what I can tell, Jameson doesn't respond.

I wonder if he recognizes me. He must. I turn my head back to watch the exchange. Continuing to stare, Jameson goes to say something but stops.

"That's Emma's twin sister, huh?" he asks.

I curl my lip up in a half-smirk.

"Boy, you're a fast learner, aren't you?" Eduardo mocks. He slaps Jameson on the shoulder.

"Fuck off. She's hot. I think I'm in love."

I smile full-on now, conveying with my eyes what's to come.

Jameson scrubs his hands repeatedly over his face as if trying to wake himself from a dream.

Still holding on to my sister, I bring her around to give my full attention to Jameson. I give him my signature pouty, red-lipped smile. "Sorry, I missed our date by the way."

Jameson's mouth opens then closes. I smile wickedly, and then I see the moment it clicks. His sight is firmly set on my lips. "That was you. It's always been you."

I nod once. Our stare-off is interrupted when Philip walks in.

Eli groans.

"What the fuck? Is everybody coming back from the dead?" Eduardo shakes his head in disbelief, dropping it in defeat.

"Too soon?" Eli says, and Eduardo snorts.

"Yeah, a bit, but I get it. It's ironic as fuck." Eduardo walks over to Emma and me, hooking his arm around my sister and bringing her in for a side hug.

"I'm just glad that it's all over," Eduardo says on an exhale as he kisses the top of Emma's head, increasing the tightness of his embrace as if he is afraid to let her go.

I smile as I watch them. Emma returns the smile and seems to understand my thoughts as twins sometimes do. She then looks up at her future husband.

"Oh, Eduardo, I have a feeling that this is just the beginning," she says, echoing similar words spoken to her not long ago.

"Fuck, I was hoping you wouldn't say that, Emma."

I wink at her. "That was one sweet chokehold release that you got out of, if I do say so myself, Emma." Her eyes go wide, and mine mimic my twin's expression.

"You saw that?" She jumps happily.

I nod and laugh. "Fucking epic, girlie. I guess you took my advice about the self-defense classes?"

Emma tosses her head back, laughing. "You could say that. So what now, Evie?"

I grab the back of my neck, wondering how to approach this topic. As if reading my mind, Mateo emerges from the shadows I stood in what seems like a lifetime ago.

"We have a lot to talk about." Mateo takes his place beside me as they look between us, and Jameson visibly winces. I'm reluctant to look away. The need to soothe and care for him overwhelms my senses. My hand twitches to reach for him.

Emma snorts, distracting me from the emotions I was almost ready to act on. "That's an understatement. I mean, what happens n-o-w?" She raises her hand above her head in an exaggerated motion that makes my heart weep at the familiarity. I stare at her with a look that promises to wreak havoc—the same look she would give me when we knew we would get into trouble.

I extend one of my black-gloved hands to Emma in an invitation, and she quickly takes it. "Well, Emma, now that you are free, tell me who you wanna be."

"Let's finish this, Evie."

I give her a nod, and that's all that is needed. I've waited for this moment, and the time is finally here. My body almost hums with the excitement of what's to come.

I grew up in a web of twisted lies, deception, and secrets. From a young age, I knew these truths were buried in our family. The hushed words that stopped altogether when I entered a room. My emotions rage beneath the surface, a swirling rise of battered waves against my black, vengeful beating heart.

My sister remains holding my hand; an unspoken solidarity thrums in our veins. I couldn't be happier at her newfound strength. She brings a sense of calm to my thunderous emotional turmoil, battling against my unruffled, carefully constructed exterior. These feelings always attempt to overtake me as I fight for control, which I need in all aspects of my life—what I eat, how I act, and how I fuck. It's the only way I know how to live now.

I look at Jameson with the need to release this pent-up anger and frustration. Who would have thought this handsome man would be precisely the person who could soothe my aching heart?

I refocus on my sister, nod once, and extend my hand toward Mateo. I don't look at anyone around us as he looks at Emma and smiles. He then extends his hand toward her. I hear Eduardo rush over to stand behind Emma.

Jameson mimics Eduardo's movements without realizing it, and I feel his warmth behind me. His body heat calms me, and my body leans closer without my permission. I take a few deep breaths to bring a meditative mind as my feelings attempt to surge out of control. Breathe the air in and blow it out. I can almost hear my therapist's voice as I count to ten the way she taught me all those years ago. Now, I have Jameson, my anchor in my sea of self-destruction.

Emma's eyes scan me assessingly, clearly not entirely understanding what is happening. I smile and nod reassuringly, silently conveying that it's okay—I'm okay with this. She trusts me explicitly and looks at Mateo, staring into his eyes—what some people call the portal into the soul—in an attempt to gain clarity. The moment it clicks, her expression softens and she takes his hand.

My family is now complete.

The short-lived moment of unity ends when I hear Eduardo growl behind Emma, staring at their joined hands. We all burst out laughing, breaking the gravity of the situation, and Mateo can't help but join in. Eduardo is so ridiculous when it comes to Emma.

"God, can you calm down? We are having a moment here. You know, even when we were younger, you had to help her off the ATV or out of the truck. No one else could even attempt to help her or you would go off on them. It was always so obvious, Eddie." I stomp my boot on the cement flooring, hearing the echo sound off.

He breaks his gaze from Emma, sparing me a glance. "You know I hate when you call me that, Evie." His voice is full of warning, but his face is dueling with putting up a show and embracing the familiarity of our beautiful memories when life was simpler. I'm sure that's partly why our parents acted the way they did, although their reasons were faulty.

Mateo steps toward Eduardo as he visibly stiffens in a protective stance around Emma. He extends his hand. "It's good to finally meet you. I'm Mateo, their brother."

I hear the words leave his mouth, and tears threaten to fall. He's never been able to say these words aloud or introduce himself as our brother. That was taken from him, this simple act of belonging.

Jameson places a hand on my hip, giving it a slight squeeze. To hear Mateo say this truth out loud... Well, let's just say that it is everything. One suppressed truth finally coming out. There are so many more left to go. I give a contemplative sigh.

I turn toward the sound of sniffles. Emma is already crying, and Eduardo looks at him in stunned silence. "I didn't know," he whispers. He drops his gaze to Mateo's hand and takes it quickly. "It's nice to finally meet you too, Mateo."

Mateo smiles at Emma and looks back at me. I nod, and Mateo releases Eduardo's hand and quickly pulls Emma into a tight embrace. They hold each other for what seems like minutes but is actually only probably seconds as Emma continues to hold on to him. Finally, she lets go, but not until she rubs her face against his shirt to wipe away her tears.

Mateo raises an eyebrow at her and then looks at his shirt. "Sis, did you just wipe your snot on my shirt?" His lips quirk up in amusement, and Eduardo scoffs.

"Get used to it. It's part of her charm." I can't help but snort, and we all burst out laughing. The noise is a welcome juxtaposition to what occurred only moments ago.

Jameson presses his chest against my back, wrapping his arms around me from behind. His warm breath lands on my neck, and I shudder at his proximity.

"You have a lot of explaining to do, Eve." I chuckle at his name for me. I once told him I was Eve, man's downfall from the Garden of Eden. It was one of our first conversations that night at the club when he asked my name before we parted ways, wanting to know if he could see me again. I gave him the only truth I could at that time. It wasn't far off from my real name then, and that's all I could do.

I didn't think that one night would turn out to be so much more.

"I agree. I do." That's all I can say to Jameson now, as I know that conversation is one I need to have alone with him. Now is not the time.

I glance at my sister and see her acutely aware of what transpires between Jameson and me. I finally point out the obvious. "As much as I'd really like to sing campfire songs and do some face painting right now, I think that we should probably get out of here and get rid of these bodies." I point to the two bodies that are laid out on the cement floor, not getting any fresher.

Eduardo speaks up first. "I can make some calls." He reaches for his phone in his pocket, but I stop him.

"I have a plan. Can you get this place cleaned up, though, Eduardo? Mateo and I will dispose of the bodies. In fact, I have 'the perfect plan,' creating the catalyst to bring out the demons who have been hiding in the dark, into the light."

CHAPTER TWO

EVIE

"PSYCHO KILLER" BY TALKING HEADS

They all go to Eduardo's and Emma's house while Mateo and I load up the bodies and head to Brownsville. We will have to wait for nightfall to see the plan through, but how splendid it will be. What fireworks to see. I become giddy with anticipation at the thought of their reaction.

But before I get ahead of myself, we first need to get some sleep before we can set this black wave in motion, return to Houston, and explain where we've been all this time. Emma deserves to know what happened the night of the fire when our parents died, but somehow I survived. I also need to come clean to Jameson. All the twisted tides pulling us into an oceanic graveyard of the condemned and damned.

Eduardo phones a team to have the area at the warehouse scrubbed, and Jameson is working on security along with Eduardo's personal security team to ensure that the surveillance won't show us being at that location.

Fortunately for us, the warehouse did not have any cameras, and I suspect that's why Julian chose that specific location to hold Emma. Now, the fucker and Cherry are corpses in the back of our van.

I smile as I file my nails into little sharp points. Mateo glances over at me, and I feel his stare. My head whips up as I hold the file in one hand. His eyebrow quirks up.

"Are you feeling a little stabby, my twisted sister?"

I laugh and continue filing my nails. Feeling like I have gotten the perfect angled points, I throw it into my bag of mass destruction.

"Always, Mateo." I look out the window at the petroleum refineries twinkling their pretty lights out in the distance. Who would think that such environmental destruction, with toxic fumes spewing into the midnight sky, could create such a perversely beautiful scene?

The lights go by, and I watch them in the passenger side mirror until they vanish from sight.

The van's cabin is quiet—too quiet—so I decided to put on some tunes. I always hated the silence. The void needs to be filled, even with someone I love and I can be entirely myself. It's my mind that never shuts off that I need to block out. The intrusive thoughts that must be kept at bay make me wonder if I will ever feel peace.

I sigh. "What do you feel like listening to, Mateo? Perhaps some Taylor Swift to lighten the mood?" I say this in jest because Mateo is not a 'Swiffy' fan, although he thinks she is hot.

He laughs. "Let's try something else, huh, Evie?"

I pretend to think it over but get my phone out and scroll, searching for the perfect song that popped into my head.

"What did you pick?" he asks impatiently, sparing me a glance. He then looks at my phone as if he can tell in that second before he darts his sight back to the straight Texas highway road.

"So impatient, bro."

I hit play. Suddenly, the driving basslines of this classic tune float through the air, with the drums flowing shortly after.

Mateo laughs aloud, a full-belly laugh as he hits the steering wheel in beat with the bass riffs. "'Psycho Killer?' Perfect. This song is a banger, Evie."

"Right? Everyone secretly always roots for the bad guys." I spare a glance at the back of the van where two cold bodies are carefully concealed. "But what about us? Some killers aren't all bad."

We repeatedly sing the famous French phrases in the song, belting out the lyrics as we drive into the night.

We pull into a dilapidated motel that is sketchy as fuck. These rooms are definitely rented by the hour, judging by the sign that reads 'Rooms for a night or a lifetime.' It's missing a few letters.

Clothes hang strung over the second-floor balcony, and bicycles on the patio are thrown haphazardly, as if they aren't worth stealing. Paint peels from every surface.

This place is where dreams go to die.

I shudder thinking about the diseases that line every surface of the rooms and what's been done in them. I, for one, will be sleeping in all my clothes on top of the bed, thank you very much. I just hope it's cleaner than the supposedly washed sheets.

I inwardly cringe at the thought of bed bugs because I suspect I will have to burn my clothes after this. Mateo and I check into our room for a couple of hours of much-needed sleep. We just can't sleep at the same time. We don't want anyone to try to steal our van and discover some dead bodies.

I let Mateo sleep first, and he verbalizes no complaint. I take my e-book reader and finish my favorite dark romance hitchhiker novel.

I look up to find Mateo staring at me as I read the epilogue's last part. "Fucking cliffhangers. Ugh. The worst." I shut my e-reader, but not before downloading the next book in the series. I stretch and get up from the chair to take his place.

He places his hoodie over his head, pulling his arms through the sleeves and tugging it down. "I'm going to grab some coffee in the lobby. I'll be right back."

He leaves, but not before I tell him to hurry back. Of course, he knows this, but I can't help it. As soon as my head hits my arm on the bed, I fall into a deep sleep.

Finally, we arrive at the location Jameson told us to be at. They drove Cherry's conspicuous bright-red car over earlier and are already returning to Houston.

We transfer the bodies and strap them into the back seats with firmly locked seat belts in place. Their heads are duct-taped to hold them up.

I take a step back and look at my work. I bring my finger up to my chin in a pensive stare.

"What do you think, Mateo? Do they look okay?" I look over at him and find him looking at me with annoyance. "What?" What died up his ass?

"Evie, what does it fucking matter? We are going to set this motherfucking car on fire in a few minutes." He raises his hand, grabs his hair, tugging it upward, and walks around in a circle.

"Calm down, Mattie. Don't get your chonies in a bunch."

He stops me from speaking further with a raise of his hand. "Please do not refer to my underwear as 'chonies.' I'm not twelve."

I laugh at the Mexican slang word we use for men's underwear.

"I just want it to look good when they burn, okay? Is that too much to ask? Have you no pride in your work?" I place a hand on my hip for emphasis.

"Fine, just stop talking about my underwear. It's weird." He huffs.

"Fine. You got it. No chonies," I retort.

I close the door and drive off, exasperated with Mateo. In the rearview mirror, I see him trailing a short distance away in the van. "He's lucky I love him and that he is my brother," I say aloud to myself, shaking my head in annoyance.

I pull up outside of the Martinez family estate—the home that Julian forced my sister to stay in with his mother and father. Pretentious fucks don't bother to live in a gated community. They think they are untouchable with their reputation, but when people think you're dead, they aren't suspecting you'll bring their dead son to their doorstep, so to speak.

I step out of the piece-of-shit sedan Cherry owned and shuffle over to the passenger seat where the window is rolled down halfway. I shut the door quietly so as not to make a racket, light a piece of Julian's shirt that I cut out and saturated in petrol and flick it through the window.

I run in between the carefully maintained privet hedges. My combat boots slap the pavement as I sprint around the block and down the street where Mateo is waiting in the parked van. I shut the door just as I hear the explosion. We drive off, headed back to Houston having completed what we set out to do.

We drive silently, saying little until Mateo verbalizes precisely what I am contemplating. "How long do you think we have until Mr. Martinez discovers it was us?"

I look over at him and shrug. "Your guess is as good as mine, but now there is no going back. We've killed his son."

Mateo's fingers on the steering wheel tighten, and his jaw ticks. He is really pissed about something. Right when I am about to ask him what's wrong, he cuts me off.

"He's going to go after Emma and Eduardo for sure. It's just a matter of time before he finds out about us, too."

It will be all out there. There is no going back.

"I'm not hiding in the shadows anymore, bro. I am all out and ready to end this."

"Me, too. I've been hiding longer than you, and I want a normal life." He tugs at his hair, and I swear the guy will regret that action when he starts to go bald.

I snort. "Normal? You think that is possible for us?"

He looks over at me, giving me a sad attempt at a half-smile. "I sure hope so, Evie. I sure hope so."

The rest of the drive is spent taking turns driving back in one go with minimal stops. Around lunchtime, we finally arrive at Emma and Eduardo's place after having offloaded the van at a location provided by Eduardo's family. A sick-looking BMW M8 in a green metallic color is waiting for us.

Mateo walks around the car and whistles. "Wow, that is one badass ride, Evie."

I snort. "Sure, that doesn't draw any attention to us, Mateo." I touch the car with my leather gloves. "If I do say so myself, it matches my eyes." I look up and find him bent over in laughter. Pointing at me, he coughs, having choked on his words.

"What?" I feign annoyance. "Spit it out already, Mattie."

"Nothing, that was just too much, Evie. Love you, sis, but come on, I'm driving first."

"Fine. Whatever." I hop in the passenger seat and grab the handle atop the window as Mateo throws it into drive, taking the corner hard. "Bro, you know I have motion sickness. Can you tone it down a notch?" I fake the vomiting motions, and he slows the car to an average speed. "Plus, we don't want to get pulled over, right?"

He looks at me and nods. "You know, you are beginning to be such a fun sucker, Evie."

"Sorry for wanting to avoid the cops after we just killed someone. And I smell..." I hesitate, sniffing my shirt. "Faintly of dead bodies and gasoline."

"Okay, fine. I get it."

Upon our arrival, he pulls into the private parking space Eduardo instructed us to occupy, and we step out of the car. I stretch out, elongating my muscles as they ache from lugging around literal dead weight tonight. I intertwine my hand with my brother's as we head into the elevator on our way up to our sister's and soon-to-be brother-in-law's place.

We attempt to knock on the door, and it opens simultaneously. Emma pulls us in, and I push her away before she can hug us again. "Emma, we need to burn these clothes. You don't want to know what's on these garments."

"Girlie pop. I am not afraid of a little blood, babes. I am an emergency room nurse. I see the worst of the worst–"

"Really? How do you feel about bed bugs?" I cut her off before she drolls on and on. "Because I swear, I felt one crawling—" I don't finish my sentence this time because she jumps backward, face contorted in disgust, shrieking her head off and calling for Eduardo.

Mateo and I start laughing uncontrollably. "Eduardo! Eduardo, come in here quick!" she screams, her arms flailing above her head as she jumps back and forth.

Eduardo quickly enters the room in gray sweatpants with no shirt. His body is sweaty, and I stop laughing, trying not to ogle my future brother-in-law. But dang-gray sweatpants and his chest glistening... my sister is one lucky woman.

"What! What is it?" He looks around, searching for the threat, and Mateo lifts his hand to calm him down.

"It's nothing, man. It's just Emma talking about how she can handle anything because she is an ER nurse. When she tries to hug us, Evie tells her it could be bed bugs from the motel room we stayed in that rents rooms hourly. We stayed there before we disposed of the bodies and haven't changed clothing since."

This time, it's Eduardo's turn to jump back, holding on to Emma.

"Okay, just hand us a bag to dump these clothes, and we'll shower." I go to move, and Eduardo halts me.

"Do not come into this house any farther." He makes us strip down in the hallway, throws our clothes into a sealed garbage bag, and leads us to the showers. Emma proceeds to spray us with Lysol as we walk by.

"Oh, God, babe. My car?" I see her twitch and rub at something on her arm.

Mateo and I chuckle as we walk over to the shower.

"We'll get you a new one," he shouts back at her as he leads us away.

Once we are out of earshot, he speaks up. "That was cruel, Evie." He shakes his head, but I know it could be possible, but more than unlikely.

"I'd rather be safe than sorry. If that were actually true though..." He finishes my thoughts.

"We'd have to burn our house." I eye him wickedly, letting the irony fall into full effect. He chortles.

"Right?" My eyes sparkle with deviance.

"Let's kill some bed bugs." He fist pumps the air. "Death by soap."

CHAPTER THREE

JAMESON

"STORY OF MY LIFE" BY SOCIAL DISTORTION

I arrive at my place exhausted. I toe off my shoes and throw my keys in a dish, then strip down out of my clothes as I move into the bedroom and throw them in the hamper. I look at the rumpled sheets of the unmade bed, wondering what she is doing now, remembering how she felt on top of me, commanding my every move and the thrill that ran through me as her sharp, pointy nails scratched down my chest.

I grab my cock and tug. A moan leaves my lips, and I hang my head down. That moment months ago got me through my ups and downs of not being with her, but now she is here, and there is no more hiding.

I enter the bathroom, let the steamy water billow across it, and step into the hot spray of the showerheads, shooting water at me from different angles. I lean against the shower tiles and lift my head up to let the spray of water hit my face as I gather it in my mouth and spit it out in front of me.

I think of Evie as she dripped whiskey into my mouth and claimed me in a soul-searing kiss. The darkness surrounded us, and the only thing visible from her mask was her jade-green eyes, similar to her sister's. How did I not see it before? Her eyes weren't as vibrant as her sister's though. Where Emma's eyes are an emerald green, Evie's have a slight circle of yellow around her pupil, giving off a feline appearance. I researched it. It's called central heterochromia. I want to know every little detail about her, down to her complex eye color.

The attraction I felt for Emma was nothing compared to my need for her sister. A need that I had to fill with my cock over and over. The feel of her wet heat saturating my dick and the feel of her mouth wrapping and sucking me so hard I had to hold on to the headboard.

I rub shampoo through my hair, facing away from the jets to wash it out, and then soap up my body. When I get to my cock, I stroke it and think of her hands. The way she would withhold my orgasm over and over, edging me to the point I thought I would stop breathing. The need for release was all I could think about. The need to come so strong that I would do anything she said just to find the release I crave. That I *need*.

I start to stroke my cock faster and twist it at the head, rubbing my thumb over the slit where the tip is already leaking. I pick up the momentum. My hand, slick with soap and water, provides lubrication, enabling quicker movements.

My breathing picks up, and I envision her eyes and lips curling up on one side, knowing what she is doing to me, how she drives me out of control, and how she is the only one I could ever want. She is the only one I could ever need.

My head falls back in a roar as my orgasm hits, and I shoot ropes of cum as I pump my cock, until I lower my head and my breathing slows.

I shake my head, flicking drops of water away from rolling into my eyes, and rinse the remaining soap and cum from my body and shower wall. The next time I do this in here, it will be me filling Evie with my cum. No more masks, no more secrets.

I shut the water off and towel off. I hang the towel on the hook on the back of the bathroom door then step out and pull some boxers and a T-shirt from the dresser to sleep in. I pull back the disheveled comforter and climb into my bed, inhaling the smell of our last time together still stuck in the sheets and fall into a deep sleep.

I hear a ding from my phone and blink the sleep from my eyes. I move around in bed and stretch over to my bedside table for my phone, seeing that I do, in fact, have a message. I click it and see that it's Eve. I sit up straighter in bed, not fully awake, and open it.

Evie: Hey. We are all meeting at Eduardo and Emma's place to talk. I hope you can be there.

I see another message sent just a few minutes after as if second-guessing herself.

Evie: If not, it's cool...

I smile when she lays it out and leaves the ball in my court.

I jump out of bed and quickly dress, checking the time on my phone—six o'clock. It's the perfect time to hit evening traffic. Luckily, I don't have far to go.

I throw some product in my hair to tame the way it shoots in all directions and brush my teeth before heading out to see my girl.

At their place, I park in the guest area and lock my car door as I run up the steps. The concierge greets me as I pass through the door.

"Hi, Miguel," I greet the middle-aged man as I walk in, having been here many times over the years.

Eduardo and I have been friends since college. He was one of my frat brothers, and I even thought about hooking up with his fiancée before she was his, but there was really never going to be an us. They have their second chance, and I have... well, I have the girl I was always meant to be with—Emma's twin sister, Evie.

I wonder if the feelings and protectiveness I had for her sister had anything to do with the fact that I felt an immediate connection to Eve—or Evie, as I found out recently. That night we met was the best sex of my life, and the connection we had was so strong. I knew then that I would do anything to make that girl mine.

I take the back elevator that leads to their floor and punch in the code. Seconds later, the doors open, and I step out into the hallway that houses only a few apartments in this high-rise. I rap my knuckles on the door and hear someone coming to answer. Emma answers the door, and I look down at her.

"Jameson?" she asks.

"Hey, Emma." She opens the door, and I step through.

"What are you—"

"I invited him over, Emma," Evie cuts her off. "I thought he should be

23

here when we explain the story from the beginning. Everyone we need to tell should be present so we can do it all at once. It is a lot to take in."

She scrunches her nose up in confusion, looking between us. Evie walks over to me, places her arm around my head, and brings it down to hers for a kiss. She plunges her tongue into my mouth forcefully, taking me by surprise at her blatant display of PDA, and quickly releases me before I try to deepen the kiss, but not before biting on my lip and retreating.

I lick my lips, tasting the coppery metallic blood that is beading on my lower lip. I wipe it away as she grabs my hand and leads me over to the sound of other voices coming from the kitchen.

"Okay then," I hear Emma say as the sound of the front door closes behind me. A low giggle is cut short when Evie looks back at her with a wicked gleam in her eye.

We walk into the kitchen, and she is still holding my hand when I see her brother, Eduardo, along with Philip and Eli, gathered around the kitchen island. Eduardo's eyebrows rise at the sight of Evie holding my hand as I stand beside her. I hold his stare and shrug my shoulders. A smile forms on his face as he looks behind me to where Emma is returning to the kitchen.

"Do you guys want anything to drink?" she asks as she waltzes in, and I notice her shorts riding up one side of her butt cheek.

I turn away quickly and focus my attention on Evie.

She has already noticed and is looking at me intently, her grip tightening on my hand. Maybe she could sense I was about to let go, but she misread my intention because I just wanted to pull her in front of me. Instead, I give her a side smile and move her over to sit on one of the barstools.

I look over at Eduardo and nudge my chin over to where Emma is now stretching upward to grab some glasses from the cupboard. Eli is looking over at her, pretending not to look, but it's obvious he is. Eduardo looks at Eli and then turns around to see Emma's shorts rise even farther as she arches on tiptoes, twisting a bit to grab the glass.

"What the fuck, babe?" Eduardo gets up from his seat quickly and places himself over her back. As he whispers something in her ear, he grabs the glasses for her, places them on the counter, and pushes Emma toward their bedroom. "Excuse us. We'll be right back." He all but pushes her down the hall, and we see them disappear around the corner, but not before we hear him growl and Emma giggle as the door shuts abruptly with a bang.

Mateo scoffs, and I can't help but laugh aloud, especially when we hear a banging sound coming from down the hall a few minutes later. The rhythmic sound tells us what is happening behind their closed bedroom door.

"Okay, then." Evie shoots out of the chair to play some music. Mateo wipes his hand across his face as if the thought of his sister getting railed in the next room is something he'd like to scrub from his memory.

"Anyone want a drink?"

I look up at Evie speaking and nod.

"Anyone else? I think this calls for some tequila shots."

"I'll get the limes and salimón," I announce and head toward the refrigerator.

I cut some limes into miniature wedges, and Evie grabs the bottle of Don Julio 1942, setting it and several glasses around the kitchen island. We each have our glasses ready to go, and Evie clears her throat. I pour some chilé on my hand between my thumb and index finger, prepared to taste and toss back this liquor.

"To getting our revenge," Mateo announces.

We all chant after him in unison, clink our glasses, and take the shots. I grab my lime and suck on it when I catch Evie staring intently at me. I wonder if she is thinking of me sucking on her clit until she drenches me in her juices.

She licks the salt hanging on her bottom lip, and I feel my cock jerk in my pants. I attempt to discreetly rearrange my cock, and it pushes tight against my pants, but it doesn't escape Evie. She moves to sit back on the barstool in front of me, and I stand at her back with my hard-on pressing into her.

A minute later, Emma comes into the room, face flushed, wearing leggings and a hoodie. She doesn't make eye contact with anyone, and Eduardo walks in, sweat trickling from his brow—no one comments.

Evie speaks up first. "Hey, Em, want a shot? We took some tequila shots while Eduardo was taking his shot."

I snort, and the guys try to suppress the laughter at Emma's expense.

Emma's face reddens.

"Fuck off, Evie," Eduardo playfully remarks.

"We'll both take a shot with everyone, and then we need you to tell us the whole story." This effectively ends the drama that would have surely ensued between the sisters.

I pull my girl back to hold her, letting her know I am here for her and not going anywhere.

We line the shots up again, and Evie makes another toast. "To all the twisted lies coming to light."

TWISTED TIDES

We down the shots and throw our discarded limes on the plate before us. I intertwine my hand with hers and wait for her to tell me the truth.

PART I

THE PAST

CHAPTER FOUR

EVIE

"SACRIFICE" BY LONDON AFTER MIDNIGHT

"Mom. Dad. I'm home." I slam the door and hear my parents calling me from the kitchen. I see a young teacher who works with my parents in the kitchen with them.

"Hey, Eves. This is Rebekah. She is one of the new teachers who recently started working at the school." The young woman, who can't be over twenty-two, waves at me.

"Hey, Evie. It's nice to meet you." She looks like she could be friends with Emma and me from high school instead of teaching in one.

"Hi. So nice to meet you, too." I look at Mom, wondering what the girl is doing here. Tomorrow is the big day when we leave for Mexico, and we really don't have time to entertain guests. We should be packing and planning our exit out of here.

Mom senses my thoughts and looks over at my dad.

"Evie, Rebekah here will be house-sitting for us indefinitely. She is new to the area and needs a place to stay. She doesn't have any family to help her, and I thought since we would be taking a sabbatical, we could use someone to care for things while we are gone."

I shake my head, contemplating this, and agree with a nod that this is not a bad idea. I wonder if she told anyone. Not sparing another thought about this anymore and trusting that Mom has everything taken care of, I look around. "Guys, where's Emma?" I attempt to walk out and call for her, but my mom stops me.

"Evie, she left a few minutes ago. You missed her."

My face falls as I hope it wasn't with who I think it is.

"Who did she leave with, and where did she go?" I say, trying to control my rage.

My parents look at me, and before they answer, I know she's with Julian. They don't even have to tell me to confirm what I know to be the worst possible circumstance.

"She'll be fine, Evie. They just went out to dinner. She'll be home before you know it, and you guys can get packed together."

I gulp down the feeling of impending doom I have and chalk it up to my usual anxiety, nothing more. But this feels so different. It feels like something ominous is looming over the house, shrouding us in darkness. I shiver at the coldness that runs through me and my skin breaks out in goose bumps.

"O-kay," I say, but the words get lodged in my throat, making it hard to get out.

Just then, the doorbell rings, and I look worriedly at my parents. My mother sighs.

"It's just pizza, Evie. I ordered your favorite. Why don't you go get your bag packed, and then you can grab a couple of slices and show Rebekah around before Emma gets back."

Rebekah looks from my mother and then back to me, trying to get a read of the room. If she guessed secrets, so many secrets... then ding, ding, ding, we have a winner.

I nod, wanting to escape the mixed stares I am getting from my parents and Rebekah. I trot up the stairs, quickly close the door, and grab my emergency backpack from the closet. Since my assault a few years ago, I have always been prepared in the event of an emergency, and this threat with Julian on my sister has caused me to take extra precautions.

I'm throwing some of my favorite toiletries I can't live without into my bag when I hear a thud, as if something has fallen. I stop packing, standing motionless, waiting to hear anything else—voices, footsteps, but nothing but silence.

"What the fuck was that?" I say aloud as I come to my senses and run out of the room, but not before grabbing my backpack and heading down the stairs.

I drop my bag when I get to the kitchen and gasp as I bring my hands up to my mouth in horror at the sight before me. My mom has her face in her slice of pizza. My dad is on the floor, and Rebekah is leaning backward in the chair. I don't have to look any further because I know with certainty that they are dead.

I stand there in shock, looking at them, unable to move. That is until I see movement in the slider patio door. It opens swiftly, and a black figure enters and shuts the door behind him.

I pick up my bag and run back toward the front door. I've seen too many horror movies to know that I will get trapped and suffer a similar fate as my parents if I head upstairs and lock myself in my bedroom, somehow ensuring my demise.

"Evie," I hear my name called, and that stops me in my tracks. "Wait, it's me."

The voice is so familiar that it sends chills up my spine, making the baby-fine blond hairs on my neck stand at attention.

I turn around against my better judgment and look into the eyes of the stranger who saved me years back. That night of my assault almost destroyed me, and it would have without all the therapy I underwent.

"What do you want?" I ask, even though I should be running far away from here.

My throat feels dry. "Evie, we don't have much time. I need you to trust me if you want to live and get your sister back."

I nod because, at this point, what choice do I have?

He holds his hand out. "Here, give me your ring."

I go to take it off and hesitate. But instead of asking questions, I remove it and hand the ring to him.

"What finger did you wear it on?"

I raise my hand where it once resided, and he moves quickly and places it on the same ring finger on Rebekah as she lies lifeless, mouth hanging open and frothy saliva trickling down her chin.

"Grab your bag, Evie, we need to leave. I didn't think I would make it in time, and I almost didn't. At least I can save you." He holds his hand out to me, and I hesitate briefly, looking at my family fallen dead at the dinner table with pizza that was barely eaten still on their plate.

"Poison," the stranger confirms.

I take his hand, and we leave through the back. I stop, remembering the most important thing.

"What about Emma?" I ask, not wanting to leave, despite knowing that staying any longer here is ensuring my death.

"We'll have to get her later. She won't be coming back here."

"I want to see first if she returns," I beg, and he takes pity on me.

"Okay, but we have to hide quickly. It isn't safe here."

We run out into the shadows and hide amongst the trees and foliage in the newly sold house on the corner lot. The new owners haven't moved in yet, so I know we are safe here. We barely get to the side of the house when a loud explosion shakes the ground, and its heat makes my skin buzz.

"What the..." I turn around to see my house engulfed in flames. I stand there, rocked to the core that if this stranger hadn't saved me yet again, I would be dead in the house along with my parents, but I guess that was the point of the explosion.

People come running out of their houses, and soon, the street is buzzing with activity. Shortly after, sirens sound, and a fire truck is coming, attempting to get control of the flames.

This subdivision has acre lots, unlike in the bigger cities where the homes are on top of each other. If that was the case, there might have been other casualties, but more trucks come, and they seem to be getting this more under control; although the house is still ablaze, it's just not spreading at this point.

The stranger speaks, and I can barely make out the words over the ringing in my ears. He turns me to face him, and he touches my face tenderly.

I think I am in shock. I feel funny, like I drank too much caffeine, and my body is light with energy that I can't contain, but my skin feels cold. I shiver, and the stranger notices.

"Here". He takes his hoodie off and places it over me.

I notice his broad chest and muscles that fill out his T-shirt and the black utility belt that holds up his cargo pants down to his black combat boots. He looks like an assassin.

"Evie."

My eyes shoot up to meet his, and his lip pulls into a smile, showing his straight white teeth. There is something oddly familiar about him, something that makes me want to lean my head on his shoulder.

"Don't worry, Evie. Uncle Andrés will send someone to meet us."

My eyes widen. "What do you mean, Uncle Andrés?" I ask, completely confused. "Who are you?" I squint my eyes to narrow my vision, hoping that if I stare hard enough, the answers will present themselves, making who this stranger is more apparent.

He takes a deep breath and stares me in the eyes. "I'm your brother Mateo. Yes, I just saw our mom get murdered. Believe me when I say that I am not okay right now."

I gasp in shock. "No. It can't be. How do I have a brother? Where have you been? Why don't we know about you?" I don't realize I am crying as tears roll down my face. He goes to answer me, but I place my hand over his cheek. "Have you been okay? Were you happy and loved, Mateo?"

His eyes snap up to mine, and he gulps. Clearly, this is not the question he was expecting me to ask. "It could have been better, Evie."

I throw my arms around him, and he hesitates briefly before returning my embrace, and there, in the middle of the night, I hold my long-lost brother, who, along with me, witnessed our parents die just moments ago.

"How did Mom and Dad let you go, Mateo?"

He hesitates but decides to tell me as we watch the chaos erupt across the street. "My dad doesn't know about me, and Mom gave me up when she had me when she was eighteen. Then she went to college, continued with her life, and met your dad there. The rest is your life, not mine."

I shake my head in disbelief. "But why not tell us about you? I don't understand," I beg to comprehend.

"It's more complicated than that, and I know we have to talk about it, but let's do that later, okay? Maybe when we are away from here."

I nod in silent agreement.

He leans over and tries to get a better look at the black SUV that makes its way over and stops down the street. I see my sister run over to the house with Julian trailing behind her. She falls to the ground, and I stand abruptly when my arm is tugged and my body is forced back down.

"No, Evie. You can't go over there. It isn't safe, and that defeats the purpose of making it look like you died in that fire along with your parents."

I turn my head toward Mateo slowly, absorbing the gravity of his words. Then it dawns on me. "That's why you had me hand over my ring?"

He nods. "Yes, the Martinez family is more than likely responsible for this, and they won't bother checking very closely to see if it's you. Julian will recognize the ring on your finger and assume the girl is you."

I hear Emma screaming, and I notice something glinting in the light. Emma slumps over, and I see Julian picking her unconscious body up and taking her to the SUV. Her head lolls to the side, her body limp in his arms, and she is once again at his mercy.

"He fucking drugged her." I point at them and look over at Mateo, disbelieving.

"Does that surprise you, Evie?" He shakes his head in disgust.

"I hate that fucker."

Mateo nods, agreeing with me. "Yeah, he's an asshole for sure."

I look over at him. Trying to get a better read on him. "That's an understatement, Mateo," I counter, but his phone vibrates, effectively cutting off our conversation.

"It's time to go."

He helps me stand with him as we head to the back of the house. Across the street, the park is shrouded in darkness, but a black pickup truck with tinted windows is idling. We look both ways and see no oncoming traffic.

"Come on," Mateo calls out and extends his hand out from behind, and I place my hand in his, effectively blindly trusting my brother that I've just learned about.

He opens the back door, helps me enter, and hops in after me. I take the backpack off my shoulders and place it between my feet.

"Buckle up, Evie," I hear a voice from the driver's seat, and my head snaps up to see Adrian, my cousin.

"Oh, my God," I gasp. "Adrian! What are you doing here?"

He smiles at me. "Well, my dear Eve's, it appears that I am saving your ass, and your sister is next."

CHAPTER FIVE

JAMESON

"LAZY EYE" BY SILVERSUN PICKUPS

I sit alone in the bar, waiting for Dax to arrive. He said that he would meet me here straight after work. I glance at my watch, knowing he should be coming through those doors any minute.

I called him up because I wanted to talk to him about Emma. I thought we had a connection, and when I left her place that night after partying at Eduardo's club, I had suspicions that he was into her. I saw him at her apartment after she sent me home insisting that she was okay and didn't need anyone, but what she meant was anyone other than Eduardo.

I saw their bodies close together as I peered up, looking into her living room window from the parking lot like a stalker. I could've blamed it on the alcohol or my mind playing tricks on me, but I hadn't had much to drink. Any lingering effects of alcohol had vanished while ensuring Emma was okay at the club. If I hadn't forgotten my wallet and tried to return to her apartment after she insisted that I go home, I would have never known she was into him.

After college, we stayed close. I worked and continued to work with Eduardo on projects at his club. He helped me once to start up my business. I know the ins and outs of his club. Some are legit, and others are not so legit, but he pays me well for my security work there, so I can't complain. I know him enough to realize that his money comes from the Mexican cartel, or at least some of it. Not that I would come out and ask him, but it is pretty obvious.

Deep in thought, I am about to sip my drink when a hand clasps me around the shoulder. "Why does it look like your fuckin' dog died, brother?" Dax drops into the seat next to me.

Before I can answer him, the waitress, Simone, saunters toward us, her breasts up close and personal. She clearly has a thing for Dax.

"Hey, handsome. What can I get you to whet your lips?"

I groan in aggravation.

She cocks an eyebrow upward to be sexy, but it has the opposite effect. Honestly, Dax and I have commented that 'less is more' regarding women and their makeup application. Still, with her painted-on eyebrows, heavy eyeshadow, and red lipstick, she looks like the Joker from *Batman.*

"I'll take a Stella beer." He tips his head in my direction. "Jameson, are you ready for another one?"

I swig back the rest and nod, placing the empty bottle on the table for her to take. "Yeah, I'll take another. Why not?"

She picks it up and nods in acknowledgment.

I think about how to bring this up when Dax interrupts my thoughts.

"You okay, bro?"

Before I can answer, Simone is back with our drinks. I wipe my hand down my face and just want her to hurry the fuck up and leave so that I can chat with Dax. She pours my drink in a frosted glass this time, and I wait patiently, trying not to rip the bottle from her hand.

This time, for fear of being interrupted again, I blurt it out. "I think Emma is fucking around with that guy Eduardo," I release all in one breath.

Dax's eyebrows pinch together in confusion. "Your frat brother?" I nod. "He told us they met in the emergency department, something similar to you and Liv, but she is on his radar now. I don't know if I want to even attempt to compete with him."

Dax shrugs. "You don't know for sure, right?"

I shake my head. "No, he is fucking her." I explain what happened and how his Porsche was parked outside after I left.

He seems to think this over and reluctantly agrees there was something there between them that night. "There was chemistry there," he comments, and then, before he elaborates, he seems to second-guess himself but decides to continue, "a familiarity perhaps." He strokes his lip as if thinking about something or someone else.

"Liv had mentioned it to me and something about flowers he sent her recently. I just thought I should let you know."

I smile half-heartedly at his reluctance to betray Liv's trust. "Thanks, man. I appreciate you having my back. It's just weird, though. I thought we had this connection. I can't explain what I feel for her. I want to protect and keep her close, but this one moment we had at the beach during spring break was… awkward? I can't find the word to describe it." Frustrated, I run my hand through my hair and can't explain it, so I stop trying.

"You know what you need, Jameson?" Dax looks at me smugly. "You need to go out and get laid. Why don't you go to The Viceroy and use the full perks of the VIP card Eduardo gave you?"

This does perk me up a little bit. "Yeah, that sounds great. Do you care for a little excitement tonight? You can be my wingman." I rub my hands together in anticipation of how this will go down as I drink the rest of my beer, ready to leave, and head to the club.

Dax hesitates, avoiding eye contact. His hand rubs the back of his neck, and he looks at me sheepishly. "Well, I can't go because Liv and I are together now."

I look at him, stunned. "She's your girlfriend?"

Dax nods in confirmation and he fucking beams. The guy seems so happy, and I can't blame him.

"I'm happy for you." I clap him on his back and throw some bills on the table.

"Where are you going, Jameson?" I hear Dax ask as I start to walk away.

I smirk, eyes alight with mischief. "To find my happy ending."

After going home to change into attire more fitting for The Heavenly Pearl, the exclusive membership-only sex club within Eduardo's dance club, The Viceroy, I enter through the discreet, private entrance that can only be accessed by using a card pressed into a scanner.

Upon entering, a hostess stands at a desk, much like at a hotel. For safety reasons, she checks my card in the system to show the times I've been there, and my fingerprint must be placed on the small scanner to accept my entry.

TWISTED TIDES

Members must comply with all the rules as exceptions are rarely granted. Then, when the hostess lets them pass through the second set of doors, the bouncer takes their phone, checks them for anything that isn't allowed in the club, and bags it for them. They get their items when they check out.

It all seems pretty straightforward, focusing solely on client safety. If you have to wonder if an item is allowed, then more than likely it isn't, so I don't bring anything that isn't essential.

I watch with rapt attention to see if anything is amiss during the intake process, but it runs flawlessly, and I smile. I was given a membership after I helped establish a security protocol for this place and ensured the members' privacy and, above all, the patron's safety. I can't say I always use this privilege, but I am grateful for times like these where I can let loose. The membership fee is expensive, but Eduardo wouldn't let me pay, so I likely wouldn't be here otherwise. I'm not ultra-rich like they are, even though my business does well for someone my age.

The idea of working for someone in a cubicle would have driven me mad, so when I approached Eduardo with my business venture before graduation, he was only too happy to invest in my start-up. Unfortunately, having him as a business associate means I know of his dealings—some legal and some not so legal—although I only participate in the legal ones he maintains on his own.

I'm no fool. I know where the money comes from; I just choose not to involve myself in that side of things, and I'm not sure Eduardo would let me even if I was given the opportunity.

Pulled away from my thoughts, I see a woman with a long trench coat, and I can only imagine what is underneath that. I take her in from head to toe as her long black hair swings back and forth like a thick mane in a ponytail worn high on her head. I gaze downward as she walks in front of me. Her black leather boots disappear underneath it, and I can imagine the point of her heel pressing into my chest as she stands above me. We walk in one after another and I watch her walk straight to the bar.

My mask is firmly in place, as is everyone else's, since it is a requirement for entry into the club. I follow her swaying hips as she perches on a seat and begins to talk to another woman beside her.

It would be more tempting if her hair were blonde, but it's dark here anyway. I've never really been attracted to women with dark hair. I have nothing against brunettes, but I have a thing for blonde hair. I go to the bar and order a drink.

I look around at all the scantily clad women. Ironically, women don't have to wear much and are not required to have memberships here. If they are vetted online, they can come, providing proper documentation showing proof of identity, a formal orientation to the club along with non-disclosure agreements that must be signed, and, most importantly, providing test results of no STIs. All of that is done online before their first visit.

The mutual requirement is that everyone must wear a mask. Some people like their identity to remain anonymous. I don't have a problem with that. Sometimes, it's better not to form attachments. I frown, pondering my words filtering through my head.

I turn sideways to get through a few people talking in clusters and hail the bartender over, ordering an old-fashioned. One thing I love about this place is that they make a mean old-fashioned.

I move my hand, and it lands accidentally on a woman's shoulder. I feel a jolt, as if I have been burned as her face whips around to see who dared touch her. That's when her jade-green eyes land on mine, and I'm suddenly bewitched.

I attempt to look away, but her hypnotizing almond-shaped eyes are captivating, and I want to yield to her every whim. As she narrows them on me, I zone in on the yellowish coloring around the pupil, causing the remainder of her green eyes to appear brighter. The tempestuous emerald green is so striking that I could drown in it for days.

I look at her, speechless, trying to form a coherent thought, and I see her lip twitch in amusement.

Way to play it cool, Jameson, I think to myself.

"Hi." That is all I can come up with.

She coolly picks up her amber-colored liquid on the rocks and sips it, eyeing me up and down. I wonder if she likes what she sees. I wait for her to say anything in return, perhaps tell me a 'hi' back, but she doesn't. She just stares, and I suddenly feel like my mouth is as dry as a desert, and I know without a doubt that I am thoroughly fucked.

"Do you come here often?" I inwardly groan at the thought of what I just asked.

Her eyebrows lift in shock as a smile plays on her lips.

Okay, that's strike two. "What's your name?" I groan aloud this time and run my hand through my hair, wishing I could recover from my mortification.

She puts her drink down and turns toward me this time to address me fully.

She seems to size me up and crosses one muscular leg over the other.

I bite my lip inwardly, begging my expressions not to betray my immense attraction to her. Her black leather corset and mini skirt squeak as she moves.

"I thought the purpose of this club was anonymity. Is it not? You know, the masks and all." Her hand makes a movement, mimicking a circle around her face.

She doesn't seem irritated by my line of potentially offensive questions, but I can sense she is as leary of me as she should be. She doesn't know who I am, and I think I might have blown my chances at getting to know her, even if it is for just tonight. I ponder on how to answer the question, and I know that she will be able to sense bullshit a mile away, so I decide to go for the truth.

"Yes." I nod in agreement. "I want to know what I should call you."

She leans a little farther into my personal space. Her scent permeates the air; I smell a mixture of spicy vanilla and bourbon. I close my eyes, trying to remain unaffected while waiting for her response.

She seems to think about it and looks me in the eye, leaning over as if she is going to tell me a secret. "You can call me Eve."

I repeat the name softly, and the one syllable rolls off my tongue easily.

"Eve." I chuckle at her response, shaking my head. "I take it that's not your real name?"

Her eyebrows scrunch together, confusion marring her delicate features. "Why are you so insistent on knowing me?" she asks.

"I just..." I sigh, knowing I must try telling her the truth, even if everything in my mind tells me to be cautious. "Do."

"I like Eve." She searches my face for an expression that will give her a reason to walk away, but she won't find one there.

CHAPTER SIX

EVIE

"CONCRETE JUNGLE" BY BAD OMENS

I straighten in my chair, giving him my partial truth, as I shimmy myself farther up my barstool. "It reminds me of man's downfall from the Garden of Eden." My tone is seductive, and I love how his eyes blaze with a commanding authority that makes my skin prickle with awareness. I feel so dopey, drunk on his essence that I want to drown in it, but I control my emotions, appearing unaffected.

He takes another drink of his old-fashioned, and I lick my lips. I imagine tasting the orange and smokey oak flavors while sucking the cherry remnants from his tongue.

I lap up a bead of alcohol on my lip before it threatens to roll off my own. My throat feels hot, and the amber liquid in my glass is only helping to stoke the fire instead of extinguish it. I'm burning, alight with lust and want that I haven't felt before.

He groans at my remark, showing just how affected he is by my words.

"Somehow, I don't doubt that at all, Eve."

I hold my head up, supported by my hand. My pensive stare holds his own, until I cannot bear to look at him any longer for fear of leaning in and kissing this stranger at the bar.

"And what about you? What should I call you, pretty boy?" But I don't have to wait long for his response.

He lifts his head and, without hesitation, replies, "Jameson."

"Jameson," I repeat, and he silently nods. I take another swallow of my drink, and I feel it go down hard, burning all the way down into the pit of my stomach.

He gulps, watching me devour the remaining amber liquid in one go. Maybe I affect him like he affects me.

"Why do I get the feeling that that is your *real name*—Jameson?" I want to see how he answers this question. I will be able to tell if he is lying.

He leans in closer. I sit motionless, feeling the heat of his breath caress my cheek.

"Because it is."

I turn slightly to look him in the eye and fight the urge to look away. Our stare is so intense that I feel as though I can read his innermost desires. I pause for a minute, contemplating my following words. "Why did you tell me your real name?" I'm confused by his brutal honesty. He is a puzzle that I want to solve.

So he tells me without reservation, "I just want to hear my name on your lips."

And there it is—the truth. My lips part, but I don't speak while his unspoken words swirl in the air, coating me with a silent embrace.

I just want to hear your name on my lips. I hear it echo over and over again in my head. I go to twist the ring on my finger out of instinct, but it isn't there, reminding me of all we lost. I clench my fists.

It was the moment that changed my life.

Sometimes, I rage so hard that I need to gain some semblance of control. The guardian angel that saved me that day was a protective force in my life and my constant the days after—my brother Mateo.

The therapy helped me cope after my assault with my frequently occurring anxiety attacks, and the self-defense classes helped to curb my ever-present anger. This anger never diminished in intensity, so I am here tonight—at The Heavenly Pearl sex club—about to lose myself in a man I just met but want to get lost in forever. His blatant honesty was refreshing. I can't wait to feel him inside me.

I clench my thighs together at the thought, except it no longer is a thought. It's a very real possibility.

I lean into Jameson and swear he thinks I'm about to kiss him. Instead, I stand and walk away from the bar. The coldness settles in as his body's warmth diminishes with each step I take away from him. I turn back to see his head hanging, and he turns to look at me with almost what can be described as sadness.

He also looks like he is stopping himself from running after me.

My lips curl up into a smile, and I lift my hand out to him in an invitation to join me. He doesn't hesitate and immediately takes long strides to reach me.

He takes my hand in his, and his eyes sparkle with excitement. I look at our hands entwined, and I feel a buzz cascading over my skin, causing my body to break out in a shiver. A warmth spreads over me, and I feel like I need to shed my clothing for entirely different reasons than just to cool off.

I lead Jameson past the bar and the small dance floor, but nobody bothers to look our way. We reach a hall, and I walk past the room numbers until I get to the one I reserved for tonight. Did I expect to use it? I was still deciding on that possibility, but after my conversation with Jameson at the bar, things have escalated pretty quickly, and I want nothing more than to use it now, with him.

I press my finger on the door keypad, and it clicks open. Due to safety concerns, cards get lost, keys are never used as they could be lost, and pockets aren't a thing here. No money is used in transactions; everything is automatically deducted from your card in real time. Your fingerprint is taken at entry to confirm and activate any rooms you may have requested in advance or at least the fingerprint associated with your name. It makes sense, and I love how much thought whoever designed the system had put into it. It's obvious safety was this person's priority, and I love that.

I push the door open, and dim lighting illuminates the room's features. Walking in, I release Jameson's hand. It falls silently, and I already miss the connection. He stands there looking at me. I undo my corset and let the string hang around the sides. I shimmy out of my short skirt and kick it off my body, tossing it onto a chair. I remove the corset and let my breasts hang as I place it near my skirt. I leave my spiked boots with red soles on because they look hot as fuck.

I can see Jameson gulp, and he stands there unmoving. His eyes roam over my body, and the desire he feels toward me is evident by his growing erection tenting his pants. He moves his hand over his hard length, attempting to be subtle, but I notice everything.

Before he can move toward me, I speak my first order. "Take off your clothes and sit on the bed, Jameson."

He tilts his head to the side, trying to understand the situation, and I raise an eyebrow at him in challenge. He quirks his lip up and nods in understanding and does as he is told. He doesn't look away but slowly undoes the buttons of his shirt, pulls his arms free, and grabs behind him to pull his undershirt off, placing it on the chair beside my clothes. He toes his shoes off and unfastens his belt and pants. I hear the zipper make a loud noise followed by his pants as they hit the floor. He picks them up and removes his socks, placing the remainder of his clothes on the chair with the rest. He remains in his red silk boxers as he goes to sit on the edge of the bed right in front of me.

Walking over to the bed, crawling onto the mattress, and moving my body to kneel behind him, I lean over and whisper in his ear, "Good boy, Jameson." I kiss over his ear and lick down his neck, sucking his flesh into my mouth. His head tilts back, lips parted.

I run my pointed fingernails up and down his back, and this time, when I come up, I move my hand into his hair and massage his scalp. My hand roams down his shoulders and his arms, kneading and touching my way around his body. Goose bumps spread across his flesh as my nails scratch around the front of his chest, drawing a circle around each nipple.

A moan escapes his mouth, and I smile, knowing how aroused he must be. The tip of his cock is leaking precum from the slit as it gifts me an appearance of this man's well-endowed cock from this angle. I am in the moment of a pure nurture mode. I want to hold and comfort him. Instead, I put my body flush with his, and my breasts touch his back.

He lifts his hand, and I wrap my arms around him, placing his hand back on his legs. I lick around his shoulder, trailing a path upward to his neck and back to his shoulder. I apply pressure with my teeth and bite him. He moans and I lift my head to look and see where my teeth broke through the skin. I love that I marked him.

When we part ways tomorrow, I will have left him with a reminder of tonight. When he sees this in the mirror, he'll remember when he was mine, even if it was only for a night.

I repeat this over several areas of his neck and back. He tilts his head back, as I kiss around, moving up to his cheek. He tilts his head forward as his lips meet mine. His hand reaches up, grabbing my hair, pushing my mouth into his. He takes over the kiss, and his tongue forces its way toward mine. Dueling for dominance, I feel consumed and struggle to regain control of my feelings.

I bite his lip hard, interrupting the moment.

Jameson sucks in a deep breath and breaks the kiss. He looks at me, and I notice blood beads on his lower lip where I nicked it, and he rubs at it. I stand and move away from the bed. He touches and licks at his lip where I bet he is wondering why I did that. I could feel myself falling and couldn't allow myself to feel more than that for someone I really don't know.

I stand before him, and he stares at me, watching and waiting for my next move. "Can you do as you're told, Jameson?"

He tilts his head, realizing what game I'm playing. He nods.

"I need your words, babe."

"I can." His eyes never leave mine.

This is the only way I can do this, but I can't tell him. I lower my thong, flicking it toward the rest of my clothing. Jameson watches closely as I discard the scrap of material. He raises his line of sight to rest on my shaved pussy. He continues to stare when I part my folds with my fingers, circling my clit. I dip a finger into my pussy and trail its wetness back up and use it to circle my clit once more. Jameson licks his lips.

"Do you want a taste, babe?"

His eyes meet mine, and the lust behind them is intoxicating. He nods. "Yes, please."

I smile at his good manners. "Well, since you asked so nicely..." I walk closer to him and stop. He wants to reach out to me, but I shake my head at him, giving him my next set of instructions. "Take your boxers off, climb onto the bed, and lie down on your back."

He immediately complies as he stands to take off his boxers, placing them next to my wet panties and crawling up the bed. I see his sack hanging heavy as his thick cock juts outward. He lays back on the bed as instructed, and I walk over to him, crawling from the base of the bed up his body.

I feel his body tighten, struggling to control his urge to flip me over and ravish mine. If I was any ordinary girl, I'd probably love that, but I'm not. I'm fucked up, and I can't let him have control. I'll unravel, and he doesn't know me or my history. I need to protect myself from him and everyone else.

"Give me your hands."

He looks at me, and I point to the cuffs hanging by the bed. They are soft and meant to restrain but not harm.

"You don't want me to touch you?" His question holds a note of hurt, but

I swallow down the words I should say. Ones meant to be cold and direct. Instead, I allow him a little truth.

"I'd like you to one day, but not today."

He searches my eyes for the truth, and they soften briefly, allowing him a small glimpse of my vulnerability. He nods, accepting this very well, knowing there may not be more than today.

He holds out his hands for me to secure to the sides of the bed. I smile at his complacency. "Good boy."

I take one hand, restrain it in the cuff, and do the same to the other. He gives them each a tug to demonstrate that he is indeed secured, and I am glad he understands my need for this tonight.

He sits back, awaiting my next move. As I move to sit on his chest, my wetness coats him, and his gaze drops down between my legs. I lean back and spread my legs, allowing him an up-close view. He inhales deeply and moans. Then he blows on my exposed lips. I feel a shiver rack my body as I look at the desire he feels for me. "Do you want to lick me, Jameson?"

He nods, making eye contact with me. "You know I do, sweetheart."

I smile at his term of endearment. I shimmy upward and see his head lift off the pillows, but it isn't necessary. I hover above him, giving him all the access he needs to lick me up and down. "Fuck, Jameson, just like that." I throw my head back, as he repeats the action. I spread my lips for him, and he takes my clit into his mouth and sucks. My orgasm that was building explodes as I almost lose consciousness. I feel weak as the last of my climax ebbs while I'm still shamelessly riding his face. My hips ease their bucking and I feel satiated. I took what I needed, and I am unapologetic for it.

As I still my movements, I feel him smile underneath me. "What are you smiling about, Jameson?" I chuckle at him, knowing how self-assured he is in the fact that he got me off—and what an orgasm it was. I shake my head as I lift off him.

With a smirk he says, "And no hands, huh?"

My cheeks are flushed, and the smile on his face is enough to knock the wind out of me.

God, he's so beautiful.

I move down where his long length is there for the taking. "Let's see if you're still smiling after I suck your soul through your cock."

CHAPTER SEVEN

JAMESON

"SOMEBODY THAT I USED TO KNOW" BY GOTYE

I went home feeling worse than when I left for the club. My spirits were lifted at the prospect of a good night to get my mind off things with Emma and Eduardo. I guess I achieved that because I had a good time and my mind is no longer fixated on my previous dilemma.

Except now it's onto something—or rather someone—else.

I realize the girl I want to see again is gone, and I may never see her again. She's fucked-up, and I'm just as fucked because I didn't want to let her go, but she makes that choice for me. She wouldn't even let me really touch her, and I wonder if there's a specific reason why she doesn't allow comfort or touch from her partner. Except that I am not her partner. I am nothing to her.

That's precisely what I felt after we left the room. I asked Eve if she wanted to go to the bar. She looked at me and said she needed to go to the bathroom. I knew from the look in her eye that she wasn't coming back, but still, I nodded and went to the bar to order myself a drink and a bourbon for her, hoping I was wrong.

Fifteen minutes passed, and I sat, staring in the direction she'd left in. Just as she rounded the corner, I stood there watching her. She paused, looking back, and smiled at me. It was a smile that said good to have known you. Maybe even held some regret.

Still, I waited. I finished her drink and left an hour later without knowing who that girl was or if I would ever see her again. It's unbelievable how, just a few hours ago, I was upset that Emma was with Eduardo. Although I didn't feel the connection I had with Eve, that raw chemistry I thought only existed in movies, I still felt this longing to protect Emma. I cared for her in a way that I can't explain. I was drawn to her, but I felt nothing that night at the beach on Padre Island during spring break when we kissed.

The kiss I had with Eve was brutal in every aspect it could be. The punishing ease with which she kissed me and took what she wanted from me was unapologetically damning to my psyche. She owned me. The brutal way she sucked my cock was the best head I have ever received, and the way she licked me all over and pulled my balls while doing it, placing each one in her mouth and kissing the area in between made me see stars.

I rub my aching cock as I remember how good it felt. How good she felt. The worst was the way she brutally dismissed me after. I thought she might change her mind when she turned around, hoping and praying to a god that wouldn't deliver. I was wrong.

I finally fall into a restless sleep, dreaming of being pulled beneath the water and carried under by punishing emerald-colored twisting tides.

Waking up to my alarm going off the following day, I hit the snooze button several times before finally rolling out of bed. I flip the light on in the bathroom almost on auto-pilot with my mundane morning routine. I turn the water on to shower, I brush my teeth at the sink as the steam lingers in the small space. I rub the condensation off the mirror and drop my toothbrush into the sink.

"What the fuck," I mumble through a mouth full of toothpaste. I move my head from side to side and see the bite marks on my neck and shoulders as I turn left and right to get a better visual of the damage that little vixen inflicted.

I hang my head back, staring at the ceiling as celestial visions of the night pass in a flurry of moving pictures. Snapshots flick through of her riding my face while I remained restrained, the way she went down on me, and the way she left me there as if it was just another night at the sex club.

I guess that's all it was to her, and I need to put it out of my mind, move on, and start dating—no more random hookups.

I see how happy my buddy Dax is with his woman Liv, and I want the same. He wouldn't have dared turn down a boy's night out, but now that he is in a committed relationship, he won't even chance it. He almost lost Liv but was given a second chance. If I ever get a second chance with Eve, I won't hesitate to hold on and fight for it tooth and nail.

Arriving at work, I try to concentrate on my tasks with a renewed purpose. The day passes surprisingly fast, and by the time I know it, it's lunchtime—my favorite part of the day because it means my work day is half over. Now, what the fuck do I eat for lunch?

My finger rests on my forehead as I scroll through my phone in search of some nourishment. Just as I decide to grab a sandwich for lunch, Eric pops his head in my office.

"Hey. I was in the area and thought maybe you'd like to grab some lunch with me?"

I laugh. "Sure. I was just scrolling through for some delivery, but I'll go with you. What were you thinking?" I try to sway his choice to what I wanted to eat before he got here. "Maybe a smoked meats sandwich or something like that?"

He snaps his fingers. "Oh, yeah. How about Schwartz's deli?"

I pretend to think about it, but hell yeah that's exactly where I wanted to go. "I could go for that." I downplay my excitement before grabbing my wallet and following Eric out of the office.

We grab lunch from my favorite deli that boasts the best Montréal smoked meats sandwiches, but instead of sitting at my desk, I am sitting with my friend. I was scrolling through social media and pulling up my newly downloaded dating app.

Eric takes a huge bite of his sandwich. "What are you doing?" he asks through a mouthful of food.

"Here goes nothing." I upload a picture that Eric took of me at the beach on spring break last year.

I take a bite of my sandwich and watch as the picture uploads to my profile. I toss my phone toward him and he takes a look.

He whistles. "Nice, man. It's about time."

I nod in agreement. "It is." I retrieve my phone, hitting the silence button, pocketing it before we head back to the office.

The day has finally come to an end, time to clock out for the day. As I shut my computer down for the night. I am looking around for my phone, remembering that I had silenced it and threw it in the drawer so I wouldn't get distracted. Reaching into the drawer to grab it so I can head out for the night, I see I have a message from the guys in our group text, so I click on it as I head for the elevators.

> Eric and Theo: Hey! Meet us at the usual spot. Happy hour.

"Perfect," I say aloud. I quickly type out a response.

> Jameson: Sure. I'll be there soon.

I pack up my shit and head out with a purpose. I'm not going to fixate on something I can't have. I will have some drinks with my friends and get out of this funk I've been in. I repeat this mantra all the way to our favorite sports bar, which is already packed.

I look around for where Theo and Eric usually sit and immediately spot them. Theo is waving his hand for me to come over, and I sidestep several people to get there. I immediately spot Simone, the waitress infatuated with Dax, and duck out of her line of sight.

The guys stand from their seats and give me a clasp-side hug as we sit, and I flag down the waitress for a beer, pointing at what they are having. She nods and goes back to the bar.

"Where's Dax?" I ask the guys, looking around as if he will magically appear. They laugh, and Theo rolls his eyes.

"Pfft. We texted him, too, but he's not coming out."

I look at him, confused. "Late night at work in the OR?" I glance around, seeing the waitress taking another order.

"Nope," Theo replies coolly. "He has plans with Liv."

Eric laughs into his beer. "I can't say I blame him. If I had a woman that hot, I'd stay home, too."

I nod in agreement. "And then there were three, huh."

"Yep," Eric says. "Just wait. I'm going to find myself one of those book girls." He says this as if he knows something we don't.

"Huh?" Theo looks at him quizzically. "Book girls?"

"You know, one of those women who reads smutty books," Eric attempts to clarify. "I've always been drawn to the sexy librarian vibe."

Before I can comment, the waitress approaches our table with my beer, ending any further questioning about book girls. As I take a long swig, something catches my eye, and I cough on my beer.

"Hey, woah," Eric states. "Are you alright there, Jameson?"

I shake my head and hit my chest, trying to say I am okay, but I aspirated a bunch of hazy IPA, so it's a garbled mess. Finally, I sputter, "Yep, just went down the wrong pipe, that's all."

Theo smacks me on the back.

I look around to find her, but she isn't there. Great, now I am seeing Eve when she is, in fact, not here. I only saw her with a mask on, but those eyes were so vibrant, I'd know her anywhere if I looked into them. *Wouldn't I?* I have got to get it together. I rub a hand down my face and stand.

The guys look up at me.

"Bro, are you leaving?" Theo asks.

"Naw, I'm just heading to the bathroom." I tap the chair and walk off, avoiding the gaze of a group of hospital employees letting loose after work hours a few tables over.

I am almost to the bathroom door when I feel someone staring at me. I look around just as someone grabs my hand. I stop in my tracks and turn to see big brown eyes searching mine.

"Amanda?" I ask. She fucking beams at me, and I just want to crawl away.

"Hey, you remembered." She twirls her hair around her finger, and I smile back.

"Yeah, of course. How are you?" I'm being polite, but I don't give a fuck about her. We had sex a while back. Although it wasn't very memorable, but the mess she left all over my sheets was. She also threw up in my bathroom afterward, claiming lactose intolerance. No one told her to drink sours. That's her punishment. We weren't drunk, but we both had a few drinks that night, and I took care of her and drove her home the following day after stopping for a breakfast burrito. This time without cheese. She was so apologetic, and I felt terrible for her then. Now, I just want to get back to my friends and our table, have a few beers before walking out the door, and going home.

"Who are you with?" she asks, looking around.

"Oh, just Theo and Eric. We were leaving soon." I try to get away, but she steps closer, hugging me and pressing her big tits into my chest.

She lifts herself onto her tiptoes and kisses me on the cheek very close to my mouth. "Maybe we can go out sometime if you want? I was just about to leave myself." She looks at me hopefully, and I hate to be rude to her.

I decide for a bit of honesty. "Um. Sorry, but I kind of met someone." I scratch my head and look over to the bathrooms.

"Oh, yeah, sure." She withdraws from me as if my fake girlfriend will suddenly appear.

"No problem. It was nice seeing you again."

She looks embarrassed. I want to tell her not to worry about it, but I also don't want to lead her on any further, so I just step backward, ready to leave. I smile at her. "Same. Take care."

This time, I make a beeline for the bathroom, and afterward, promptly head back to the table to hang out with my friends.

We try to play some trivia, but soon, they decide to head out, and I am pretty tired after the night before. We ask for the check, and the waitress returns, saying it's all set.

"What do you mean?" I look at the guys, and they seem as surprised as I am. "Well, who do we have to thank?" I look around and don't see anyone that is looking our way.

The waitress chuckles. "She didn't say. She just said to cover the drinks, dropped some cash, and left about a minute ago."

The guys are already heading to the door, but I can't shake the feeling I had of being watched all night, and I have to know.

I stop the waitress as she begins to walk away with our glasses and tug her arm momentarily. "Sorry to bother you, but can I ask what she looked like?"

She shrugs and says, "Short, but wearing high-heeled boots, blonde hair, nothing uncommon except for her eyes. They were bright green." She walks off, and I'm stuck there open-mouthed.

I hear my name called and look around, but I know the waitress said she left. What are the chances she was here? Does she live around here, too?

Theo calls out, "Hey, we're out of here. Catch you later, bro."

I nod and walk toward the entrance as he walks out the door. Eric is probably already home. When that guy says he's out, he doesn't hesitate. As I walk to my car, the feeling of being watched intensifies. I can't shake the feeling that I'm not alone. I'm being ridiculous, but God, I just wish I could see her again.

I open the door, throw my keys on the counter, and head to the bathroom, forcing myself to shower even though all I want to do is crash.

I'm physically and emotionally drained after meeting this woman. A total mindfuck.

I pull back the crisp sheets of my bed and dive in. I set my alarm and notice there is a message on my dating app. I click on the message and immediately sit up. The picture is of a girl with short blonde hair slicked back. She's facing away from the camera. She looks like an emo girl with all-black clothes and black combat boots. Even though she is facing away from the camera, I recognize her body. A body I had the privilege of getting acquainted with most intimately. Without a doubt, I know that if she turned around in that picture, her eyes would be mesmerizingly green.

"Fuck." I take a deep breath and open the message.

CHAPTER EIGHT

EVIE

"CHERRY WAVES" BY DEFTONES

I knew I should have left him alone. There were so many things that I should have done, yet I don't regret a single thing. I don't regret taking him up on his drink offer at the club. I don't regret having mind-blowing orgasms with him. I don't regret making sure he got home okay after I pretended to be unaffected by his touch while I left him there wondering if I was coming back.

However, I do regret not being able to keep him.

Leaving him there was one of the hardest things I've had to do, and considering all I lost, that is saying a lot.

I can't believe he waited for me all that time, knowing I would probably not return. I stared at him, holding myself back from returning, but I knew it would be a mistake, so I forced myself to put one foot in front of the other and numb myself to the repressed emotions that threatened to resurface after spending only one evening together.

I've never had that kind of connection to anyone before. Following Jameson to work, and then to the bar afterward, was wrong, but no one said I was normal. I've accepted that I wasn't an ordinary girl long ago. I was made this way out of deception, lies, and abuse. I was forced to develop my own form of coping skills.

So here I am, at the bar Emma frequents, watching Jameson meet his friends sitting at a high-top with him in my line of vision.

Emma left as we arrived, sitting with her usual coworkers, but he didn't notice. I took a seat, sipping my seltzer water and watching from my spot in the corner with a view of the whole bar. Mateo was put off by my new obsession, but for someone who looks out for the same things I do, he's one to talk.

As fucked-up as I am, I didn't feel that way last night with Jameson. I felt seen. After hiding and pretending I was dead along with my parents in that fire, I must remain invisible to everyone. I rarely talk to anyone besides Mateo, and have never had a relationship.

After Mateo saved me from being attacked long ago in that alley, I was traumatized, but with the help of a therapist, I was able to pull myself from drowning in flashbacks of that night. Even though I was just bruised, my injuries were invisible—and my spirit was broken. I had to learn how to take back the control that was taken from me that night. I did that by speaking about my anxiety, and self-defense classes to combat my fears. I swore I would never let anyone have that kind of power over me again. I will be the only one in control of every aspect of my life.

I have held true to that, even when it comes to being intimate with someone.

Let's be honest. There is no intimacy with the one-night stands that I have. Sex for me is an act used to release tension that has built up to the point of rage. I have had sex with men in the past, but never anything more than that—except for last night. I felt seen and treasured when he looked into my eyes like I was someone who mattered to him. I wasn't just Evie, the sister who died and stayed unseen to protect Emma.

I was an actual person who sought the things all women want. I want to be the center of someone's world. I want to be held and cherished as if I am the most essential thing to their existence. I felt that possibility for a small amount of time, and even if I never have that again and all our plans go to shit, I can say that without a doubt, for that moment, I mattered to someone. I felt cared for and treasured, which is absolutely absurd, since we were both at a sex club. I'm sure we won't be telling this story to any grandkids.

Finding him on that app was pure luck, but once I saw his profile, I knew that I had to reconnect with him again. Maybe just one more time to indulge myself in something I can't have. So I threw caution to the wind and decided to send him a private message.

I want to explain to him that I didn't want to leave but that it was for the best. It's a mistake to talk to him and get him involved any further than he already is, but I can't stop wanting him. He's like a drug, and I need my fix. I pick up my phone and hit send.

> Eve: I want to see you again.

One small phrase that should get my point across.

I've never been a jealous type, but when I saw that girl push up against him at the bar, I wanted to scream in her face that he is mine and rip her hands off him. They had a familiarity of having been intimate. I've never felt so many emotions at once: anger for touching what's mine, jealousy that someone else knew him in a similar way I had, and a longing that makes me want to be held the way I imagined he would have night—the night when I walked away from the one thing I wanted to be selfish with.

I drive home where I reside with my brother Mateo. The traffic here is insane, and I wish for a simpler life. I'd like to pick a place I want to live versus someone dictating where I have to live. Living in Houston isn't the best, and I loved the simplicity of living on Padre Island, but Julian found Emma, and Adrian convinced her to move here with Liv, so here we are. The timing was perfect, and the reason held true—to be a friend to Liv and help her with her transition to a new city after the accident at the beach. I can still hear the screaming.

I remember that day and the first time I saw Jameson at the beach.

I blended in with the crowded beach area, pretending to be any girl indulging in the moment. I hid behind my sunglasses and hat while Mateo hung out with girls wrapped around him. He said it helped provide cover, but it sure looked like something else from where I sat.

I watched my sister with her friends and felt a twinge of sadness that I couldn't tell her that I was there. Instead, I watched from afar and bided my time—all to keep her safe.

Day turned into night, and the party continued. The crowds had lessened, and Mateo and I were farther away from where we originally sat, closer to the shore. We had the van parked farther back now as the tide came in, but we were still close enough that I could keep an eye on Emma.

A thump startled me from my thoughts, followed by a high-pitched wail, and finally muffled sounds all coming from the van. Thank God he shoved his hand over that bitch's mouth.

Just when I thought I could get a moment of reprieve, it started rocking, and I snorted, "Fuck this." I put on my Van sneakers and walked in the shadows when someone called out my sister's name.

"Emma?" I heard a voice call out. She looked zoned out until she realized someone was calling her. "Do you have to pee or something? You can't keep still?"

I looked to see where she was and turned to talk to a guy with brownish-colored hair, average height, and a toned body.

Her laugh carried on the humid coastal breeze. "What gave it away?" she asked playfully, and my lips turned up in a smile.

"Oh, I don't know. It looked like you had ants in your pants," he retorted, displaying a beautiful smile across his chiseled jaw. He was handsome and anything but average in my eyes.

Emma threw her hand around. "Ha! I hope not. What do you think about escorting me to the bathrooms? I need to pee, but I don't like that it's so secluded over there and..." I saw her throat bob as she formulated her following words. "Dark."

My heart broke hearing that she was still acutely aware of the dangers that lurk in the dark. I wanted to go to her. To shout, 'I'm here, Emma.' Instead, I stood silent and continued to watch over her.

He smiled at her and reached for her hand. "I'd be happy to escort you." He swung her arm back and forth playfully. "Come on. Let's go." They walked hand-in-hand, like school-aged children, to the portable bathroom stall closer to the sand dunes.

I walked behind the dunes, watching and waiting to see if I needed to intervene.

"Do you want me to wait here?" he asked respectfully. "I'll give you some privacy."

Emma chuckled. "Nope, no privacy needed," she retorted. "Can you wait right here, right here?" She said it twice for emphasis as she pointed to the spot in front of the stall before stepping in to relieve herself.

"Of course," he replied, standing there waiting for her. I heard the stall door close. Then I saw them coming my way, but before they got to the sand dune to cut back to their friends, I saw him stop and face her, bringing her into him. He placed both hands on her cheeks, staring down at her. I couldn't see his eyes, but I could feel the desire he felt for her radiating off in waves.

I swallowed in anticipation of what she'd do. I couldn't help but feel a longing. I saw myself there with him. I envisioned him gazing down at me. I felt his hands on my cheeks, and he watched me with the same longing desire, but this time for me, burning me up inside. My clit pulsed, and I saw him pick her up. Her legs wrapped around him. I sucked in a breath, begging for them to silently stop. I wanted to throw up.

One arm went to grab her ass, holding her up, and my face turned red. The other arm reached across her back, and he looked intently at her as if he saw no one else.

Has anyone ever looked at me that way?

I felt it when their lips touched, and I touched my lips as they tingled from the sensation that mocked me. He deepened the kiss, kissing her passionately. I watched them through blurred vision. Wetness coated my eyelashes, and I've never wanted anything so bad. The ache in my heart widened as the need for this man took hold of my heart and squeezed it painfully—a reminder that I couldn't have him. Their kiss ended as fast as it started, and he stared at her in confusion.

He dropped her legs from his embrace, and Emma righted herself. She looked around, then back at him awkwardly. "Um," I heard her say. "We should get back. They will wonder where we went soon."

He nodded and held her stare as she looked anywhere but at him. "Sure," he said, rubbing his hand at the back of his neck. I'm sure he wondered what the fuck just happened.

"Me, too," I said aloud to no one in particular. Just then, I felt a hand on my shoulder. I stiffened. "Pfft, took you long enough, asshole." I didn't have to look around to know that Mateo had seen me staring at this guy. I watched them walk away, and before I could give Mateo hell for fucking someone in the van, we heard a scream.

"Help! Someone help!" Mateo and I followed Emma, who ran alongside Jameson, to where a large crowd had gathered.

The sound of my phone interrupts my intrusive thoughts. I lie there staring at the ceiling. I got tired of waiting for a response, but then I thought maybe he hadn't seen the message yet.

I hesitate to pick up my phone. A series of questions float through my mind. What if he doesn't want to see me? What if he is already dating someone from the app? What if I didn't really matter to him, and he is this way with everyone? What if I'm not that special?

I pick up my phone and hover over the little pinkish square of the dating app. I see a message from Jameson and let out a breath before opening it.

Jameson: Sure. Coffee?

I look at the cuteness of the place he wants to meet. Unfortunately, I can't meet him for coffee. Maybe not ever.

Eve: I have a better idea. I'll come to you.

His reply is instant, and his confusion is apparent. I smile, thinking about how that night will go.

Jameson: What? When?

I hover over the text and type out a reply before I can second-guess myself.

Eve: I'll come to you—your place. I'll be in touch soon.

I'm about to click out of the app before another message with his address comes through. I can't help the laugh that escapes me now.

"Cute, he thinks I don't know where he lives." I shake my head at his innocence and feel like I have something to look forward to for the first time in forever.

I get under the covers. This time sleep comes the easiest it has in a very long time, and I dream of Jameson smiling up at me as I come undone, riding his thick cock.

CHAPTER NINE

JAMESON

"EMERGENCY CONTACT" BY PIERCE THE VEIL

I hate to say that I've been checking my phone frequently on the off chance that Eve has sent me a time when we will meet up. It was unexpected to hear from her after I had already told myself that I probably would never see her again after that one amazing evening together. I reluctantly watched her leave and immediately regretted letting her turn that corner and walk away. Still, it's been weeks, and I haven't heard from her after that last text message via the dating app, so maybe she had a change of heart.

My phone rings, and I look down at the name flashing across the screen. *Eduardo.* I quickly think of all the reasons he may want to talk to me, and all the reasons involve Emma. With her on my mind, I hit the answer button without a second thought.

The traffic was brutal, so finally an hour later, I am pulling into the rear parking lot outside of Eduardo's nightclub, The Viceroy, as I was instructed to do. He'd said he needed to talk to me about Emma's safety, so I'd left before we even hung up to see what he needed from me.

I'm escorted through Eduardo's office door and notice two security guards present. I know one is Philip, who is responsible for following Emma and driving her places. The other is staring at him with disconcertment.

"Jameson, good to see you, brother. I am glad you were able to get here so soon. Like I said earlier, it's important." He sits forward in his chair. "Eli, I'll call you when we are done with Philip."

The door to his office closes, and I hear footsteps retreating from the entryway. I eye him skeptically, wondering where he is going with this. "You mentioned safety and Emma's name in the same sentence, which is why I am here so fast," I clarify. It makes him furious as fuck, and I wonder why I even said that. It's not as if I am in love with his girlfriend, but I feel a strong connection to her—one that I can't explain.

"Right," he says with as much indifference as the guy can muster, but I notice the tic of his jaw and the clenching of his teeth holding him back from saying what he wants to.

He gets up from his desk and moves to the front, bracing his hands against the front of the desk and kicking his legs out in front of him, crossing them at the ankles, appearing aloof and unaffected. I know that move is one of power and intimidation, but he is my frat brother—I've also cleaned his puke out of the backseat of my car.

I cock one eyebrow upward, urging him to get on with it. He nods in understanding.

"Jameson, I called you here because you care about Emma, and we need your help. What I am about to disclose to you is to stay between us in this room and no one else. It is about her safety, and I can't jeopardize that."

I sit up immediately, interest piqued as I look between the security guards and Eduardo. He waits to hear me verbalize my understanding.

"I understand," I inform him as I sit in my chair, waiting for more details. "What can I do to help? Is she in trouble?"

He hesitates, biting his bottom lip before he responds. "I don't know the history between you two..." He pauses, and I wait for him to elaborate, but he doesn't. He wants me to tell him without drawing inaccurate conclusions. That fucker.

"Yeah," he continues, "I have known Emma for most of my life."

I must look confused because he tells me that their families were business associates and they recently reconnected. He tells me about her abusive relationship with a man named Julian and then about her parents' death and twin sister.

My head shoots up. "Twin sister?"

He nods. "She had a twin sister named Evie, her best friend. She misses her terribly and blames herself for their deaths."

I take this in and slump a little in my chair, letting my hand rub up and down on my pant legs. The rage inside is palpable.

I stand up. "He is still after her? He was here tonight?"

He nods in confirmation. That's all I need to know. I already know that I will help him however he needs me to.

"I need your help looking at the security feed to see if I missed anything, and I also need you to wipe it a little bit or just a certain section of it."

My confusion is evident as he continues to explain the reasoning. "Well, since you installed it, you know more about the system than anyone else would, right?"

I nod, confirming that he isn't wrong. "Um... why do you need it wiped?"

His smile is one of a criminal thug at his finest. He looks over to Philip then to me, and he says, "Philip here has to die, and I don't want there to be any evidence."

Okay, that is not what I imagined he was going to say, and I can't be an accomplice to murder. Can I? I am just contemplating Philip's murder, and he must notice because he snorts, breaking my concentration.

"You're fucking joking, right?" Because now I think they are fucking with me.

"Mostly," Eduardo counters. Seeing my ethos winning the internal war that wages on my morals, he rolls his eyes, putting me out of my misery. "I need it to *look* like I killed Philip, but he will stay hidden and keep an eye on Emma—from the shadows," he clarifies, rolling his eyes.

"With everyone thinking that he is dead, that will give him the upper hand so he can go unnoticed. People won't suspect he is secretly watching out for the person giving Julian information if he is considered dead. We need to find out who that is before they lead him to her and he gets to Emma."

I glance over at Phil and then back at Eduardo before quickly responding, "Okay, I'm in."

After Philip is presumed dead and I wipe the surveillance feed, Eduardo invites me back to his office for another chat. He is more direct this time. "I want to know what happened between you and Emma. I know that you have feelings for her."

I sense the struggle between wanting to know and knowing he may not want to know about his girlfriend. He is staring at me as he blows a long breath and visibly tenses.

I look up at him, running my hand through my hair. "Nothing." He waits patiently as I find the words to describe it. "We met on Padre Island during spring break. That's when Dax met Liv. He was a patient in the ER and we all met up at the beach the next day. We shared a moment, but then she came here. And she saw you. I don't know."

His breathing has increased, and I can sense that he thinks I fucked his girlfriend. I decide to put him out of his misery. His fist clenches and unclenches on the desk, and I know he will lose it very soon if I don't clarify. There were times when his volatile temper got the better of him in college.

"A moment?" He tilts his head and glares at me. "Did you fuck my girlfriend?" And there it is. His voice is laced with barely controlled anger. He finally asked me what he really wants to know.

"No," I reply without hesitation, meeting his glare so that he understands that it is the truth. "We had an awkward kiss, and that is it. I think Dax and Liv thought there was more between us, and I wanted there to be, but now she is with you."

He steps away from the desk, rubbing his face. "Awkward kiss?" he questions, wanting to know every fucking detail. Why does he want to torture himself with all of this?

I rub the back of my neck, trying to explain the kiss we shared in the least embarrassing way. "Yes, bro. Awkward as fuck. It felt like I was kissing my sister, despite being super attracted to her." He snorts. "I can't explain it, but I feel super protective of her, too, but not in a romantic way."

He smiles. "Okay, sister fucker."

We laugh.

"Nice, bro. Thanks." And that breaks the ice a little. "You have nothing to worry about. I care about Emma, but if she is happy with you, I just want her to be happy." I shrug noncommittally.

He stands and clasps my shoulder. "I'm glad to hear that. Now, I need your help with a tracker for Emma."

"Unbelievable," I mutter as I walk through my door a little after midnight. The things that motherfucker roped me into doing tonight. "Only slightly illegal," I loudly mock Eduardo's tone.

In need of some alcohol, I turn on the lights and head to the fridge to grab a beer when my phone buzzes in my pocket. I take a long swig and look at the message. I swear, if he needs one more thing, I will lose it.

I hit the button and see that it's definitely not from Eduardo. I smile, seeing that it's from Eve. I almost drop my phone, thinking about seeing her and the excitement that elicits.

> Eve: Can I come over?

Those four words make my heart race in excitement. I stare at the phone in wonderment. It's as if she knew the exact moment I got home.

I take my beer, walk over to my balcony, open the slider, and walk out. I stand there looking over the street, wondering where she is. I take another swig of my beer, wondering what to tell her. I'll be damned if I am going to turn down her request to come over tonight. She reached out, so who am I to deny her?

I shrug the doubt away and decide to respond sooner rather than later, having been so anxious to hear back from her in the past weeks. I don't want her to disappear again, but I don't want her to think she can just come and go. Reluctantly, I need to know, so I text her back.

> Jameson: I didn't think you were going to reach out. It's been a while.

I immediately hit send, then regret doing it. What am I doing? A sexy woman wants to come over to my house, and I'm guilt-tripping her for leaving me hanging for weeks. I groan and hope that I didn't just ruin everything. Minutes go by, and I swear that I fucked up royally. Why couldn't I have just said, 'Hell yes.'

> Eve: I was away but reached out as soon as I was free. Is that a no?

I don't want there to be any more confusion. I want her. I wanted her yesterday, and surprisingly, I want her for my future. So, I respond as directly as possible to prevent any other confusion.

> Jameson: That's a fuck yes. Come.

I laugh at the double entendre in that sentence. God, what I wouldn't give to have her come over and over on my tongue and around my cock as I thrust into her. I rub my aching dick as it pushes against the tight confines of my denim jeans, trying to alleviate the throbbing, and needing a release.

> Eve: I'll be there as soon as I can. Leave the door open and the lights off. Be a good boy and wait for me naked in your room.

> Evie: Don't touch yourself. That's my job ;)

My body thrums with excitement as I read her message and then re-read it to make sure I didn't miss anything. Eve that night was a woman who knew what she wanted, and I was turned on as fuck as she rode my face. Her take-charge attitude was a complete turn-on, and I loved every second.

I groan, thinking about that night and wondering what tonight holds for us, and with that, I take a quick shower. Stepping out of the fastest shower I have ever taken, I throw a towel around my waist, unlock the door just as she instructed, pick up my beer from the table, and finish the rest. I shut off the lights and head into my bedroom, stripping off my towel just as I step into the room.

Whenever a woman tells you to wait for her naked and in bed, it's best if you just oblige.

CHAPTER TEN

EVIE

"LOVE THE WAY YOU LIE" BY EMINEM

I've been busy these past few weeks and haven't been able to reach out to Jameson since I sent that last text message on the dating app. Pretending you are dead and trying not to be seen is more complicated than one would think. My Uncle Andrés summoned us to meet with him in Mexico about the incident with Emma in her apartment.

Emma and Liv were catching up and visiting, since Liv spends most of her time at Dax's place. Julian must have been in Emma's apartment and wrote a message on her mirror. This prompted Eduardo to race to her apartment and drag her out with a bag. I had been watching the apartment as they drove away.

After that incident, it is clear he is in Houston and has found her. We just don't know how, but we have to be smart about when to anticipate his next move.

She's been at Eduardo's ever since that night. He has provided around-the-clock security detail for her. Someone takes her to work, or he personally takes her places. She is even working the night shift at the hospital now. We hope it is safer that way.

Emma was back at the apartment today, and we were on high alert. Their friends from Padre Island are here and unpacked their stuff hours ago. Watching them tonight proved to be an act of patience. I was at The Viceroy Club with Mateo, watching Emma and her friends from afar. Eduardo allowed her out of his sight as long as she brought the girls to his club, where he could have his security and bouncers watch over them closely.

I had been waiting at the club. Her friends from Padre Island and her best friend, Liv, walk in. The girls are excited about tonight, but Emma is frowning, looking at her best friend. Concern etches her face as she tries to have fun but will not leave Liv's side. I immediately notice Liv looking a little peaked. Despite her best performance, the girl seems one step away from puking in a trashcan.

Always watching and never participating, I feel like I'm living my life through Emma and her friends, except I'm not; I'm nobody. I sigh.

Suddenly, I see a man approaching Emma and her friends dancing. On high alert, I sit up straight on my barstool and send a message to Mateo, but he's already on the dance floor watching Emma as this random girl grinds on him. I'm also watching Emma, and she seems to notice something is off.

Security is around the dance floor talking into their headsets. I walk toward the dance floor's perimeter, wondering if this is when my cover is blown, but Mateo and I make eye contact. The girl he is dancing with has her head buried in his chest and is holding onto him. He shakes his head at me, and I immediately go back.

A big, muscular guy wearing a tight-fitted Henley shirt with tattoos in places similar to Eduardo's approaches Emma with a predatory gleam in his eye. He starts to dance closely against her, and a small commotion occurs on the dance floor. A very pissed-off Eduardo tells the guy something in his ear while looking at my sister. He nods in recognition when he realizes his error. Emma is led off the dance floor hand-in-hand with Eduardo, and I visibly relax. Then she turns back and rips her hand away, running to Liv.

Liv is holding onto a barstool, swaying as if she is one breath away from passing out of the floor. She motions for Eduardo, and he quickly calls for security. Liv is picked up and taken upstairs to what I assume is Eduardo's office. Emma and the girls follow her upstairs past the VIP areas and into the back hallway. Mateo abandons his partner on the dance floor and walks to me with purpose.

I toss back a shot of tequila and pass one over to Mateo. He takes it from me and throws it back in a similar fashion. He wipes his mouth with the back of his hand. I lean over to talk with him. The music is unforgiving, but I can't wait and need to know now.

"What happened? Did you see what went on?" I lean in closer to hear him better, but then pull back. "Ugh, you smell like a brothel." The cheap perfume is so sickly sweet that it's nausea-inducing. "Is this what Liv smelled?"

He shakes his head.

"You're so dramatic, Evie." He moves closer, despite my wrinkling my nose and the stench emanating from his shirt.

"It really does smell bad. I'm allergic to cheap perfume."

He ignores me.

"Yeah, that guy with Emma was a distraction. I saw another guy walking around that was staring at Emma. It's probably a good thing Liv had to be carried away. It brought extra security around them, honestly."

I see a bouncer escorting a man through the crowd and walking toward the VIP rooms. I nod.

"Wanna bet that's Liv's boyfriend?" Mateo snorts at his own question.

"Wanna bet that girl's pregnant?" I counter and look over at my brother with one raised eyebrow.

"You think so?" He looks at me like that is impossible. He shudders. "Kids."

"Who knows?" I've already lost interest in Emma's 'best friend.' "I guess it could be a stomach bug." I roll my eyes for emphasis, just in case he didn't pick up on my sarcasm.

"Maybe," he answers in more of a question than a statement, still not grasping my condescending tone.

I look up to the balcony, and see Emma hanging over, looking down at the crowd dancing below. Her friends are around, and she is watching someone walk in. I look at her line of sight and freeze when I see Jameson approaching Eduardo's office. Mateo catches my eye.

"What are you doing, Evie?" I want to get up and run after him, but I can't. My fist is clenched, and the other holds on to the barstool, preventing me from running after him. I look back up and see that Emma has returned to her friends.

"Let's wait and go back to see what we can learn from there." I go to stand, and Mateo grabs my hand. He must see the anxiety rising to the surface, coming over in waves. I take a deep breath to calm myself.

"Come on, sis. I got you."

We leave the club, and I hold onto my brother like a lifeline—the only man who has been there for me.

We waited but never saw Jameson and Philip exit the club. I did see another man they called Eli drive off with Emma and the girls, undoubtedly to take them home. Mateo followed them, and I took off to our apartment alone.

Instead of going there, I detour, taking the on-ramp heading to Jameson's place. I'm parked outside, stalking him, and I'm excited to see him. I didn't think it would be this long before I saw him again, but here I am debating on whether or not to end the torture I've felt, not being able to reach out to him because I was out of the country.

Seeing him walk into the club, and how good he looked made me stabby—even seeing my sister taking him in sent jealousy coursing through me. She has her own man, but the reminder of her legs wrapped around him at the beach sends a bolt of anger rushing through me as my face begins to feel too hot. I turn up the air conditioning and adjust the vent to hit my face, trying to calm the surge of anger.

He pulls into the parking lot, and I watch him jump out of the car and lock it with the key fob. He's sending a message, and I immediately wonder who he is messaging. I look down at my phone. Nothing. It's not me, but why would it be. I've left him hanging.

I rub at my temples, with the impending headache that threatens to erupt. I open the app where my text message was sent to Jameson some time ago.

'Come.' One word has me shivering from head to toe. Goosebumps break out along my arms. I know he sent the message like that because he knew how it would affect me. I have been recounting the events of our first evening together—reliving the experience with Jameson.

My connection with him was one that I have never felt before or with anyone else. I have never allowed myself to become attached to anyone, but with him, I want to try. He makes me feel so much, too much, and that in itself is a scary thought.

Eve: I'll be there as soon as I can. Leave the door open and the lights off. Be a good boy and wait for me naked in your room ;)

I grab the mask I wore the last time I was with him at the Heavenly Pearl Club. I shouldn't even be seeing him. I should stay away, but I can't.

I get out of my car. I parked down the street from his house, and the lights have been off for over an hour. I take in a deep breath, as I open the door, fighting all of the reasons why I should get back in my car and just drive away. Instead, I push open the door and walk into his place.

The lights are off, and I touch my mask to ensure it is in place. I lock the door behind me and take in my surroundings. I walk over to the balcony where I saw him standing weeks ago and take in the view. I want to see it from his point of view. I imagine myself watching him from my car and him looking out, unaware of me.

I touch his sofa. My hand brushes along the soft leather. Its coolness nips against my skin as I walk down the hall toward his bedroom.

And there he is. Lying on his bed. Just as I asked, he is naked and lying flat on his stomach. His even breaths let me know that he is asleep. Did he go to sleep thinking that I had stood him up, that I wouldn't come?

I go to his chair and sit across from him, staring at his perfect form in front of me. His muscular ass is barely visible in the dim moonlight coming in through the window blinds.

When I look back up to his face, I see his eyes open and looking right back into mine. A small smile plays on his lips, and I can't help but reciprocate. I reach down and take off my combat boots. I shimmy out of my knee-highs and leather skirt. My tank top is pulled over my head, and I stand there in nothing else except my lacy black bra and a matching thong.

Jameson turns over without breaking eye contact, and his fully erect cock is there for the taking. His tip glistens with precum; I salivate at the thought of tasting him. I reach around and undo my bra, letting it fall to the floor.

I pull down my thong, and wetness pools around my center. The sight of him turns me on.

He groans. "Eve, you're killing me here."

I walk over to him and crouch over his body. I lick at the tip of his thick erection as a milky drop leaks from the slit, and I lap it up, tasting his saltiness. He lifts his hips, and I take him in my mouth. Before he can grab my hair, I release him with a pop.

I move slowly up his body, leaving kisses along the way, and when I reach his neck he grabs my face between his hands and he kisses me with everything he has. Our kiss turns sloppy and hungry as if he can't get enough of me. I understand the feeling. I run my center up and down his dick, soaking it with my wetness. I line him up and drop down onto his thickness, feeling so full.

"God, Jameson, I've needed this," I admit shamelessly, showing him a vulnerability that I refuse to give anyone else. I want him to know that he is different, that what I feel for him means something to me, and that in turn, he means something to me.

I moan and start riding him. His hands go to my hips, pushing me down hard with a punishing force. I place my hand over his, not turning away his touch, but for the first time embracing it.

God, how long has it been since I've allowed anyone to touch me like this? It turns me on so much, and I hold his hands there, pinning them to me. I'm lost to the sensations as I bounce up and down on his cock. I hear his breathing become labored.

"Eve, I need you to slow down." His hand goes up over his head, and his head moves back and forth as if he can fight off the impending orgasm from crashing over him.

"I can't slow down, it feels too good. I need this Jameson. Please let me have this." Because I'm almost right there with him. My hands are on his shoulders, and I rock into him as he pushes up into me, meeting me thrust for thrust, both of us lost to the sensations.

"Oh, God." I pant. "Jameson."

He brings my face down to him and kisses me, thrusting his tongue in and out along with the pace of his cock. His chest is covered in a sheen of sweat, and my juices run down his cock, soaking his balls. The sloppy sounds of our fucking fill the room. He grabs my ass and brings me down more forcefully, and I swear he is so deep, hitting that sweet spot no one could ever find.

"That's it, Jameson. Keep doing that." I throw my head back, and he meets me thrust for thrust. My walls start to convulse as I come so hard that I almost black out.

He fucks me through the orgasm, and he comes after a few more deep thrusts. He brings me down to him, threading our hands together as he kisses me. I collapse onto his chest, and he strokes my back gently. And I allow it. Wetness fills my vision, and everything is blurry.

"Where have you been all this time, Eve?" he whispers, but I don't think he expects an answer, and I certainly don't offer him one.

Not once does he ask about my mask.

CHAPTER ELEVEN

EVIE

"DECODE" BY PARAMORE

I watch Jameson sleep, and I can't help but stare at him. He looks so peaceful, and I bet he does it without a care in the world. He probably doesn't even dream. I envy him for that. To be able to sleep without waking up from a nightmare that you relive whenever you begin to think you feel safe, but I haven't felt safe in a very long time.

Retrieving my clothes, I quickly dress and stare at his sleeping form before leaving. I'm trying to take a mental picture of him this way. Instead, I take out my phone. *Click.*

Without looking back, because if I do I may do something crazy like crawling back into bed and staying. For once, I felt seen, and I don't want to go back to being invisible.

No more masks.

Grabbing the mask, looking down at it one last time before letting it fall onto the table. I vow that the next time I see him, he will see all of me—no more hiding, at least not from him. Reality, on the other hand, has different plans for me. I have to put my happiness on the back burner if I want to help my family. The only family I have left are my siblings.

I take one more look around his apartment and walk out the door with a silent prayer falling from my lips that maybe one day I can have him. I can choose to be selfish and have my happy ending, too, but for now, I can't let this continue. I have to keep Emma safe. This thing we are doing is a luxury that I can't have. If I just keep repeating it over and over to myself, I just might start to believe it. Our need to get revenge is more important. I can't have any more distractions, and Jameson is a huge distraction for me.

When I get back to my car, I slide into the driver seat and just sit there with the engine idling. I don't want to leave, but I force myself to pull away and drive back to my place, leaving a piece of my tattered heart behind as I drive away.

As I pull into my parking spot just before dawn, I see someone jogging out of the complex, and another is leaving for work. I always feel like a loser when I arrive home in the early hours of the morning after a night out at the club. My sister calls it the 'walk of shame,' and it's tough to head to bed while everyone else is just starting their day.

I drag myself up the stairs and open the door when a big yawn escapes me, scratch my head, and throw my bag on the kitchen island. I fill a glass of water, turning around to lean against the counter, when I come face to face with Mateo staring at me.

"Dear God!" I jump back, sloshing half of the water out of my glass. "Bro, what is wrong with you? You almost gave me a heart attack. Don't sneak up on me like that." I flick the water off my tank top, now sporting a huge wet spot in the center. I frown looking down at it, then grab a towel to pat myself dry. I chug the remaining water and place the glass in the sink. Mateo is still staring at me. "What?" I look at him, trying to decipher what his deal is.

"Oh, looks like someone had a rendezvous. Did you see that guy again?"

I look quizzically at him. "Who?"

He snorts. "Don't play dumb, sister. It doesn't suit you."

I smile, displaying my straight, white teeth. "You'll have to be more specific, Mattie. I'm not twelve." We laugh and then realize the implications of that comment as our laughter dies out.

We didn't get that chance to have that relationship because he was sent away. I didn't even know I had a brother until recently. Now, he and my sister have become the most important people in my life. Another part of me thinks that maybe Jameson can be my person, too.

A hand lands on my shoulder. I jump at the unexpected touch.

"Relax. I didn't mean to startle you." He brings me into him and kisses the top of my head.

I force myself to relax into his embrace.

As if hearing my thoughts, Mateo speaks. "I love you, Evie."

I raise my hand to my heart and rub the ache that threatens to take up residence there. The physical aching from someone telling me I am loved is a welcome feeling.

"I love you too, Mateo."

He takes a sniff. "Now, who smells like a brothel? You smell like sex." He pushes me away.

"Yeah, alright. I am going to shower. Great moment." I walk away, and he calls me back.

"Oh, Uncle Andrés called right before you got here. I guess Eduardo called him up asking for Emma's hand in marriage."

"No shit. Um, wow. She's getting married?" I don't know how to feel about that.

"He told Tió that he would keep her safe."

I think about how much time has passed since they were younger. I guess when you know, you know. "Maybe I'll get to go to the wedding," I reply snarkily.

Mateo nods. "Yeah, and maybe I'll finally meet my sister," he speaks hesitantly.

God, I am such a bitch. When I think about all I've lost, I realize that Mateo has had it so much harder than I have.

"One could only hope, Mattie." I smile sadly at him as I walk off toward my bedroom and close the door behind me.

Flopping on my comfy but empty bed, I slip on my favorite sleep shorts and tank before throwing my outfit from last night in the hamper, mimicking a two-point shot. *Swish.* Snuggling down under the covers, I wrap myself in my blankets, refusing to shower so Jameson's scent can envelop me in a feeling of peace where my mind can finally be at rest.

I wake up to the bright sun shining through the blinds. I lazily walk to the bathroom, turning on the shower to let it heat up so I can shower quickly and get some things done. Walking out of my room and into the living room, I see Mateo sitting on the couch watching television. He stands quickly, turning the TV off.

"Come on. Let's get some tacos. I'm starving."

I walk over to grab my bag. "You don't have to tell me twice, bro. I love tacos."

When we get to our fave Mexican spot, we ask to sit outside on the covered patio. The ceiling fans are going, giving us a nice breeze. When our waitress comes over, we order a plate of tacos. Mateo gets a beer, and I get an iced tea.

"No beer?" Mateo questions.

"Nah, I am thirsty, and nothing quenches my thirst like an iced tea."

He tries to hide his laughter but just shakes his head at me. As the waitress returns with our drinks shortly after taking our order, I eagerly grab my iced tea and take a big sip, feeling the coolness of the drink refresh me. However, as I put the glass back down, I notice some moisture pooling on the surface, making me shudder a bit. I quickly reach for a tuxedo wrap and wipe off the excess moisture. Mateo shifts in his chair.

"You really hate condensation, don't you?" He takes another drink, shaking his head at me in jest.

"Ha, you have no idea. Emma and I both do." A smile plays on my lips, thinking of my sister with good memories instead of the bad ones.

I gaze at my brother's profile, searching for any resemblance between us. Despite looking light-skinned while he is an olive tone, and having green eyes while his are as dark as night, I can't help but wonder where his features come from. As he catches my stare, his expression softens, and he smiles, revealing Emma's smile. This gentle reminder tugs at my heart, reminding me that everything could change at any moment. However, I hold onto the belief that we will be reunited soon.

"So, tell me about Jameson?"

My eyes shoot up to his as I ponder his question. What do I tell him about Jameson? Hell, I don't even know much about him, or how I feel about him, except that I found a deep connection to him that I just can't explain. I was able to let some of the control go as he held me. He actually fucking held me. It was almost sweet, as if he understood that I had some issues, yet he still wanted to consume me. It didn't feel like just a fuck. It felt like something more.

"I pick at the napkin around my glass, avoiding his gaze. "I like him." I stop and meet his eyes. They soften.

"I can tell, and I'm happy for you, Evie. You deserve to be happy."

I frown. "I just need this to be over so that I can tell him everything, but when will that be, Mateo? You know, I saw him that night at the beach when Brodie had that accident. I liked him from that moment without even knowing him, but he was interested in my sister then." I look over at Mateo, and his head tilts to the side.

"What do you want to ask me, Evie?" He stares at me instead. I push through and ask my question, verbalizing my biggest fear.

"What if he likes me because somehow I remind him of Emma? I mean, she is my twin." I bite my lip. I hate the vulnerability in my voice. I look across the street at people walking by, taking in the ease with which they walk without a care in the world. I see a woman walking up to a man. He wraps her in a hug, kissing her, and grabs her hand possessively as they walk off. God, what I wouldn't give to have that—to be the center of someone's whole world.

"Evie, do you really believe that?" he asks with concern etched on his features.

"I don't know, Mateo. I mean, no, not really, but he did have a thing for Emma, but she is with Eduardo now. What if I am just second best?" I immediately hate the words when they escape my mouth, but now that they are out there, my worst fears are voiced.

"No, Evie. You are nothing like Emma. You may share looks, but other than that, you are so very different from her. I see a strong woman in front of me. One that loves fiercely and protects what she loves at all costs."

I smile. "Thanks, Mattie. That means a lot to me. I wouldn't know what to do without you."

He shifts awkwardly in his chair but smiles at the compliment.

"Enough about me. Tell me about you. Any special lady in your life?"

He shakes his head. "Now? Nope, no one special."

I shrug, deciding to pry further and invade his privacy. "So what do you do when you leave the house and come out here?"

He chuckles. "You promise not to laugh?" He shakes his head.

"Oh, boy. Now, I have to know. What do you do?" I repeat, almost bouncing in my seat with excitement, and I know that I am so going to enjoy this.

He begins but then stops mid-sentence, pondering his following words. "Fuck it." He rubs his hand over his face. "I went for a walk to think, and I found this cafe by the water. I started having my coffee there and watching the ocean waves. It brings me a bit of peace, you know?"

I nod my head in acknowledgment because I totally understand how peaceful the waves can make you feel.

"I met this older man, he was playing chess alone. I would just sit and watch him play, then one day, he asked me if I wanted to join him."

Wow, that wasn't what I thought he would say at all. I look at my brother, shocked. "You've been playing chess with an old man in your spare time?"

He rubs his hand across the back of his neck. "I mean, I guess, yeah." He snorts, almost embarrassed. "We talk about nothing and everything. His wife died, and he doesn't talk to his son. I think he is just lonely."

I nod in understanding.

"I mean, he is nice, and it quiets my mind."

Silence falls between us. Looking over at my brother, my heart aches as I realize the depth of his loneliness. It's heart-wrenching to imagine how he must be feeling, especially after being abandoned by those who were supposed to be there for him. He didn't have a real family, despite my uncle and aunt raising him as best they could. I can't imagine how tough it must have been for him not to have parents wishing him a happy birthday. Looking back, I now realize how fortunate Emma and I were. I also know how he feels when he says that it quiets his mind. Isn't that what I seek out, too?

"Is it fun?" I ask, wanting to know.

He laughs. "I mean, yeah. I enjoy it. I actually look forward to our time together. Is it weird to have a friend who could be your grandfather?"

I finish my drink. "Nope. Not at all. Hey, do you think maybe I could join you sometime?"

Surprise registers on his face. "Um. Yeah, sure. If you'd like to hang out with us, we meet once a week," he responds shyly. He smiles and shifts his attention to the waitress coming over with a tray of tacos.

The smell hits me, and my mouth begins to water. I swear I can taste the crispy mahi-mahi from here. The conversation halts as the waitress lays out our food in front of us, and I moan at the first bite of my crispy meal. Mateo and I sit there in silence, devouring our weight in tacos.

CHAPTER TWELVE

JAMESON

"CREEP" BY RADIOHEAD

I wake up the next day hoping that Eve will still be there, but as I go to touch the other side of my bed, I already know what I will find. My fingertips brush the cool sheets, and it's obvious Eve has been gone for a while. I stretch out and swear I can still smell her on me. The spicy vanilla scent is the one I wish I could spray on my sheets so that every time I lay my head down, I can envision her being here with me.

I turn my head into the pillow her head rested on last night and inhale deeply, committing it to memory in case it's the last time. I look up at the ceiling, not wanting to think about that but knowing very well that it's a possibility.

As I get out of bed, I whip the covers off my body. I try to remove the crumpled bedsheet from my bed, but I find myself hesitating as I find myself transfixed on the empty space where I had Eve lying just a few hours earlier. I drop my head and realize how fucked I really am if I can't strip my bed and rid myself of her scent just yet.

"Just one more day, and then I'll change the sheets," I mutter like a lovesick fool. I can't help the smile that pulls at my lips as I straighten the sheets and duvet as best I can before jumping into the shower. As I get dressed, I reflect on yesterday's events.

Last night at the club was so messed up. I didn't appreciate the danger that Emma is in with that psychopath ex of hers. Has she been dealing with this all this time? Was that why she appeared so skittish and afraid of the dark when I first met her during spring break on Padre Island?

My phone vibrates with an incoming text message, and I stop thinking about Emma. Instead, I only have thoughts of Eve and hope that it is her texting me. When I turn it around and click on the message, my shoulders slump forward when I see it is from Dax.

> Dax: Hey. Can you meet me for lunch? It's kind of important.

I wonder what could be so important, but then I remember that Liv was taken to the emergency department last night. Geez. I run a hand through my hair. I hope she is okay. Dax is so in love with her.

I frown when I remember Eduardo's request, reminding me I must go to work today to sort out the details of Emma's tracker. I also know I have to be there for Dax, so I decide I need to meet him today as well.

> Jameson: Sure. I have to go to work for a bit, and then I'll be there.

I finish lacing up my sneakers as I open the refrigerator door, wondering if there is anything I can take with me to eat that isn't spoiled. Another text comes in, and I pick up my phone and see the details from Dax.

> Dax: Usual spot. Noon.

I type out my reply and shove my phone into my pocket.

> Jameson: Gotcha. I'll be there.

"Not much to eat here." I close the refrigerator door and open the pantry, searching aimlessly until I see an almost empty box off to the side. I grab a protein bar and rip it open after deciding I'll meet him for lunch today so I will get a proper meal in a few hours, so I probably don't need much to eat before then.

"That should do it," I voice aloud my happiness at my progress in developing a tracker for Emma. I turn it around in my hands, admiring my work.

The GPS tracker should be easy to place in a pendant or locket. It can be worn with a necklace or a bracelet. It even has an SOS button on it.

I look down at my watch and notice it's 11:30. I start picking up my items and placing them into a little velvet purse-stringed bag to take to Eduardo's place. I know he wanted to give Emma a present.

I chuckle at the murderous look Eduardo gave me when I had to tell him about the awkward kiss Emma and I shared, but it was only a kiss. They are obviously madly in love with each other, so it really shouldn't even matter. But there's only one woman who consumes my thoughts on a daily basis, her presence lingering in my mind with every passing moment.

I arrive at the sports bar we usually frequent after work for happy hour. Dax hasn't been here in months, since he has been spending all his time with his girlfriend, Liv. I knew that from the moment he met her in the emergency department that day during spring break, he was a lost cause. He was a wreck after he left her that night, but they seemed to have their second chance, and I couldn't be happier for him.

I see him sitting at our usual table and plop myself down, clasping my hand to his shoulder.

"Hey, bro. How are you?" He looks tired but smiles like the cat that caught the canary. I steeple my hands, placing them in front of my face. "So, it looks like you have some good news. I was worried about Liv when she was taken to the hospital. I assume everything is okay?"

He nods enthusiastically. "Liv's pregnant. We are going to have a baby."

I am just about to speak when Dax looks past me, and I turn my head slightly, seeing Simone, the waitress that has a thing for Dax, stare at him with her mouth agape, opening and closing it like damn fish. She goes to speak and then stops. We both stare at her until she says, "I'll give you some more time to order," and scurries off, obviously shaken at the news of Dax becoming a daddy.

"So," I chuckle, "I guess you are officially off the market, huh?" I drink my ice water, relishing the cold drink from recently after getting out of the hot Texas heat.

Dax laughs. "Yeah, I am. That girl owns me, and the thought of her belly swollen with my baby very soon is making me all kinds of possessive of her." He runs a hand down his face. "Fuck, honestly, I can't wait to do it again."

I look at him in shock because this is not the same person I knew a while back. The guy who would not fuck anyone without a condom.

"Congrats. I am happy for you, man." I clap him on the back and he gives me one in return.

"Thanks man. I just wanted to tell you in person. We are both still in shock, but we are so excited. I'm also going to ask her to marry me. I just went out this morning and bought her the perfect ring."

He looks proud of himself, and I can't help but sputter in disbelief. "You're getting married?"

He nods, confirming my question with a wide smile.

I run my hand through my hair. "Wow, this is a lot to take in." I laugh, and he just shrugs.

"This baby's going to come sooner than later, and I want Liv to know I am all in. I don't want there to be any doubt in her mind." He removes something from his pocket and shows me a velvet box. As he carefully opens the box, my eyes are immediately drawn to the shimmering engagement ring. She is going to absolutely love it.

I whistle. "That's a huge rock."

Simone comes back to take our order and sees Dax with the ring. We both look at her as she walks off without taking our order.

"Bro, thanks a lot. Now we are never going to eat."

He laughs. "Do you think we should go somewhere else?" He looks around the sports bar.

"Naw, it's all good."

Simone never returned to our table, which was okay with us. After finally placing our order with a different server, we ate quickly as most of the time was taken up by waiting to place our order. We made plans to get together before he left on holiday break.

I'm just walking to my car when Eduardo calls me. He usually sends a text, so I wonder what the urgency is. I quickly answer the phone as now we are working together with a singular purpose.

"Hey, man, what's up?" I hit the button on my key fob, start the car, and wait until the phone picks up on Bluetooth.

"Hello," I hear Eduardo say into the speakers.

"Yeah, I'm here. I just got in the car and am headed to your place. Are you at work? The club?" I stop at the light and something catches my eye one block from the restaurant—a woman with short blonde hair wearing combat boots, leggings, and a crop top. Oversized sunglasses cover her eyes. The light turns green, and I speed up as she enters a bookstore. "Fuck," I curse, hitting the steering wheel.

"Jameson, you all right?"

Silence.

"Huh? Oh, yeah, sorry. I thought I saw someone I know, but I lost them."

Eduardo chuckles. "Alright then. Are you coming over to drop off the trackers? You finished already?" Hope radiates in his voice.

"Yes, I worked all morning on them, and I have what you need. I'll drop them off and explain what we need to do and how they work."

This seems to make him happy, and I can sense the worry leaving his voice.

"Great, I appreciate this, man. More than you know."

I end the call and pull up to his club, parking in the back.

Eli meets me at the door, patting me down. I am annoyed that I have to go through these measures, but in the world Eduardo lives in, I guess no one, even people you've known for years, can be trusted.

I pass through the hall that leads up to the Heavenly Pearl and wonder if Eve has been by the club recently. Has she been with anyone else? The thought makes me murderous, and I clench and unclench my hands as we walk up to the hall that leads to Eduardo's office.

Eli knocks on the door, and I hear the lock click meaning Eduardo hit the button on his desk to open the door for us. Eli walks in, and I follow, plopping myself into one of the chairs.

I run a hand over my face, and Eduardo stares at me.

"I'll ask you again. You okay, Jameson? Is there something you need to tell me about Emma?"

I see the worry on his face, and I shake my head. "No, I was just thinking about someone I met a while back."

He smiles and runs his hand over his face, rubbing at the scruff. His eyes are alight with amusement. "You met someone?"

I hear the door close and realize Eli left us alone together. I nod, confirming as much but not willing to give anymore details right now. I pat my pockets, pulling out the velvet purse-stringed bag.

"Here. I have what you asked for," handing it to him.

He takes a seat across from me and empties the contents on his desk. He looks up at me. I quickly explain what it is.

"This is the GPS tracker for Emma?"

I nod. "You just need the jewelry. You need to buy something like a pendant to put on a bracelet or necklace." I motion with my hand at the small tracker.

Eduardo's smile is wide as he opens his desk drawer and removes a large blue velvet box. "You mean like this?" He opens the box to reveal a stunning emerald pendant. There is a necklace and bracelet in the box.

"May I?" I ask before I pick it up.

"Of course." Eduardo hands the box over to me, and I pick up the pendant.

"This is perfect, Eduardo."

He smiles. "Yeah, it reminded me of Emma's eyes, and I had to have them."

I hold onto it, and a strange familiarity works its way into my memory of similar eyes that shone through a mask at me, once at the club and once at my home. I touch the green of the pendant and run my hand across the flawless gemstone. I straighten my shoulders. "Let's get this thing installed, and I'll show you what to do."

CHAPTER THIRTEEN

EVIE

"THROUGH GLASS" BY STONE SOUR

I've spent most of my days stalking Cherry after I found out she was harassing my sister and her friend while they were shopping. I saw her in the shop talking to my sister with a snarled expression, like the bunny boiler that she is. That girl is certifiable, and I swear if I didn't need her alive to lead me to Julian, I'd dispose of her properly.

I'm torn between following her to see what she is up to, but then I would have to leave my sister. I immediately call Mateo, but he isn't in the area, and I've lost that god-awful box red-dyed hair of a disaster walking out through the crowded city streets.

"Ugh." I stomp my foot, causing a woman to startle, jumping back and cursing at me under her breath. I see Liv laughing, arm in arm with her best friend as they enter a restaurant to have lunch. I've become an intruder in their life. I am no longer my sister's best friend; I am just a lonely woman looking through the glass and watching what should have been my life, too.

My nights are not spent any better. My mind is consumed with pining over Jameson or watching him from afar. The holidays are approaching, and I've never felt more alone.

At least I have my brother.

Mattie and I have plans of our own. He was invited to spend the holiday with the older gentleman who he plays chess with. I am supposed to meet him today, and I am glad that my brother has found a friend, albeit a seventy-year-old elderly one. Apparently, he is alone for the holidays as well, so it seems like the logical choice, throw in being by the shoreline and we will take it. I am hopeful that this will be our last year in hiding.

Walking along the boardwalk, I see Mateo on the pier overlooking the water. I stop where I am to take in the sight of him. He's tall, over six feet, with a solid build. The guy is not someone I would describe as lean, more so the type that is built for cage fighting. He is ruggedly handsome with his olive complexion and soft, wavy hair that falls into his eyes. His dark brown eyes stare at you with the innocence of a child, but I have also heard Mateo with some of his conquests and innocent is something he definitely is not. I also know he wasn't afforded that luxury, having grown up in our family and being a soldier for our uncle.

At times, something about this appearance is familiar, but it is probably because I have spent more time with him in our hunt for Julian and to keep our sister safe.

Some college-age girls pass by him and attempt to gain his attention, giggling as they pass. I smile at them, wondering if my brother would have had a girlfriend like that. If he had gone to college instead of working for our uncle, he would never be free to choose his path.

He senses me approaching and turns, his eyes soften when he sees me, and I can't help but skip a little as it turns into running towards him. He laughs, shaking his head at my antics.

"You're late." The lines around the corner of his eyes show his increasing age and sun-kissed skin, and he places his hand over his eyes to shield them from the bright Texan rays.

"I was busy," I counter, a pout forming.

He rolls his eyes along with his head and then shoots me a look that screams bullshit. "Does it by any chance have to do with a certain guy named Jameson?"

I stab my pointed fingernail into his solid chest. "None of your business, Mattie."

He leans away from the pier, standing tall as I fight the sunshine reflecting off the water to stare up at him.

"Right, then. Let's go. I want to introduce you to my friend."

I loop my arm in his as we approach their frequent meeting place.

The bell chimes above the door as we enter the cafe, and I am immediately hit by the aroma of rich coffee mixed with the scent of cinnamon. From the entrance, I can see an elderly gentleman placing a cup of coffee on the table by the widow. He beckons us with his hand as he sees us approaching his table. My mouth immediately starts to water. I grab Mattie's arm, and he halts midstep. He looks back at me quizzically.

"Nothing," I state. "I just want to know if you'd like a coffee. I am going to grab one for myself, and I see your friend already has one." I gesture with my hand over to his friend, who is now smiling at us and watching our interactions with amusement, his smile reaching his kind eyes.

"Yeah, thanks. I'll take an iced coffee, nothing in it."

I nod. "Right," I counter, "a black iced coffee to match your soul." I smile cynically, my full lips pulled wide, displaying my straight white teeth.

"Ha. That's a real knee-slapper, sis. Har-har." He smacks his outer thigh for emphasis.

Turning I head to the counter, whipping the ends of my shorter hair across my cheek, not acknowledging his stupid joke. I scan the menu that is displayed across the counter, squinting at the almost illegible scrawled cursive-colored chalk, *until* I see the Mexican latte that makes my mouth water.

I order a kolache to go along with my latte and Mateo's black iced coffee, then move down to hang out by the end of the counter while I wait for my order to be ready. I click on the dating app and notice a message from Jameson. My heart races with anticipation.

Jameson: When can I see you again?

I stare at it, knowing I can't see him again, but I want to. I left my mask there the last time with the full intention of never returning, but I am going to make a liar out of myself, and that man will be my sole reason.

Eve: I'm still trying to figure it out.

I bite my lower lip, thinking about it. I begin to type and then backtrack and stop. Do I lead him on? What if I can't see him ever again, and it makes me a liar? Without second-guessing whether I should see him again, I reply.

Eve: Soon, hopefully. Very soon.

I click out of the app and place the phone in my pocket, my emotions somber. I hate this and the way it makes me feel.

My order is ready, and I see the handsome guy in front of me. He is smiling at me. He seems... I pause, trying to find the right word for him.

Sweet.

I smile and grab my items from him with a thank you, pocketing my kolache for later, and tipping my cup at him. I approach the table where Mateo and his elderly friend sit, setting up their chess game. I hand Mateo his coffee.

"Thanks. Evie, I want you to meet Ramón Martin. Ramón, this is Evie, my sister." He looks between us and smiles.

"Evie, it's very nice to meet you," he says with accented English.

"Likewise, Mr. Martin. My brother seems to enjoy your company. I hope he isn't too much of a chore to entertain. He's quite serious, you know." I place my head on Mateo's shoulder, letting him know that I'm joking.

He pats my hand, resting on the table lovingly. Mateo laughs, pointing at my drink. I look at him as though he's lost his mind.

"Please," Mr. Martin replies, "call me Ramón."

"Okay, Ramón. It's very nice to meet you." I look over to Mateo who is fixated on my cup before returning to my conversation.

The elderly gentleman graces me with a smile.

"What's the matter with you?" Mateo startles me away from my pleasantries. He turns my drink around and I look at the guy's number written in black marker on the side with his name.

I look over to the guy at the counter and he is staring at me, face flushed with embarrassment. I turn back to look at the name.

"Dylan," I say aloud. I shrug and take a drink of my coffee. It's delicious, and the burst of spicy cinnamon chocolate hits my taste buds with a flourish.

I am struck with a sense of nostalgia, reminding me of a time when I was young during the Christmas holidays in Mexico. My abuela would make the best hot chocolate over the stove by melting a thick, dark Mexican bar of chocolate. She'd allow me to stir the tantalizing concoction until it was fully melted, mixing in some milk and a little sugar and a dash of spicy red pepper at the end that always made my mouth water in anticipation.

I remove the lid on my coffee on autopilot, still submerged in my visions, blowing on the top to cool the caramel-colored liquid as I take another drink from my cup.

"Mmm," I hum in appreciation.

Ramón breaks me from my trip down memory lane, and I look at him, realizing he said something. "What was that?" I ask.

He places his chess pieces on the board and lifts his chin toward the guy who gave me his phone number.

"I'd throw away that number away if I were you," he says nonchalantly.

I cross my arms over my chest defensively, look at Mateo, and then back at him. Sitting back, I kick one foot out in a relaxed pose.

"And why is that, Ramón?"

He sits forward as if he has some secret to tell me, and I find myself leaning forward, mimicking his position as if he is one of my friends from high school.

"I saw his wife with their baby in here the other day..." He lets that sink in, and I immediately sit up straight, my nostrils flaring.

"So he's a cheater?"

He places his hands up defensively.

"Hey, I don't know if it is his wife, but it sure seemed like it, especially when she left with the kid waving its little cute chubby hand in the air, saying, 'Say bye to Daddy.'"

Mateo almost chokes on his iced coffee, and I glance at him, daring him to breathe another word.

"Geez, calm down. I wasn't going to call him, but now I'm annoyed that his name and number are on my cup." I point at the offending cup with my hand. I look at the scribbled marker, and a thought comes into my mind of taking his number and giving it to an escort service who...

Mateo has his hand on my arm, stopping me from plotting and scheming the downfall of Dylan, the barista.

"Evie, whatever you are thinking, let it go." His penetrating gaze reminds me so much of my sister's. She would give me a similar look when I wanted to take revenge on someone or get even. I nod once and smile up at him.

"No problem, Mattie. It's already forgotten." I glance over at Ramón.

His look tells me he isn't so sure, but he nods at the chessboard and speaks to Mateo. "Are you ready to lose, buddy?"

After Mattie and Ramón played a few games resulting in Ramón sweeping Mattie best two out of three, we say our goodbyes, and make plans to get together again soon. We are in the car driving to our apartment, which resides between the beach and the city. It was a compromise for both of us because we knew where we wanted to be and where we had to be. Conflicted, we opted for the halfway mark, much like we do with everything in our lives. Breaking the silence engulfing the car, I look toward Mateo, his expression one of contemplation.

"Mattie?"

His eyes crinkle in confusion as I pull him away from wherever his mind is. "Yeah, Eves?"

I fidget with my hands. "I like your friend. He, um, seemed... nice."

His eyes soften. "Well, he seems as lonely as we are, so I thought maybe we could all get together and maybe not be so lonely together."

I nod in understanding.

He takes his eyes away from traffic again, sparing me a quick glance. "You look like you want to ask me something." He poses this as a statement when it's more of a question.

I swallow, done with the motions and vulnerability, deciding to take a chance. "I'd really like to see Jameson."

He shakes his head. "I don't know, Evie. He's friends with Eduardo. The whole point is to keep you hidden, to keep Emma safe."

I attempt to bite my nails in frustration but just end up stabbing my lip. I look down at them and frown—maybe a little too pointed. I flick my hand out, admiring my filing job. "Okay," I almost whisper.

He pulls my hand away from my mouth. "Maybe wait a little while longer, yeah? See if he can be trusted. Maybe feel him out by talking to him first. The holidays are coming, so get to know him and size up his character."

I smile, now having something to look forward to for the first time in a very long time. "I could do that."

He smiles back at me. "Just keep me posted, okay?"

I happily agree because this gives me hope—hope that I could be something more than what I am now, hope that I could be something to someone. So, I grab my phone out of my bag and I send a message—one of many that will get me through the time and the holidays until I can see him again.

CHAPTER FOURTEEN

EVIE

"DEEP WATER" BY STRAWBERRY SWITCHBLADE

Ramón has become a permanent fixture in Mateo's life, and he seems equally smitten with the old man. They have a weird connection that makes me jealous.

We spent the holidays at his house, and I'm delighted that we did. It was clear that he was indeed lonely, and I think we brought him a sense of family interactions that he was missing. For some reason, he no longer sees his son, and I don't really know much about it. It's not really any of my business to pry. What I do know is that he doesn't have any other family besides him. His wife passed away, leaving him to spend his days in the company of a young man and his sister.

In a way, I think we all helped each other have a feeling of the things we miss around the holidays. This won't last forever. When we end this, I am confident that we will have the biggest family get-togethers. But until then, I'll be longing for the times when we can have a moment of peace all to ourselves. If I keep believing this, perhaps I can manifest it. Maybe we will even bring Ramón with us into our family—our found family.

There hasn't been any other interest in Emma these past couple of months. Ever since Eduardo proposed and gave her a massive engagement ring, she has had a couple of people who dated Eduardo make some unsavory comments toward her about his past.

I am concerned with the woman who used to work at Eduardo's club. Cherry threatened Emma when she saw her out at a store when she and Liv were shopping. When I found out, I was livid. Adrian told us that Eduardo admitted he used to screw her at the club, and I swear if he weren't as devoted to Emma as he is now, I would have made sure he suffered for that. It all happened before he reconnected with Emma, but the fact that she is coming at my sister because he is with Emma now is disturbing.

During Emma's and Eduardo's stay in Mexico over the holidays, we were surprised to discover that Philip is still alive and undercover, watching Emma's every move. It would appear that Emma has a few people walking amongst the shadows, watching her and looking for unsuspecting threats.

Tonight will be difficult to navigate without being noticed. They are going to a gala to benefit the hospital where Liv's husband is employed. His parents support the organization, and his mother is the chairperson for the gala. All the proceeds are utilized to provide a selected unit within the organization with state-of-the-art equipment that helps their hospital stand out in the community, making a difference in patient care.

I awoke late in the morning after spending a long night on the phone with Jameson. We have fallen asleep together, and I imagine myself sleeping next to him. I heard his light snores coming from the phone earlier, and I touched my lips and then the phone, wishing it was his mouth I was kissing before getting up from bed.

I haven't seen him since that night when we were physically together, but we have had phone sex. We seem to be having a lot of that, and I long for the days I can have him again. I get to explore things with him that I doubt I could do in person.

I found that I know the sounds he makes before and when he comes. He tells me what he wants, and I feel empowered to give it to him. I let him tell me the things he wants to do to me, and I imagine my hands are his, moving over and inside me. The control that I desperately need is in my hands.

I don't know if he realizes this is like therapy for me. I can only hope that when I am with him again, I can relinquish the control that I require and allow him to take it. To be able to take me and make me his in the physical sense, because I already know that I am his in my mind. We are getting to know one another, and I hate that I give him half-truths, but someday, I can tell him everything. I just hope he sticks around to learn it all, because I know we can have it all if he does.

I'm just stepping out of the shower, towel drying my hair, when I hear Mateo on the phone with someone.

"Yes, Tió. I will." He spares a glance at me with an evil smirk while he is apparently speaking with my uncle. "She is very excited to go to the gala tonight. You know Evie. She loves a good party."

If he hadn't turned his face away from me, I am sure I would have punched him from spreading such vicious lies about me. He knows I hate parties. Also, there is no way that I would find attending a fundraiser to be a good time. "Tió Andrés is very concerned about the gala tonight," Mateo says as he disconnects the call with our tió. The mocking tone is evident in his commentary.

I pick up the coffee pot and pour a mugful, noting the lack of steam rising. I touch the pot and find it's cold.

"Ugh. No coffee?" I hold out the offending pot to Mateo.

He shrugs. "There was some earlier, but someone slept in."

I don't have to guess who that someone is, but it is apparent he is set on talking in riddles this 'late' morning. I walk with the mug to pour it down the drain but stop, thinking better of it. Instead, I just pop a cup into the microwave.

"Are you listening?" Mateo side-eyes me, but I can't be bothered because I haven't had my motherfuckin' coffee yet. I will shank this bitch. Don't even test me.

I raise my hand to halt his words because I literally can't right now. "I need coffee first, Mateo."

My head is hung, and my arms are slumped over, resting on the counter. The microwave chimes, and I grab my coffee from it. I lift the steamy brew up to my mouth to sip the strong cup of black coffee. I pull out one of the two barstools from the kitchen island and plop myself there. I push my shoulders back, waiting for what he has to say.

I crack my neck from side to side and look in his direction. "Okay, what?" When he doesn't speak, I lift my arm to him, rolling my hand around so he can get on with it.

He shakes his head back and forth as if clearing a lousy memory. "I have a bad feeling about tonight."

I continue to sip my coffee, staring at him. "What do you mean?" My eyebrows pull in, unsure of what to make of this statement.

He begins to pace around, biting his fingernails. It's a nervous tic he has that makes me cringe at the irritating sound grating on my every nerve. His comment makes me feel uneasy. His eyes soften when they meet mine.

"We haven't heard from Cherry, and things have been quiet. I don't want to lose my sister before I have had the chance to meet and get to know her." He drops his head and braces himself on the island where he stands next to me. I soothingly run my hand on his back.

"Mattie..." Emotion clogs my throat and I clear it away. "I genuinely believe that we will all be together again."

He raises his head, meeting my eyes once again. When he looks at me, the sadness there is heartbreaking. "I just want my family, Evie."

My heart breaks for the boy who didn't have one. I at least knew what it was like to have a family and be brought up with loving parents, but he didn't.

"You'll have us always, Mattie, and once Emma and I are reunited, we will always be *your* family."

He turns around and pulls me into a hug. I gulp down the emotions threatening to leak from my eyes, and I hold my brother, determined more than ever to reunite us and get our revenge against the monster that took it from us.

The event is held in Galveston along the seawall, and the historic-looking hotel is breathtaking. The decorations are nothing short of elaborate. I wish we could arrive and valet park, but that would draw too much attention to us, so we park a short distance away and walk in through the outside area where a small group of people are congregated.

It gives us access to anyone who is pulling up as well.

I am sipping on my tonic and lime when I see Eduardo stepping out of his SUV, holding his hand out for Emma to be assisted out of the back seat. He holds her arm lovingly, she looks at him as if he has hung the moon and stars just for her. I almost audibly sigh because it's just so fucking cute, and then I realize where I am.

"Okay," Mateo explains the plan. "So we know they are here, so let's just stay out of their line of sight. If they see me, it doesn't really matter, but *you* need to remain hidden, and when I tell you, make sure to keep your head down."

I pick at my hair and feel the weird texture assaulting my fingers. "Do you really think they will notice me with my short hair in this wig?"

He stops to take a look at me. "No, it looks good on you though. I was more concerned about your eyes, but with the contacts in, it's not too much of a problem now."

We walk past another couple, and they smile at us, clearly thinking we are together.

"I look like shit."

He takes my arm, guiding me around another couple of people stopped in conversation regarding the hospital.

"You do not. You look beautiful as always." As he says this, a tall woman in a red dress with long blonde hair makes eye contact with him, licking her lips. He winks at her, and I snort.

"Great, now that's not awkward as fuck."

He huffs. "Why do you say that?"

I throw my hand out as we reach the other side of the bar, hidden away from the larger crowds gathered inside. "It looks like my date is cheating on me."

He laughs. "You're my sister."

"That's not the point!"

He shakes his head. "I don't get it."

"Of course, you don't. The point is that she has no respect for me. She doesn't know that I am your sister."

He turns to face me. "I swear you always try to pick a fight with me."

"I do not," I counter, pouting at him for calling me out. "Forget it, let's focus here, Mattie."

He stares a minute longer at me and then looks over my head at something that caught his eye. I know the moment he spots Emma and Eduardo because he stiffens.

"Let's move to our seats. I think the speaker is walking up to the stage, and I see people returning to their tables." He leads me to the table we are assigned to in the back corner.

Thank goodness. I notice Liv, who is noticeably pregnant now, and Dax walking over to my sister. Dax walks beside Liv with a hand around her lower waist, guiding her possessively to their table. Emma shoots up from her seat, embracing Liv.

The speaker announces herself as Isabella, and everyone turns their attention to her. I keep an eye on Emma and her friend. Something is going on over there, and I see Liv put the phone up to her ear. She draws the attention of a few others as she does the same thing a few minutes later, except this time, she leaves the table, heading toward the bathroom.

Mateo and I excuse ourselves, keeping my head down as Mateo instructed as I walk out in the same direction Liv went.

Emma excuses herself and makes her way into the bathroom, as we wait nearby to see where she goes next. Moments later she walks out of the bathroom, when a man dressed in a suit bumps into her. His hands raise to apologize, then they drop into a defensive stance. Her face whitens, and then she runs off, chasing Liv out the door.

The man looks as if he is going to follow her but decides not to at the last minute. I want to see who he is. I want to see who it is that has scared her this way.

We approach him. As he turns around, I am so caught off guard that I almost stumble back as Mateo holds onto me.

"Mateo…" I stop, realizing my error as his razor-sharp eyes look at me in recognition and then at my brother.

CHAPTER FIFTEEN

EVIE

"WRITTEN IN BLOOD" BY SHE WANTS REVENGE

I swear all the air is sucked out of my lungs. I gasp, and I must look like a flopping fish out of the water, an angler who holds me bound by an invisible line suspended mid-air as he stares at me with an unadulterated hunger.

He steps closer, and I instinctively take a step back, self-preservation mode kicking in. He smirks, clearly enjoying the recoil his mere presence brings, much like his sons'.

This must be what it feels like when a predator holds his prey, and you are locked in their sights with nowhere to flee.

Mateo grabs my arm and stops my retreat. He raises his chin to the man with similar eyes. I never knew it before, but that is what I always found familiar when I'd stare at my brother. The sudden realization makes me want to vomit.

I see the evil glint in his eye, almost giddy at seeing my brother. He knows this is something big, and I wish we never found out this way, but there is no denying it. If I didn't know him better, I'd assume he was almost... proud.

"Mateo," he drawls, and I hate how he says it.

Mattie squares his shoulders, attempting a stand-off with this man, and I visibly stiffen.

"Yes, and who are you?" my brother asks.

But I don't want him to know the truth. I already know it, and I don't like it. Does Mateo not see it? I want to say to him that we should run. We should run far away from here, take my sister, and move back to Mexico, but then this would all be for nothing.

The man smiles sinisterly at him and puffs his chest out. "Well, that really is the question, but you should always be weary of the questions you ask, Mateo."

Mateo snorts, his arms crossed over his chest in a defensive stance. "Oh, really? And why is that?"

I grab his arm, pulling it down, and that makes the man's face light up with amusement. He spares me a glance before returning his focus to who he is really interested in now.

"You might not like the answer," he states with a touch of humor that seems to annoy Mateo.

"Oh, is that right?" my brother growls.

I watch this volleying of responses. A long moment lingers between us, and when I don't think he will answer, I contemplate walking away and leaving, but I can't. I find myself stuck in this spot, unable to move. I wonder if I will have to be physically dragged from here. I always considered myself to be strong, but his revelation has ungrounded me. It has made me question everything that my family ever told me. It has made me aware of the fact that maybe I didn't really know my parents at all, especially my mom. She has a story that I will never get to hear from her. So many twisted lies and secrets that just keep coming to light, and it's blinding.

Finally, after the tense moment, he speaks, confirming all my thoughts that Mateo is now going to be living a nightmare. "Let me introduce myself. My name is Mr. Martinez, Julian's father."

I see Mateo clench his fists and unclench them. His jaw is set so hard that I think I can hear his teeth grinding. But what he says next is the most unsettling.

"*Your* father."

I gasp, and Mr. Martinez looks at me quickly before his gaze returns back to Mateo. "I'm glad to meet you finally, son."

I see the shock register on Mateo's face, and then disgust oozes from every pore. He stands back, full of contempt. "I'll never be your son."

He grabs my hand, but we hear a commotion from outside before Mr. Martinez can make a rebuttal. I see Eduardo running out of the door, Eli and Dax crouched down, and Liv slumped to the floor, crying hysterically. Dax picks her up bridal style and carries her out. Her head is pulled into his chest, and Eli has his arm around Emma. As they walk out the side, I see Eduardo pulling up with the SUV, and they all climb into it and take off.

Mateo and I are close-behind as we get into our cars and pull away from the venue.

We pull into the emergency department entrance to see everyone in the SUV running in through their front door. The words 'trauma bay' are illuminated above that entrance where there are several ambulances parked outside. I don't know what caused everyone to come here so quickly, but I can guess it has something to do with Liv's friends, since she was the one crouched down, sobbing inconsolably against the wall.

We sit there after they enter the emergency department and wait to see what happens next. The silence continues until I can't take it anymore. "Are we going to talk about the big news we were just blasted with, Mateo?"

I look away and stare out the window. I can hear Mattie's breathing pick up. I know that he is still processing the clusterfuck that is the news of hearing that Julian's father is his father and, worse, that the person who had been hurting his sister was, in fact, his half-brother, Julian. If I am frank, I also have a hard time with this.

"I can't," he finally says. He shakes his head, and I understand. It is all too much, but what I can do is offer my brother the support he needs.

We sit there in silence for a couple more hours until I see my sister wrapped up in Eduardo's arms and Emma's pregnant friend, Liv, being held up by Dax. She is crying hysterically, and I can only assume it is not good news. They pull out of the parking lot and follow suit, returning to our place.

A week passes, and we find ourselves at my least favorite place. There is peace you should have knowing that your loved ones are no longer suffering and their souls are laid to rest, but that isn't always the case. Some of the souls were taken before their time, driven from their bodies by someone or something that took their life. They took them from their families, children, and left them to figure out things independently. To live a life without them. The last time I was here was when my parents died.

The last time I was here was to attend my own funeral. I got to experience what a person would feel like if they could hear everything that was said, and experience all the sadness of the life they left behind.

I listened to my sister crying, and I wasn't able to console her. Julian had her wrapped around him forcefully. He fully supported her financially, but without her consent in anything, and he appeared to everyone as the ever-doting boyfriend.

Not everything is as it appears.

Loud thunder cracks across the sky, pulling me from my morbid thoughts. It is fitting that a storm should be approaching. It feels like an omen of what's to come. It's as if the angels are weeping with us. I see my sister and all she has had to go through. She is so supportive of her friend, but she truly had no one there to support her when we were laid to rest? Julian may have been there, but that was all for show. That was before Eduardo came into the picture, and before she became best friends with Liv. But our cousin got her out and away from Julian, and she found her way back to Eduardo who has been keeping her safe ever since.

Jameson is there, too. He is sitting silently near Eduardo and Dax. He is alone and stares out across the cemetery. I can't take my eyes off him; he looks so beautiful—and mine.

I want to go to him and let him know that I am here. I want to have him support me as Eduardo holds onto Emma, like she is something so precious to him. I close my eyes and imagine that Jameson is holding me. His strong arms envelop me in a solid embrace. I tilt my head back a bit. I can almost smell his musky scent of steamy nights mixed in with my earthy scent of questionable intentions, making the perfect scent for just us.

I decide to send him a text to let him know that I miss him, but his reply is always the same.

Jameson: When can I see you again?

I want to go to him, but I can't. I decide that after I return, I won't let myself be away from him any longer.

Evie: I have to go away for a while, but when I get back, I would like to see you.

It feels good to tell him this, but I just hope he can wait.

> Jameson: How long will you be gone?

I bite my lip, not looking at the phone, trying to determine how long we will be away.

> Evie: I'm still trying to figure it out. It will take a couple of months at the most. I have some family business I need to tend to.

I am waiting for his reply, but I don't get one. I look over at him, see him reading the text, and then placing the phone in his pocket. I slump my shoulders in defeat. Does this mean he isn't going to wait for me? Are we over before we have begun? I panic, not even thinking before I send off the message.

> Evie: Please wait for me...

That's all I can say, and I hope I'm not too late. I curse myself, and this makes Mateo look at me with concern. I shake my head, not wanting to talk about it. It will just make me sadder than I already feel. Besides, Mateo has enough going on in his mind to worry about something that should be a priority at this point. Literally, everything else is more important than this, except it isn't to me. It's just my happiness, but that is something I haven't been allowed to indulge in.

The priest talks about the Kingdom of God in a long-winded speech about His son returning to be united with Him. I look around at all the people who made the trip for this young man whose life was taken too soon.

As the ceremony ends, everyone is walking to their cars. I have already been sitting in ours as Emma is in the SUV watching from the window at her friend suffering alone by the gravesite, refusing to leave.

She stands there holding her single red rose and staring down into the grave. It's as if she doesn't want to throw her flower in the grave because that will be it—the final goodbye. She releases it, and I can't help the gasp that leaves my lips. I almost didn't expect her to do it. I almost wish she would have walked away with it, but what's the point? Acceptance is all there really is to move forward now. She looks up at the sky as if she is cursing at her God.

Tears fall down my cheeks, witnessing such a private moment. I swallow the sobs that threaten to escape. I wipe my tears from my cheeks and look at my brother. I grab his hand for support.

"Come on, Mattie. Let's go home."

We have a lot to discuss when we get home—the only home that we have to go to now. Just when I think I can't feel any worse, I feel my phone vibrate.

Jameson: I'll try for you.

I take a deep breath, and I feel like I am losing him. I feel him pull away; if I didn't know that, I could see it. I watch him answering his texts just as we are pulling away to head to the airport. He hesitates, looks away, and then pockets his phone. He rubs his temples as if I make his head hurt. He is tired of waiting on me, and why should he? He is an attractive man. I know that, but I can't help but want to selfishly keep him, and make him mine. I wish to possess his mind, body, and soul. I have never felt this connection with anyone. I also wish I could relay all my thoughts and the intensity of my feelings for him without scaring him away.

Taking our seats on the airplane, the flight attendant comes around to make sure our items are stowed away correctly. I rest my head against the seat and think about everything that happened earlier today and hope that I am not away for too long. I take out my phone and send one last text to him.

Evie: Please.

I set my phone down, the flight attendant giving me a dirty look as I was told repeatedly to turn off our electronic devices. I tuck my bag under the seat, but keep my phone out. I'm getting ready to turn it off when I see a message pop up.

Jameson: I'll wait for you.

That's all it says, and that's enough to put a smile on my face and ease some of my tension for now.

CHAPTER SIXTEEN

EVIE

"RUNNING UP THAT HILL" BY KATE BUSH

The plane touches down in Mexico, and I feel the anxiety creeping in. Mateo and I didn't speak much during the flight. The night that we found out about Mr. Martinez being Mateo's father, I knew that a long-overdue visit to Mexico was needed to finally find out what the actual fuck was going on. We have so many questions that need answering, and I want to be able to see our uncle's face when he tells us the truth.

"How many more lies are they keeping from us?" I mumble under my breath. It's not a question because I know that there is definitely more to come to light.

Mateo glances over at me, but doesn't respond. He runs his finger over his lip, probably wondering the same thing. I look out the window as the plane is taxing into the gate.

This is *our* family, and there should not be any secrets between us if we are to succeed in bringing the Martinez family down. I know every family harbors some secrets, but this is beyond normal. This is the mother of all secrets, so to speak, and I can't believe my own mother kept this from us and that, worse, no one told us anything about it after her passing. Wasn't it significant enough to warrant a discussion? I want to find out why my brother was sent away from us and we never knew anything about him.

We grab our luggage from the carousel and walk side by side out of the baggage claim area. As soon as we get outside, I am assaulted with the heat that only comes from a desert-like climate. Spring is hot in Texas and is similar to south of the border, but what a heat wave it is. The heat creates a visible mirage glaring off the pavement in wavy lines. I place my hand over my brow to reduce some of the glare when I see Adrian pull up.

"Eek!" I drop my luggage handle and run over to hug him. I know that Mateo and I are close, and it stings something fierce to know that they are cousins, too. The unfair balance of family dynamics is unsettling and puts a damper on my reunion.

He runs around to the side of the truck, and I can't help but jump into his embrace, messenger bag and all.

"Hey, cousin. How are you?" I drop down from my koala-like hug and fling my messenger bag over his shoulder before he can reply. I jump into the front seat of his truck before Mateo can get in there.

"Shotgun!" I ring out as loudly as I can. I hear Adrian greet Mateo while simultaneously throwing our luggage and my messenger bag in the back.

"I see she is just as pleasant as ever," he remarks, and Mateo snorts.

"Oh, you have no idea. Remember, I live with her."

Adrian laughs. "Right, my condolences."

They both get into the truck, glancing my way.

"Hey, I can hear you guys. You know that right?"

"Um, Evie, we were not saying anything you didn't already know, and we weren't exactly trying to keep that from you." Adrian chuckles, placing the truck into drive.

No, but what else are you keeping from me, cousin?

I roll down the window as we take off toward our uncle's house, the only consistent home I've ever had and filled with many good memories. I stare out the window, wondering at the possibilities.

We are barely settled in at the house and are about to have lunch when our conversation is interrupted by a phone call from Eduardo. My uncle heads to his office, and Mateo, Adrian, and I all run toward him, following like children to eavesdrop when he takes the call.

My uncle ushers us in, as he shuts the door when I slip in last, taking my seat. The emotions on my face quickly decline as my mind turns into a downward spiral of what-ifs. Mateo tucks me into his embrace, standing by my side as always while we wait to hear what Eduardo has to say. He places the call on the speaker and places his finger to his mouth, a gesture letting us know to be quiet.

"Eduardo. To what do I owe the pleasure of this phone call?"

The urgency in Eduardo's voice makes me want to run back to Houston to see if my sister is okay for myself. Mateo squeezes my arm, trying to comfort me.

"I just spoke to Emma, and she informed me that Mr. Martinez, Julian's father, was at the gala last week, and he cornered her outside of the bathroom. She just told me after a week. A whole fucking week, Andrés!"

He sounds upset. My shoulders relax as Mateo and I saw this account firsthand. I know he didn't have time to tell her anything, but he does know where she is now. Unfortunately, that's the least of our concerns at the moment. After our brief, but informative visit with Mr. Martinez, we now see much more is going on, which is more unsettling than today's news. After all, that is why we are here visiting our uncle.

Uncle Andrés knows this too, and judging by his expression, there's more. They discuss strategy, and he lets Eduardo know that he is coming up with a plan but has an emergency he needs to take care of at the moment. They disconnect the call and Tió points to the chairs that he would like for us to take a seat at. I'm already sitting, but before Adrian joins us, he decides we might need a different approach.

Adrian walks over to his dad's cabinet and pulls out a bottle of scotch. He grabs four glasses, pours some Buchanan's into each glass, giving one to each of us. I, for one, don't waste a minute before I throw back the entire contents in one go, smacking my lips in the process. Adrian wrinkles his nose as he looks at me like I am a disgrace to the family.

"Pfft, please." He wouldn't be incorrect, but there's a lot of 'disgrace' going on in this family. I place my glass on the table before smacking my lips at the flavors assaulting my taste buds. My uncle looks at me with a slight quirk on his lip. "Something you wanted to say, Uncle?"

He steeples his hands, observing us, and Mateo's knees bounce in anticipation of what he will say. I look him up and down. Maybe he should have drank the scotch in one go also. Bro looks like he can use about one or twelve.

I frown, looking his way, but he doesn't notice. He doesn't notice anything except the person sitting at that desk about to make his worst nightmare come true. He is focused on anything that may leave our uncle's mouth. I turn back to him, and then he confirms what we feared.

"Mr. Martinez is your father."

Mateo blinks a few times before he drops his head down, and I move my chair over to offer my brother some emotional support. To be told that that monster is your father is the worst news that anyone can get.

Tió continues, "Julian is your half-brother."

And I think I lied to myself because it definitely did get worse. Mattie shakes his head in disbelief, but he knows it's true. He just doesn't want to admit it, and I second that.

"How?" he says. "When?" He shakes his head in disbelief, but he knows it's true. He just doesn't want to admit it.

"Your mother dated Julian's father during her first year of college. She was on her own, like father and son, he had a similar infatuation with your mom as Julian did with Emma. She found out she was pregnant with you and came home one weekend to speak with us about it. She explained that she had been sexually active with Mr. Martinez in a consensual way, but when she told him she was leaving college to return home, he wanted her to take time off and have her stay there with him. He was very insistent, and she was wary of his intentions. She swears he must have tampered with the condom, but before she could end the relationship, she found out she was pregnant with you. She was in her first trimester, and we discussed various options."

Mateo visibly tenses with this, and I know immediately what he is referring to by this. I hold onto Mattie's hand out of instinct, and he leans into me, unsure if he wants to hear anything further. Tió holds his hand up to let him continue with what he is saying.

"I want to be clear. She always wanted to keep you, and anything else than not having you wasn't an option for her, but she also knew that if she told him about you that he wouldn't let her leave and his controlling behavior would just get worse. He would hold you over her forever, so she left the beach of South Padre, which she loved so much, and lived here with us."

"I did believe her when she told us that Mr. Martinez had tampered with the contraception. This wasn't what she had planned. Our parents were pissed, but they supported her decisions, when she came back home to have

Mateo. She also discovered that her best friend and dorm mate was now sleeping with Mateo's biological father, so she felt he would soon forget about her."

"But he didn't forget about her, did he?" Mateo mutters under his breath.

"Our father thought it was best for her to go to another college farther away, and they decided to raise Mateo along with my wife and me."

"So, why didn't she give me up for adoption?" I look over at my brother and selfishly thank my mother for keeping him close. He saved me, too, so there's that. If it wasn't for him, who knows what would have happened to me, but I do know. He would have broken me, and then I'd be dead, too—like my parents.

"She couldn't possibly let him get to you, and I think she wanted to keep you close because she couldn't let go. Anyway, later, she received a letter forwarded from the PO Box we had on file at the school containing a wedding invitation from her ex-boyfriend and ex-best friend. We thought that was the end of it, and for a long time, it was.

"When your mom went to this new college, she met a man there and fell in love with him—your father, Evie. She wanted to come back and be closer to you, but we all decided that you could never know about her, Mateo, and that she was your mother. She begged and pleaded with us, but we were insistent and wouldn't hear of it. You were safer that way. We all were."

He takes a big gulp of his drink before placing it down. "She eventually moved back to the town she loved so much after she had you girls, which was still close to us. She wanted her kids to be born in the US, and her husband was a US citizen. They had you girls and came to visit frequently, but then Eduardo and Emma became close."

He left that to simmer for a bit. "He seemed almost obsessed with her, and he came from another mafia family. Your mom didn't want that life for Emma."

I notice Mateo visibly stiffening in his chair. Anger radiates off him, and I can understand that. "But she didn't care about that life for me?" He slams his fist on our uncle's desk.

"Let me be clear. We discovered Mr. Martinez wanted to trap your mother because of her family ties. He realized she was the daughter of a major mafia player in the Gulf Coast area, and he wanted to tie himself to the family through an heir. That was why he could never know about you."

I turn to look at Mateo and my uncle. I understand his reaction. He has a lot of anger, and things are undoubtedly unfair. He never had the chance to meet his mom and have the family he deserved. In fact, when we were there in Mexico with our mother, Mateo wasn't. He was sent off to boarding school, and now we know why.

"So why was I sent off?" he spews, but I already know. "Was it because they didn't want me around when her new family was here?" The anger is palpable, and I recoil at the viciousness his words yield.

My uncle is quick to reply. "No, it's more than that, Sobrino." His eyes soften, and this is the first time he has referred to Mateo as his nephew.

I almost choke out a sob and try to rein it in, looking away from my brother. His expression would gut me. I see from my peripheral vision as Mateo's head drops, and I know that he realizes as much as I do that there is something broken in my uncle's voice that is more like regret and sadness.

"I don't remember her being here," Mateo admits. His voice cracks, and I almost want to cry for the little boy that wasn't with his real family. "I remember you and Adrian, but I don't know them." He looks over at me, and sadness stretches between us. I glance up to meet his eyes—a bridge of tears that brings us closer to understanding the truth of what happened all those years ago.

"We left and went on trips. You always loved the beach." He smiles, remembering all of it as his memories wash over him in nostalgic waves. He pauses. "As the girls got bigger and my wife passed, I couldn't handle it anymore. Grandpops passed away, and my mother had suffered from dementia for years and was in an assisted living facility with round-the-clock care. Her memories were stolen from her, and she didn't even know who we were."

Adrian stands up and pours us all another glass of scotch. Tió empties his glass's remaining contents and holds it out to his son for a refill.

"I decided to send you off to school so that you could have a better education. Then, when your mother cut off ties with us, we brought you back and made you part of the organization—a soldier—in case we needed you to take a stand.

"Mr. Martinez might have suspected you could be alive, but he never saw any indication that the rumors were true, until he recently had everything confirmed with his own eyes."

I look at my brother in panic, and he stares back at me, the same emotions flaring to life.

"Emma was falling down the same path with Eduardo, and I think your mom overreacted and never returned to Mexico. Eduardo's family is heavily involved in the mafia, and she wanted a different life for her kids."

"Well, that worked out well, clearly." I point around us. "You know what they say about the 'best-laid plan' and all."

"It might have been. Except Eduardo was always in love with Emma. That time the kid returned the following year, and he left heartbroken. A shell of himself. I had to tell him to respect your mother's wishes. But who knew that history would repeat itself and Julian would get his claws into Emma." He pauses, looking around at us.

"This is so fucked up." I stand up and walk around the office. Mateo is still sitting there, until he finally speaks.

"Does Julian really need Emma now that I am alive and have a real connection to him and this family? The bond that ties us all?"

Uncle Andrés finishes the rest of his drink and stands. "Now that, my nephew, is the real question, and more importantly, what happens now?"

CHAPTER SEVENTEEN

JAMESON

"JUST PRETEND" BY BAD OMENS

As promised, Evie has kept in touch, and when she returns back from her family business she had to attend to, we will finally make plans to meet up.

There isn't a day that has passed that we haven't chatted since she asked me to wait for her and I said I would. Sometimes, I send a quick text about what I think about getting for lunch. Sometimes, she texts me with a food recommendation about what I *should* get for lunch. I like learning about all of her interests. I long for the day that we will get to meet for lunch, and we can order together.

Theo and Eric think I am nuts waiting for a girl for months without physically touching her. I think back to the times that I did and our connection with each other. You can't fake that type of chemistry; the physical attraction is off the charts. If I had to wait an eternity for this girl, I would. Nothing has felt more right.

Today, she sent something that surprised me. She snapped a picture of two people holding hands. I don't know who they were because the image was not meant to show their faces but what they represent. It displays their backs, as if she discreetly took a private moment from them from behind and sent it over to me. The text under the caption read: *'I can't wait until this is us.'*

I stop and look at it, wondering what she is implying. Is it the couple? Us being a couple out in the open for everyone to witness. Is it me holding her hand casually? Or is it something deeper? Whatever her reasons, I will make sure that it becomes a reality. I want to be the person who helps her achieve all her dreams and be the partner she trusts completely. I think we both need that more than anything.

I know the girl has her secrets, and that they had to be the reason why she sought control over everything, especially in the bedroom, which I didn't mind too much. Despite that, I am bewildered as to why this can't be us now.

For a brief moment, I wonder if maybe she is secretly married to someone else or in a relationship, stringing me along, but there is nothing that makes me question this chemistry between us.

When I looked into her eyes that she hid behind that mask, as she rode me from above, my hands held back with a tie; I almost felt like I had seen her before. It was powerful, and it was raw. The emotions she carefully hid behind her mask showed me a person who wanted to be held. To be cared for. And most of all, to be free of fear so that we could live out the rest of our lives without this invisible weight she carries.

How we would get to that point, since she wouldn't let me even touch her, was beyond me, but that night at my house, something changed.

She left her mask, and I thought that that was the last time I would see her again, but she clarified her meaning by saying that she would never hide from me again. That next time it would be without any mask, inside and out.

I find it ironic that she has been gone all this time, and I just have to believe her when she said that it was for work and family business. Besides, tonight I won't have to wonder anymore because I feel that after we see each other with no sneaking around or wearing masks at clubs, we can finally move on to having a real relationship.

She's told me different things about herself without fully divulging too much. It's only a sliver of what I want, and I'm greedy enough to devour it all. Whatever she is, I want to know it.

She wants me to know her real self, no more pretenses or masks to hide behind.

Speaking of masks and covering up faces with costumes, there is a Ghost concert that Eduardo is taking Emma to tonight, and in case he needs me for anything, which I doubt, I plan to be somewhere nearby to get to them.

Emma is obsessed with this band, their lore, and the comradery of their fan base. Thankfully Emma wore and loved the jewelry with the GPS tracker, and SOS button I had made for Eduardo. She wears it religiously, making him and herself feel more secure, knowing he can get to her location should anything happen. Philip and Eli will also be there tonight, so I am confident they have everything planned to optimize Emma's safety.

Eve and I plan to meet for dinner and drinks. As I arrive at the restaurant and take a seat at one of the high-top tables by the bar, I have a clear view of the entrance and can see anyone approaching from the giant glass windows that span the entirety of the front of the restaurant.

The server takes my drink order, and places a glass of water in Eve's empty seat. After fifteen minutes, I notice a woman with blonde hair and wearing boots approaching through the doors. I sit up a little straighter in my chair, excited to finally get to see Eve up close after months of torture and only phone sex to occupy my nights. She follows behind a hostess, and when I see her face, I immediately deflate, looking at her brown eyes and round face. Eve has more of a heart-shaped face, and her green eyes are unmistakable.

After another fifteen minutes pass by, I realize she isn't coming. I flag down the server for the check because I know when I've been stood up and I don't want to embarrass myself anymore by waiting another minute. I pay the bill and feel my phone ding with a text notification, but before I can look at it, my phone begins to ring.

I look at the name and answer the phone call from Eli. "Hey, what's up?" He sounds anxious on the other end, and I hear footsteps like he is running, and a door slam.

"Jameson, they've taken Emma. Eduardo is following her on the GPS tracker."

I start running to my car.

"Where is she? I'll meet Eduardo. Wait, I'm calling him now." I disconnect the call and ring Eduardo. "What's going on?" I ask directly into the line, needing to know what is happening.

"Jameson," Eduardo answers out of breath, "where are you? Someone has Emma, I just know it."

I had pulled up the app Eduardo insisted I have on my phone in case something like this happened—a double safety feature should this actually happen and Emma was taken. I look at the address. "I am at the restaurant down the street. I'm leaving now. I'm on my way." I thought he was being overprotective and utterly ridiculous when he insisted I have it just in case, and now I realize that he was so right about all of this.

He responds quickly. "I see her in this warehouse not far from here. Do you see her, too?"

The star-shaped icon on screen continues to move. Just when I think it couldn't get worse, we all get the SOS alert from the location where Emma has now stopped moving on the map.

Eduardo verbalizes my concerns.   "Oh, shit. Emma is in trouble."

I just hope we are not too late. I speed to the location where the SOS came from.

Arriving at the warehouse where the tracking icon had stopped and hasn't moved since, we scan the area. Nothing looks out of the ordinary and the warehouse is dark. As I run across the street to regroup with Eduardo and Eli, Eduardo has a few of his men around the perimeter that are ready to intervene if necessary.

As Eli, Eduardo, and I go to enter the building, trying to be as discreet as possible. Eduardo pulls his gun, as does Eli, they give me one should the situation arise and I need it. It's better to be safe than sorry.

The door is open as we step into the almost pitch black room. However, I catch sight of golden hair and see the moment Eduardo recognizes his whole world is tied to a supporting column in the middle of the room.

A light shines, and I see Cherry; her face is messed up. Eduardo is standing here, assessing Emma for injuries, but there don't appear to be any. However, Cherry's eyes are bruised over, and it seems her nose may be broken. From the looks that Cherry is giving Emma, I believe that Emma acted in self-defense, and I have never been more glad to see her okay than at this moment.

Emma's eyes look over to us and then lock on Eduardo's.

Julian steps in from the corner with his gun pointed at us. "Drop your weapons and kick them forward."

We all lower our guns and drop them, doing as he says. Just as Cherry puts a knife to Emma's neck, and I place my arm out to stop Eduardo from charging over there to rip that bitch a new one, but now between that and

Julian having our firearms, there is not much we can do.

Julian steps in front of Emma, blocking his view. "Don't even look at her. She's mine and for my eyes only. You remember that."

Eduardo clenches his jaw, and I swear I hear his molars crack. The murderous look in his eyes would have lesser men recoiling.

I notice Cherry's head snapping up and staring at Julian in disbelief. "What do you mean she's yours?" she spits spitefully. The feral, unhinged look in her eyes is scary even for us to witness, and I see Emma cringe inwardly. Cherry snaps her sights on Emma. She is defenseless as Cherry lunges for her.

She screams out, "I'll fucking kill that bitch! She can't have you, either! I did everything for you, Julian!" She goes to attack Emma, and I see Emma brace for it, but Julian intercepts her and pushes Cherry onto the floor.

"No one else hurts Emma. She is only mine to hurt." The spit flies from his mouth, and he is indeed the monster Emma thought he was.

Cherry lies on the floor and attempts to get up. We watch, frozen in our spot. Julian walks over to her, and instead of helping her up, he points his gun at her.

"I can see you are going to be a problem. I was hoping we could have some fun together, but I don't think it will work out anymore, Cherry." With that, he lifts his gun and shoots her twice in the chest.

She lands backward as red appears on the ground, pouring from her chest wounds, making the red of her shirt even darker. She places a hand on her chest as blood comes out of her mouth in a cough that sprays blood all over the floor. Julian lifts his gun once more and shoots her in the head. Three bullets, and Cherry is gone.

Emma stares at her dead body. Cherry's eyes are fixed, locked on something she no longer sees. I know that she is gone. Emma shoots her gaze to Julian, who has already lost interest in Cherry—if she ever held any interest to that man.

He walks over to Emma, and Eduardo is trying so hard to restrain himself from lunging forward. Julian stands by her side. "I think this has gone on long enough, Emma, don't you? Why don't you tell Eduardo who you really love?" He looks over at Emma expectantly. Eduardo attempts to lunge forward, and Julian watches as I hold him back.

He lifts his gun at Emma. "I wouldn't do that if I were you, Eduardo." He tsks. "If you claim to love her as much as you say, it would be in your best interest not to move any closer." He moves closer to us and kicks our weapons out of the way.

I look over at Eduardo and Eli. We all have the same pained expression of anger and sadness in our eyes.

"Say it, Emma!" he screams at her, and she looks him in the eyes, not backing down.

"I'll never say that to you, Julian," she says low enough, but we all hear it. It has its desired cruising effects on Julian.

His eyes narrow, and then he lifts his gun to her. Emma locks her eyes with Eduardo and mouths, *'I love you always.'*

PART II

THE PRESENT

CHAPTER EIGHTEEN

EVIE

"TEAR YOU APART" BY SHE WANTS REVENGE

We stand there in shared silence trying to process the events that have happened from our point of view and lives that led up to this moment. Jameson pulls me back to hold me, letting me know he is here for me and not going anywhere. We line the shots up again, and I make another toast.

"To all the twisted lies coming to light." I lock eyes with Emma and she nods.

"I'll drink to that." She lifts her drink up and taps the table like I've seen her do so many times with her friends.

I frown, recalling this as Emma commits such a common action with no thought to it, as she tosses her shot back. We down the shots and throw our discarded limes on the plate before us. Jameson intertwines my fingers with his, sensing my downward spiraling mood. He silently encourages me with this action, but patiently waits for me to tell them the truth.

I look at our entwined hands and it gives me strength to get it out there. To place my past before us. To verbalize the words that I want to suppress more than anything because of all the feelings that arise from the torment of reliving it through my vivid memories of past events.

And I do—the long, sordid tale of those past events and leading up to all that transpired just yesterday. I speak of what happened while we were disposing of the bodies. The empty vessels. The people who caused us so much pain, but we know that it doesn't end there. We know what's to come, just not when. That is an unspoken truth that lingers in the air like the calm before the storm.

Hours later, he is still holding my hand. I stop and look around at everyone, and I suddenly feel so sleepy. It's as if all my energy has been zapped from my body. I know that I am, in fact, more emotionally drained than physically. The thought of just telling everyone the entirety of our sordid tale has taken so much out of me, and to be honest, it has the same effect on Evie and Mateo as I stare at their resolute expressions.

Eduardo is the first to break the silence. He claps his hands together. "Okay, I think that we should all get a good night's sleep and then reconvene in the morning. It has been a long couple of days." He brings Emma in and kisses the top of her head.

We look around at each other to process the conversation and decide to table it for another day. I look at Mateo, and he shakes his head, reading my thoughts of silently imploring him to take us back to the apartment. "Not a chance in hell, Evie. I am staying here tonight."

Eduardo grabs Emma's hand. "You are all welcome to stay. In fact, I insist. There is room for everyone." Emma kisses Eduardo's hand before releasing it.

"Babe, will you help me get everyone settled into a room?" He looks at her lovingly.

"Of course, baby. Do you need me to grab you any extra sheets from the linen cabinet?"

She nods. "Yes, and a fitted sheet for the sofa, too."

Mateo starts to walk toward it, already choosing his place to retire for the night. "I'll take the sofa, Emma." He drops his bag near it, and Eduardo comes back from down the hall, carrying linen for the bedding. Mateo takes the items and makes himself comfortable on the sofa.

"Eli and Philip can take the game room and the couches there," she indicates with a nod of her head, turning toward the hall, then she turns to speak to Gus.

He lifts his hands. "I'm going home. I have somewhere to be."

Eduardo laughs. "You mean someone to do?"

Gus shrugs the comment off. "Same thing. Laters." He walks out the door, I grab Jameson by the hand, dragging him toward the hallway.

Emma calls out before we make it to one of the rooms, stopping us. She runs over, grabbing me in a solid embrace. "I'm so glad you are here." She kisses my cheek as I hold onto Jameson's hand, my eyes glistening.

"Me too, Emma."

I spare a glance at Eduardo, who is looking on with adoration just as Jameson is looking at me. I know they think that we are unbelievably brave, and I know that we are going to need to continue to be strong and support each other if we are going to get through this.

I enter the spacious room with a sleigh-style bed in the middle of the room against the wall. The room is tastefully decorated in beige, gray, and neutral tones. The earthy color scheme boasts a beautifully understated and classically elegant style, except for the crystal chandelier that hangs in the middle of the ceiling. Two tufted chairs are placed in front of the window, and a table is in the middle where one can look at the cityscape below and gaze at the wonder of a multitude of flickering lights, while looking out onto the city.

"Wow, what a view."

The billowing curtain sways with the air vents that are currently pumping out some central climate control in the room.

I perch on the seating provided at the foot of the bed to remove my shoes. I place my feet on the rug and tuck my boots into the corner of the seat. I run my feet back and forth on the luxurious fabric before I stand and walk to where Eduardo has left my bag. I step around and look up to find Jameson staring at me.

He smiles. "I'm going to take a quick shower, okay?"

I nod, blinking away my lust-filled thoughts, and continue to organize my stuff. I hear the shower turn on, and the steam billows around the bathroom, creeping out into the bedroom space.

I stand there, conflicted. My clothes are in my hand, and I don't want to intrude on his shower, but I really want to join him. I figure if he did want company, then he would have asked. So, I continue to stand there waiting.

I hear the shower shut off and a repeated squeaking sound coming from the bathroom. I look up and see his reflection in the mirror as he wipes the condensation and the surge of stormy fog away from the mirror. Our eyes meet in the reflection, and I can't look away.

TWISTED TIDES

Water drops from his wet hair, landing on his chest. His blondish-brown hair appears darker when saturated with water. I can't help but ogle his body and how incredibly handsome he is—the first two times we were intimate had been under a disguise. I was hiding my face and, more than that, my emotions under a literal mask.

After all the time we had apart, we had explored each other without touching. His voice echoing through the speakerphone, telling me to touch myself—to pretend it was him. The way my hands obliged and pretended they were, in fact, his as I made myself come over and over the past months I was away from him.

Seeing him here right now, naked and wet in front of me, is surreal. Although nothing was confirmed about our relationship status, I know in my heart that I am his and he is mine. I hope that the intimacy we shared remotely can be reciprocated tonight. I want to release the control I've come to need and give it over to him.

Let him take me. Claim me. Make me his.

I walk into the bathroom, facing the shower. I undress without looking back at him. I step into the shower as he stands there, watching me enter. The transparent glass leaves nothing to the imagination. I wash the day's grime away from my body and the twisted lies that spewed forth from my mouth earlier as they swirl in a bubbly tide of water down the drain.

He doesn't move from his spot; he just continues to watch me. The fact that I hold him captive is alluring and empowering to me. I run the conditioner through my shorter hair, and it doesn't take long to rinse it out.

I shut off the water and hear a cabinet open and close. When I step out of the shower, Jameson is holding a towel open for me, and I turn around as he wraps it and his arms around me. I am immediately enveloped in the fluffy cotton and his warm embrace.

I hold it hitched around me as he takes another smaller one and towels off my hair. He wrings the water from it and fluffs it around, much like he did on his own hair. I can't help but smile at the simple yet kind domestic act. I rock up on my tiptoes and back down again like a kid waiting for their birthday surprise. He pulls me in for a hug and holds me there, as if he's afraid I will pull another disappearing act. I ease his concerns.

"I'm not going anywhere, Jameson." I let him know so he understands I am staying here this time. That this time is different. He kisses the top of my head, as I release the towel from my grasp. He feels it fall from my body, his body tensing in response, and then he looks down at it pooling around my feet. I step back and look up at him. I smile seductively.

I drop my head down, unable to meet his eyes. "I want you to touch me." He lifts my chin upward to meet his. The fire in his eyes makes me shudder. I gulp before speaking, licking my lips. "Will you show me how much you've missed me while I've been away?"

His eyes alight with desire, accepting the challenge. "Baby, I would like nothing more. I can't wait to make you come on my tongue, fingers, and cock."

He bends forward and takes my hand in his. His other hand caresses my cheek as his lips touch mine. He presses soft kisses to my lips, down my cheek and neck. He slowly licks his way up my neck to my ear, pressing light kisses that make me giggle as his facial hair tickles my sensitive skin. When he sucks my earlobe into his mouth, tugging lightly before he returns his path to my mouth, I meet him without hesitation. I open for him as his tongue swirls with mine in a tangle for dominance.

He moves his hand in between my legs, brushing a finger across and then through my folds. He pushes further inward, parting me, moving the moisture that has pooled around my core and bringing the wetness upward to make little circles around my clit.

My head falls back slightly as he bends lower to kiss my neck, sucking in the exposed skin. I am sure it will make little marks where his mouth has been.

He pushes a finger inside me, and I can't help the moan that leaves me. He takes his other hand, and places it on my breast. He moves his fingertips over my erect nipples while tugging and flicking over the sensitive peaks. He adds another finger, scissoring them inside me, making me even wetter. When he adds a third finger, I gasp as he fucks me, making me feel so deliciously full. I start to pant with longing, seeking the much-needed release only he can provide.

"What do you need, Evie? Tell me, baby," he almost pleads, desperate to hear my answer.

I don't make him wait, the truth falling from my lips. "I only need what you can give me, Jameson." I can sense this pleases him. The upturn of his smile tells me so against my bare skin. "I need your fingers," I continue as his fingers thrust in faster, and I feel my climax approaching. "I need your mouth." I whimper as he sucks hard on my neck, undoubtedly leaving evidence of his claiming my body. "I need you to make me come."

He curls his finger upward as he hits the exact spot I need to make me see stars as I come undone from his ministrations.

"Oh, God." I take a few breaths to regulate my racing heart. He removes his fingers, and I see evidence of my climax on his wet fingers as he takes a fingertip and traces my lips with it.

I lick my lips, tasting myself on them, and his eyes flare with pure, unadulterated lust, as he watches the motion. "I need..." I hesitate, wondering if it is wise to reveal so much vulnerability because that would give up any bargaining chips.

He would know my true feelings, bearing it all to him.

Instead, I throw caution to the wind and, for once in my life, decide to relinquish the control I so desperately crave and need. I choose to rip myself open at the seams for the possibility of what we could be.

"I need your heart."

His eyes meet mine, and the surprise that registers is quickly replaced by a fierce determination.

He smiles widely and then kisses me so deeply that I feel it all the way down to my toes, and I know that, somehow, we are going to be alright.

He takes my hand and leads me out of the bathroom and onto the bed. For once in my life, I put my body and soul into someone else's control. As we lay there wrapped in each other's arms, I can feel the weight lift from my shoulders. The regret that I live with, the same that Emma lives with, feels lighter as I release the burden I have always carried. The lies between everyone is a cross that no one should bear. And for once in my life, I feel free.

Jameson grabs my hand in his as we lie in bed. Our legs draped over one another as our bodies mold together. I close my eyes, drifting off to the sound of his steady breathing, and I realize that this is our new beginning.

CHAPTER NINETEEN

JAMESON

"CULT OF PERSONALITY" BY LIVING COLOUR

Mateo and I decide to bring back some breakfast for our family. Eli and Philip left this morning with nothing but a cup of coffee to join Gus—Eduardo's primary personal security detail and long-time trusted friend. I mean the entire group that had gathered around the island, our found family, have returned to ensure everything is running smoothly at the clubs while we strategically plan our next move. We are still waiting for Mr. Martinez's response to our blatant attempt at retaliation and expect him to bring hell to our doorstep, but his fury has yet to make an appearance and come our way.

Mateo pushes the seat back in my vehicle to accommodate his large frame as I start the car. I connect my Carplay, and one of my favorite songs starts playing. I hit the air conditioning button several times to full arctic blast mode to combat this Texan heat in a city that just seems to bake on the concrete slab it resides upon. I saw Theo cook an egg on the hood of his car once in high school, proving it could be done. Unfortunately, it also took away some of the paint.

I smile. Lesson earned.

Mateo glances over at me, seeing me lost in my thoughts about my idiot friends, as he turns up the dial and starts bobbing his head to the music.

Well, look at that, bro has good taste in music.

I look over at him and witness my girlfriend's brother. He shakes his head, singing and playing air drums. "The only thing we have to fear is fear itself." Taken from the "Day of Infamy" speech is one of my favorites, and apparently Mateo is fond of it too, especially in this particular rock song.

I slow down as I approach the local taqueria and ease up on the gas as I pull into their drive-thru entrance. There is a long line, but things progress quickly, and I lean back so Mateo can lean over toward my window and order when it is our turn. He has the list, and he knows what he wants, too.

I pull up when our turn comes and scrunch up my nose at his order. "What the hell is nopalitos?" There's another car in front of us receiving their order, and he looks at me and laughs.

"Cactus," he replies cooly.

I pretend to gag, now knowing what it is. "Why the fuck would you eat that? Great fiber?" I'm now trying any excuse to guess at why he chose that out of everything they have on the menu.

"Well, I like it for one, and it is better than what your girlfriend ordered," he counters.

I gulp dramatically. Curiosity winning, I take the bait. "Okay, enlighten me. What did she order?"

He looks me up and down, trying to decide if he wants to tell me. He smirks evilly at me and then replies, "Tacos de lengua."

I shrug. "I have no idea what that is. It sounds good, though." I counter.

Mateo nods, agreeing with me. "Yes, delicious, if you like beef tongue."

I look at him in horror.

"That's what it is?"

He nods, confirming. "I've had that before. It tastes..." I look for the right word. "Salty."

He nods again, agreeing.

"Yep, I agree. Definitely salty."

Suddenly, all the saliva floods my mouth, and not in a good way. I need to change the conversation. I don't have to wait as the server at the window repeats our orders. Mateo looks over at her, winking, and I see the blush forming on her cheeks.

"Here you go, boys, and I threw in something extra."

I grab the bags, hand them to Mateo, and thank her for the food.

"Do you want to know what tripas are?"

I hold my hand up, halting this conversation. "Definitely not."

He laughs loudly, slapping his leg. Tears spring from the edges of his eyes as he fights back the fit of laughter.

"Save it. I'm so done. If it tastes good, that's all I need to know."

He tightens his hold on my shoulder as he slaps my back while I am driving. "Bro, welcome to the family."

I smile. Indeed.

We walk through the door with the bags. Evie and Emma come over to take them from us. They unpackage everything, and I see Evie frown. I look over at what she is holding, and she lifts a paper.

"Sylvia?" she reads. "What the fuck is this?" She looks at me, and I feel like taking her against the counter in response to her outright act of jealousy.

I find it to be such a turn-on, knowing that the thought of another woman flirting with me consumes her with fury. I already know my little vixen has a temper, and I'd love to test it out, but maybe without an audience this time.

Unless, of course, it is back at Eduardo's club in a voyeur room.

I inwardly moan at the thought of angry sex with Evie, if it is anything to go by that night we shared back at his club. I shake my head, blocking that thought because if anyone else saw her naked, I'd have to gouge their eyes out.

I realize I have zoned out and laugh.

Evie is still staring at me, assessing and, no doubt, plotting my demise. "It's not mine," I reply, lifting my hands in surrender. "Ask your brother."

She looks at Mateo, who seems unfazed by her dramatics. He rolls his eyes. I guess that's what happens when you live together for a while. He reaches her, snatching the paper out of her hands, and quickly shoves the paper napkin into his pocket.

"For a rainy day," he remarks absently. "Now, let's eat."

We sit around the island like last night, but it's time for breakfast and coffee instead of tequila and limes. I look over at Eduardo, who is striding into the kitchen, freshly showered and ready to start his day of mafia dealings. Now that everyone is on the same page, there is no use in sugarcoating anything.

Eduardo is eating his tacos, and he moans around the food. "I love when my tripas are extra crispy."

Mateo snorts. "I know, but don't tell Jamesy here what it is. He doesn't want to know." His hands are raised in a halting motion, and he is not attempting to hide his mocking tone.

I look at my plain bacon, egg, and cheese taco, shrugging off the comment. "Some things are better left unsaid."

"Agree." Eduardo laughs, knowing my sensitive palate full well. "It's bad enough that I discovered Evie ordered cow tongue tacos." I place my food down, taking a big swig of orange juice.

"You said you liked my tacos." She looks at me, puzzled, and dare I say offended.

"I do, but they are salty."

She leans forward and murmurs in my ear, "I love salty things, baby." She licks my ear, and Emma coughs, speaking up.

"Okay, can we please get through breakfast?"

Evie shoots her an ugly look, and Emma beams at her.

"What the fuck kind of family have I gotten into?" I say, barely audible, but apparently not low enough because Eduardo chuckles. Great, now I am sitting here with my taco and a hard-on after Evie's comment. I adjust myself as discreetly as possible.

My phone chimes, distracting my thoughts just as Emma's does simultaneously, and we both share a look.

Eduardo straightens upright and looks between us with an expression of displeasure and wondering what the message could be that involves Emma and me, but not him.

Evie's jaw tightens, and I touch her face and turn her toward me to kiss her quickly before showing her my phone. "Here, read it for me. My hands are greasy."

She smiles, knowing full well that I am doing this to show her that I have nothing to hide from her.

I know we have many things to work on, and the first one is trust. I need to continue building trust between us, and this time, there will be no more secrets. It is a group text from Liv and Dax. I see the recognition on her face as she reads it, and then a smile spreads when she sees the picture of a baby boy taking up the screen, and his weight and length are displayed under his name.

"Kaden Brodie Johnson," she reads aloud. "He's beautiful, Emma."

I look up to see Emma touching her phone. Tears run down her face, and Eduardo kisses her cheek and licks away her tears. I look at his devotion to her and finally understand his feelings toward Emma. I only wished back then that I could have those feelings of love, protectiveness, and utter devotion to someone. They were childhood friends and then became so much more.

Evie senses me looking at something and looks over at her sister as well. I see the same realization on her face. It's not one of jealousy. Her features soften, and I squeeze her hand. She looks up at me, and when our eyes connect, I express with as much emotion as I can the feeling I have and the hope for us to have a similar connection. She squeezes my hand before releasing it and walks over to Emma.

Eduardo shrugs. "You guys go. I have some things to take care of here, and if you are there with them, Jameson, I would feel much better." He clasps me on the shoulder and starts to walk off.

"Wait," I hear Emma call out to him.

He stops quickly and turns toward her, immediately concerned for the panic rising in her voice.

"Yes, babe. What is it?"

She walks over to him. She bites her lip, and I can see the wheels in her head spinning about how to phrase her following words.

"Um." She twists her engagement ring around. "I was hoping that maybe I could tell Liv the truth. I have been feeling guilty for lying to her for a while now, and I really want her to know how much I value her friendship and maybe allow her to get to know the real me."

Her shoulders slump forward, and I realize how much she looks like Evie in this instant. The thought that they have gone through so much is terrifying to me. All Evie has been through was also without anyone there to hold her and love her. I know she had her brother with her, but it is not the same. Eduardo is so devoted to Emma, and she has relied on his strength to get them through some of the most challenging times, but who did Evie have?

"Hey, sis. Do you want some company to go and see your friend?" I see Evie's look of uncertainty flash across her face before she shuts it down and looks to Emma for an answer. She thinks Emma will blow her off. The vulnerability she tries to hide behind a strong façade is heartbreaking. She braces for her response as if the words Emma speaks could physically crush her.

Emma doesn't hesitate before she replies. "You mean, do I finally get to introduce my sister to my other bestie?"

Evie lifts her head in surprise and happiness. Emma quirks an eyebrow upward, and Evie cannot contain the laugh that bursts forth.

Looking at them both, I can tell they will get there sooner rather than later. Their pieces are now whole; now that Mateo is in the picture, they have come full circle and have their family back together.

I walk over to my girlfriend and take her hand, bringing it to my lips. I kiss it gently and then drop it. "We should all go," I say, looking at Emma. "Me, Evie, and you?" I ask so they don't think I would leave Mateo out. "Do you want to go, Mateo?"

He is quick to reply with a, "Fuck no. I need to sleep, and I mean for a whole day. I'm tired as fuck."

I place my hand behind Evie's neck. "We should probably go and get some rest, too." I look over to Emma. "When do you think we should go?"

Emma scrunches her nose up in thought. "Well, she just got home from the hospital, and we need some time to plan for any retaliation from Mr. Martinez that should be coming our way soon." She looks over to Eduardo, and he confirms.

"Yes, babe. Maybe give her some time to rest, and then you can all go over to visit, or if Jameson can't go, then I can take you girls to catch up." He thinks about it for a second. "How about this weekend? I have some work at the club, and you can spend some time with your friend and let her know to plan for them to visit her and to..." He pauses and swirls his hand in the air. "Whatever it is you want to tell her."

The girls nod in unison and agree to make a date to visit this weekend to see Dax and Liv's newborn.

"I can take them then," I confirm with Eduardo, and he agrees that it is still a better choice. "I'd like to catch up with Dax if he's home." Which I suspect the fucker took advantage of some paternity leave if he could.

Eduardo claps his hands. "Okay, it is settled then. Jameson will take you girls, but now I need to see what I can find out about Mr. Martinez."

Mateo stands. "I'll meet up with you in a bit. I have somewhere I need to be, and then I'll meet you at the club?" he asks, and Eduardo nods. "Jameson?"

I shake my head no.

I grab Evie by the hand and drag her out. "We have some catching up to do."

Evie barely has time to grab her bag as I'm ushering her out by the arm. I hear Eduardo laugh, and I get it. If I spend the rest of my life telling her how much I love and cherish her, it still won't be enough for the rest of the time I wasn't there with her. The only thing I can do from this point on is devote myself to her.

CHAPTER TWENTY

EVIE

"ALL AROUND ME" BY FLYLEAF

"Hurry up, Evie. I don't want to be late to meet Ramón!" Mateo shouts from the kitchen.

Where did I put my bag? I lift the pile of clothing from my bed and see the offending object. "Okay, just a sec."

I hear him pacing around out there. Bro needs to calm down before he goes bald from tugging at his hair. Sure enough, as I proceed to sling my cross-body bag across my shoulders, letting it rest over my right front hip, I see his hair standing erect on one side. I walk over to him, lick my hand, and smooth the hair down on that side.

He steps back, I'd say disgusted if going off his facial expression. "What-the-ever-loving-fuck?"

I shrug. "Your hair was sticking straight out on the side."

He lifts his hand up in protest. "So, you thought you should just…" He motions with his hands flying back and forth between my hand and face.

"Lick your hand and rub at my hair?"

I chuckle. "Um. Yep, that's exactly what I did, bro." I grab my water cup and swallow the ice-cold brew that resides there instead of the H2O that *should* occupy the space, but I'm not one to do things I *should* do.

He shakes his head in defeat. "Whatever. I just can't with you today." He walks out, and I follow him, locking the door behind me. I hurry to catch up with his long strides.

"Mattie, are you okay? You seem all…" I move my hand upright, making a circle around his person. "Tense," I finish.

He continues walking, sparing me a side glance so I can see just enough of his exaggerated eye roll as he continues ignoring my question.

"Are you suffering from FSB or something?"

At this, he stops mid-trek to the car. He pivots and turns around to me. "I'm afraid to ask…" He rubs a hand down his face. "But I will against my better judgment anyway. What the fuck is FSB?"

I smile slyly. "Why, fatal sperm build-up, of course."

He rolls his eyes upward as if they will pop right out of his head at any moment. He pivots and turns around without further comment. I can see the remark hit its desired mark because, if I am not mistaken, I see his shoulders rising as he tries to stifle a laugh.

Walking up to his usual coffee spot where he meets Ramón for chess, as I follow behind like a scolded child. I guess he is still sore about the saliva thing.

I walk in and see Dylan at the front counter. He sees me and smiles brightly. I don't return the enthusiasm, but I am not a total bitch, even though every bone in my body wants to scream *'cheater.'*

I notice Mateo is already seated with Ramón, and I once again feel like an outsider hanging out with them, as if I am intruding, except now that we had spent some time with him over the holidays. I see how much he enjoys his time with Mateo and how lonely he is. Two men finding a sense of purpose with one another—filling a missing familial void.

I get a text message and glance quickly to notice that it is from Jameson. My smile widens, but the text message has me a little confused.

Jameson: Where are you?

I look at my phone, wondering why he is asking this when I already told him we were coming to see my brother's friend.

Evie: I am with Mateo.

I snort as I type this. What is he getting at? Does he think I am lying?

Jameson: Where are you both?

Okay, I didn't tell him where, but we are still near Houston.

Evie: We are in Galveston?

I type it out because I don't want him to worry. This line of questioning is kind of worrisome. He has never been like this, and it is starting to make me nervous. I can see that he is typing, as the three little dots show under his message.

Jameson: Who are you with, and where?
I need all the information Evie.

I am now starting to panic. I look around the coffee shop and don't see anything conflicting or unusual that would make me suspicious. I am pretty good at sensing danger at this point. Nothing is screaming 'dangerous situation' at me.

I feel Mateo looking at me. I meet his gaze, and his expression remains neutral, but his eyes are questioning. I ignore it and look back at my phone, typing out a response.

Evie: I am at the usual coffee shop with
Mateo and his friend Ramón.

His response comes quickly.

Jameson: Perfect.

I make a jerky body movement, and annoyance starts to creep in. I type a nonthreatening questioning response.

Evie: WTF?

I see his following message and throw my phone down on the table.

Jameson: I'll explain later...

I don't bother responding this time. I'm just annoyed, but I am sure there has to be a good reason for that line of intense and very specific questioning. I cross my arms over my chest and kick my feet out in front of me in a pissed-off stance.

I look over to my brother and see him and Ramón staring at me and wondering why I have been reacting to my messages in that manner.

"Jameson is being vague. And super annoying," I say to them with an eye roll.

Mateo laughs, and Ramón smiles. "Ah, young love," he comments with a faraway look in his eyes, as if he is remembering a moment that is now just a distant memory—a blip in time. Maybe he is thinking about his wife. Whatever it is, he doesn't elaborate or comment further.

They return to their game, and I sit there wondering what is going on right now.

Bored with my situation, I stand up and leave them to their game—Ramon is clearly winning this round—and walk over to the water station and fill up a cup of iced water, adding a lemon to it.

I stand looking over at the sun reflecting off the water outside. I feel someone looking at me, and I turn to see Dylan. I lift a challenging brow. He looks as if he is going to walk my way, and I almost want him to do so, so I can let him know what I think of him. I am saved by the bell when a young woman comes through with a stroller, her eyes bright and cheerful. Dylan turns to her in surprise and then spares a quick glance my way, schooling his features.

I sip my drink, watching the interaction from a few feet away. She removes the clasp on the carrier and lifts a little girl from the stroller. She is wearing a little pink dress with a pink hairband holding back her little blonde curls surrounding her cherub-like face. She is beautiful, moving her chubby little hands back and forth and sticking her tongue out.

"We just came to see Daddy before lunch with Grandma and Grandpa." She coos at the little girl, adoration and love spilling forth for her little bundle of joy.

Dylan is rigid, knowing that he is officially busted. I take a long swig, watching the exchange and wishing I could help his unsuspecting wife in a way that lets her know she deserves better.

I turn to look at Mateo, and he is watching me. His eyes are pleading, asking me not to cause a scene. I nod once, and he visibly relaxes and returns his attention to his lost cause of a chess game.

Dylan takes his baby girl and kisses her on the top of her head. I see that he loves her because of the way he carries on about her. I mean, who wouldn't? She is so perfect.

It's at this moment my resolve softens, and as much as I think Dylan is the scum of the earth for attempting to give me his number, I don't know his situation. Looking at them, I don't see wedding rings on either of their fingers. *Interesting.*

I walk over to them, drawn to the sight of the baby and all its cuteness. I decide to just pass by and walk to our table when the baby drops the little doll that she had just had in her mouth. A long line of saliva falls, chasing after the little toy.

I pick it up for the young mother and hand it to her. She smiles at me, and Dylan just watches me to see what I am going to say. The little girl looks at me and shows a complete, gummy smile that radiates sunshine and happiness.

"She's beautiful," I whisper, not intending for that to slip out. I straighten my posture rigidly. I speak up. "You are both so lucky." I smile at them, and the mom beams at the compliment.

Dylan speaks. "Thank you. She is the best thing that happened to us."

I walk away and hear the woman ask Dylan if he has any plans tonight or if he is free to watch their daughter. It is then that I realize maybe they aren't together and I might have misjudged the situation. I frown as I walk back to the table.

When I hear the woman leave, I look at Dylan. My eyes soften, understanding the complexity of his situation. Dylan's cheeks blush as he looks down and walks off. I watch him retreat, wishing him positive vibes so that he can find happiness and find a person who will love him and that sweet girl unconditionally.

It's then that my jaded heart cracks just a little more with sympathy and compassion for another person instead of jumping to conclusions and seeing only the worst in everyone.

I sit there and reflect on the events in the coffee shop, waiting for my brother and Ramón to finish their game of chess. Mateo, in fact, loses the game. Shocker. They pack up their chess game, carefully putting away the pieces into the velvety cloth drawstring pouch. He helps Ramón put it into his messenger bag as we stand to walk out.

Dylan is at the counter, trying not to make eye contact with me. I walk over to him, and he looks up in surprise.

"Hi," he says shyly.

"Hey," I counter. "I just wanted to let you know that I have a boyfriend, but if I didn't, it would be such a turn-on to see such a man taking responsibility and caring for his daughter. I'm Evie, by the way." I extend my hand out to him, and he takes it, smiling.

"Thank you, Evie. I appreciate that."

I turn around, and before I leave, I wave. "See you around, Dylan."

The door chimes as I step out into the blazing heat. My hair is frizzing by the second. I pluck the sunglasses from my head and place them over my eyes to combat the blinding sun rays. I see Mateo and Ramón standing by the pier waiting for me.

Mateo shakes his head at me. "You just couldn't help yourself, could you?" He looks almost disappointed in me.

"I didn't say anything wrong. He isn't married, and he seems like a doting father. I just wanted to let him know I have a boyfriend, and his little girl was cute." I shrug.

Mateo looks at me. "Hm." That is all he says, and I see him look at Ramón, who smiles without comment. "Okay then. Let's go. We will drop off Ramón at his house after his doctor appointment, then head home, okay?"

I place my hand in my pocket. "Sure, no problem."

With that, we walk over to where we parked and get into our very hot car. Mateo opens the windows to allow some of the heat to escape. As we drive, I look over at the boats on the bay, the calmness, and the sound of seagulls flying carefree. It brings me a sense of peace when everything around me is spiraling out of control. I like things I can control.

> Jameson: Are you dropping off Ramón now?

I look up at the door, frowning at the question. I turn around and look out at the empty street, but I don't understand this line of questioning. *Can he see me?*

> Evie: Yes, we are headed there now. It took a while after his appointment. He had to see a doctor today.

I need to know what is happening, but I sense that we will not like the answers. He starts typing then stops. I stare at my phone and frown, but don't comment. No further messages come through.

Mateo pulls into Ramón's driveway, and he assists the older gentleman, helping to get him to his door. Mateo disappears inside the condo, and I wait for him. My phone dings moments later, and I notice another text message from Jameson.

> Jameson: You and Mateo meet me at The Viceroy after. Eduardo and I will be waiting for you.

I'm reading the last message as the door opens, and Mateo slides into the driver's seat. He looks over at me, then backs out of the driveway, pulling onto the feeder road to get on the highway. He looks over at me, sensing something is wrong.

"What? What's going on, Evie?"

I shake my head, confused as to what they need to discuss with us and why all the evasive questions.

"Not sure, but Jameson said we should go over to Eduardo's club. They want to talk to us there." I look over at my brother to see what he thinks about this.

"Did they hear back from Mr. Martinez yet?"

I bite my nail, shrugging my shoulders. "He didn't say, but I have a bad feeling about this, Mattie."

"We can speculate all we want, but it's best just to go now and see what they have to say."

I nod in agreement. We ride the entire way into the city, absorbed in our thoughts, wondering when the other shoe will drop.

CHAPTER TWENTY-ONE

JAMESON

"TOO SWEET" BY HOZIER

I get a call from Eduardo to meet him at his club. He doesn't explain the reason for the meet-up, but I know it is important if he called me at work to meet him.

I promptly gather up my belongings and rush out of the office, rushing to his club. I park right next to the door in the back alley and hit the button on my key fob to lock my car door as I am met by Gus. He leads me down the hallway and up the familiar set of stairs to Eduardo's office. Gus doesn't knock. He opens the door, and I see Eli and Philip already there. I enter, looking back at Gus, and take the only remaining seat across from Eduardo's desk.

"You aren't at the gym today?" I know he isn't, so it's more of a rhetorical question, if anything.

Still, he shakes his head in a nonverbal answer to my stupid question that really didn't need an explanation in the first place. His hands steeple over his mouth in a contemplative gesture as he carefully chooses his following words.

"I received a phone call today from Evie and Emma's uncle in Mexico."

I straighten in my chair, immediately on edge as to what this could now mean for us. "Did you speak with Emma? Does Evie know?" I look back at Gus, who walks closer to us and leans on the wall, crossing one foot over the other—his half-effort at getting comfortable.

Eduardo shakes his head. "No, he just called and told me about something exciting, and because of this new development, I need you to get me a camera." He looks over to Eli and Philip.

"What is this about? How can I help?" I look back and forth at anyone who could put me at ease because I don't like how my stomach drops at the uncertainty of the situation.

He hangs his head and then directs his focus at me. "I just found out that Mr. Martin is actually Mr. Martinez."

I look over at Eduardo, who is waiting for me to react. I just don't know what he's talking about. Perhaps if I had more information, I would respond differently.

"I'm confused. Mr. Martinez?"

Seeing my confusion, Eduardo quickly brings me up to speed for the urgency of this meeting. "The same as Julian and his father. As in the same grandfather to Julian. That Mr. Martinez."

I sit there frozen. "Ramón?"

My brain takes a moment to compute the gravity of the situation. This past year, Mateo has found a friend in this older man. I thought it was odd that this gentleman wanted to hang out with him so much.

"That's his grandfather?" My hand falls over my mouth. "Evie has been over there multiple times, and they were with him over the holidays because the man didn't have any family," I say, my pitch getting higher, as my anxiety rises through the roof.

Good God, how could we not have known? All this time that Mateo was spending time with this man along with my girlfriend was because he didn't have any family, when in fact, Mateo *is* his family. This is so fucked.

"Is he the enemy? Are they in danger?" I jump up quickly, my chair toppling to the floor as I move haphazardly, unsure of which direction to go. I imagine myself having a meltdown.

My body moves one way, and my mind moves another. My movements are jerky and erratic, causing me to almost misstep and tumble over the toppled chair. A loud thud echoes in the lofty office space.

I lean forward on his desk. My breathing picks up as my head hangs down. I try to calm the panic that Evie could be in danger. She has been going to this man's house and hanging out with him and Mateo frequently. If I recall correctly, they were even meeting him today.

I lift my gaze to Eduardo and see the same concern for his fiancée's safety. He holds his hand up as I am starting to ask another question.

"From what I can tell, he has been without contact from Julian before he died or from Mr. Martinez. I just don't know how he met Mateo and Evie. I think it seems just a tad bit coincidental that he meets them both and hangs out with his grandson without him actually knowing that Mateo is his biological grandson."

I look over at Eduardo's security detail and trusted friends. "Is that why you want the camera? To see if something is going on?" I take the object from my bag and place it on the desk. "What do we do now?" I throw that question into the air and see who grabs at an answer. The room remains silent. *Does no one know what we should do?*

I look to Eduardo for guidance. He has been doing this longer, and while Emma was my friend and I helped to keep her safe, this hits a bit differently. Now it's Evie, my woman, who is in trouble.

Eduardo sighs and rubs at his temples, like he is waging a war against an impending migraine. Everything is headache-inducing. The situation is complex and tiresome. Will we ever be able to just relax and hang out without worry? College was long ago; even days spent on Padre Island seem eons ago.

"Do you have everything I asked you to bring?"

I'm pulled from my thoughts and look at him, nodding that I do and pointing to his desk where I placed a bag with the contents of a camera inside.

He smiles. "I have an idea, but where are Mateo and Evie now?"

I take out my phone and send a text to Evie. I thought she was with Mateo in Galveston today, but I want to be sure. A moment later, she replies. My annoyance must show, so I quickly thumb through the reply, followed by two more. I put my phone down.

"She's with Mateo and the old man in Galveston."

Eduardo shoots a quick look at his best friend, Gus.

Gus steps off the wall and puts his hand out. He must sense my question to his outstretched hand. "I need the camera."

I look to Eduardo, who smiles and then begins to explain. He hands the camera over to Gus, who hooks the bag over his shoulder.

"We are going to plant it in Mr. Martin's house and see what he's up to. It just seems all too coincidental, don't you think?"

I nod in agreement. "I do. Coincidental as fuck." I point at the camera I brought and explain how it works, but there isn't much to it.

With that, Gus leaves for what I assume is Mr. Martin's place. Since he is out of the condo now, it should be an okay time to get this done.

I send one more text to Evie and ask her to let me know when they are on their way from dropping off Mr. Martin. We need to come up with something and make a plan to handle this new and unexpected development.

The phone rings in Eduardo's office. I look over in puzzlement at the source of the intrusion. Eduardo picks it up and smiles slyly. "Excellent, Gus." He looks over at me. "I'm sure Jameson can get it up and running here, and we will see you soon." He hangs up the phone, and I'm still staring at him, waiting to see what this conversation was about.

He feels me watching but ignores me to grab himself a drink as he hovers over the bar area in the corner. He grabs a glass and pours some amber drink into a glass. He looks over at me and tosses it back.

"What?" He stares at me in confusion.

I start to laugh. "I didn't think you still had a landline."

He looks at the phone and then back at me. "So." He shrugs. "It's for the club, and if anyone needs to call me."

I nod, accepting this excuse. I look around.

"What are you looking for?" He seems to be helping search for the unknown item.

"Nothing, I was just curious where your fax machine was." I start laughing, and he pours himself another drink.

"You know, I was going to offer you a drink, but now, I'm not feeling so charitable." He chuckles. "Dick."

"I'm just kidding, bro, but what did you need me to do? I heard you mention something to Gus."

Eduardo's smile spreads into an evil grin. "Yes, we have the camera up in Mr. Martin's house. It's time to find out what that old bird has been hiding."

I get the app up, and we look through the phone to see Mr. Martin standing in his kitchen. Eduardo called him an old bird, which isn't far from the truth. Ramón is under six feet, but that's not what makes Eduardo's comment accurate. He has a hook nose that mimics a beak. His eyes are beady and elongated in an obsidian black color, much like the color of

Mateo's eyes and Mr. Martinez's black ones that match his heartless soul. This combination gives him a bird-like quality that makes his comment laughable and highly on point.

I motion with my hand over to Eduardo. He peers over my shoulder. "Put it on speaker."

I do as he asks and place the phone on his desk. Eli and Philip move over to see him on the screen moving about in his kitchen. The clanking of dishes in the sink sounds through the phone as he sets the clean dishes down on the rack to air dry. Suddenly, a sound pierces the room, and Philip looks over at Eli.

"What's that noise?" Philip comments.

I laugh at his question. "I know, right? You should ask Eduardo," is all I say as Eduardo scowls at me.

Mr. Martin dries his hands on a towel as he walks over to answer the phone on the wall. They start laughing, but it dies down as soon as Mr. Martin answers the phone.

"Hello." He folds the dish towel over the sink and braces himself on the island. "Yes, I went to the doctor today, and Mateo took me." He adds the last part hesitantly. He appears to be in physical pain as he shifts his weight from one leg to the other. Whether the pain is related to his doctor's appointment or this phone conversation, we don't know.

We hear in a hushed tone, "Please don't ask that of me." His head is bent down as his hand rubs at his hair, much like Mateo does.

I look over at Eduardo, and he listens intently to every word of this one-sided conversation. It funnels in through the speaker in a whirl of acrid sounds as if he is afraid to miss any detail. "Okay, son. Yes, I will."

With that last sentence, I let out a breath I didn't realize I was holding. He hangs up the phone on the receiver. I sit up straight and watch as Ramón hangs his head and cups his face. He stands abruptly and walks off out of view into the bedroom.

A moment of silence passes before Eduardo speaks, confirming what we all know to be another truth. Ramón definitely speaks to or is in cahoots with Mr. Martinez, Mateo's father.

"Well, I guess we have our answer." Eduardo looks over at us as we consider the gravity of the situation.

"So, who is going to tell them?" I ask.

As soon as Eduardo's office door opens, Mateo and Evie walk in.

"Who's going to tell them what?" Evie says just as Eduardo groans.

"Fuck. You always did have perfect timing, Evie."

CHAPTER TWENTY-TWO

EVIE

"FOR WHOM THE BELL TOLLS" BY METALLICA

I walk into who knows what conversation as Mateo trails a few steps behind me.

"Perfect timing to tell me what the fuck is going on," he grumbles.

"With pleasure, Mateo. That's why we asked you over here. It certainly isn't for your smashing personality." Eduardo retorts.

He walks over to us, ushering Mateo and me into the already cramped office space. Mateo looks around at the solemn faces and whirls around to Eduardo.

"Why do I sense that we are going to get another piece of fucking information that I know we aren't going to like?" Mateo pulls at his hair again.

I grab his hand. "Stop that. You're going to go bald. I know you will hate that look."

He stops to roll his eyes at me, but I can tell I at least distracted him from escalating further.

Eduardo goes to his desk, grabs another drink, and pours a large amount of an amber liquid into a glass, as he puts the bottle back. Before I think what he will do with it, he hands the glass over to Mateo. He stares at it questioningly. One eyebrow arches up, but Mateo accepts the glass from Eduardo, although hesitantly.

"O-kay." That's all Mateo says as he waits to hear what happened.

Eduardo walks around to his desk and sits behind it before delivering the news that I'm sure will wreck us.

Mateo takes a sip and waits patiently, without rushing the words Eduardo really needs to spit it out already because he is drawing out the waiting period agonizingly slow, if you ask me.

His fingers drum on the edge of his desk. He shares a look with Jameson and he frowns at me. I swallow all the saliva that has now pooled in my mouth, suppressing the feeling of an imminent vomiting episode. I gulp, and Mateo takes the rest of his drink and downs it in one go.

"Tell me already," he says as he places the empty glass on Eduardo's desk with a resounding *thunk*.

Eduardo moves away from his desk. He stands with his feet placed apart and his hands crossed over his chest in a confrontational manner. "There is no easy way to say this, and I want you to hear me out before you jump to questions."

Mateo nods once, and that must give Eduardo the encouragement he needs to continue. "We had suspicions that Mr. Martinez was getting his information from someone, and it was confirmed when your uncle called to inform us that Ramón is the one who has been feeding him the information about you and Evie."

He pauses and the room is silent. It takes a minute for Mateo to process what Eduardo says, his breathing increases in intensity, as if he is trying to take a deep breath to contain his brewing anger.

I can't take it anymore. I speak up before this gets ugly. "Why do they think that…" I pause as the words I want to say escape me. "I mean, are you sure?" I look at Mateo, who is not moving, but his fists are clenched and knuckles are white as he holds onto the chair with a death grip.

Eduardo looks over to Jameson and Mateo, and I turn my attention over to him. "What's going on, Jameson?"

He walks over to me and grabs my hands. "When I asked you about your whereabouts today, it was so we could plant a camera in Mr. Martin's home."

Mateo stands, knocking the chair back. Jameson startles at the sound and looks his way.

"You went into his home and invaded his privacy? For what, a hunch?"

He is furious and wants to take his anger out on someone; however, his anger is misplaced. He is still protective of Ramón, and I can understand why. He was the closest thing to a father figure, and once again, he feels betrayed.

I can't help, but I feel the same way. I understand what it feels like to be lied to, and everything that you knew or thought you knew was all just a lie concocted for the benefit of someone else. Good intentions are a waste, if you ask me. To believe that we were conned by an elderly gentleman and then were in his home for the holidays… how could he have faked that kind of emotion?

Jameson doesn't miss a beat. "It was more than a hunch, and we confirmed it when he was talking with your father on the video feed. Albeit reluctantly, he was, and it sounded like he was asked to do something he didn't want to do."

Mateo rushes at Jameson and grabs him by the shirt. "Don't you ever call that fucking monster my father!" Spit flies from his mouth as he attempts to control the rage that courses through him in waves. I immediately step in between them.

"Mateo. Get your hands off of Jameson. We need to hear the rest."

Mateo slowly releases Jameson's shirt from his fists and steps back. The anger is still there, while he is attempting to control his emotions. The fury is just barely contained under his skin, waiting to erupt at any given moment.

Mateo turns to Eduardo, and I take the opportunity to throw my arms around my boyfriend, relieved that no punches were thrown.

Eduardo lifts his hands. "Mateo, there is more, but I need you to keep your cool as I tell you the rest because it is a lot to take in."

My brother returns to sitting in the chair and leans forward, hands steepled together like a kid praying at the altar. I hope he is praying to a god right now to have mercy because I can't imagine anything else being as wrong as what we heard. The betrayal that he must feel right now, his trust once again broken. My heart aches for the life my brother has had to endure, and I want nothing more than to take the pain and ease the burden from him.

Eduardo stares at him, waiting for him to regain his composure, and whatever Eduardo is looking for he must see because he continues and delivers the final blow. "Ramón is your grandfather."

And there it is, the final death punch.

Mateo hangs his head in defeat. I suck in a breath, causing Jameson to look at me in concern. I must sound like I am having an asthma attack, but no air comes out. I look around and the faces that stare at Mateo are solemn. They know how close my brother has become to Ramón, and now this news? It is just too much.

I leave Jameson's side and run over to my brother. I throw my arms around him in a protective embrace, leaning into him, and rubbing circles around his back. His hands go up to his face, and from the rise and fall of his back, he is crying. One by one, the guys clear out of the room and leave us as Mattie, my strong and protective brother, falls apart in my arms.

Jameson gives me a kiss on the forehead. He whispers near my ear, "I'll be right outside if you need me." With that, I hear footsteps retreat and the soft closing of a door as Mateo and I are left alone in Eudardo's office.

I stroke his hair. "I love you, brother. So much. It's okay. You have us, and we love you so much."

His sobs increase and a heart-wrenching cry comes out of his mouth, causing tears to flood my eyes as my vision becomes blurry. I have never felt something so heartbreaking. The loss of my parents, finding out the truth of their deception, what they did to my brother, and even Emma being kidnapped is nothing compared to the feeling I have for the man who is breaking down in my arms.

I want to protect him like he protected me, and I vow that I will hunt this man down and make him pay for all the pain he has caused my family. I wish I could go back in time and knock some sense into my mother and tell her not to go out with Mr. Martinez, but then I wouldn't have Mateo, so what is done is done. We can only move forward from here and end it once and for all.

I don't know how long we stay like that, but the door opens again, and I expect it to be Jameson or Eduardo coming in to see how we are doing. What I don't expect to see is my sister walk in and rush over to us, throwing herself into Mateo's lap. She hugs him so fiercely, and he shakes all over again. Emma tells him how much she loves him just like I did, and we all hug each other in a tight embrace.

Emma stands and reaches for me, and I grab her hand, pulling her into my side. We extend our hands to Mateo, and he looks at us with red-rimmed, swollen eyes. We smile at him in adoration of the boy who protected us, despite being denied the family he should have had all along. We each hold out a hand to him as he rises and takes them. We form a complete circle. Our family.

Emma speaks, looking straight up at Mateo. "We are here for you always, Mattie. You are our brother, and we love and support you no matter what. We will finish this."

I nod and squeeze both of their hands. Mateo goes to hug Emma and rests his head on her shoulder. He runs his nose along her collared shirt, and my hand rises to my mouth as I stifle a laugh. Emma visibly tenses, slowly releasing Mateo's embrace, and her head shoots to the side where Mateo has left a slimed trail of mucus along her blouse. Her eyes narrow and shoot over to him accusingly. He wipes his face with his hands, and a smile is left on his face as they lower to his side.

"You did that on purpose, Mattie." She pretends to be angry.

He smiles. "Must run in the family, sis."

She laughs with her head thrown back. "Touché, bro."

I let out a laugh, as does Mateo. We hear the door open, and Eduardo peeks his head in. His eyes go to each of us, and sensing the mood in the room, he motions outside to his entourage to come back into his office.

"Everything okay in here?" Eduardo looks to Emma, and she saunters over to him. His expression is guarded. It pains him to see Emma angry, and he would do anything to prevent her from feeling anything other than happiness.

He pulls her into him and kisses the top of her head. Her arms are wrapped around his lower back as she snuggles into his embrace and sighs in contentment.

I look over to Jameson, who is watching me keenly. I shrug, and he comes over to sit in one of the chairs, pulling me on top of his lap.

Mateo clears his throat, breaking the silence. "So what do we do with this information, Eduardo? What's the plan?"

Eduardo looks at my brother and studies him for a moment. "What do you want to do, Mateo? Do you want to confront him?"

He seems to think about it and eventually nods. "Yeah, I think I do. We are meeting next week at the café. I plan on asking him there."

Jameson looks over my shoulder at Eduardo. "I think that is a good idea, and maybe this week we will find out something else from the camera feed."

I glance quickly over at Mateo and his jaw clenches. I can tell he isn't too keen on the idea, but it must be done. I think he recognizes this and nods.

"Yeah, okay. Sounds good." With that he stands. "I think I have had enough excitement tonight. I'm going to head home. You need a ride, Evie?"

I stand and pull him into an embrace. "No, but I will meet you back at home tonight."

Emma comes over to hug him goodbye, and he waves as he leaves the office. No one says anything for a while, but Eduardo looks over to Emma, who is biting her lip with worry.

"Don't worry, babe." He grabs her hand. "It will all work out."

I stand and pull Jameson's arm to bring him to an upright position. "Let's go. I'm so tired, and I need to think."

He nods, telling Eduardo to call him if he needs anything else as we leave not much after Mateo does. Climbing into Jameson's truck, we pull out into the bustling traffic.

"Your place or mine?" he asks me because I know, after all that went down at Eduardo's office, he doesn't want to leave me alone tonight. That was a lot to take in, and his need to make sure I'm okay is palpable.

"Mine. I want to make sure Mattie is okay." I turn my head to look out the window, and after the bomb that was dropped, my mind is a whirlwind of rising emotions.

CHAPTER TWENTY-THREE

EVIE

"I JUST WANNA RUN" BY THE DOWNTOWN FICTION

We get to the apartment to find Mateo isn't home. I check his room and find it just as he left it earlier, which means that he never came home after leaving the club.

I hate to admit that I am worried. I have never seen Mateo cry. Not even after our mother died, when he learned about Emma and I being his siblings, and even when he learned about our mother giving him up to be raised by her grandparents. None of that had the reaction that I saw from him today in Eduardo's office, when he cried over the news about Ramón that was difficult to watch.

Is he really that close to Ramón? Maybe it was just that last scoop added onto the heaping pile of shit that is our life. Maybe it was just too much for him to handle—the straw that broke the proverbial camel's back and all. The last Jenga piece placed haphazardly that caused the whole tower of emotions to come tumbling down in one fell swoop.

I return to the kitchen where Jameson is standing with his hands in his pockets watching me with a myriad of emotions displayed on his face. I walk over and stand in front of him with my arms crossed over my chest. He looks into my eyes, and I keep his stare, but it is hard to return it. I want to break like Mateo did, but I can't. I won't let myself be weak any longer. I made a promise to myself years ago that no one would ever break me again. I guess we all go through shit, and some things just tip us over at some point.

Today was one of those days.

I feel like Jameson can see into my soul and all the rot that takes up residence there rent free. He sighs and removes his hand from his pockets and places them on each side of my arms, running them up and down as if he is trying to warm me up from a chill.

He smiles coyly at me. "How are you holding up?"

I shrug, and he keeps running his hands up and down my arms. Now I do feel chilled. It elicits goose bumps on my arms from where his touch leaves and then returns. I involuntarily step closer as if I am being pulled by an invisible thread that tethers his heart to mine.

"It was a lot to take in."

He searches my eyes for the truth. "Was he okay when we left the room?"

My voice cracks at first, and then I clear my throat. "Not really. He has been through a lot. It was heartbreaking." I press my cheek up against his chest. The sound of his heart thumps louder. The rhythm is strong and soothing to my rising anxiety.

He places his chin on the top of my head, and my arms feel cold when his hand leaves them to rub circles on my back. I feel like I'm shivering yet burning up as he stokes a flame that needs just a bit more fuel to fully combust.

"I wish I could save him the way that he saved me."

I hear him start to say something and then stop.

I lift my head from his chest and look up at him. Jameson gulps and then looks away. "Did you want to say something?"

He turns back and nods. "I want to know everything about you, Evie. I want to know the good and the bad. I want to be there for you and be someone you can trust and rely on."

Now it's my turn to gulp back the lump that forms in my throat as the intrusive memories try to resurface. All the memories I have been attempting to suppress rise along with my stomach bile. I fight the nausea, and it makes me flinch as if it just happened yesterday.

I pull away from him and he tenses, thinking he did something wrong, that maybe he pushed me too far, but he doesn't realize how much he has already helped me.

I tug at his hand and pull him toward the couch. "Come on. Let's talk about this while I'm sitting on the couch. I need to be a bit more comfortable for what you want to know about me."

We walk over to the couch and sit side by side. Jameson turns his knees angled in toward me, and I do the same to give him my full attention.

"You know, I loved art. I wanted to be an artist. That is until everything happened and I could only see the ugly in the world. I refused to make anything that was as dark as all the emotions that shredded my heart and the depravity of what I thought in my head. I wouldn't give it a name or face, so I stopped painting and drawing."

He takes my hand in his. "Take your time, babe."

I clear my throat and continue. "When I was fifteen, I had to stay after school to finish up a project I was doing for art class. We didn't live that far from school, so I thought I would just walk home. I took a shortcut through the center of town and through an alley. I was almost through it when two men came out of nowhere."

I can sense Jameson getting angry, but I ignore it and continue. "One grabbed me from behind, and the other stepped so close he sandwiched me between them. I bit one of the guy's hands when he clasped it over my mouth and nose. I felt like I couldn't breathe. I thought I was going to pass out, and I was in self-preservation mode. Maybe not thinking clearly, but at that point what was the right choice here? Getting raped? He called me a bitch for it. I screamed before the other one slapped me so hard across the face, my vision blurred." I wince, remembering the sting of that slap and the tingle that spread across my body at the violation my body felt afterward.

"He... ugh." I pause, looking away from Jameson as I get through the next part. He runs his thumb across the top of my hand to soothe the emotions running through me. I'm finally calm enough to finish.

"He said, 'I'll give you something to scream about' as he cupped his hand hard in between my legs as he mimicked thrusting his erection on my leg."

I feel Jameson tense and I spare a glance at him. He nudges me with his hand on my leg to continue. I tense, remembering the feeling, and he removes his hand from my leg and holds both my hands in his. It is as if he can sense my discomfort and tries to lessen my burden.

This feels so intimate and stifling, but I know that he is only trying to provide me with comfort, and I know that I can get through this. I can do this for him. "I didn't hear anything, but more like I felt his presence. Then something landed on my shirt. Something warm and wet, and when I looked down, there was blood on the front of my shirt.

"I was pushed forward and almost tripped over the dead guy who just had his hands on my most intimate parts a moment ago. He was lying on the ground in a pool of blood. His life gone. I saw a young man walking toward me, and the assaulter who held me against him along with his dead accomplice started running to get away. He tripped, and I turned to look up at my guardian angel of death before he put a bullet in his head and killed the second assaulter."

"I heard sirens, and the young man that just saved me from an unknown fate comes up to me and tells me I am going to be alright. The sirens get closer; I look over to the police running my way. I turn back to thank him, but he is gone."

Jameson pulls me into a hug. "That was Mateo?"

I nod. "I just didn't know it then."

Jameson looks at me quizzically, but encourages me to go on with my recounting of events that night.

"Later on, when Emma met Julian, I was hit and left unconscious in another alley. You think I would have learned my lesson about alleys, but I was with Emma, and she wanted to get some food from our favorite street truck after her shift at the coffee shop... I mean, it was still daylight out," I stammer, still trying to comprehend how I let this happen to me again, as if the excuses I make have anything to do with the ordeal being my fault. I didn't ask for any of that.

I shake my head thinking about it. "Julian and his dickhead driver pulled up, and he tried to make Emma go with him. Long story short, the driver punched me and Julian took Emma. I came to, awakening with Mateo holding me in the alley until I was able to go home. He walked me home and then took off."

Jameson curses, and I look to see how angry he is. "Did you know that he was your brother?"

I shake my head. "No, I mean, I didn't even think that. I thought he was just someone my uncle had watching over us after I told my mom about it." I laugh, but it sounds evil when I get it all out.

"After we told my mom about Julian and Emma, she mentioned it being Uncle Andrés's security detail. Not my fucking brother or her son. Can you believe that?"

"No," he replies. "That's just so fucked-up, Eve's."

I nod in agreement. "It is, and I didn't see him again until he saved me from the house explosion and finally told me that he was my brother. My own parents didn't even tell me. They never told us the truth."

All the twisted lies. I run my hand down my face, and Jameson grabs my hands in his.

"You are so incredibly brave, baby, and I love you so much for all of it."

I freeze. I don't think he realizes that he just told me he loves me, but I can feel it.

"You love me?"

He looks me in the eyes and brings my face to his. He kisses me. "Yes, Eve. So, so much." He pulls away and studies my expression.

I bite my lip and smile up at him. "I love you, too."

He swallows. "Is this why you didn't like for me to touch you when we first met? The times we were intimate?"

I stand and pace away before I turn to him. "I went to Krav Maga classes after the incident. I didn't ever want to feel that out of control of my life again. To have those feelings like I had years ago. Defenseless. Helpless. I felt so down on life, and I hated being a victim. I thought that I could take back my life if I could control everything about me. Maybe a little too much." I shrug, and he stands up.

"I have an idea. Do you trust me, baby?" He looks at me with so much devotion in his eyes that I can't say anything but the truth.

"Yes, completely."

He smiles, showing a full set of pearly whites, and my heart dances around in my chest, excited to see what he has in store for us.

"I'll be back in half an hour. Go run yourself a bath, and I'll be back before you know it." He winks at me and then leaves the apartment on a mission, for whatever he has planned, I know that he would never hurt me.

CHAPTER TWENTY-FOUR

JAMESON

"COME UNDONE" BY BAD OMENS

I drive back over to Eduardo's club and park out back. I open the back door and run up the stairs that lead to his office. I see Gus walking out and he eyes me suspiciously.

"Everything okay?"

I smile. "Yes. Is Eduardo in there? I have to ask him something, but it's of a personal nature."

He nods. "Sure thing. Just knock per usual. You know he doesn't usually lock his door. No one would be stupid enough to go in there."

Not that they'd live to tell about it. I think of that psychopath, Cherry, and shudder.

"Got it." I thank him and run off.

I knock on the door and Eduardo's voice gives me a resounding, "Enter." He looks up from his computer as I walk in. His expression turns to worry and I put my hand up.

"It's nothing, I just want a personal favor for Evie."

One eyebrow lifts up, and I wonder if he realizes that he does that so well. It's almost comical.

He sits back in his chair and steeples his fingers together. "Go on. What is it?"

Taking a breath before I ask, "Now, I hate to ask this, but I think it could really benefit Evie, and if I am being totally honest, it would help me a whole lot, too."

He just stares at me, waiting it out to see where I am going with this.

"I was hoping to borrow some supplies from the club next door," I get out all in one breath.

He tilts his head to the side. "My sex club?" I nod. A smile spreads across his face. "And why is that, James?"

"Just call it therapy," I counter.

He laughs. "Sure. I'll let them know that you are going in and will 'borrow' some items." He emphasizes the word *borrow* in air quotes. "Just make sure that you return them and disinfect them before we also disinfect them. Okay?"

I'm already heading to the door. As I open it, I give him a thumbs-up, and I can hear him laugh as I close the door behind me.

I enter the club with a mask on, disguising my face much like I did when I first met Eve here. Wow. To think so much has changed since then.

I approach the hostess station, scan my card, and let them know that I am here to borrow a few things. She seems skeptical, but after a quick call to her boss, I am escorted to one of the rooms where I pick a few items out that she helps to place in a garment-like bag. Once it is zipped up and discreetly hidden away from prying eyes, I leave the club through the back entrance and tuck the items in the back seat of the pickup and leave in a hurry to start my first session with my willing girlfriend.

I don't really have an idea if this will work, but I have to give it a chance. I want Evie to trust me while simultaneously helping her overcome her fears. We have made such good progress, but I want to be able to do more. Although she may not ever fully recover from her trauma and hold onto tidbits of that memory and fear, I can help her overcome the part that affects us and our relationship.

As I contemplate all the therapy sessions we will have tonight, I barely register pulling into the parking lot. I grab the bag out of the back seat and run up the stairs, taking them two at a time. I unlock the door with the key that Evie gave me before I left and place it back on the foyer table, calling out to her as I make my way into her bedroom. "Evie? I'm back."

"In here," she says.

She is towel drying her hair and rubs some products into it that smell like lavender and other botanicals. She tosses the towel to hang over the hook behind the door as I place the garment bag on her bed. As I fully unzip the bag for her, she looks at each item I have, receiving an eyeful of the toys I intend to pleasure her with.

Before she can ask, I let her know my plan. I walk over to her and take her hands in mine. "Remember when we met at the club that night for the first time?"

She smiles mischievously at the recollection of the events that unfolded that night, and I know exactly what part she is remembering.

"Of course."

I smile in return. "Well, I stopped by the club earlier and thought maybe we could create some more memories in the safety of your bedroom."

Her smile increases. "I like that plan. What do I get to use on you? Do you have a certain thing in mind?"

"I do," I reply. "I want for you to have an open mind."

She eyes me suspiciously and I can't help but encourage her. "Do you trust me?"

"You know I do."

But I can tell her hackles are raised and she is hesitant to learn of what I have planned because she is right. It is something to be concerned about, and I just hope that I am not making a colossal mistake and taking her too far out of her comfort zone.

I remove the first item from the bag—a pole with a leather padded attachment called a flogger. I place it on the bed, and I see her stare at it. I bring the next item out of the bag—a silk scarf. That is obvious, but the last one causes her to shuffle backward.

I remove the leather restraints from the bag and place the four items together on the duvet. Lastly, a pole is placed with the cuffs. "It's a spreader. It keeps your legs apart."

She looks at the items and then at me. "I don't understand."

"I think you do," I counter.

I approach her, and her body stiffens. I bring her closer to me. My hand is on her waist, and I look down into her eyes. They seem guarded, and they should be because we are going to test some limits, and I want her to get past this fear. If I can help her, maybe she can heal and learn to trust me as her partner and lover.

I run my hand down her cheek, and she leans into my touch. She stares up at me. I bring my lips to her and kiss her softly. "You know that I won't hurt you, right, Eve?" She nods, but doesn't speak. "We can stop at any time if you are uncomfortable. You know that too, right?"

She nods again. "Do I need a safe word, Jameson?"

I kiss her lips and trail kisses down her chin and neck. I pepper light kisses along her chest as she tosses her head to the side, granting me more access to the place she wants me to move. I oblige and then answer her.

"No. No safe word, baby. You just tell me to stop and I will. That's all it will take."

She smiles. "Okay. I want to try it for you."

I grab her hands and place them above her head. She keeps them up as I pull her tank top off her body and throw it over her head. I kneel at her feet and look up at her, bringing her sleep shorts and panties down her legs as she steps out of them. I toss them behind me and place a wet kiss on her pussy, swiping my tongue through her folds. She stares down at me with a hooded gaze. I stand up and point at the bed.

"Lay on your back in the middle of the bed, baby."

She quickly turns around and jumps on the bed, eager to follow directions. I strip all my clothes off agonizingly slowly, even though I want to peel them as soon as I can from my body so I can bury myself in her tight cunt.

I groan at the thought and palm my dick to stifle the ache that is building at the idea of her wet heat engulfing my cock. A bead of precum drips off the tip, and I need to progress this if I want to make it through all the things I want to do to her.

I pick up the scarf and twirl it in my hand. "I am going to cover your eyes, so you are going to need to trust me, okay."

"Okay. I can do that." She looks at the other things on the bed as I kneel on it and move on all fours toward her.

"You have already seen what I took out of the bag, so you know what is coming, okay. This is about you turning control over to me and learning to trust. I would never hurt you, Evie."

I place the scarf over her eyes, and she lifts her head so I can tie it around her head loosely, but effectively. "Can you see, baby?"

She shakes her head now, and I smile.

"Okay. I am going to put the cuffs on your hands and feet now." I pick up the cuffs, and the chains make a noise that causes her to flinch. I trail my finger over her legs and bend over to kiss her feet before placing the cuff on one leg and then repeat the same action on the other one. Once I have the cuffs on her legs, I attach them to the spreader that will keep them apart as I lock it in place.

I move over her body, my hand rests on her flat stomach, and I touch her lightly, running my hands under her breasts and everywhere except where she wants them. I see her lift her chest up in offering, hoping that I will put one nipple into my mouth, but that will come later.

I lift off and entwine my hands with hers as I raise them above her body and attach the cuff to them. My erect dick leaves a trail of wetness on her chest and hovers just over her neck as I move forward to attach the restraint to her metal headboard. As I tighten the last one, I feel her tongue dart out to lick my cock as she runs her tongue along the side.

"Fuck, Evie. You want to be a good girl and suck me off, baby?" This was not the plan, but if she is offering... I want to make her happy.

"I do." She licks her lips at the drop that falls from my tip.

"Open wide for me and stick out your tongue, so I can feed you my fat cock."

She obliges, and I grip it at the base as I scoot up and place the tip on her tongue. She licks the tip, and I inch more into her mouth as she hollows out her cheeks and takes me in deeper, until I hit the back of her throat. She doesn't gag like I thought she would, and I retreat out a bit before I push it back in.

Her tongue swirls around at the tip and licks the underside as I pump in and out of her mouth, but this wasn't the plan, so I pull out of her mouth with a pop as saliva trails down her chin.

She pouts.

"This isn't about me, baby. It's about you. Your mouth is sinful, Eve."

She smiles when I call her that.

"You are definitely my downfall, and I'll ride that train straight to hell if you're driving, sweetheart." I kiss her, and she lifts her head to deepen the kiss when I pull away and step off the bed. I pick up the flogger.

"What are you doing, Jameson?" she asks nervously.

"Nothing you won't like, baby."

I see the rise and fall of her chest quicken as she becomes anxious of what's to come. I don't keep her waiting long as I grip the flogger and place the cool leather trailing a path up her arm and down her chest. I circle her nipple with it and then repeat the same action on the other side. I trail it around and then bring it down quickly on the underside of her breast in a quick snap to her flesh. She gasps, but realizes what happened.

"Jameson," she moans.

I trail the flogger down her leg and up the other until I reach her pussy. I give it a quick snap with the flogger and wetness pools down her leg. She tries to bring her legs together to relieve some of the ache that is forming between them, but the spreader bar is there preventing her from moving the way she would like to. I place my head between her thighs and blow on her glistening pussy.

"You are so wet for me, baby."

"Please, Jameson. The anticipation is killing me."

I don't give her a chance to say anything else before I devour her. I hold her lips open as I fuck her with my tongue then come back out, finding her clit as I pull and suck it into my mouth. She comes with a scream. I tuck one arm under her hips to help bring her closer to me as she bucks and thrashes around while I continue to suck on her clit.

Wetness pools underneath her as I wipe the mess from my chin. Her breathing starts to slow, and I undo the spreader bar. I toss it off the bed and climb forward as I run my dick through her wetness. I line up with her opening and surge forward, causing Evie to cry out. I stall.

"You okay?" She shakes her head. "Use your words, baby."

"Please fuck me, Jameson."

And I do. I won't last long. But I want her to come again, so I suck on her nipple and toy with the other as I fuck her hard, hitting that spot that makes her see stars. I know I've reached it when she gasps.

She screams, "Right there. Keep going." She squeezes my cock as she comes, and I follow, climaxing along with her.

I collapse on top of her and swirl my tongue around her over sensitive nipple. With my dick still inside her, I undo the restraints on the headboard and hover over her as I remove the blindfold from her eyes. I look into her eyes and she smiles.

I kiss her and feel my cock harden again. I start to move and she wraps her legs around my waist. This time I fuck her softly, letting the gravity of what we just did register. She trusted me, and hopefully that's enough. She loves me, and I know that's everything.

CHAPTER TWENTY-FIVE

EVIE

"ONLY HAPPY WHEN IT RAINS" BY GARBAGE

I don't know when we fell asleep, but I was fucked into unconsciousness. I'm awake at three AM, the witching hour. It is the time of night that nothing good happens, when evil is meant to be at its strongest and the supernatural run rampant, spreading lies and deceit through the remaining hours of nightfall.

I hear a crash and sit up quickly. Jameson is already out the bedroom door to investigate the disturbance. I throw on his shirt when I see him helping my drunk-as-shit brother up off the floor. The guy is piss drunk and reeks of cheap thrills taken in a dive bar bathroom stall.

I hope that I am exaggerating, but he does smell heavily of booze and sickly sweet perfume. His zipper is down and his dick is sticking out slightly and I wince, looking away just as quickly. I hope that he was trying to take a piss somewhere and it's not from anything else.

"Yikes. Commando. Agh. My eyes." I rub at them, but some things cannot be unseen.

"Evie." Jameson startles me from my verbal diarrhea. "Help me get him to his bed, please."

I jump into action as I round the other side of Mateo and fling his arm around my shoulder. Jameson and I struggle but manage to bring his dead weight over to his room and attempt to lay him on his bed, but he bounces as we drop him there. He groans as if in pain.

Just wait until tomorrow. I shake the thought away with a violent shudder, remembering how that time felt and vowing never to feel that hungover again. That out of control.

"Yeah, that wasn't fun for me either, bro."

I tug his shoes off, and Jameson helps to remove his pants. I don't want to see any more of my brother than I already had to this early morning, so I run over to the other side, lifting the covers as Jameson lifts his legs up and I swoop the covers from under and pull them upward and over his body.

I go the kitchen to grab a Gatorade and water bottle along with some pain medication. I know he will need it to help with what I am sure will be a raging headache when he finally wakes to welcome a more sobering day.

He will definitely regret this later.

After we place him on his side with a trash can in case he decides to puke, we close the door. I follow Jameson back to my room, and I swear I can still smell his scent of questionable morals lingering in a claustrophobic blanket of despair over my body.

Jameson is behind me now, waking me from my thoughts. He quickly kisses my neck, nuzzling and breathing in deeply. "Wow, he stunk," Jameson says as he steps away from me, frowning as he sniffs his arm. "Can you still smell it?" he asks me, and I giggle, nodding.

"Right?" He grimaces. "Damn. I thought so."

"Should we shower?" I think about it, but I am beat and want to go back to bed.

"We are getting up soon, so why bother? We can shower in a couple of hours when we have to get up anyway."

He nods in silent agreement.

He rummages through the bathroom cabinet. "I found it." He looks victorious as he waves my favorite lemon verbena spray and starts spraying our room and sheets with it. "There." He puts the bottle down, sniffing the air.

"Good lord, it does smell a little better now." He sniffs his arm again, but the overpowering fresh scent of lemon is all I can smell.

"Can we finally go back to bed now?"

It doesn't take much to convince Jameson as he pulls the covers over his shoulder, tucks himself into me, and is asleep before his head touches the pillow.

Hearing him breathe so relaxed and deep makes me tumble into an equally deep slumber where dreams evade me and my mind is clear from the dark waves of emotions that constantly wash over me.

Emma called and asked if I wanted to join her to visit Liv. I had my reservations, but she convinced me to go. Jameson is going to drive us, since he is friends with Dax, Liv's husband. They are going to catch up while he is home on a brief paternity leave with Liv.

I am sitting, having my morning coffee and cursing Mateo, when she pulls up to my house at around ten. Jameson says something about disinfecting some equipment before returning it to Eduardo's club.

He walks out of the bedroom and places the garment-looking bag on the side of the couch. My face reddens looking at it and thinking about how we used most of the equipment in varying positions. I got used to feeling restrained around him, and the way Jameson fucked me like a champ all night left me pleasantly sore between my legs. I slept so soundly afterwards, until I didn't.

The doorbell rings, and I get up to answer it. Emma is at the door and waves to someone as she enters.

"Was that Eduardo?" I close the door behind her, and she waves to Jameson, who is scrolling through his phone with his cup of coffee.

She places her mug on the table. "Yes, of course, it was. You know how he is." She looks around and walks to the refrigerator. She opens it and she fist pumps the air. "My favorite cold brew. How did you know?"

She opens it and pours a generous serving along with my oatmilk, which is hidden off to the side and covered by Mattie's gallon of whole milk. So infuriating. Why did I somehow miss the lactose enzyme? She places her top back on her cup and takes a long sip.

She sighs dramatically. "Absolute heaven." She looks around. "Hey, where is Mateo?"

I shoot a glance over to Jameson, and he looks at me, then proceeds to avoid eye contact with Emma.

She stands. "What was that look for, Jameson?"

He won't look at her. "I have no idea what you mean, Em." He continues to scroll through his socials, and I scoff.

"Geez, at least I know you are a bad liar." Emma focuses her attention on me. "What is it, Evie? Is our brother okay?"

"No, he isn't okay. He was given some pretty devastating news yesterday, remember?"

Emma starts to walk over to his room, but I pull her by the hand away from the door.

"He came home so drunk last night, or rather this morning, around three AM. We had to help him to bed, and it was a sad sight. He smelled horrific, and I swear I need to burn his sheets."

She rolls her eyes. "Don't be so dramatic, sis."

Jameson finally looks up and holds his hand up. "Hey, I have to agree with Eve on that. He was so saturated in booze and cheap perfume that I think it is better just to do that. In fact, I think he should bathe in more alcohol to burn the germs off. I just hope he was careful and didn't fuck anyone without protection."

Emma winces at the visual that Jameson painted for her.

"I told you. He was in a bad way, Em. I was going to check on him, but I honestly thought it would be better for him to sleep. He'll need to sleep off that hellacious hangover."

"I agree," Jameson says.

Emma looks toward Mateo's door and frowns in displeasure. She relents. "Okay, I guess you're right. Let's let the guy sleep, but later, he is free game."

I feel bad for Mateo if he has to hear her bitch at him this afternoon.

I stand, placing my now empty mug of coffee in the sink, and Jameson follows suit. He comes over to me and gives me a quick peck on the lips, pulling himself close to me and wrapping his arm around my waist before he lets go. He claps his hands together, rubbing them together.

"Are you girls ready to leave here and see a baby?"

Jameson agrees to drive us over there, and I climb into the front of his truck. Emma hops in the back, and Jameson gets in on his side, starting up the truck. I roll down my window to let some of the heat out. Jameson blasts the air conditioning, but it doesn't feel cool until he pulls onto the interstate. The cooling seats are magnificent, as the leather doesn't seem quite as hot as before.

My thoughts go back to last night and all the delicious things Jameson did to me. I wanted to admit I wasn't okay, but I didn't want to upset him. I felt better when I practiced my breathing techniques and remembered that I was in a controlled environment.

Even though I gave control to him, I never felt like I wasn't in control. He told me if I wanted to stop, we could. There were too many reassurances for me to feel anything other than safe in his arms.

I understand it is because I trust him, and the comfort level is there. I had so much therapy before, and my partners were never someone as close as Jameson is to me. We are in a relationship built on love, respect, and now trust. He knows all my secrets, fears, and, more importantly, my dreams. He wants to be a part of that, and it's more than I could have ever hoped for in a relationship.

I smile, thinking of him coming with a roar in my ear as he nuzzles into my neck, causing a tickle there that made me squirm and laugh. If he had tickled me while I was tied up, I would have been pissed.

"What are you smiling at, Evie?"

His question pulls me from my thoughts, and I look over at him. I'm biting my nail, and I'm sure my cheeks are pink from the memory of him fucking me hard as the headboard knocked against the wall.

Oh my goodness. My poor neighbors.

"Never mind," he says as he looks over my shoulder to merge into the other lane.

Emma chimes in. "I don't think I want to know."

We pull into Dax and Liv's place, and Emma starts toward the door, while Jameson comes over to my side of the truck, where I step down onto the pavement. I look up at him as he pushes me against the truck. His erection grinds into my stomach as he bends over to kiss me. I push him away and swat at his arm.

"Stop."

He laughs and closes the door, locking it with the key fob and adjusting his erection as Emma watches us, shaking her head with her hands lifted above her head. She knocks on the door, and Dax opens it. I'm already ahead of Jameson, and he jogs to catch up. "Hey, ladies. Liv is through that way in the room off the kitchen."

Jameson mouths 'Have fun,' as I follow Emma to see Liv's new baby, Kaden Brodie Johnson.

Liv is snuggled into a chair with baby Kaden in her arms. She stands when she sees us. She shuffles over to Emma, and Emma wraps her arms around her best friend and looks over at the little boy in her arms. She looks up to stare at me and looks over at Emma.

"Holy shit. You have a twin sister?"

Emma winces. "Yes, Liv, this is my other best friend and sister, Evie."

Liv looks at me, and then Emma and I can sense the hurt radiating from Liv and how she never knew about me. It's not as if Emma could have told her, but I am beginning to understand why I am here and the support Emma needs to tell her best friends the truth. It's time for all the lies to stop.

"Liv, I am here today not only to see you and the baby but also to tell you the truth." She bites her lip and looks over at me. I stand near Emma to give her support.

Liv nods and then points to the chair for us to sit. She settles the baby into her lap, and I put my hands out to offer to hold the baby for her.

Liv looks over at me hesitantly before handing her baby boy over to me. She crosses her feet under her and places her hand in her lap, waiting for Emma to speak.

"Liv, there is so much I want to tell you, and I have kept so much from you, but you are my best friend. It is time to tell you the truth. I can finally tell you the truth about my family and why I was so secretive. There were so many times that you asked me something, and I wanted to tell you, but I couldn't because it wasn't safe for me to do so."

Liv leans closer, as if the secrets will appear if she squints hard enough. Emma twists her hands in her lap, and I move side to side, trying to comfort a sleeping baby, but perhaps I'm the one who needs the soothing.

"I knew Eduardo from when we were kids, and my mother kept us apart. The reason is that his family is in the mafia."

Liv blinks and then looks away. "Emma, I kind of already knew that. I mean, Jameson said that he went to college with Eduardo and didn't come out and say it, but that's what I suspected."

Emma smiles. "Yes, you are right, but what you don't know is that my family is, too." This news shocks her, and her hand goes up to her mouth, stifling a gasp.

"I was on the run, Liv. I had a stalker ex-boyfriend that abused me, and he and his father killed my family. I was taken by him, held captive, and escaped when my family in Mexico came for me. I recently learned that my sister wasn't dead and that I have a brother."

Liv jumps off the couch and throws herself at Emma. "Oh my God, Emma. Why didn't you tell me you were in danger?" She pulls back, and Emma is trying to hold back tears that threaten to fall from her eyes at any given moment.

"I didn't want to put *you* in any danger, Liv. I thought I was doing what was the safest for you, especially since Julian was still trying to find me."

Liv shakes her head. "Is he still after you? Are you safe now?"

Emma looks over to me. I speak maybe out of turn, but I want to give Emma a moment to recover.

"Julian is no longer a threat." Liv audibly gulps, and I continue. "But his father is. We are handling it, but Emma brought it up at our family meeting, and here we are. She wanted to purge the secrets she's kept from you, so I hope you will keep this to yourself?"

Liv is quick to reply. "Of course. Of course."

I smile, satisfied that she will keep our secret. "It's also really nice to meet you, Liv. I feel like I know you, too. I used to watch over Emma and always wanted to hang out with you guys and your other friends at the beach and club, but you know... being dead and all," I trail off, and I swear I see her hide a smile.

"Yes, I see how that could be a problem, Evie." She looks over at Emma, who is analyzing our interaction.

"Now you see why she hid from me and I had to keep her a secret? Troublemaker, this one." Emma laughs, pointing a thumb in my direction. The tension in the room seems to lighten after our banter.

"So..." Liv starts. "You and Jameson, huh?" She waggles her eyebrows up and down.

Baby Kaden starts to fuss after being placed back in Liv's arms. I snort. "Yeah, I know."

Liv and Emma start laughing as baby Kaden begins to cry. Jameson walks in with Dax and looks over at me. "Ya know what, Evie?" he repeats my words, asking a question, although with a hint of mischief in his eyes.

CHAPTER TWENTY-SIX

JAMESON

"BAD COMPANY" BY FIVE FINGER DEATH PUNCH

"So, you and Evie, huh?" After spending some time catching up with our mutual friends and hearing about Dax's new position as a full-fledged partner in his father's practice, I'm surprised it took him this long to discuss the elephant in the room.

I take the soda he offered me, electing for a more alcohol-free drink this morning full of sugar and caffeine. I swear I still smell that jackass's stench on me. Dax must see the downturn of my mouth and interprets this as something wrong with Evie and me.

"Am I wrong?" he asks, concerned.

"Huh? No, sorry, but we had a little problem last night, and I was just trying to think of the best solution to fix it." Dax rubs his hand over his chin, trying to ascertain if I need help or not. I hold my hand up to him.

"It's better if you don't know." He looks at me and then nods in understanding.

"Of course, but if you..." he trails off, letting me know that he is here for me should I need him, and those unspoken words mean the world to me.

I place my hand on his shoulder. "Thanks, bro. I appreciate that."

He smiles, and I hear a wail coming from the other room. Dax stands immediately to tend to his son, and I follow.

"Man, that kid has some lungs." The crying, along with Evie's dipshit brother coming in at the asscrack of dawn, has my head pounding.

Dax chuckles. "You have no idea, Jameson. Just wait. It will happen to you, too."

We enter the room just in time to hear the end of their conversation. I wonder what was said before I entered the room. Whatever it was will have to wait, and baby Kaden is having a complete meltdown, and Liv needs to feed him. We take this as our cue to leave.

We make rushed goodbyes with a promise to meet up very soon. We walk down the stairs, and I look back, extending my hand to Evie's as we walk to my truck.

I shake her hand, nudging her to look at me. "You okay?

She shakes her head. "Yeah, but dang, there was a lot of screaming in there."

I bring her hand up to my lips. "You mean you aren't ready to have little Evie or Jameson running around yet?"

She stops mid-stride, and realizing she is no longer walking with me, I turn back to look at her. The sheer terror on her face makes me go back to her.

I approach her carefully, like a skittish cat that will run off if you advance too soon. "Baby, I was just kidding. I'm not ready to have kids right now. It was a joke, and by the looks of it, maybe a very bad one."

She relaxes into my embrace. "I'd make a terrible mother," she almost whispers.

I take her face in both hands and bring her close. "You are brave, protective, and love so fiercely, Evie. I think those are the best traits for a mother, and I think you would be the best mom someday."

She searches my eyes for the truth. And I know when she finds it there as she melts into my embrace. Sometimes, I forget that even though she puts on a brave act, she is still vulnerable and needs reassurance, just like we all do.

She tilts her head in my hands, and I bring her lips to mine in a soft kiss. She leans into me, and I hug her, kissing the top of her head. When we turn around, Emma is standing there with tears in her eyes. She looks away and walks ahead of us to the truck without looking back.

The ride back to Evie's and Mateo's place is quiet. Entirely too quiet as we are all lost in our thoughts. I look in the rearview mirror and see Emma looking out the window. She must sense me staring because she looks my way. Her eyes meet mine and she beams at Evie and smiles. Then she looks back at me before returning her attention to the passing cars on the interstate.

We pull into the complex and see Mateo is still there. Emma is out of the car as soon as it stops, jumping from the back seat like she is propelling herself at a forty-five-degree angle, posing as a stunt double in an action-packed movie.

I cock my head sideways as her little legs take her up to their apartment. Where she is curvy, my Evie is toned and just perfect. I stifle a laugh, and Evie swats my arm.

"Stop already with the short jokes. It hurts her feelings."

I raise my hands defensively.

"You know we are twins, right?"

"Okay. Okay, but I didn't say anything. And for the record, you do not look identical."

We've almost caught up to Emma as she has to wait for us at the door since we have the keys. I wave them at her, and her nostrils flare with annoyance. She takes both of her hands and twists them in a scooping fashion toward the door, urging us to hurry up. Evie scoffs, taking them from me and tosses them to her. She opens the door seconds before we arrive and, immediately, the cold air-conditioning hits my face.

"Geez, what is it, like sixty degrees in here?" Evie goes over to the thermostat, turns it up, and the air conditioning cycles off.

Mateo walks into the living room with gray sweatpants and no shirt while he towel dries his hair. We all stare at him as he rolls his eyes at us and saunters off.

"Oh, no, you don't, Mattie." Emma starts marching over there.

"I'll be right out, and you can yell at me in a second. I just need to put this towel away." He disappears into his room but reappears with a bottle of water.

He slumps into the recliner, placing the cold water bottle on his forehead. Evie and Emma sit on the couch as I stand up, leaning against the wall staring at us. Mateo downs half the water bottle's contents and leans forward to place it on the coffee table in front of him. He slumps forward and runs his hand through his hair, tugging at the ends. He moves them to steeple under his chin and waits patiently for the chastising to begin.

No one says anything.

I look over at Evie, and she seems genuinely sad for him, while Emma looks pissed.

Emma shoots up off the couch, startling Mateo, causing him to lean back and away from his firecracker of a sister with an equally volatile temper. She raises her hands in the air. "What the fuck Mateo! You cannot get shit-faced like that and just disappear."

Mateo hangs his head like a child being scolded.

"You scared Evie half to death coming in last night drunk off your ass and smelling like it, too, from what I hear. You cannot bury yourself in booze and pussy because you were feeling sorry for yourself."

He looks up at Emma with a scathing look. "And why not, Emma? Huh? Maybe I just need to forget what my life is like sometimes. Maybe I just wanted to feel something, or maybe I just wanted to feel nothing at all."

Emma sits back down on the couch, crossing her arms over her chest.

Evie leans forward, this time to say her peace. "Mattie, I was so scared when you came home like that. I worry about you. Just like you worry about me. You are my brother. My family. And I've lost so much already. I couldn't bear to lose you, too. I don't think I could recover if I lost *my guardian angel.* My protector. My brother." Evie hits her chest with each spoken word, like a vow she makes to him in return.

Mateo gulps as a multitude of emotions flash over him. He withers into the chair like he is empty and defeated. Beat down.

Evie walks over to him and squats at his level. She takes his hand in hers, and I want to hold her. I want to tell her how amazing she is, but I just sit there, taking in the scene as she comforts her brother.

"Mattie. It's okay to feel alone, to feel shattered, and to take others' feelings for granted. You have been through a lot. We all have. Just remember that you have us. You're family, and we love you. You are not alone anymore. Collect your broken pieces and fix you, Mattie, because if you don't, one day your life will be nothing but regrets."

His eyes shimmer with unshed tears, and then Evie leans in and hugs her brother.

Emma walks over to Mateo and throws her arms around him. "Please don't forget that again, Mattie. We love you." Emma speaks softly into his shoulder as she leans on the recliner side, hugging Mateo.

He pulls her in closer and kisses her on the cheek. "I love you too, Emma."

She smiles in return and then smacks him on the arm. "But if you ever do that again, Mattie…" She doesn't finish that sentence before Mateo tickles her side, and she falls off the chair laughing.

I walk over to the couch that is now free as the girls are huddled over with their brother on the recliner. "Mateo," I speak up, and the room is silent as Evie glances over at me, forehead scrunching. "I have a concern."

They all look over to me, and Mateo nods, encouraging me to speak my piece. Emma bites her lip, forcing herself not to speak up to defend her brother and wait until I get out what I have to say.

"What will we do about Ramón now that we know he is working with Mr. Martinez?"

The girls both look to Mateo for answers as I wait patiently to hear his response.

He clears his throat. "Well, I think I need to confront him, but I don't think his house is the best place. Maybe at the cafe where we usually play chess?" He looks to me for what I can only assume is my opinion on the matter.

I nod. "I just worry about Evie because she always goes with you. Maybe I can tag along, or Emma, Eduardo, and I can show up there for your next meet-up?"

He seems to ponder the idea over and nods in agreement. "Yeah, I think maybe that would be best."

Evie squeezes his hand, walks over to me, and sits on my lap. "When do we see him again, Mateo?" She shifts her hips over my thigh, making my cock jump into action. She feels it as she wiggles her ass over the rigid outline as it is trying to push upward as if it has a mind of its own.

I hold her from shifting further and stifle a groan. She giggles, and Emma squints her eyes as if she has x-ray vision that allows her to see through clothing.

Mateo speaks, interrupting my thoughts of slipping my rock-hard cock into Evie's slick heat. "We are set to meet on Friday around midday."

I look at Emma, and she nods. "I can be there. I'll bring Eduardo. Just give us the details, and we'll see you there." She stands, and Mateo rises with her.

"You leaving, Em?"

"Yes. I have to work tonight. It's such a zoo there, and nights are the worst, but Eduardo thinks it is safer. I don't work much now, but it's part-time. At least for now, until I do other things."

Evie and I look over at her, and Emma walks toward the door. Evie turns to me and mouths 'other things.' I shrug, not knowing what that means as we walk to say goodbye to Emma.

She kisses her hand and then waves. "Love you, but I gotta run, or Eduardo will throw a fit before he takes me to work." With that, she closes the door, and we stand in the window watching her sashay to her BMW Eduardo had dropped off to her earlier, as she drives away.

Evie scoffs. "Let's not pretend that Eduardo doesn't always know where she is."

As if right on cue, another vehicle with someone who strangely resembles Philip follows Emma out of the parking lot and onto the street.

"Told you," Evie barks out, pointing to the car driving off after Emma.

"Baby, that's not the half of it. And I can't say I blame him."

Evie looks over at me, searching my eyes for something she won't find. Because if there is one thing that I have learned from Eduardo, it is that there is nothing we wouldn't do to protect the women we love.

I pull her to me as I hear Mateo move away.

"I think I'm going to order some greasy food and go back to bed," he says.

I tug Evie toward me. "I think we will skip the first part of that and go straight on to the second." I lead Evie back to her room and close the door.

CHAPTER TWENTY-SEVEN

EVIE

"LOVERS ROCK" BY TV GIRL

Midweek, I decide to call Emma and see if she wants to have a girl's day. I know she doesn't work tonight, so she agrees. We are meeting up with everyone this evening for dinner to brainstorm ideas for when Mateo will confront his grandfather, Ramón, on Friday. The anxiety of that meeting has me on edge, and I need a distraction. What better way to do that than to go for afternoon margaritas at our favorite Tex-Mex restaurant? It might be fun to see if Liv wants to come along.

I remember all the times when I witnessed Emma and her friends out and about having a good time eating lunch or clubbing at night. I felt that pang of jealousy as I watched from the shadows, never to be invited or even known about. The sister who died more than anyone else would ever realize. I died a thousand deaths in the shadows, feeling dead inside.

Now, all these feelings rise to the surface, overpowering me as a turbulent storm of emotions which constantly swirls around me, trying to break through my carefully crafted façade. Since Emma told Liv about us and our family, it seems like a weight has been lifted.

I feel lighter. I feel free. I feel seen.

I thought the day would never come when I was able to sit at their table, talking and laughing with my sister and her friends. To partake in conversation and camaraderie is something I have longed for and will never take for granted.

"I'll take the Texas Skinny margarita, please," Liv tells the waiter and gently places the menu on the table.

I frown at her choice because she just had a baby and that shouldn't mean that she needs to go on a diet. I don't know her well enough to tell her that I think she looks fantastic after giving birth, so I offer her a small smile instead.

Emma takes forever to pick something, and it makes me roll my eyes. I want to cut in but mind my manners as the waiter ogles her, and she remains oblivious. I look over at Liv, and she suppresses a laugh with her hand, hiding her smile as she looks away. Emma bites her lip in concentration, and he licks his lips. I can only imagine what he is thinking at the moment, and I cock my head to the side, assessing to see if I need to intervene.

"I'll take the Some Like it Hot margarita." She places her menu down and doesn't even look at the guy. She nods at me as if letting me know it's my turn to order. She must feel his stare on her; this is her way of kindly turning him down.

So done with this, I roll my eyes and snap my menu down, startling the waiter and Liv, who snaps straight and makes a startled noise similar to a baby bird. The waiter faces me, seeing the smirk that forms on my lips, letting him know I saw him. Emma's eyes twinkle with hidden laughter. I look at his name tag as if I am getting a hard look at it, squinting my eyes for the full effect.

"I'll take the Smoky Mezcal, please, and if we could get a vat of guacamole with chips and salsa, please, Cole."

He nods and leaves us without another word.

Emma scoffs. "I hope he comes back soon with our order. I think you might have scared him off."

Liv watches the exchange between us and doesn't comment.

I roll my eyes at her naivety. "Sorry, but I really didn't want it to get back to Eduardo, and then I have to listen to it because we are all meeting tonight for dinner, and we have much more pressing issues to discuss."

She nods her understanding. "Agreed."

The waiter returns with our drinks and apps, and we give him the rest of our food order. I take a big scoop of guac and practically orgasm as the taste of spices and cilantro hits my mouth.

I sip my margarita and look up at Liv and Emma, who are curiously eyeing me. I dab the salt off the sides of my mouth and sip my margarita once more. I put it down and look at Liv, who is staring at me like I'm Uncle Eddie in my favorite Chevy Chase Christmas movie.

"Sorry, but that is the best guacamole ever."

Liv gives me a genuine smile and loads up her tortilla chip before she bites into it, sending crumbs splattering over the table. She makes a similar noise of pleasure.

"Agreed." She says this with a mouth full of food, mimicking Emma's comment earlier.

Emma laughs, throwing her hands in the air. "Okay, now it's my turn." She holds her chip mid-flight as I scoop up more with my tortilla chip. "Don't you dare try to stab me with your chip." She snorts.

"I would never stab my own sister, Emma." I wink at Liv as she snaps her attention over to me and then to Emma, as if she sees Emma in her truest form for the first time.

I grin widely. "She's just kidding, Liv. I am usually the stabby one."

Liv almost chokes on her drink as Emma moans loudly, licking the excess avocado from her lip. We all look up to see our waiter, Cole, standing there with a food tray in his hand and his mouth open as he stares at Emma.

"Oh, hey, Cole, just in time," she comments as he distributes our food quickly and leaves without further comment.

Liv's hand goes to her mouth as she laughs. This causes Emma to snort, and I watch them in amusement, thinking that I have not had a better day in what feels like forever.

As we finish up our food and drinks, Cole approaches us, asking if we need anything else.

"Then thank you, ladies. The bill and tip have been paid in full, and I thank you for your generosity. I hope to see you again soon." He leaves us, and Emma throws her napkin on the table.

"I don't know about you, but I need to be assisted out of here. I ate so much. I don't think I can breathe, much less stand."

We all get up to leave as Philip brings the car around the front of the restaurant to take us home. Liv gets into the back seat with Emma, and I sit in the front. As I buckle up my seatbelt, Liv touches my arm, startling me, and I fight the urge to pull back. Her touch is gentle and non-threatening. "Evie," she says softly.

I turn back toward her. "Yes."

She looks over to Emma and then to me. "I just want you to know that I had so much fun with you and Emma today, and I am thrilled to have another friend."

I look over to Emma, who is smiling at me and Liv. I am not used to feeling this way, and the thought of having another friend catches me off guard. I haven't had many close connections, and this feels like a huge step into living.

I touch her hand in return. "Thank you, Liv. That means more to me than you know. I really appreciate your friendship."

Emma turns her attention to Liv. "Hey, I wanted to let you know now that I can talk freely in the car that we may be gone for a while. Something has happened that may be a bit dangerous, and we need to leave."

Liv looks between us. "Where are you going?"

Philip looks at Emma in the rearview mirror, and Emma nods. Ignoring Philip's pleas to stay silent she, of course, does the exact opposite.

"I told Liv no more secrets, Philip." She brushes back her hair that has fallen out of her loose bun and inhales deeply, closing her eyes.

Liv waits patiently, as if she's almost afraid to blink.

"The man that killed my family lives in Brownsville, and we are going to hide out, assessing the situation to ensure the next part of our plan to take revenge for our family is implemented."

Liv snorts. "Damn, Em. You say that like it's a nursing care plan you used to write for school."

Emma laughs, and I look at them, not understanding the joke, but I am sure I won't get many of their private jokes.

"Well, I do have a fully furnished condo near Brownsville, and it sits empty now, if you need a place to hide out, just so you know."

Philip looks at me, and I place my hands together.

"Oh, a secret hideaway lair. How perfect." I rub my hands together like an evil overlord plotting Earth's demise.

Emma slaps Liv's leg, startling her. "Liv, that might just be what we are looking for. Do you need to ask Dax, though?"

She shakes her head. "Nah, we can't use it now anyway, and I'm sure he's offered it to Jameson also. Not a problem. Just let me know, and it's yours if you need it."

"It's right on the beach, too, huh?" I ask anxiously.

Liv nods. "Yep, you'll love it."

She sits back, and we laugh and talk about normal things women our age would. They catch me up on their friends back in Padre Island, since we are on the topic of it.

Soon, the trip is over, and we make plans to do it again soon. They drop me off next, and I tell Emma that I'll see her later. As I am walking to the door, I hear the car door open. Emma comes running over to me and tightly hugs me.

"I am so glad that we have the chance to do this, Evie."

I hug her back. "Me too, Em."

With that, she gets back into the car and drives off as soon as I enter my apartment. With everything that will happen in the near future and all the unforeseen complications with Mr. Martinez and now Mateo's grandfather, it was nice to have a sense of normalcy, even if it is just for a brief moment.

Jameson, Mateo, and I drive over to Eduardo's and Emma's place since we planned on meeting there to discuss our next step with Ramón. We found out that Ramón is Mateo's biological grandfather and Mr. Martinez's father, so we have to decide what this could mean for all of us. Eli, Gus, and Philip are there. We are all gathered around the island. Eduardo comes out of his office with his laptop.

"I have a few people who are going to be on a video conference with us."

"Who is it, babe?" Emma plops herself onto Eduardo's lap, and he pulls her in tight, moving her off to the side as he tries to shift himself discreetly. Emma tries to move over, and he halts her, whispering something into her ear. Her face blushes, and she nods once.

Mateo's eyes narrow, and I cough to hide the laugh that threatens to leave me.

Eduardo clears his throat. "My dad, for one, my brother Ramiro and his fiancée, Anna—" Emma cuts in.

"Oh, that call. Our Uncle Andrés and cousin Adrian, too then?" Emma announces.

I can't help the question that leaves my mouth. "Why is your brother's fiancée listening in?"

Eduardo leans over the island, pushing Emma along with him. "We don't keep secrets from each other anymore, Evie. We are family, and all of us here, whether related by blood or not, are family. Our own family is built on love, trust, and respect for one another. No more secrets."

Emma leans over to him, nuzzling her face into his neck. "I couldn't have said it better, my love."

Eduardo claps his hands. "Okay, ready to get this started?" He logs into the video conference call, and faces pop up on the computer, letting us know that they are all there and ready. After a few rounds of 'can you hear me?' and 'how do I turn on my camera?' we are finally ready to formulate a plan together.

"Absolutely not!" Eduardo booms loudly through the kitchen as he stands up abruptly, almost knocking Emma to the ground before he catches her around the waist as if she weighs nothing. He kisses the top of her head, placing her gently on her feet. "I won't put Emma in harm's way."

I look at Jameson, and by his expression and the tic of his jaw, I don't think he likes the idea either as he shoots daggers at my brother. If looks could kill, Mateo would be dust already.

"Look, Liv offered her condo down in the valley to us, and it's literally right there by Brownsville. No one would know that we were there."

"I think it is the best idea where we are all close together. Until I meet with Ramón and find out what he and Mr. Martinez want from me, I'd like to have my sisters close-by and hidden." Eduardo rubs his hand over his face.

"I have an idea," Ram's voice comes through the speaker.

"I sure hope it is better than Mateo's." He shoots my brother a look that would make another man wither, but my brother is no other man. He was a soldier for my uncle and brought up the same way Eduardo was.

"I'll come up and take over the business for you while you go down to Brownsville with the girls. With you and Jameson there and their family just a stone's throw over the border, I would feel okay with the plan."

"Oh, you would have no problem if this was Anna? If it was your fiancée there instead of Emma?"

Ram hangs his head down and looks over to his wife. He grabs her hand and kisses it. "Maybe, but I think that this is the best solution."

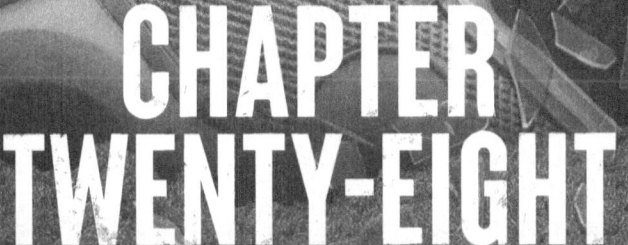

CHAPTER TWENTY-EIGHT

JAMESON

"ROMEO AND JULIET" BY DIRE STRAITS

Last night, I dreamt that I lost Evie to that monster. I can't imagine how Emma felt thinking her sister was dead all this time, especially after losing her parents as well. I know that she was the closest to Evie, and as she lies beside me, I can't help but hold her, bringing her closer.

I kiss her neck as my hand splays across her abdomen. She pushes her ass into my hard cock, causing it to weep. I trail my fingers lower to her panties, feeling her sweet heat. Then I throw one leg over her, bringing her closer to me still, and feel her waken as I palm her pussy. She moans, and I slide my hand under the hem of her panties, pushing through her folds as I move my finger through her slick seam. She turns her head slightly, and I move over her more, kissing her. She brings one arm around my neck, pulling me to her, and I think back to when she couldn't do something as simple as this.

It took a while of being away from each other, getting used to her touching herself, pretending it was me, and then slowly taking my hand over hers until we got to this—the point where she trusts me completely not to hurt her, and I would rather end my life than hurt this woman. Who knew she would be so perfectly damaged and fit my own missing piece of a puzzle?

I circle her clit with my thumb and plunge one finger into her hot, wet pussy as it sucks me in greedily. I add another finger, and she opens her legs wider for me, allowing me more access. I add a third finger, and she throws her head back. Wetness drips down my fingers as I finger fuck her, and she rides my hand as I suck on her neck, marking her.

I pull my fingers out of her, and she whimpers at the loss. I flip us and place her on top of me. I bring my fingers to my mouth and suck off her sticky wetness one by one. She watches me with hooded eyes, yet I am the one drunk on her. She rocks back and forth, seeking friction from my hard cock as her panties dampen further.

"Gotta take these off, baby."

I grab both sides of the sparse material and pull it apart, leaving a little mark on her hip. It pulls there, and I tap her bottom. "Come up here, Eve, and ride my face. I want you to come all over my mouth. I'm dying for you, sweetheart."

I lift her ass up and move her along as she almost falls forward. Her breasts land right in my face, and I lick and suck. She grabs my hair and pulls me to her. I tweak her nipple with my other hand, pulling and tugging as her pussy drips onto my abdomen. "Can't let that sweet juice go to waste, can we?"

I pull her all the way up, and she hovers right above me. I can smell her, and it is heaven. I push her legs apart with my forearms and hook them around her thighs as I bring her core right to my face. I swipe my tongue through her folds. "Part those sweet pussy lips for me, baby. I want to eat you."

Evie uses one hand to place on the headboard, and the other hand goes to separate herself for me so I can easily get to her pretty, glistening cunt. I admire it for a split second before shoving my face into her as she soaks me in her juices. She throws her head back.

"Ride my face, baby." I bring her down more and nip and lick her. I eat her like she's my last meal. I am starving for her and only her.

"Oh God." She is lost to the sensation.

I shove my tongue in, swirling it around, and sweep upward, biting at her clit. I feel her quiver, and I suck hard while she convulses under me. I feel a squirt and stick my tongue in her pussy, licking up as much of her wetness as I can before she goes still, and then I lap at her clit before she starts to shake again.

I sweep her off me, and she falls onto the bed like a dead weight. I drop down on the bed and hook her legs over my shoulders, bringing her back to me. I thrust three fingers in at once while I suck her clit into my mouth. Her body bows off the bed as she cries out with another orgasm.

I sit up, wiping my mouth as I stand up off the bed, pulling her down toward the end where I stand in between her legs, placing them over my shoulder. I lean down and lap at her beautiful tits before kissing her, letting her taste herself on my lips.

I stand back, lining my painfully hard erection up with her slickness as I drag myself through her cum. She rocks her hips, trying to get close to me, and I don't make her wait any longer as I impale her on my cock, taking her to the hilt in one go. She's so wet after two orgasms that I slide in without much effort.

I play with her tits as I plunge into her, mercilessly fucking her hard. The headboard hits the wall over and over again. I'm sure Mateo, as well as the neighbors, can hear it, but I don't give a fuck as I chase my release. I swirl my hips around and then lower her legs and myself to her as I rut into her over and over. I tongue fuck her mouth as I feel her walls spasm, gripping my cock, and I come, cursing as I fill her. I pull out of her as I start to soften up.

There is sweat glistening over her body, and I see my cum dripping from her opening. I run my finger over it and drop down to my knees, bringing her close to me. I lick her softly, as I push my cum back into her.

"Jameson, what are you doing to me?" she whispers.

I swirl my tongue around her swollen clit, and she shudders. I suck gently on her bud as she throws her head back, riding out another orgasm. I drop to my ass, sitting on the bedroom floor as she has one arm flung across her face.

I hear the front door slam and Evie snorts a laugh. "I think you pissed off Mattie."

"Whew, I think I will skip the gym this morning." Sitting back, I'm unable to move.

"I think I am going to go back to bed. I think you broke me," she says as I rise to stand over her bending to kiss her. She pulls me in, and I kiss her again as my dick springs back to life. I pull her up with me, and she falls into me with a laugh.

"Come on, you little hellion. You're going to shower with me. You got me hard, and now you're going to drop to your knees and suck me, swallowing my cum." I swat her ass, and she laughs as she walks over to the shower, winking at me as she sways that sweet ass into the bathroom.

> Jameson: I need to drop by this morning.
> Are you around the office?

I sit at my desk, wishing I had my coffee, which is probably sitting just where I left it this morning. I was in such a hurry to leave after giving Evie a few orgasms, then she sucked my cock so thoroughly that I forgot about everything else, including my favorite beverage.

> Dax: Yeah. Come by, and I'll have them send you back.

The receptionist walks through the door, dropping off a package left at the front.

She stands there waiting, but I continue with my message. If I don't get Dax now, then I could miss my window of opportunity, and then he will be off seeing patients.

> Jameson: What time?

He replies immediately, and I mentally give myself a fist pump. I'd like to get the keys to that condo, just in case we need them sooner rather than later. You never know when the need to leave will arise.

> Dax: 10:30. I have a free moment before I have
> to go to the hospital for a scheduled surgery.

I look at my watch, noticing that I'll have to leave soon if I want to make it to his office with lunch-hour traffic by that time frame.

> Jameson: Great. See you then.

I place my phone down. "Hey, Marie. What's up?"

She fiddles nervously with her blouse and approaches me. "I've worked here for a while…" Marie saunters over to me. "And I thought maybe you'd ask me out, but you didn't." She puts her head down and looks upward at me through her curled lashes, a pout on her lips. "I thought you were interested at one point, but then you haven't looked at me since, so I thought I'd make the first move."

She picks her head up and walks over to me, her intentions clear. I put my hand up to stop her advances when I see someone standing in the doorway. I immediately stand to stop her advance, but she doesn't see Evie there. When she comes closer to me and raises her hand to my chest, I grab it just as Evie walks in with my coffee. I immediately drop Marie's hand, dismissing her, and walk over to Evie who is watching me with a mixture of trepidation and annoyance.

"Oh my God." I take a sniff of the magnificent smell that is rising from the cup. "Baby, did you bring me my coffee? I left it at home. You distracted me so much."

She laughs. "Yes. I felt bad seeing it on the counter this morning."

I see movement in my peripheral vision, realizing I totally forgot that Marie was there propositioning me. I'm not going to lie, I did think she was hot, but that was before I met Evie, and well, now that isn't an option for me anymore.

"Marie, this is my girlfriend Evie. Evie, this is Marie, our receptionist."

Evie looks her over and waves her little pointed fingernails painted red with black tips.

"Nice to meet you, Evie. I'll just be going." She mouths, 'Sorry' as she is leaving, and I shake my head and drop it to my chest.

Evie lifts it for me to look at her. "If I hadn't come in when I did..." she trails off, not finishing her sentence or needing to, for that matter, because I can sense the question and apprehension, but what kills me is the vulnerability in her eyes. She gave herself over to me entirely, and now she wonders if that is too much.

I bring her to me. "Evie, you have nothing to worry about. I am totally in love with you, baby."

She brings her forehead to my chest and then looks up at me.

"I am yours, and you are mine," I assure her.

"I love you, too. It scares me so much," she confesses in a whisper.

I kiss her forehead and bend to kiss her lips as she reaches up to meet mine. "I know," I whisper back. "Hey," I say a little more loudly, electing to lighten the mood. "Want to give me a ride to Dax's office? There is something I need to pick up there on the way."

CHAPTER TWENTY-NINE

EVIE

"A BEAUTIFUL LIE" BY THIRTY SECONDS TO MARS

As I walk down the pier with Mateo, I can't help but feel like someone is watching us. Throughout the years, it has happened, and I've become acutely aware when something just isn't right. There are some telltale signs. The way that my skin tingles. The prickly sensation that causes the hair on my arms to stand on end, much like static electricity. Except, this is more of a feeling, an instinct of self-preservation. I doubt anyone is, but I also wasn't aware of Mr. Martin. Not once did he give me bad vibes. Mr. Martinez, Julian, and Marcus, Julian's driver, always gave me the instinct to flee and to do so fast.

I should feel creeped out that this older man whom Mattie has come to love so much could betray us so badly. I'm trying to give him the benefit of the doubt because I know that Jameson mentioned that he looked defeated, dropping his head down when he repeated that he didn't want to do that while he was on the phone with his son, Mr. Martinez.

The camera they secretly installed in his place captured that one-sided conversation. It made it seem like he wasn't complacent in this, but instead, he was doing it out of necessity.

We won't know the whole story until we walk in there and learn the truth from Ramón.

Mateo opens the door, spotting the little traitor in the corner with his coffee and chess set. His bright eyes, usually alight with humor, are dulled. There is a worried expression replaced by a furrowed brow, his thoughts miles away from this café.

He's taking the board out as Mateo walks over to him, and I turn around to grab our usual coffee orders. That's when I notice Dylan, the barista who wrote his name on my cup months ago, standing there.

I misjudged him, thinking he was cheating on his wife when she was, yes, the mother of his child that they were co-parenting and not in an actual relationship with. He looks skittish, displaying a recent black-and-blue eye. He won't look at me, and it sets me on high-alert for some reason.

"Dylan."

He looks up at me before looking around, but no one else is in here right now except for us this Friday afternoon.

"Are you okay?"

He ignores the question, acting like he doesn't know me. "What can I get you?" He avoids making eye contact with me as I repeat the same thing I order every time I come in here. He turns around to get us the coffee and rings me up. Taking my payment, I slide him a note telling him to meet me around the back by the bathrooms. He nods once, and I take the coffees over to Mateo and place mine there as well.

"Hi, Ramón," I say to the man who shares the same blood as my brother. I give a little wave, and he smiles, not knowing that he is about to meet with a few intimidating people in a few minutes. "I'm gonna run to the bathroom quickly before I watch Mattie lose."

Mateo makes a 'hmph' noise as I walk off in search of Dylan.

As I turn the corner, an arm pulls me into the back, and I almost lose my footing, ready to give the guy another black eye.

"Evie, I wanted to warn you, but I'm afraid."

My hackles rise. "What do you mean, Dylan?"

He looks around, as if potential danger lurks in the broom closet. "I was approached by a man the other day asking about you and your sister. He said his name was Mr. Martinez."

I look at his black eye. "Did he give you this?" I reach out to touch it and he winces.

"Yeah, well, not him, but another guy that was with him. He also had a couple more men at the door watching. He snuck in at the last minute when I was closing up. I don't really know why he was asking these questions, but he threatened me and my family. He wanted to know when you came in again."

I nod.

"Evie, if I don't tell him, he is going to hurt me or, worse, my baby."

I shush him as I think about it some more. "I appreciate you telling me. I have my family coming here in a few minutes. After we leave, you call him and let him know that Mateo and I are here."

He shakes his head. "No, Evie, I can't let you get hurt because of me."

I smile at him and how sweet he is. To think how badly I really misjudged him. "It's okay, Dylan. You tell him, and then you will have done what he asked of you. He won't hurt you or your family, okay? Can you do that for me?"

He bites his lip, thinking it over. "Okay, but be safe."

I assure him I will as I head back to the table, knowing that this will take a different turn very soon. It's obvious that Dylan's black eye happened recently, meaning he is still in town, so he knows where we are.

I return to my seat, and Mattie looks at me. He can sense the change in my posture, despite my attempts to keep my mood light. I don't get the chance to direct the attention elsewhere because Eli and Philip flank Eduardo, Emma, and Jameson as they walk in through the coffee shop like they own the place.

Dylan scoots back from the register and busies himself, pretending to refill coffee beans. I shake my head and smile, trying to reassure him that no harm will come to him, but he can sense the danger these men bring to the table.

They take a seat surrounding two tables, moving them closer to us as chairs screech across the floor. Jameson puts his arm around me, bringing me into him. A blanket of warmth and safety envelops me, making me remember when Mateo was the only one who helped save me. Now he needs our help, and I'll do anything for him, including laying my life down to protect him like he did for me those times before.

Ramón looks over to Mateo in question. He just shrugs. "I think we have some things to discuss, pops."

The look of shock and what I can only describe as fear, envelopes Ramón as he crumples his shoulders in defeat. His head hangs low, but when he raises it, there are tears in his eyes.

"You have no idea how much I wanted to hear you call me that. I have come to know you over the past months, but for you to say that to me now means that you know something, but not everything. I can assure you things are not always as they seem. But today, I will ensure you learn all of it."

His determined expression shows that he was strong in his day, a force to be reckoned with. He did raise Mr. Martinez and with a grandson like Julian... I can't even finish that thought.

Goosebumps rise on my arms, and Jameson interprets this as me being cold. He moves his arms back and forth on me in an attempt to warm me up. Emma sits there silently, and Eduardo looks murderous.

"I think you should get talking, *Mr. Martin*." Eduardo stresses his name, letting us all know that his real name is Martinez, much like the animal he sired.

He nods. "I knew your mother."

Okay, woah. That is not where I thought this was going.

"She came to me when she learned she was pregnant with my son's baby and asked for my help. I was a lawyer, much like my son who is following in my footsteps, but that is where it ended. He had big aspirations, and one of those was to marry your mother and have an heir that would give him the connection to the Ortiz mafia family, which he needed so much to further his political endeavors.

"I learned that he was physically abusive, and she wouldn't let her unborn son be used over her as leverage to return to him, so she came to me asking for help to get away. I kept her secret, and we formed a plan to move my son's focus onto the gold digger, who was her best friend at the time and roommate—Julian's mother.

"Your mom already knew that he was sleeping with her, and it wasn't too much later that she ended up pregnant. They even sent your mom a wedding invitation to show her how much of an afterthought she was."

Mateo looks over at me, and I shrug.

"So she planned that?" Matteo asks in confirmation.

"Yes," he states. "And her plan worked. She had you and kept you hidden. She went off to college and met Evie and Emma's father, who wanted no part of that life. I think that it was a relief for her to discover that. She didn't want that for her other children either."

Emma squeezes Eduardo's hand. "Yeah, she almost cost us our happiness in the process."

"I think she cost us a lot of unhappiness." Mateo hits his hand to the table.

Mr. Martin nods. "I think it was hard for her, and unfortunately we may never know what she truly would say to it all. What her answer would be to those questions because of my son's actions."

Jameson scoots his chair closer. His fingers tighten around my hip. "Your son terrorized my girlfriend, and she almost died in that fire alongside her parents, if it wasn't for Mateo. He saved her on more than one occasion."

He holds his hand up to halt the conversation. "I haven't talked to my son in years. I disowned him and my grandson when I saw their depravity. They were evil, and I wanted no part of them. I didn't know what he was doing until recently when he told me his son died and that you left his body placed in a car belonging to some woman and set it in a fiery blaze outside his home to find."

Evie feigns indifference. "It was the least we could do to that sick fuck after what he did to my sister, and it's only fitting that he died similar to my parents. An eye for an eye, right?"

Mateo glances over at Eduardo. "So what now?"

Eduardo stands with Emma, and they both look at Ramón. I can sense that Eduardo would have no remorse if he killed him if it meant that Emma would be safe.

"That depends on what you have to say for yourself, Mr. Martin. Are you working with your son to take us down?"

Mr. Martin looks at Mateo but answers Eduardo's question. "Absolutely not. He is forcing me to help him, or he threatened to hurt my grandson. I was hoping to get him to work with me, but I just couldn't bring it up. I had a phone call the other day, and he is in the area now. This needs to end, and that means my son needs to die."

Eduardo nods at his two men, and they get up and walk to the front and back entrances of the coffee shop to look out. "We heard your conversation with your son at your home."

Ramón looks up in disbelief. "You bugged my house? When?"

Eduardo waves his hand away, and Jameson beams, proud of the part he played in keeping us safe by stealing a page out of Eduardo's playbook. "That's not important. What is important is what he said to you."

Eduardo and Mateo exchange a look, which I don't understand.

Ramón nods in understanding. Recollection of that conversation is fresh in his mind, and he spares not a single minute to share the details of it. "He wants you to take over for him. To be the heir he wanted all along to solidify himself a place in the mafia world. His true heir. With those types of connections, he feels his political standing will soar, as will his wealth in the illegal drug trade across the border. He wants you, Mateo, and I am entrusted to deliver you to him." He stands up.

"No, Mattie. You can't go. I won't let you." Emma stands, too, pleading. "He is a monster, and I've seen it with my own eyes. I've been on the receiving end of it with his son, too. You can't leave us."

Mr. Martin looks at Mateo. "I don't think any of you understand here. He doesn't just want his son, his only heir, to take over his business. He wants his sisters, too."

The room is so quiet you can hear a pin drop. The anger that radiates off Eduardo is palpable. The air grows thick. He stands abruptly, toppling the chair over.

"Over my fucking dead body will he take Emma from me." His words are deadly and vicious. His chest heaves as he restrains himself from having a fit of explosive rage.

Emma places her hand on his, and he breathes in deeply. He closes his eyes, trying to collect his hot temper, which only a few have had the displeasure of witnessing.

He looks over to Emma, and he seems to calm a little at her soothing touch. She calms his inner monster and makes him a better person. We all know this.

I look over to Jameson, and he is entirely rigid—his lips parted. I swear he has stopped breathing. I place my hand over his cheek, and he sucks in a deep breath, like he is revived by my touch alone.

"Fuck, no," he says angrily. "He can't have you." I look over at him but talk to everyone around us.

"He has already been here. He knows where we are, and he wants us. You see that guy behind the counter with the black eye?"

They all turn to look at Dylan, and he visibly pales at the attention of the angry group in my blended family.

"He knows that we come here. Dylan told me when I got here. He threatened *his* family, and I told him to call Mr. Martinez and let him know when we leave."

Everyone looks at me, saying my name in unison. Jameson turns my face to look at him, ignoring the angry cries contesting my decision, but it's already been made.

"Why, baby? Why would you tell him to do that?"

I look down before meeting his eyes. "So many people have been hurt to help us, and he has a baby. A baby, Jameson. A defenseless baby that Mr. Martinez threatened to hurt."

Emma gasps, and a small sob comes out of her as Eduardo soothes her, running his hand through her hair, murmuring loving words to her.

"It's time, Mattie. You have to go with Ramón. You have to end this. If that means we must go with you, then so be it. He stole our past. It's time we reclaim our future."

CHAPTER THIRTY

JAMESON

"NITRO (YOUTH ENERGY)" BY THE OFFSPRING

"When did you get this?" I hand the keys over to Eduardo. "Evie stopped by the office the other day, and she gave me a ride over to pick it up. Dax didn't ask any questions, but Liv told him we needed the condo in Padre Island to hide if things went bad. I think this is truly the definition of 'if things went bad. Don't you?"

He nods in agreement, biting his lip in concentration. "Yeah, I think it is."

I planned this thinking that it would just be a precautionary measure, that we wouldn't need it. I mean, I hoped we didn't need the keys, but I am glad I had the foresight to get them. Otherwise, it would be hard to know if we are being watched and then needed the keys before Emma and Evie are forced to leave with Mateo. Because they are going to have to leave with him. I am still unsure about Evie and Emma having to go, but we will get a better idea when we hear it directly from the source. When we have an idea of what he really wants with our family.

Dylan, true to his word, called Mr. Martinez as soon as we left, and now Mateo and Ramón are headed to his place to meet the monster we call Mr. Martinez. Hearing that Mr. Martinez threatened Dylan and his baby solidified the notion for me that he would stop at nothing to get what he wants. I don't think it is really about family but about him getting what he wants from the wealth and power his alliance and connections with a mafia family would provide.

Mateo has a burner phone hidden. He thought it would be a good idea to have a separate phone that isn't tracked, just in case his phone is looked at by his father or any of the security details that his father has back at his house. Being a politician allows him to have security for his home, but more people realize that it is more to his connection in an illegal trade that requires this level of protection and secrecy.

I recently placed cameras, which allow us to at least listen in on the conversation. We will have a heads-up to see what is coming our way. Will they make them leave right away? Ramón mentioned that he wanted Evie and Emma to go with Mateo, but I can't imagine why. Will he keep them as collateral to keep Mateo in line, or will it be for some other advantage?

We've had preemptive talks with Mateo and Ramón, so they know to keep the conversation flowing around the island or near the kitchen so that we can hear what they say more clearly. Now it's time to see how well Mateo has perfected his acting career.

We speed to Eduardo's office and huddle around his desk, watching the screen. We text Mateo when we get here so that we don't miss a thing. He and Ramón plan to finish up their chess game, allowing us time to make it back to Houston. The drive back is quiet. Each of us is in our heads and not speaking about the what-ifs.

Eduardo calls his brother on the way, putting it on speaker, and I watch my friend closely. "Hello? Ram?" There is a moment of silence on the line as the international call connects.

"Hey, little brother. To what do I—"

"Ram, I need you," Eduardo cuts him off, " and I need you to call Father and let him know that things have turned for the worse over here in Houston."

Without hesitation, Ramiro asks, "What do you need? I can be there soon to take over the business if you need to go?"

Eduardo looks over to Emma and tells his brother everything without another thought.

"I'll be there and have Dad call you. Do not worry about anything over here. Just go to keep Emma safe and do what you have to do. They are messing with the wrong people. Dad will call Emma's uncle and join forces to do whatever needs to be done. She is your fiancée, and no harm will come to her if we have a say in it."

Eduardo grabs Emma's hand and kisses it. "Okay, Ram. Thank you, and hurry, brother. See you soon."

"See you soon," is echoed on the other line before it dies.

Now we wait to see what they say at Ramón's.

They leisurely head to Ramón's place to put the plan into action as if there are no pressing issues, such as a psychopath waiting to take them away at any given moment.

We hear the door open, and Ramón walks through, followed by Mateo on his heels. They are around the kitchen island talking about predictions for when they will have to leave for Brownsville.

"I should grab my bag from my room just in case we have to leave soon." A look of confusion passes on Mateo's face as he disappears down the hall, but then his head jerks toward the door opening a moment later.

And then we all actually see him—Mr. Martinez.

He approaches Mateo slowly, like a predator circling his prey, except Mateo is no one's prey. His eyes narrow, calculating and assessing his biological father as he steps closer and is now standing before Mateo.

It is hard to dismiss his similarities to this horrible man. They are of similar size and stature: brown skin, brown eyes, and a full head of hair. Mateo's hair is dark brown, and Mr. Martinez's is streaked with gray, but it doesn't take away from his striking features. He could easily pass for his son, but whereas Julian had more of his mother's facial features, Mateo has strong lines and a square jaw.

Mr. Martinez studies Mateo, sizing him up. Mateo assesses him in return. When their staredown is interpreted by Ramón coming back from the room with his bag, he sets it by the sofa, and Mr. Martinez raises one eyebrow in question.

"Going somewhere, Father?"

Ramón simply shrugs. "I'm not sure, son. Are we going somewhere?"

Mr. Martinez raises his hand. "Not until I have had the opportunity to talk to Mateo. Have you told my son anything yet?"

We see through the camera's eye Mateo stiffen at the use of the word 'son,' but Mr. Martinez doesn't seem to notice. Ramón shakes his head, saying no.

"I told him you wanted to talk with him and that he would learn of everything soon."

This seems to please him, and he turns his focus to Mateo. "Well, this has been a long time coming. Your mother kept you from me, and now that my son, Julian, is gone..." he trails off, looking at Mateo. If he is looking for any admission, he won't find it on our brother's stoic face. "You are my only remaining son, my only heir." He reaches to place his arm on Mateo's shoulder. "My firstborn."

"You mean I am the only heir, and my mother's family is also part of the Ortiz mafia that suits your financial endeavors, am I right?"

His smile widens. "Yes, well, that, too," he admits, running his finger over his bottom lip. "I believe we can do great things together, son."

"Did you kill my mother?"

His hand falls off Mateo's shoulder. Mr. Martinez's eyes narrow, and he visibly shakes.

"That lying cunt stole you from me. She left and married that pathetic and weak excuse of a man who couldn't offer her anything. We could have had it all, but she chose poorly and suffered the consequences. She left you and me."

Mateo nods, trying to appease the crazy in this man who claims to be his father.

We move closer to the screen, and I watch Mateo's features. Emma has her hand over her mouth, waiting to hear what he will say next.

"Yeah, she did leave us both." His head is bowed down when he says this, and I know that the emotions shown on his face are real. This is his family and he doesn't hide his feeling from them and only them. He looks like he feels every bit of her leaving him, and he may never get over that fact. For whatever reason, she thought it was in his best interest to do so.

But when he raises his head to meet Mr. Martinez, his following words are spoken as an act, but still gut his family as they fall from his lips. "What do you need me to do, Father?"

Emma chokes on a sob, and Eduardo brings her closer to him as we stare at Mateo on the screen.

Mr. Martinez laughs sinisterly. "I knew you'd come around, son. We are going to leave here and go to our new home. Everything I have will be yours now, and we will grow our business, and then... you will take over. We will force the Ortiz family to play nice and accept our terms. I need the connections to bring my drugs over the border, and they have the connection that I need. I have them here." He lifts his palm up to Mateo to signify that he has them in the palm of his hand. "You see, it's a mutually beneficial agreement."

Mateo rubs his chin, pondering the things Mr. Martinez has said. "I don't know if you are aware of this, but they sent me to boarding school, and I don't think they will be willing to accept that deal from me. They barely acknowledge me as their own."

For some reason, I see the shared look on Evie and Emma's face, it's obvious that they, too, feel the raw emotion that comes through in his spoken words. Despite the performance he is portraying for Mr. Martinez for our benefit, there is some truth radiating from the harshness of his tone.

Ramón steps closer, and so does Mr. Martinez. He leans forward on the kitchen island.

"Well..." He cocks his head to the side. "They might not be with you, but when we take your sisters with us, then they might have to reconsider."

Eduardo stiffens, rage building in him. Gus, Eli, and Philip exchange glances with each other, and the room is so quiet you can hear a pin drop.

I hold Evie closer, and she leans into my embrace. We listen and wait for the rest of the story.

"You'll make them come with us, and then we will marry them off to the highest bidder."

There is the slightest tic to Mateo's jaw, indicating that he is much displeased with this direction of conversation, but he doesn't say as much. We look at the screen, dumbfounded.

Eduardo stands up, and Emma almost falls off his lap. However, his usual firm grip around her waist allows her feet to land on the floor instead. He is shaking with uncontrolled rage.

"Motherfucker! I will fucking kill you! You're dead!" Eduardo is yelling at the screen with spittle flying like a rabid dog. He's fuming and shaking with so much unrelenting anger, and Emma hits his arm, trying her best to calm him enough so we can hear the rest of the conversation.

"Highest bidder, huh? I don't know about that. Father, I don't want my sisters being offered up like cattle."

Mr. Martinez shrugs. "Makes no difference to me." He pretends to pick an imaginary strand of lint from his suit jacket.

Mateo is deep in thought and then snaps his fingers when he is struck with an idea, although I don't think he had thought about it long.

"I got it," he says, and Mr. Martinez looks over at him. "What if we have a party announcing their 'availability' and then have suitors come and discuss a mutually beneficial agreement."

He seems to think about this, and then his smile broadens. "You know, son, I think that would be a great idea."

Mateo nods. "We need strong allies if we are going to make this business venture beneficial with powerful players in place, but also, we want to be able to control the narrative. We should pick the best suitors who would make a more profitable alliance, right?"

Mr. Martinez soaks this up, and at the moment, I am afraid that Mateo may have switched sides. He is so determined to bring us down that I believe him.

He turns toward the camera and winks. Emma reaches over to Evie, and she nods that she saw that, too. Evie sinks into my lap in relief because Mateo's story was too believable for our liking.

Mr. Martinez must buy the act too because he claps his hands together in an excited fashion. "Okay. When do we leave?"

Mateo makes his way toward the door. "No time like the present."

Ramón has been watching this entire exchange without interruption, but as Mateo moves to leave and passes him by, he stops him.

"Where are you going?" Ramón looks over to his son sheepishly and then at his bag. "Do you need me to go with you, Mateo?" The look in Ramón's eyes says that he is afraid to be alone with his son while Mateo is away.

For some reason, I believe that his grandfather cares for him. A person can't have that level of concern for another without it meaning something. I just hope, for Mateo's sake, that they have some salvageable relationship after this is over.

Mateo looks over at the camera as if he is speaking to it. "I am going to bring my sister's back over here so that we can begin a new life."

With that, he exits Ramón's place and gets in his car to drive back to Houston, where our whole world is about to get a lot more complicated.

"I'll be waiting, son."

Everyone hears as the door shuts as Mateo walks out.

CHAPTER THIRTY-ONE

EVIE

"LET'S HAVE A WAR" BY FEAR

We sit there stunned into silence. My breathing picks up, and Jameson's grasp on me tightens. I practice my breathing like I was taught so long ago in therapy. When my thoughts go dark, I think about the therapist who helped me so much back then, but it feels like all the same emotions are just beneath the surface, threatening to break me. Amid a violent storm that threatens your life amongst the chaotic seas that rocks you to your core, you must get through it because at the end of the storm, there is calmness and peace.

The sun breaks through the stormy clouds, and the water reflects the light off the peaceful waters. This storm has been brewing for years, and now we must face it. No matter how strong I tried to make myself, I knew that this time would come when I would face all my fears and our family would have to come together to win a war—a war that was started so long ago over greed and power at the cost of those that weren't born yet.

And we will have to suffer the burden to end it all.

I am pulled from my thoughts as Eduardo roars and throws everything off his desk. It all comes crashing down—his anger, frustrations, and helplessness at the failure to get his reason for existing, as he says to her so often in anyone's company, are all his emotions swirling as he refuses to let her go.

Emma sobs into her hand, and he goes over to her, kneeling at her feet. He takes her hands in his, pulling them from her tear-stained face.

"I thought I was free, but will we ever be free from this, Eduardo?" she asks him so innocently that my heart breaks for her.

She suffered so much brutality from Julian. We ended his life, but his father is still alive and now wants to sell us off as if we are his possessions to do so.

"I am not going to let anything happen to you, baby. I promise."

I rise from Jameson's lap. I extend my hand to my sister much like I did that day we ended Julian's life in that warehouse. I knew that this time was coming. The time when we would have to fight for our family.

She looks up at me, and her face is streaked with tears, but tears no longer flow from her eyes. There is a look on her face that I haven't seen before. She looks pissed.

She places her hand in mine and rises as Eduardo moves aside, allowing her space to stand alongside me. She looks into my eyes, searching for something she must find, and then she looks at Eduardo.

"I am so tired of this fucker, and I want to see him suffer a cruel death deserving of the sins he has committed. I want to see him die, witnessing the moment his life fades from his eyes. I want to know that we did that and that he lost. Everything he wanted. His hopes and dreams are to be extinguished so he can burn in hell with his son."

I've never heard Emma speak this way, and it empowers me to know that she can and will be brave enough to see this through.

Jameson is shaking when he takes my hand, pulling me out of my trance-like state, seeing my sister finally become the woman I knew she could always be. There is no place for weakness now, and knowing that she can be strong enough to do this helps me. I can't be strong for the both of us, and Eduardo, as much as he wants to keep her safe, understands that she needs to be strong, his equal, if she wants this type of life with him. We all do. We are all part of this life together, and together we will fight to keep what is ours.

Someday, Eduardo will take over his father's business and take his place as the head of the family. He was raised for this. Knowing that Emma can be by his side, strong and assured in her role as his wife, is all I ever wanted for my sister. I want all of us to get what we deserve–the happiness and peace we so desperately seek. This is the moment where it starts. It's time to finish this. So, I say, "Let's have a war."

Jameson takes me to my apartment, and Emma will meet me here. Mateo has already texted us and told us he will be here soon, so we can be ready. I step through the door and walk to my bedroom. I stand there looking around the space I have called my own, but not my home.

Jameson comes around me and wraps me in a solid embrace. He is so warm, and I shiver—not from being cold, but from my comfort when he is here with me. I lean into him and tilt my head to the side. His warmth caresses me as he leans in to place soft kisses on my neck.

"When all this is over, Evie, I want you to move in with me. I want us to pick out a place together that is just ours. I want you. If I have learned anything from being with you, it is that life is fleeting. I see the dangerous life we live and the enemies that will stop at nothing to take what doesn't belong to them in the quest for more power and control."

I turn around to look him in the eye. I am amazed to hear his words spoken and the truth that he loves me written on his face. Jameson wears his heart on his sleeve. He may not be the alpha male that Eduardo is, but that doesn't mean that he won't risk his own life or do everything in his power to keep me safe. Eduardo was born into a different life than he was, but being Eduardo's friend means that he needs to be a strong man as well.

"Maybe we can get a place in Eduardo's building? Even Mattie, too. We can all have separate places, but still be there for one another."

He nods. "That sounds amazing, Eves. I like that idea so much, and it will be the only thing I will look forward to when you are in that monster's house. I won't be able to keep an eye on you like I want to, but I will be able to at least track you." He pulls out a box from his pocket. "Here. I had these made and picked them up the other day."

He hands me a little black velvet, heart-shaped box. I stare at it, afraid to open it. "What is it?"

He looks at me, amused. "Well, why don't you open it, and you'll find out?"

I look at him, assessing, until my curiosity wins out. I step away from his embrace, turn to look at him, and open the box.

"Wow, I don't know what to say. They are beautiful." I hold a box open that contains a set of two large emerald hearts. I pick them up, noticing they are a little heavier than I expected. "They are beautiful, Jameson."

"I agree," he says, "and practical, too."

I look at him curiously, wondering where he is going with this. "Well," I say, thinking about it, "I do wear a lot of green, and they do go very well with my eyes, making them very matchy-matchy." He chuckles at my comment. "You don't think so?" I raise an eyebrow at him in question. I take the earrings out of the velvet holder and put them on. "They are also screw backs, so they won't come off." I list all of the valid points as to why they are such a perfect present.

"Sure, I do think about all those things. I also think that they will let us know where you are at all times and let us hear you if we need to." He waves his tracking app on his phone before stuffing it into his pocket.

I laugh aloud. "Of course there is." I shake my head as I tighten the last earring, securing it in place.

He looks delighted with himself as he rocks on his heels and back to the balls of his feet in one fluid motion. His hands are in his pant pockets, and he looks absolutely delicious. I lick my lips and he seems to understand the look of hunger in my eyes as he approaches me slowly, calculating his next move.

"One's a speaker." He touches one of my earrings. "The other is a tracker with an SOS feature, much like Emma's bracelet Eduardo had me make for her."

My hand drops from his gift. "Practical and beautiful," I whisper.

His body is flush with mine, and I breathe in his masculine, earthy scent. It envelops me, and I want to remember it, to bottle it up and take it with me. I want to commit it to memory, so that I can take it with me and cherish it when I am alone and in my bedroom without him, waiting on someone else to determine my future for the last time. I don't voice the thought that I may never see him again because I have to believe in our blended family and know that they will do everything in their power to see him through to the end.

"I agree. So beautiful." His words tickle my ear as he sucks and tugs on my earlobe, sending a tug at my core. I moan and tilt my head, giving him better access. He licks down my neck and places kisses all over my face, until he plants a soft kiss on my lips. He hovers over my mouth, until he brings me in close, parting my open lips farther with his tongue. My body is pulled into his, and I can feel the rigid outline of his cock.

He leads me backward to my bed until my legs hit the edge of the mattress. He pushes me back and takes off each of my shoes, and then my pants and panties in one go. He undoes his belt, letting his pants pool around his ankles as he steps out of them.

"Take off your shirt." His voice is desperate. Pleading. "We don't have much time until everyone gets here."

It's like having cold water thrown on my face to wake me from my lust-filled gaze. He watches me as he pulls his shirt over his head and then grabs my shirt, ripping the thin, lacy material. It smarts against my skin, and I look up at him, ready to say something, but he doesn't let me.

He pushes his cock into my mouth as my teeth scrape lightly along his velvet skin. He is trying to get me out of my own head, and it's working. He always knows to give me what I need, and right now, I need his cock choking me, filling me.

He crouches over me, holding my head up as he fucks my face. I hold onto his ass, and my fingernails in their usual pointed shape dig into his cheeks as he pauses, holding himself to me. He hisses and removes his cock as dribbles of saliva trail down my chin. He drops down to my legs and plunges his tongue into my entrance. My legs spread wide, giving him full access to my pussy.

Jameson licks around my entrance as he lashes out at my clit and sucks hard. My back bows off the bed. I open my eyes, seeing him watch me from below. He places kisses to each side of my leg, wiping his mouth on my inner thigh. He brings himself up and hovers over me, aligning himself with my entrance. He drives in one thrust, and I cry out. He fucks me mercilessly, as if this is the last time.

We are loud and wild. I grab his hair and tug him to me. He kisses me hard and grabs upward, using the wrought iron to pull him into me more forcefully. I've never been fucked harder, and when he hits that spot deep inside of me, twisting his hips, I cry out.

"Fuck me, Jameson, that's it. Right there. Keep—Oh God, keep going. Oh…" My mind stops working, and my body shakes, convulsing with an orgasm so strong, I spasm, turning rigid under him, and he fucks me through it until I open my eyes and see him again.

He kisses me lightly, so different from the man who owned me and possessed every ounce of my body a moment ago. "I love you, Evie. Come back to me."

Something wet hits my cheek, and I see this man crying for me. It is almost my undoing as I shed tears that I haven't in so long, when I vowed never to be weak. To never show my emotions. He drops down onto me, covering me in his full weight.

"I promise," is all I can say because I will do everything I can to come back to this man. To come back to my family and have the life I deserve and the happiness I have now in Jameson's arms.

He doesn't just own my body but my heart and soul, too.

CHAPTER THIRTY-TWO

JAMESON

"ZOMBIE" BY BAD WOLVES

"I better take a shower."

She gets up and walks to her dresser, retrieving a pair of panties and bra set. I take them and toss them onto the bed where her suitcase lies open, waiting to be packed. I tug her back into me. My hand splays over her flat abdomen, and I trail my fingers down to her slick, wet folds. I gather up our cum dripping down her legs, pushing it back up into her. She is sticky, and the thought of her filled with me, with us mixed in our sexual act, has me already hard.

"Leave it. If you must leave me, take a piece of us with you." I breathe out slowly and drop my head onto her shoulder. She tilts her head to look back at me, but I can't meet her eyes. I am in a bad way at having the best thing that has happened to me leave and walk straight into danger. To be sold off to the highest bidder.

What if we can't get there in time to save them? What if I lose her forever?

I shudder underneath as the fearful emotions roll out of me and onto her.

She turns around in my embrace and picks my head up. "Okay." She looks into my eyes, and sadness pools in hers. "I'll take you with me." I nod and kiss her. "Always," she breathes onto my lips.

Our moment is interrupted by the front door closing. We realize our time is up. Our moment finished. We step away from each other.

"I'll just change." She walks into the bathroom, and there is a knock on her door.

"Evie?" Mateo asks from the other side of her bedroom.

I walk to it and step out, closing the door behind me. "She is just finishing up packing."

He nods, and there's another knock on our apartment door. Mateo looks out the window and sees Emma and Eduardo outside. He drops his head for a moment, then opens the door. It's time, and we have run out of it on our end.

Eduardo enters the apartment, bringing in all his tension and rage. The room feels incredibly small with all of us here. The anxiety I am feeling is crippling, especially with the impending doom I feel at Evie and Emma walking through that door with Mateo, knowing that he is going to take them straight over to Mr. Martinez and Ramón. They will all go to Brownsville and be kept at his house until Emma and Evie are to be married off for the benefit of Mr. Martinez's political associations and financial security.

Eduardo is holding Emma's hand in a death grip. Her eyes are wide as she looks over every apartment space to see if Evie will magically appear.

"She's getting ready. Almost packed."

Emma nods. I look over to their clasped hands, and Eduardo's fingers release Emma's hand and then regrip it firmly. He's holding her emerald heart charm in his hand, and I snap my head up, attention piqued.

I've known Eduardo for a long time. Part of being friends for so long is that we can read each other perfectly without any words being said. He's asking me about the bracelet and the earrings I had made for Evie. I nod very subtly and then fix my sights on Mateo. We purposely didn't tell him about this. The fewer people that know, the better it is to keep a close eye and ear on the girls.

They both have SOS options on their trackers. Evie also has a small microphone to pick up conversations in her earring. I am sure their bags will be looked at or maybe even confiscated and disposed of. We don't want to risk the chance that they are taken anyway.

"Emma's suitcase is in the car." Eduardo looks over at Mateo. "I trust you, Mateo, to guard your sisters with your life."

Mateo steps forward, never breaking eye contact with Eduardo. "I have always guarded my sisters with my life and would gladly give up my own for their safety. They are the only reason my life is worth living. Without them, I have nothing else. They are my family."

Emma leaves Eduardo's side and runs to her brother, throwing her arms around him. I look to the door of Evie's bedroom, wondering where she is, but she is there standing, listening to the entire conversation. I don't know how long she has been there, but it must have been long enough because she joins her siblings in a group hug.

Mateo kisses the top of each of their heads. "I promise to do everything in my power to get us through this. He pulls back, looking down at their short statures.

"I just want you two to know that there may be times when I have to act or behave a certain way. I might be cruel or say things that are very out of character from the brother that you know. The brother you know would never say or mean those things, but it is something I might have to do. I have a part to play, and you do, too. Let's do everything we can to stay safe and do what must be done."

Mateo looks over to Eduardo, who is speaking to him. "I have to know that he dies and this is over. There is no other option, Mateo."

"I'll make sure to get word to you when to come."

They nod in agreement. "We will come, Mateo. I promise."

"Okay," he says to Eduardo. "We better go before Mr. Martinez gets suspicious."

We close up the apartment that Evie and Mateo have stayed at the longest together, and I feel like we are closing a chapter in their life. Mateo turns back to look at his place, standing in the middle of the parking lot. He is silent for a while, until he finally speaks as we wait for him to load his vehicle.

"I hope that when we return here, it is to start a different life. A life where we all are free to live, fulfill our passions, and pursue our dreams. I don't know who I am anymore, other than Evie's guardian angel or Emma's savior—their brother. I want to live a life for myself and maybe, just maybe, find the happiness they have with a partner that is so in love with me that we cannot exist without each other. I can only dream of having a life like that one day."

I clasp my hand over Mateo's shoulder. "Let's play our parts and get this done. Then we can all get our own happiness, however that may be."

We load up the cars, and Mateo starts the engine on his. He blasts the air conditioning, trying to cool off the vehicle. It hasn't been that long since we arrived from the coast, but the city has a way of making it hotter than average.

Eduardo and I shake Mateo's hand and watch Evie and Emma get in. Mateo shuts his door and puts it into drive, pulling out of the parking lot. I stare at them as they drive away.

As they turn the corner, I see Emma's hand on the window with tears streaming down her cheek. Evie stares straight ahead. I know that she is trying to be brave. She can't risk falling apart, and if I know her as well as I think I do, she is counting her breaths and holding them in a practiced fashion the way she was taught to do when she is about to have a panic attack. She is so controlled now, more than ever, and someday I wish that she won't have to put on a fake act and be able to show me the most vulnerable side she has. I want to swim in a rocking sea of her salty tears and lick them away from her face as she looks up at me through those tears-stained eyes, knowing that I am the only one that will ever see the real her.

I continue to watch them drive away until there is nothing there except an empty street. I turn my attention to Eduardo. Gus comes out of the car and walks over to us. I lift my chin in an informal hello, and he does the same, but his main focus is on Eduardo.

"Are you ready to go, boss?" he asks. His sights never leave Eduardo's.

"I'll be there every step of the way, too, buddy. We need to stick together. We have a new priority. *Operation bring them home.*"

Eduardo looks over at me. "I'm glad you said that, Jameson, because I'm going to need you close to bring our women back and get our family back together as soon as possible."

"I want that more than anything." I slap my hand on his back, as he walks over to his car, Gus following. He turns back.

"I expect you to bring your shit and move in until they are back home safely."

I look at him to see if he is joking.

He continues, "I need all the surveillance ready to go and the station with all the manpower to leave at the drop of a hat. Bring your equipment and get everything ready in my place today."

I run my hand through my hair.

"Yeah, I guess that is the best way. Be there in a couple of hours." With that, he drives off.

I am left standing alone, and the gravity of our situation finally hits home. With a newfound sense of purpose, I run to my truck and drive off in a hurry to get to Eduardo's place. But first, a stop at my mine to start *'Operation bring them home.'*

I fight the traffic and lose miserably. I end up three hours later at Eduardo's place, well into the evening. I shoot him a text letting him know that I am here and need help getting my shit into his house. I understand this is a secure area, but I don't want to make several trips back and forth to get everything. The elevator door opens into the garage, and out steps Eli, Philip, and Gus.

Eduardo isn't present, but I expected this. I know that he is home because his car is here. What I don't expect is for him to get out of Emma's metallic-green BMW and walk toward me. I don't have to wonder why he was sitting in there. I know that it was to feel closer to her and breathe in her scent that envelops him in her car.

Avoiding looking at him, I allow him his own private moment and sling my bag over my shoulder and grab my laptop. Each of the guys grabs a box that is filled with monitors and speakers to amplify the sounds from Evie and Emma's trackers. I also have a separate screen showing where they are in the house. I have a blueprint of the mini-mansion that Mr. Martinez calls home. I have also tracked his wife's routines. I like to know where she is at all times. I am sure that with Evie and Emma in her home, things might take a turn for the worse. I want to be able to get to her—mostly to tear her throat out if she so much as lays a finger on our women.

We ride the elevator in silence, and the tension rises with each floor we ascend.

As soon as Eduardo leads me to our workstation, I quickly get everything situated and in working order. I don't know what happened when Evie, Emma, and Mateo left us to meet Mr. Martinez and Ramón back at their place because they never returned there. Shortly after he left their place, Ramón and Mr. Martinez left as well to an undisclosed location. We know that Ramón already had his bag packed, so the element of surprise is gone.

Mr. Martinez doesn't want to risk getting caught at Ramón's place if Mateo breaks his newly formed trust. He wants to ensure that he can witness it for himself. It seems too good to be true that Mateo went along so quickly with everything that his sperm donor said. That's what we have been referring to him as—the sperm donor. Usually, when things are too good to be true, they are, so he has every right to be cautious.

"There," I say, pinning the blueprints of the house on the cork board. I take a look around the workspace that looks like a crime center at first glance.

On the GPS monitor, I see the girls traveling in a car heading on Interstate 37, showing their every movement. Eduardo steps into the room, handing me a can of beer.

"I thought you would be drinking something stronger?" I take the beer can, open it, and take a large pull from it. My throat is dry, and my heart is aching, but I keep it to myself.

Eduardo shakes his head. "No, I have to keep my wits about me in case I need to leave. In case something…." He doesn't finish that sentence, but he doesn't have to. I already know what he was going to say. "Come on. You need to eat. I ordered everyone pizza, then we can get back to work."

CHAPTER THIRTY-THREE

EVIE

"IN THE END" BY LINKIN PARK

Mateo drove us to the place Mr. Martinez told him to on the phone. We heard his phone ring, and when he answered, he looked at us. Without saying a word, we knew the plan had changed.

Now we are in a Walmart parking lot, of all places. It is packed, and I guess that is the point. We were transferred to another vehicle, this time a black SUV similar to the one Julian rode around in when Emma was with him. I say the term "with him" loosely because she did not have a choice toward the end. The end of where we ended his life and then set Cherry on fire in her own car in front of their house.

I notice Emma tense as she walks over to it. Every instinct she has for self-preservation screams for her to run from this SUV. Do not get into the vehicle, which is blaring with loud red sirens.

We ignore that loud warning bell and walk with purpose to the SUV.

We slide into the seats as the doors close in the back, locking us in—as if we would try to run at this point.

Ramón is driving Mateo's vehicle, and Mr. Martinez and Mateo are in the middle section with Marcus, along with another scary-looking man with a bald head and a gold front tooth that eyes me lasciviously from the rearview mirror. He licks his lips, and I look away. Marcus laughs in the front seat, but no one says anything as we drive out of the parking lot.

Our hands have been ziptied since we left Houston, and they ache with the need to rip them apart. To free myself from these physical confines. Having to use the restrooms outside the gas station we stopped at was difficult since we didn't have the luxury of having free hands. Now, I sit here in silence with only another few hours remaining before we get to our new prison.

I don't know how I could have fallen asleep, but I wake up with a jolt as the SUV door slams shut, and Emma looks over at me. Our door opens, and that scary man that was lusting at me in the mirror opens my door, grabbing me over the seat and hoisting me out of the car. His hand lands on my breast, and I flinch, almost falling over as he leans over me, catching my fall while his erection digs into my backside.

As he struggles to stand me up, Mateo is striding over to him, pushing him away from me. He snarls at the man, and he smirks at my brother, knowing very well what he is doing to aggravate and get a rise out of him. Mateo stands straight, demanding respect.

I look over at Emma, who is watching along with Mr. Martinez, who is watching the exchange with amusement.

"My sisters are going to be promised to some very wealthy men. I won't have you tampering with them. We need them, so if I so much as see you look at them in the lustful manner in which you did before, I will cut your eyes out, am I clear?"

The guard looks over at Mr. Martinez.

Mateo slaps his face, getting his attention back to him. "Do not look to my father to save you. I am his son and heir. You will listen and respect me, or I will beat it out of you until you understand. You work for me. You got me?"

He must understand whatever he was looking for in his employer because he changes his tune quickly. "Of course, boss. I understand now."

Mateo nods, and we walk to the house. Still zip-tied, Emma and I walk in front of our brother as Mr. Martinez and Ramón enter the house.

We walk through the opulent and gaudy interior of the home, and I hate to say that it screams *I want to be important*. It is so flashy that my eyes cannot look at one thing. The mismatched designs and bright colors are in opposition with themselves, and I become dizzy trying to make sense of what is going on here. It is the exact opposite of class. The design is... I'm-trying-too-hard with a splash of desperation sprinkled into the home's interior design.

My boots echo on the open foyer as we stop, taking a look at our temporary home. A woman comes through shortly after and greets Mr. Martinez, welcoming him home. She is young and very pretty and I suspect she is there for things other than being the estate's stewardess. I wonder how Mrs. Martinez feels about that.

"Adalia, this is my long-lost son, Mateo. I have finally brought him home."

Mateo nods at Adalia, and she blushes. Of course, she does.

"It's so nice to make your acquaintance, Mateo."

I roll my eyes, and Emma just watches the exchange.

He nods. "Adalia, these are my sisters. I trust that you will keep an eye on them and give them whatever they need to make their short stay here as pleasant as possible."

Adalia spares a glance with a small smile before returning her full attention to my brother. "Of course, sir. I can absolutely do that for you. I can do anything that you need me to."

Ramón coughs. Mr. Martinez looks at her sternly, and I am sure she will be punished for that comment later. I don't wish that on my worst enemy, especially if he is anything like his son.

Emma gulps loudly, and I can only imagine the memories that are brought up now, being in this house once again.

"I'll show them to their rooms, sir," Adalia says.

Emma and I start to walk off, but Ramón calls out for us to stop. He walks over with a pocket knife in his extended hand. Mateo immediately takes the knife from him and comes over to us.

"Here," he says, pointing at the zip-ties.

I wordlessly extend my arms out to him, and he cuts through my ties and then does the same thing to Emma. Immediately, we attempt to ease the tingling in our wrists from being in that fixed position for the last ten hours.

Mateo's eyes hone in on the redness that encircles our wrists, but he doesn't comment. The tic of his jaw is the only sign that he is upset at the pain he was partially responsible for, but we all have our parts to play. His parting words echo in my mind, easing some of the feelings brewing.

We follow Adalia as Mr. Martinez says, "Come on, son. Follow me. I have much to talk to you about."

I hear their footsteps leave us as we hit the home's second level and walk to our gilded cage.

We are in a bedroom that is connected to a bathroom—a Jack-and-Jill style.

"Here you go, ladies," Adalia says as she shows us to our room. "Your suitcases are here, and I believe they have already been checked, so if your things seem to be rummaged through, then you would be correct. Can't be too safe these days."

I want to say safe from who, but I can't find it in me to talk to this poor, brainwashed creature.

"I suggest getting a good night's sleep because breakfast is early." She heads toward the door, but I stop her.

"We are eating breakfast with our brother?"

She turns back to address me, her hands intertwined in front of her. "Oh no, you will be served breakfast and lunch in your rooms."

I nod in understanding. They are truly locking us in here.

But she adds, "You will have dinner tomorrow night with everyone present where they will let you know what is expected of you."

With that, she leaves and closes the door behind her. We hear a lock, and then her footsteps trail off until there is nothing but silence. Suffocating silence.

I study our surroundings and then look at Emma. She sits on the bed, hugging herself. I walk over and sit beside her.

"Will you sleep with me, Evie?"

I nod. I don't want to be alone, either. Even though our rooms are connected through a Jack-and-Jill style bathroom, it feels too far to be away from one another. I'd like for us to stick together in this place.

"Mateo won't let anything happen to us, Emma." I don't know if I say that to reassure her or myself because right now, I am feeling anything but safe in this palatial prison.

I walk to the bathroom with my toiletries and belongings under my arm to shower. As the water runs, I undress. The images of Jameson just a few hours ago seem like a lifetime away, but I can still smell him on me, and that thought brings me comfort.

I reluctantly step into the shower, not wanting to wash his last memory off me, but I need to freshen up from the trip. I let the hot water warm me up. Even though it is a hundred degrees outside, I feel chilled to the bone. The warmth of the water seeps into my skin, absorbing the heat and moisture past its protective dermal barrier.

After I'm done, I step out and towel dry my hair. I touch my earring and remember that Jameson is here with me, and that gives me a sense of comfort. Emma is waiting to shower after me. I brush my hair in front of the mirror. I wonder if he can hear me.

"We made it. Emma is in the shower. We have adjoining rooms on the second floor with a bathroom in between, Jack-and-Jill style. Emma wants me to sleep with her tonight, and honestly, she didn't even have to ask me twice."

I put some product in my hair, slicking it down. "They locked us in here. They said they will feed us breakfast and lunch here, and then we are to join them for dinner to learn what will be expected of us. I am sure they would love to discipline us if given the chance. I'll try my best not to cause any trouble." I pick up the blow-dryer and dry my hair.

I look up to see Emma standing in the doorway of the bathroom, looking at me. I apply some moisturizer to my face, stand, and walk past her returning to the bathroom to brush my teeth. When I step back out, she is braiding her hair where I was just sitting.

"It helps to keep the curls if I do it this way."

I didn't ask her, but I feel it, too. There is a need to say something, anything, to make the feeling of normalcy return to our lives. Except this isn't anything normal. We are locked in a room of the house of an evil man, going to be auctioned off to the highest bidder through a forced marriage all to help Mr. Martinez gain power through our family connections.

Walking over to my bag dropping it to the floor, I start taking things out of my suitcase, standing up pissed. "They took my Kindle, those assholes. I thought maybe I'd get to read, but nope. It's not like I can access the internet. It would just be to read what I had on there. I have a lot of books on there. It would have helped to pass the time." I throw my head back, fighting the tears that threaten to fall.

Emma shrugs. "Well, that is one thing we have..." I pause, looking around and then back to meet my sister's eyes, wondering what she means by that comment.

"Plenty of time," Emma explains. She walks over to the bed, pulling back the covers. She climbs in and pats the side of the bed. "Come on, Evie. We should get a little sleep. Who knows what will happen tomorrow."

I walk over to the bed and climb in. "The bed is comfortable. I'll give them that." I pull the blankets over my chest, and Emma leans into me.

"Good night, Evie."

I place my head on hers. "Good night, Emma. Maybe when we wake up tomorrow, it will all be just a bad dream."

I feel someone pulling me. "No, I don't want to go with you. Please, just stop. You're hurting me."

But he just shakes me over and over.

"Evie," I hear my name being called, and I sit upright in bed in a place I don't recognize. "Evie, it's me, Emma. You were having a nightmare."

I notice a pale light coming through from the window drapery. I lay back down.

"Great, I woke up from one nightmare just to realize I'm living in another one."

I feel the sweat cooling on my skin as I take a deep breath and count my breathing to stop the anxiety and panic from creeping in. I don't want Emma to witness it. I've always tried to keep it from her.

"Do you have dreams like that a lot?" she asks, and I look over at her.

I bit my lip with worry. "Sometimes, I guess." I shrug it off, trying to make light of my nightmares. "I haven't had one in a while."

I've changed, and I think it has a lot to do with Jameson being in my life. He has been there for me, loved me, and made me feel safe. My brother may have saved me from several close encounters, but Jameson saved me from myself. From being in my own head. He gave me the time and patience I needed to learn how to trust someone and relinquish the control that I sought to maintain after I had none with the assault, and later in the situation with Emma's own abuse.

I remember waking up unconscious in an alley from one of Julian's abusive encounters. The memory makes me shiver. I was alone and vulnerable there, unconscious. Anything could have happened, but Mateo saved me.

I just pray he can do it again.

I must have had the same dream because, once again, I feel like I am not in control of my life. I am at the mercy of Mr. Martinez. I just hope that we come out of this. If we do, it will be on the other side, finally waking up from this nightmare.

CHAPTER THIRTY-FOUR

EVIE

"GIRL YOU'LL BE A WOMAN SOON" BY RAFFERTY

We were served in our room like we were told we would be yesterday by Adalia. The food, shockingly, wasn't bad. I would even consider it some of the best I've had in a long time. I expected to be served subpar meals, but then again, nothing has been what I've anticipated since arriving here.

We are getting comfortable the best we can, lounging on the bed, deep in our thoughts, when there is a knock at the door. I flinch, and Emma sucks in a breath. Is this it? Is it time for them to drag us out of here like cattle to the auction barn? We were not expecting anyone after our meals, and we don't know what time it is. The sun is still shining outside.

Emma grabs onto my hand just as the door opens. Adalia enters, breezing in with her skirt flowing behind her and carrying two packages in her hands. She has a beaming smile plastered on her face, and I can't help but wonder if she is possibly drugged. No one can be that delusional, but wait, this whole house is.

Maybe it's something in the water.

I quickly look over at my empty glass as it sits on the counter, condensation pooling around the bottom, and I snicker, thinking how Emma is silently cringing at it. If it didn't bother her, then we indeed have more significant problems.

"Hi, ladies. Your wonderful brother asked me to bring these to you. He is sorry he couldn't visit but he is so busy with his father."

I look over at Emma, whose nose is crinkled up at the tip, trying to hide her disgust but failing miserably. I stand, trying to sound excited. "Oh. I love presents, Adalia. What is it?"

Emma is now staring at me, wondering what I am up to.

Adalia practically jumps up with glee. "Dresses!" she exclaims. "Beautiful dresses." She claps her hands. "Isn't that great?"

"Wonderful."

"Can we open them now, Adalia?" Emma asks, joining us, and I bet it kills her to be this type of fake nice to her.

Adalia picks one package up and hands it to Emma. "Of course, silly goose."

Emma accepts the package and mouths, '*Silly goose.*'

I quickly turn away to hide my chuckle. "Is that mine?" I point to the other remaining package.

Adalia nods and hands it to me. I open the package, and in it is a red fitted dress that should come to land around mid-thigh. It is short. A pair of black patent red-soled stiletto shoes complete the ensemble.

I look over to Emma. She opens her box, which holds a green halter dress with a similar style and length along with chain-style black leather red-soled shoes. She holds up the shoes, and her eyes light up.

"Not bad, Mattie." Emma clicks her tongue.

Adalia squeals in delight. "I knew you'd like them."

I nod in agreement. "It's like Christmas." I look over to Emma, and she snorts.

"Literally, green and red. Our favorite colors."

Adalia looks over at the dress. A slight frown forms on her lips. They purse when she notices the green and red colors clashing like a Walmart Christmas portrait people mock on social media sites.

I reach out to her and grab her by the wrist to get her attention. Her eyes dart over to me, and I drop her wrist.

"They are really lovely dresses, Adalia. Will you please thank our brother for us?" This seems to make her spirits rise a bit. I cringe at my fakeness spewing forth.

"Of course!" she exclaims, clapping her hands together.

Emma and I hold our boxes, wondering what we are supposed to do now. We look at each other and then at Adalia, who is standing there.

"Um," Evie starts off, about to say something.

"Oh, right. The dresses are for the party this weekend. We just want to ensure they fit, so I need to see them on you. I am to report back if anything needs to be switched out."

We look at each other then walk into the large bathroom to change, and as soon as we shut the door, Emma starts to speak.

"What happens—"

I put my hand over her mouth, shaking my head. I place my finger up my mouth and point to the door, indicating that Adalia is listening and will likely report back anything we say.

We get dressed in silence, and I glance in the mirror. The dresses are pretty, but together, they scream 'holiday party.' We walk out, and Adalia frowns.

"Well," I hold my arms out, twirling a little, "What do you think?" Emma doesn't do anything but stand there holding her hands like a little girl seeking approval from her mother.

A sigh comes out of Adalia's mouth. "I don't like the colors together. I am switching them to both be red. What do you girls think?"

I look over to Emma. She shrugs, and I nod. "I think that is a good idea. I do like the colors though."

We step out of the dresses and hand them over to Adalia, and she walks to the door but hesitates before she leaves. She turns around to face us. Her eyes narrow.

"Don't screw this up for Mateo. There will be a lot of important people at that party, so your complete cooperation is expected. Otherwise..." she trails off. Her smile widens. "Mr. Martinez has the final say on who you marry, and he might not be very cautious about whom he picks for you from the potential suitors. We have all ages with varying specifications for their future bride. Or even worse, if he allows Oro to punish you, I can guarantee that you won't be able to walk well for about a week if that happens."

I hear Emma gulp.

"Dinner is in a couple of hours, so be ready. Someone will be up to escort you to the dining room, so I suggest you are both on your best behavior."

TWISTED TIDES

I look over to Emma as I hear the door close. I walk over, and she throws her arms around me, hugging me. We change into one of the few outfits we were permitted to bring with us and wait. We sit there in silence, deep in our thoughts, not wanting to talk about what we fear and what may happen this weekend. Without a clock or watch, we have no idea how long we sit there waiting.

Suddenly, the door opens, and our brother walks inside. We both jump off the bed and hug him tightly. I step away to look at my brother as Emma still holds on to him. That's when I notice he isn't hugging us back.

"Emma," I say, and she looks at me in question, still holding onto Mateo, then notices what I noticed moments ago—the resemblance.

She steps back, looking at the man we came to love, and wondering if this is an act or something else. Did he betray us?

"Sisters, follow me." He walks out the door, and his polished shoes click on the tile floor as we follow him down the hall.

The scary-looking guard with the gold tooth, who they referred to as Oro, is leering at Emma. His lip curls in a sinister smile as we walk past. Emma turns her head just as he winks at her, licking his lips and staring at her ass. Mateo doesn't notice, and she doesn't comment if he does notice. We continue to walk behind our brother in what I assume is the direction of the dining room.

Enter the dining room, where a large ornate table lies in the middle of the room under a crystal chandelier, there is a serving station with wine and champagne resting in their respective glacettes. Adalia picks up a bottle of red wine and serves Mrs. Martinez.

Mateo pulls our chairs out, and we take our seats in the spots that he selects for us. He then goes to sit across from his father and grandfather.

Adalia stands there along with the butler, who brings everything out to the table. He has a plate full of raw filet mignon steaks that he brings over to Mr. Martinez for approval. I watch with interest at the exchange. Mr. Martinez nods, and then the butler walks over to the guéridon trolley to begin cooking the steaks.

The steak is placed over heat, and brandy is poured into it to begin the flambé process. The fire roars to life, and the meat sizzles, causing my mouth to water. The smell of perfectly cooked meat fills the air, and I realize how hungry I am.

A multitude of trays line the table under heated flames to keep the food warm while the steaks are cooked to perfection. No one asked me how I like my steak cooked, but as I watch this demonstration, I can rest assured that they will be cooked perfectly to a medium-rare temperature.

Adalia picks up a bottle of wine and some champagne from each glacette and fills our cups. I select the champagne, as does Emma. I feel someone looking at me as I turn toward Mrs. Martinez. She is sizing me up with a look of distaste. Mr. Martinez laughs at something Mateo says, and her gaze moves toward him. If she looks at me with distaste, then the emotion on her face as she stares at Mateo is with a look of pure hatred.

She must sense my continued stare because she turns back to me before I can look away as she finishes the rest of her wine in one gulp. As soon as she puts it on the table, it is promptly refilled. I wonder if I should be worried about her lack of restraint. Nothing good could come of a drunk wife around my brother who has quickly taken her son's place.

I've barely taken my last bite of food as I set my napkin on my lap, when I hear a throat clear. I turn to see Mr. Martinez wiping the corners of his mouth like some kind of aristocrat instead of the corrupt politician that he really is.

"Ladies, I hope you have enjoyed your stay here because it will be short-lived."

Emma and I both look at Mateo, and his expression is emotionless. A robot would have more compassion than my brother.

"As much as I would have liked to have punished you, Mateo assured me you would behave while you were here, and he was right. This weekend, we will have a party for you where you will meet your potential suitors. By the end of the night, we will have chosen the best addition for this family to become your new husband, binding us to the Ortiz mafia connections across the border. This will solidify our ties and ensure a prosperous business venture."

He clasps Mateo on the shoulder and squeezes. "My son is home, and I look forward to the continuation of my legacy. Now to find my son a bride of his choosing."

Adalia perks up at this with her delusional smile plastered to her face.

The smile Mateo gives Mr. Martinez is all white teeth and most award-winning. The happy moment between father and son is short-lived as red wine drips from my brother's face and saturates Mr. Martinez's white shirt. The crimson color streaks the front as it rolls down the fabric and onto the floor. I hear a gasp from Adalia, but Emma and I sit there frozen and unflinching, not wanting any attention to be distracted from the wrath that will be coming.

Mr. Martinez stands up abruptly, and his chair falls back, hitting the floor with a loud thud. Mateo grabs the cloth napkin from his lap and wipes the excess wine away from his face. He is wearing a black dress shirt, so the wine coloring isn't visible, but I can tell most of it was meant for his face.

Mrs. Martinez must be drunk or stupid because even I know to be scared, but any common sense has left the building along with her sanity. She stands up, her finger pointing at him as she leans over the table. I don't know if she is using her grip on the table to hold herself upright or to keep from swaying at this point as she slurs obscenities at her husband.

We watch the exchange with our heads volleying back and forth as if we are watching a tennis match where the winner is an obvious unanimous decision.

"Your son. Your son!" she screeches, and I almost go to put my hands over my ears to ease the high-pitched sound that threatens to rupture my eardrums. "Our son is dead. My son is dead. He was the rightful heir, and this bitch killed him. I want her dead. I want them both dead." She is looking between us and Mateo, but Mr. Martinez just laughs at her.

"Do you think I give a flying fuck about what you want?" He mocks her. *"I want them dead."* He shakes his head. "Was their mother not enough for you? You've always been a jealous bitch and a lousy lay." He looks over to Adalia and winks at her. Now my steak threatens to come up because I know that she is fucking him.

Mrs. Martinez takes her new glass of wine and begins to chug it.

"I think you've had enough to drink for tonight." He takes her drink from her and places it away from her reach.

"Fuck you," she spits at him, and he is so quick that I don't hear the smack until a second after it happens.

She holds her cheek as anger radiates from her body. She stares at him defiantly, and I shift down farther into my seat, not wanting to see what will happen. "Fuck you!" she screams.

He nods. "Maybe that is what you need then."

Her eyes widen almost as if the demon that took over her body has been exorcised, and she is just realizing what she did. Although, now, her eyes widen in fear.

"Oro!" Mr. Martinez yells, and the large tatted-up man enters the room.

"Yes, boss," he says as he stops right in front of Mr. Martinez.

She backs up, realizing her mistake, but it is too late.

"I need you to show my wife what it means to be fucked."

Oro chuckles. "Oh, I can certainly do that, boss."

"No! No!" She begins to back up and looks around. If she is looking for help, she isn't getting any from us. No one is saving her. Her cheek is bright red from the slap Mr. Martinez gave her.

Oro stalks toward her, and she attempts to kick him in the balls, but he anticipates the move. He leans in and punches her in the face, and she goes down like a ton of bricks. He picks her up as if she weighs nothing and flips her over his shoulder. One shoe falls to the floor as they turn the corner and disappear.

Emma and I stay there sitting quietly.

"Let this be a lesson to you to understand what will happen if you don't cooperate this weekend at your party. If you step out of line, I'll let Oro teach you some manners." Mr. Martinez leaves the room.

We hear a door open. The sound of muffled cries echoes down the corridor before it disappears along with my dinner as I throw up the entire contents of my stomach onto the high-polished floor.

CHAPTER THIRTY-FIVE

JAMESON

"HEY MAN, NICE SHOT" BY FILTER

I have hardly slept. Eduardo and I listened to Evie talk to us through her speaker via the microphone earrings I gifted her before she left me. My stomach twists with sickness as the small device picks up her words with almost perfect clarity—both a blessing and a torturous curse simultaneously.

We learn that she and Emma are being kept in a shared room on the second floor, and I see exactly where it is via the GPS tracking device. Emma also has hers, but Eduardo has had no relief in knowing where she is at all times. According to him, he has failed if her heart is not alongside his.

I draw out two hearts in the center of that room, marking it on one of the blueprints hanging in our office, and stare at them, both of us trapped in our own hellish silence.

What really broke me was listening to her scream in the middle of the night and not being there for her. Her nightmares have returned, and for good reason. She's living a nightmare that she can't wake up from.

It killed me, and a part of my soul dies not being with my other half, not being able to comfort her or to find comfort in her embrace.

In this short time, Evie and I have become so close that I swear we are one of those couples I used to envy that could complete the other one's sentence. That's what hurt the most. Emma was there for her and comforted her when I wasn't there to do so, and it damn nearly killed me. I bring my hands up to my face to fight back the tears that blur my vision as the anger rises inside.

"Motherfuckers!" I hear Eduardo shout as his glass hits the wall and shatters into a million pieces along with our sanity.

Emma grounded him. She tamed his inner beast that always hid behind a firm handshake and a narrowed glare. I haven't seen him this volatile since our college days, which were a haze of debauchery and frat parties. That is, until Emma returned to his life. I didn't realize that she was 'the Emma' from his tattooed knuckles that he frequently used to beat the shit out of anyone who gave him the slightest reason.

Evie wasn't lying when she said she hadn't had a nightmare in a while, but I know that it is the feeling of the unknown that caused it. Not being in control of herself and at the mercy of a cruel monster. Being in the same house with Marcus, her assaulter. It brought back all the memories of a time when she was helpless and at the mercy of someone who had dominated her. Anyone would be scared, and if it was a person other than Emma and Evie, they would have fallen apart already, but these sisters are strong and resilient. I know that if anyone can overcome this, it is them. I have to believe it is for me to continue with this plan and not damn near run into the house and drag her out, even at the possibility of not coming out alive to join her.

Eduardo's hand hits my chest, breaking me out of my self-loathing. "Shh. Did you get that?"

Eduardo is already going to the board to write down the name Oro and the date for when they will be sold off to the highest bidder or the suitor with the most assets to give Mr. Martinez the money and resources to optimize his business relationships. I look over to Eduardo and don't understand how he could be so calm now when he was all fury just a moment ago. Now, at the mention of his fiancée being married off like some prized cow, he is almost gleeful. I must look confused when Ram speaks up.

"So what's the plan?" Eduardo's brother asks.

The guys have been here since day one to help out. His brother has taken over at the club so that Eduardo can concentrate on bringing Emma home. That is his sole focus now, as is mine.

I have shut down all contracts because I cannot concentrate on anything work-related when Evie is held prisoner in the Martinez house. To think that I may never see her again...

The memories of our last night together run through my mind on a constant loop, repeating the sound of her moans as she came on my fingers, tongue, and cock. I sent her away with my cum dripping down her leg and wouldn't let her shower. Now, I know it is all down the drain along with our hopes and dreams. I just pray that she will be safe and back in my arms again soon.

"This week, we will bring them home."

I am startled from my thoughts again at the plan Eduardo begins to bring forth.

"How?" is all I say. I want to believe that this time next week, I will have Evie home with me and this will all but be a distant memory while we forge ahead, creating our own memories together.

Forged hearts. Stronger and unbreakable.

"We move out in the morning to Brownsville and move into Dax and Liv's condo."

I nod because we need to be there closer to them. In the morning, we take off.

"I've already contacted Andrés and Adrian, and they are going to meet us there with my father. If we all can't bring them home, then no one can. The girls may have brought on this war, but with all of us combined and as a united front, we will see to it that it ends now."

We all get up early the next morning and make the five-hour trek south. We make no stops and take no breaks. Eduardo insists on driving the entire way. Ram stayed behind to run the business, and by the time we get into town, it is evening.

We pull up to the condo and remark on the beautiful sunset. I'm thinking about how much Evie would love it. I would love to sit out here and watch the waves crashing along with the sun setting in the background. It is breathtaking.

We gather our bags and open the door to our new home for the week. I must remember to thank my best friend, Dax, after this is over. After this weekend, we will be free. There is no option of failure. I can't think of the alternative where Evie isn't with me.

I know Eduardo feels the same about Emma. He hasn't been himself since Emma left, and he doesn't even want to eat, only consuming alcohol. Now, he hasn't touched a drop as he is committed to the plan. The guy is miserable without her, and I now understand how Dax felt with Liv.

When you know, you know.

I set up the equipment in the living room and it appears that the girls are having dinner with the family. It sounds like a pretty good dinner, from what I gather, but then I hear Mrs. Martinez comment about Mateo not being the true heir. The punch that echoes in the room when Oro knocks her out makes me visibly recoil.

We all stop moving around and listen carefully to what transpires next. I hope Mateo is watching out for them. I can't believe they are there. If he lets that happen to his own wife, then what is he capable of if the girls mouth off? For their sake, I really hope they don't make this harder than it has to be.

I know that Mateo won't allow anything to happen to them, and if Mr. Martinez tries something, the plan will be ruined and the guise will be up. I don't hear a peep out of Mateo the entire time, and I would wonder if he is really there if it wasn't for the comments made about him in his presence.

"So, it's happening this weekend?" I ask Eduardo.

He nods as he sips his coffee lost in thought, almost like he isn't really here. He doesn't answer me. He is here only in the physical sense because I know that his mind and soul are with Emma.

Nothing else matters.

We hear a knock at the door, and I get off the couch to answer it.

"There's your answer," Eduardo replies, void of emotion.

I look at the window and then through the peephole to see who is on the other side. When I recognize the faces of Evie and Emma's uncle and cousin, I open the door.

"It's about time," I say, relieved, and welcome them wholeheartedly. I give them each a hug, patting them on the back silently and thanking them for their assistance in getting the girls back home.

"Think nothing of it. This was a long time coming, and I am glad to see this finish so that maybe my sister's soul can finally be laid to rest."

I quirk an eyebrow up, clearly not believing any of this spiritual stuff, but Eduardo does, and he makes the sign of the cross. I almost roll my eyes at the irony of these men who also release people to the spirit world more than I'd like to know about.

"Thank you for coming," Eduardo replies while walking over to them.

Andrés just nods, acknowledging his thanks. They enter the condo and get settled. We discuss the plan and fill them in on what is happening. We relay all our news and show them where the girls are being kept.

"I have some news," Andrés says.

Eduardo nods, urging him to continue. I bite my nails in frustration, not wanting to hear, but then feel compelled to listen to anything that could help bring my girlfriend back home as soon as possible.

"It was brought to my attention that the police chief that is in the pocket of Mr. Martinez is upset."

Eduardo nods, encouraging Andrés to proceed with his discovery. I lean in closer to what he says next, hanging on every word.

"It also came to our attention that his pixie-looking daughter's life was threatened to encourage his complacency with Mr. Martinez, who has been slowly overtaking things here in Brownsville. His insistence on bringing illegal drugs across the border has had the police chief turning his attention to anything other than the drugs that are being smuggled across the border by Mr. Martinez."

"How did he threaten his daughter?" Eduardo asks out of curiosity.

Andrés doesn't hesitate to answer. "Some guy named Oro who is one of his enforcers and security detail. He is considered a brute and does anything Mr. Martinez asks of him. He sexually assaulted the chief's daughter and threatened worse next time if he didn't have his full support in his endeavors."

We nod, remembering the knockout ordeal with Mrs. Martinez for spitting at Mateo and throwing her wine at her husband. It was all so much to take in, but Mr. Martinez didn't have any of it, so he sent her off to be punished by Oro.

I shudder at that mental image of Emma and Evie in that house, along with that monster that threatens them if they step out of line. It makes me want to gut someone, but I control my temper and wait for further instruction. I know that we can all keep them safe. We just have to formulate a plan to ensure it works.

CHAPTER THIRTY-SIX

JAMESON

"INSANELY ILLEGAL CAGE FIGHT" BY DAL AV, JACKSON ROSE

We set a meeting with the chief of police mid-week. He was hesitant when he initially received the request from Eduardo and Andrés, but as soon as they mentioned removing the threat to his daughter, he was full steam ahead in assisting in any way he could.

When the day to meet him finally rolls around, I wake up early and purposefully. I have a few questions of my own for this man, and the thought of him having any information about how to handle this situation or working together toward a common goal would also be considered a win.

The store is empty at this hour. The large chain bookstore has a sizable cafe in the middle that allows us some discretion but isn't too big so that we can't see someone approaching. This is the perfect combination to allow us the opportunity to have this meeting.

We have a clear view of the front doors from where we sit and will notice when he enters. I've never met the man, but by looking at his pictures, we should be able to identify him quickly.

I approach the counter, placing our order for some coffees. I peruse the menu further, considering the 'buy one, get one half-off' cookies, but decide against them.

That's when I notice the barista's book recommendations placed in front of the cashier. A sign that reads, 'Only five dollars with purchase of a beverage' is placed between the cookie display and the coffee cups. It's a romance book.

My upper lip curls in a half smile, making me chuckle aloud. I tilt my head to get a better look and contemplate whether I have seen this particular book at the apartment. I wonder if Evie has read it. She and Emma like to read about kick-ass heroines in polyamorous relationships. I could never be in one of those relationships because the thought of sharing Evie with anyone makes me want to commit all kinds of crimes.

The barista notices me checking out the books on display and raises an eyebrow. I place the book back on its shelf and shrug. "My girlfriend likes to read these types of books." I raise my arm toward the stack for purchase. The cover model is a scantily clad woman. Her harem of men surrounds her while they all touch her, and their stare shows to anyone looking that her presence consumes them.

I have to admit, it looks hot.

"She has them lying around throughout the apartment," I go on, my hand reaching behind me as if our apartment is there and she can see all the books. I pick up the book and fan through it before placing it back on the holder. It appears a little crooked, so I straighten it.

She laughs, causing me to look up at her. "Sure. Whatever you say." She looks behind me, raising her chin upward to the person ready to get the next order.

I feel my face heat and then step away, and when they finally call my order out, I pick up the cups in a holder to return to our table. I hand out the black coffee and wait to see when he approaches.

Right on time, a man in his late forties with a salt-and-pepper military-style buzz cut that matches his mustache enters, head held high, and heads straight for us.

We stand and offer him a seat. It draws the barista's attention, but she pretends not to notice us. Clever girl, I think to myself. Our table screams danger, but we only want to harm those who have taken something that doesn't belong to them, and we intend to right that mistake very soon.

"Please, call me Santi." He holds out his hand to Eduardo, who is leading the meeting. "I was told that we could be mutually beneficial to each other."

Eduardo nods, and we all stay silent and pensive while observing his reactions to Eduardo's following words.

"I understand you have had unpleasant dealings with a certain public figure in Brownsville."

We notice Santi visibly tense, and we spare a quick glance at one another to see if they picked up on it, too. He sits upright, no longer relaxed and wary of his following words.

"I–"

Eduardo holds up his hand. "We are very aware of your problem with Mr. Martinez and him threatening your only daughter. I believe we can help one another because, you see, he has two young women, sisters, that belong to our family. We understand what it is like to have someone take and hurt your family." His eyes shoot up to mine.

"What did he do to your sister?" His hands ball up in anger. His rage is barely contained beneath the surface.

Eduardo shakes his head. "Not my sister, but my fiancée and her twin sister, who is also my friend's girlfriend." He gestures in my direction, and I look at him. I'm sure my eyes are pleading with him to help us.

Andrés speaks up, causing us all to turn our attention to him. "She is my sobrina."

Adrian speaks after his uncle. "My prima."

Santi nods in understanding. "They are your family."

Eduardo looks around at the group gathered at the small table in the cafe. "They are our family, yes, Santi. Mr. Martinez has taken them to sell them off to the highest bidder all because he wants to further his assets and solidify partnerships through their marriage. They are selling them off like cattle, and I want my fiancée and her sister to be back home with us where they belong. With their family."

He nods, determination lining his facial features. "They threatened my daughter, Meli. If I didn't turn my attention away from his drug smuggling, he would retake my daughter, and, this time, she might not come back. Meli—" He stops to compose himself before continuing.

"That monster, Oro, assaulted Meli, and she wonders if she'll be retaken. If that happens, I know she won't survive mentally or physically." He rubs his face as if attempting to erase the bad memory from his mind.

Andrés leans in. "Help us get rid of him, and you have my word. He won't hurt Meli or anyone else again. Any of them."

Santi nods. "What do you need me to do?"

Eduardo looks over to Andrés, and he nods, giving him permission to relay the idea we came up with earlier.

The remaining days pass in a whirlwind of planning and high emotions. We all realize the severity of the consequences if we fail. Eduardo was a wreck the night before, but I convinced him to ride it out without alcohol.

The time frame is too delicate, in case we need to go in there and break them out, but this way is much better than that. We just have to be patient for a few more hours.

Tonight, we strike when they least expect it. They are undoubtedly planning for us to sneak around like thieves in the night to steal Emma and Evie away, but *they* are the thieves, and we are merely there to take back what belongs to us—our family.

"Did you get the tuxedos?" Andrés speaks to Adrian as he waltzes into the condo with a few takeout bags. He places everything on the counter and drops the bag he carries with his teeth onto the table.

"Yes, Father. I just couldn't carry it all." He scoffs. "Can you help out?"

Seeking any excuse to make the time go by, I jump at the offer. "I'll go."

I spring up from the desk chair and practically run out the door to make myself useful. I have been monitoring things at the mansion, but I am so nervous about tonight. I feel the need to release some of this pent-up anxiety. I wish I could go for a run to expel all my nervousness, but I can't bear to be away from the computer screen for too long.

What if I am out running and then miss a crucial element of the conversation and events of tonight?

I know that we pretty much have the situation handled, but I still think knowing everything possible is helpful. There is no room for errors tonight.

I open the door as Adrian unlocks it with his key fob. Seven tuxedos are lying on the back seat. We will all play our part at the party, but we won't be on the guest list. In fact, they won't even know we will be there until it is too late. With blueprints and reinforcements coming in to stay at a safe house located between here and the border, which, mind you, is a few miles away, it should be quite the show.

Adrian and I enter the condo and walk toward the back bedroom where we hand out the tuxedos in the closet. After having a meeting with the police chief, our men, and our family gathered here at the condo, I believe Eduardo when he says that this unified front is enough to bring the girls home and to show these men that they are messing with the wrong family.

Eduardo has reiterated that it isn't about just bringing the girls home but also teaching a lesson to our enemies who may try to repeat events such as these. The family must show them that they are strong and have the power to defeat their enemies and keep the organization strong. It's been a long time since someone has dared to challenge them for power, and, like always, the strongest prevail. Luckily, that is us, our blended family, but it doesn't stop someone from trying to take what is yours.

Eduardo picks up the bag of tacos and takes two. They are passed around until only a bag with a styrofoam-enclosed plate is left. He looks curiously at it. "What's in there?" he asks, going to open it, and I reach out for it.

"It's mine." I take a whiff, and my mouth waters. "It's a taco salad."

Eduardo raises one eyebrow. "A taco salad?"

I open the container, and the spiced chicken and veggies smell permeates the air. Nom. Nom. I smack my lips in anticipation.

"A fucking taco salad?" he asks again.

I take a bite of the salad that rests inside a crispy corn shell. It crunches, and light flakes of corn tortillas fly away from my mouth.

"Hm. Yes, bro. It's the best."

Eduardo just shakes his head, chuckling. "Whatever you say." He finishes his tacos in a few bites and walks out of the room, tossing his bags and trash out on the way.

I call out to him over my mouth full of food. "Where are you going?" I take another heaping forkful of my food, groaning as the flavors assault my taste buds.

He turns back to me. "To get ready. I want to look my best when I rescue my fianceé." He winks at me before he disappears behind the door.

It takes everyone a while to get ready, but there are a couple of bathrooms where we take turns showering and getting changed into our tuxedos. We call up Santi to see how everything is going on his end.

"Santi, is everything a-go for tonight?" Eduardo has him on speaker so that we can all listen to his response.

"Yes, I have all my men in place, and they have been made aware of what will happen tonight."

"What about your wife and daughter? Are they at the safe house now, just out of an abundance of caution? We want to ensure their safety. When we eliminate the threat, they can return home."

There is silence on the other line, but we can hear his breathing pick up. He blows out a breath.

"That would be great. Thank you, Eduardo. We want to help you, too, and it has been a long time coming."

Although we can't see him, I imagine him nodding in agreement.

"It has, and I am glad that it will soon be coming to an end. I'll see you soon, then." He hangs up the call, and Eduardo tucks the phone back into his tuxedo pocket.

"Okay. Let's go over the plan one more time."

I nod, as does the rest of our blended family, and we go over one last time on how we are going to get into the house and bring our family home.

CHAPTER THIRTY-SEVEN

EVIE

"SON OF A PREACHER MAN" BY DUSTY SPRING-FIELD

"Here you go, ladies." Adalia enters the room without knocking. Her sheer, flowing dress billows about as she rushes in with two packages—two boxes I recognize from the other day. She places them on the bed, looks at them, and then back at us. She lifts her hand to the packages. We watch her with curiosity.

"As promised, here are the dresses, both red this time so we don't have the 'holiday theme.'" She makes air quotes and rolls her eyes. "I remember the words you spoke when I brought them in for you to try on."

I open the boxes to see that the dresses now match. "Thank you, Adalia. That was very kind of you." I give my best attempt at sincerity, and she beams at our praise.

With her head held high, Adalia turns to walk out the door with a flourish of iridescent fabric trailing behind. Before she exits, she turns to us.

"You have someone coming in. Make sure you are waxed and made up before you slip into your dresses. I suggest you don't give them a hard time." She waves, and the door shuts behind her.

"Pfft, I was almost going to say she isn't that bad." Emma snorts as we stand in our robes, dumbfounded at the exchange just as another person enters moments later.

This time, a young woman enters wheeling a cart in front of her, and a bag is slung over her shoulder. She doesn't speak; she just goes about her business while we stare at her.

She gently places the bag on the vanity and opens it, and a multitude of makeup and hair products spill forth. Next, I notice the heated wax on the silver cart, which makes me sweat. She grabs a stick and places it into the waxy mixture, then sets it down, testing the readiness of the substance as she claps her hands together in glee, ready to inflict pain on someone's lady parts. As if there was any question about her role in this room, she immediately clarifies it.

"I'm going to help you ladies prepare for your party. Who wants to get waxed first?" She looks excited, and I look like I'd rather bathe in the hot wax as punishment.

The question lingers in the air as neither of us answers. She looks from me to Emma and then back again, wondering when someone will answer her. I glance over at Emma, who is standing there open-mouthed.

"I'll go first," I volunteer for what I suspect will be a Brazilian wax. "How do you want me?"

She points to the bed. "Lay on your back with your knees bent and legs open like a butterfly." She demonstrates the motion with her hands. "Let your knees drop outward."

I do as she says, and Evie looks away, pretending to look over her dress to give us some privacy.

"Yes, that's it."

Moments later, as the hot wax spreads over my most sensitive areas. The hair is removed in one quick sweep. Before I can think of it, I feel the sting, and my eyes fucking water.

"Oh, wow. That was intense." I shift uncomfortably.

She nods in understanding. "We are almost done."

I look up at her. "Really?"

"Nope. Just a few more passes, though."

I almost pass out with the thought of continuing this for a few more rounds. I think my skin has gone numb as a protective mechanism. I didn't know I even had hair there. I must have cleared my mind with my meditation techniques.

Before I know it, Emma is in my place, and the cool, soothing gel really did help to alleviate the minor discomfort of having all my hair ripped out at the follicle.

Emma howls, and I hold her hand, looking away out the window.

"So dramatic, babe." I look down at her as she just glares daggers at me.

Before we know it, we are dressed, hair done, and makeup, too. I take in my appearance in the floor-length mirror and admire her grooming work. I look refined and sophisticated in the outfit. I look every bit the mafia princess worthy of a maximum payout for her hand in marriage.

I just hope Mateo comes through for us. We haven't seen him since that horrific night at the dinner where Oro carted Mrs. Martinez away before our eyes. I shudder at the thought of him punishing her. Although we weren't present to witness what happened to her, the screams that came from the room were enough to imagine the horrors she endured as part of her punishment.

The young woman is putting away her things, and we watch her, wondering what we do now.

"Is someone coming to get us?" I ask, and she raises her head to look up at me before continuing to put away her accessories.

She shrugs. "I don't know. I was just told to get you ready like your life depended on it."

I recoil at her choice of words. She doesn't seem to notice my reaction. She leaves precisely how she came in—without acknowledging us. As she opens the door, we can hear the commotion of an event consisting of chatter and a band playing classy lounge music. I imagine guests walking around with a cocktail or champagne as Emma and I await certain doom.

A knock at the door lets us know that our time has come. Emma winces at the sound, and I hold onto her arm for comfort. She squeezes it in return, thanking me for my support.

In walks Mateo, and boy, is he a sight for sore eyes. Emma is about to run up to him, but the scared look in his eyes lets us know that that is a bad idea.

I hold her back, stopping her from going any farther and for him to have to physically reject the affection. There are bags under his eyes, and it looks like he hasn't slept in ages.

"Are you ready, my sisters?" he asks with a pleading look on his face.

I answer for Emma and me. She is incapable of words at the moment. I don't know what she thought was going to happen. He has a part to play, and so do we. We just have to trust that everything will come out okay.

To put your blind faith in someone is hard. You just have to trust them to come through, and not seeing anyone this week has really made it hard not to feel abandoned. Yet here we are, placing our faith in our brother to end this war that has been a long time coming.

I shake Emma's arm, and she looks at me. Her eyes harden, and I smile.

"Let's do this. Lead the way, brother." I motion with my hand in front of me.

He nods, a slight smile to his mouth as he turns around, and we walk out to the party where shit is about to get real.

We walk down the hall as the music and noise get louder. "Walk behind me, please."

As we arrive at the grand staircase, we are met by Mr. Martinez and his father, Ramón. Mr. Martinez looks us over with his hungry gaze that makes me want to vomit, but I won't show him any weakness. Mateo and Ramón move to flank Mr. Martinez on each side of him, thereby hiding us from view.

"Can I please have your attention?"

The music stops, and the crowd grows silent. I can't see anyone from here, but I know there are many guests present for this. The faces blend into one another as if they are melting.

"I'd like to welcome you to my home and, for some of you, into my family. You know my father, but you may not know my son, Mateo. Much like the prodigal son, he has returned home, and I welcome him with open arms. He is my true heir, and he brought us our very special guests for tonight. They are quite lovely, and I know that two of you here tonight will be fortunate enough to make this collaboration worth every penny. I will pass this over to my son to make further introductions."

He slaps Mateo on the back and hands him the little microphone. He smiles widely with excitement.

"Hello. As my father introduced me a moment ago, I am Mateo, his son. Thank you all for coming, and I look forward to doing business with you in the near future.

"Without further ado, I know that you are here for the lovely women we are offering tonight, so I'd like you to meet them."

Mateo motions for us to come forward, but I cannot move. I am the center of attention, and the hushed whispers make the perspiration drip down my back. Marcus is at the top of the stairs and pushes us forward.

"My sisters, Evie and Emma Ortiz Taylor." Mateo holds out his hand for us to take, one on each side of him.

The music starts up again with a bass riff and a flute, lightly fluttering notes in the background. The singer belts out jazzy vocals as we begin our walk down the long staircase toward an uncertain fate.

CHAPTER THIRTY-EIGHT

EVIE

"SEVENTY THORNS" BY JONATHAN DAVIS AND KIM DRACULA

One thing I notice straight away is that there are a lot of men here. I gulp, holding onto Mateo's hand with a firmer grip. The second thing I notice is Oro, standing by the large picture window, flicking his tongue at me. My nostrils flare. He's provoking me. His laughter rises up above the crowd to mock me. My anger takes over as my primary emotion as I envision his head exploding. Gray matter flies out of his brain with force as a projectile shoots through his skull, causing his head to crack open like a watermelon. I hear the gasps as people duck and run.

I blink, but the image stays.

That's when I realize he *was* shot, and what I was envisioning wasn't my imagination, but it really happened.

The band breaks into another song with harsh lyrics and death metal vocals. I feel like I am in one of my nightmares—a kaleidoscope of images and lights flickering from one scene to the other. Too much is happening that I can't focus on one thing. The images shift and then disappear as bodies fall to the floor as the sound of gunfire echoes in the mansion—dead men who wanted to purchase two young women.

A person jumps through the fractured glass, causing me to gasp in surprise. The glass further shatters the remaining window pane as men in tuxedos and skull face paint begin to surround us.

People run for the door, hit with bullets before exiting and landing facedown, taking their last breath before the light vanishes from their eyes. Blood pools all around, and the screaming and yelling escalate along with the frightening lyrics that continue to play forth from the band, making for a hellish sight. The security guards turn their fire onto the crowd.

I hit the SOS button and see one of the masked men shift his face to me. *Why is he looking at me? Did he hear it? How could he possibly...* Then recognition hits.

It's Jameson. He's here. I look around at the other masked men, now approaching us at an alarming speed. Knowing who they are, I smile, and Jameson's smile mimics mine. He strides toward me with purpose but gets punched by a man with a bald head. He is not one of the paying guests, but as it turns out, he is one of Mr. Martinez's security detail.

I turn around to see Marcus coming at me. He grabs my wrist, and I pull it toward me and push it out of his hold as my other hand hits him with the flat palm of my hand, striking him with a hard upward motion straight to his nose. I feel the crack under my palm. He raises his hands to stop the blood pouring out as I knee him in the balls. He drops forward onto his knees, not knowing what to hold.

Mateo takes his gun out and shoots Marcus, while Emma pushes his collapsing body over the balcony railing, where he falls in a freakish fashion. When he hits the highly polished flooring, his legs and arms are bent unnaturally. His eyes are open, staring into nothing. Blood quickly drains from his lifeless form, pooling underneath and outlining his body.

Mateo has his back turned, so he doesn't see what happens next. Mr. Martinez makes a rush for him. His gun is raised as he points it with his sights locked on Mateo's chest. I hear someone call his name, and he turns to see where the voice came from.

"Mateo. Watch out!"

Mateo turns his head to lock stares with his father, who now has the gun pointed firmly at his chest.

"Son, I thought better of you. I didn't think you, of all people, would betray me. Your own father." He walks closer.

Emma stands still, and I beg her not to move. To cause him to have the trigger pointed at her instead.

"What a disappointment."

We see and hear the gun go off. The bullet is set to hit its target right as Ramón jumps in front of his grandson, pushing him out of the way. The force of the bullet causes Ramón to fall backward and tumble down the stairs. Mateo runs after him, halting his rapid descent.

I watch in disbelief that Ramón saved my brother from his father. I breathe in a deep, meditative breath to calm the anxiety rising up, threatening to throw me into a panic attack. I hear a grunt and open my eyes to see Emma standing over Mr. Martinez.

"You sick fuck. You thought you could sell us. You and your son, Julian, are the worst kind of evil, with no chance for redemption. Now, I can end this, and I hope you meet your son where you both can rot in hell where you belong." Emma holds the gun at Mr. Martinez's head.

He sneers. "You don't have the—"

She fires, as blood splatters over Emma's chest and face. She looks like an avenging goddess covered in her tormentor's blood. She drops the gun and rushes over to me.

"Deep breaths, Evie, I've got you. I've got you like you've always got me." Her hand runs over my forehead as I kneel on the floor, sucking in lungfuls of air without the feeling of my lungs fully expanding. I can't get enough air to breathe, and I'm starting to panic.

"Evie!" I hear a familiar voice as my vision starts to go.

"Emma!"

Jameson and Eduardo are here with us. Eduardo is kissing Emma, despite all the blood covering her chest and face. I am immediately engulfed in a warm embrace, and Jameson's soothing voice helps me calm my breathing.

"Count, Evie. Hold it in for two counts and slowly let it out. Okay, now do it again, baby. I've got you. I'm here. Let's get you both out of here."

I stand on shaky legs. I can take a deep breath once again. I nod. Now, Emma is next to me. She holds onto my hand as we descend the stairs and sees Mateo holding Ramón. Emma runs down the remaining stairs to help him.

"Mateo, how is he?" She drops beside him, feels his skin, and checks for a pulse. Blood coats his arm where a bullet intended for Mateo grazed him, but otherwise, it did not injure him.

Emma rips his shirt and assesses him for other gunshot wounds. "It's just a graze, Mateo, but we should get him to a hospital after that fall. Something could be broken."

Another man in a tuxedo with a skull-painted face approaches.

"Does he need an ambulance?"

Eduardo answers while looking at his fiancée for further direction. "Emma?"

She shakes her head. "I'm not sure of his injuries. If we call an ambulance, it might bring attention to us."

The man talking to Eduardo looks over to me. "The area is secure. No one will say anything, and the property has been searched. We found a dead body in the basement. A middle-aged woman. I believe it was his wife, Mrs. Martinez."

I look over to Emma, and she nods knowingly. I'm glad they are all dead. "Let's get Ramón to a hospital. He saved my brother, and I consider him part of our family now."

Eduardo nods. "Agreed. Let's get him help."

They carry Ramón out of there, and we follow. Jameson holds my hand. I can't help but look at where the band played a while ago and think of how differently this night started.

There is a large SUV waiting for us. Eduardo opens the door, and Emma gets in. Jameson pulls me in and onto his lap. I sit there curled up in his warm embrace as he rubs circles on my back. The vehicle idles. I'm waiting for us to leave when a blaze erupts from my peripheral vision. Jameson's hand tightens around me, and I focus on the beautiful fire that engulfs the house.

"That is how it all started, you know," I say aloud to anyone and no one.

Jameson places a kiss on my neck, trailing up to my ear, and places another soft kiss there. "And this is how it ends," he whispers in my ear.

I bury my head into his chest and cry, and he lets me, just content in holding me tightly to him as I unleash all the emotions I have kept hidden. I cry for my parents, who died in that fire years ago, along with a part of me. Emma thought I was dead, and I might have been if it wasn't for my brother, who saved me that night.

We drive out of the property gates and onto the highway, leaving behind our past forged in fire. The tides turned that day. Julian took everything from us, yet we rose from the ashes and came out stronger after it all.

I once told Emma that when something bad happens and causes everything you once believed in and loved to burn to the ground, you have no choice but to rise with an unbreakable strength amid the flames.

Those intense periods of pain became our black wave—unrelenting. We persevered. We spread our wings and soared away from the past and into our new future, transformed and resilient. Despite it all, we now have a newfound strength to help us heal our family—our forged hearts. The rising, falling, and turning twisted tides broke free, crushing all our enemies in their wake, ensuring that for once, we are finally free.

CHAPTER THIRTY-NINE

JAMESON

"THE SUMMONING" BY SLEEP TOKEN

W e meet Mateo at the hospital and sit in the waiting area waiting for an update. I look over to Emma and wonder if she is thinking it's like déjà vu remembering how Liv, her best friend, received some terrible news about her ex-boyfriend. Now, we wait similarly for news about Ramón's progress.

Ramón saved Mateo, there is no denying that. Anyone can see that he loves his grandson. The countless hours he played chess with him, without any agenda other than spending time and getting to know him. For whatever reason, he had to do what he did. I am sure we will hear about the true reason for his actions, when, or if Ramón makes it. I bet there is more to that story than what we know now. I just hope there are no more lies to be revealed. Now is the time for healing and forgiveness. This self-reflection needs to happen if we are going to get through this together.

A few hours later, a surgeon approaches us, as Mateo stands up. We knew that he was in critical condition due to the severity of his fracture, but I also know that Dax highly recommended an amazing surgeon. When I called him to tell him about Mateo's grandfather falling, he didn't ask any questions; he just called up his buddy, and he went to evaluate him in the emergency room and prepped for surgery a few hours later.

"He did extremely well. I don't anticipate any problems with his recovery," the young surgeon states. "He will be waking up from anesthesia shortly, but why don't you go and get a good night's sleep and return in the morning? I will personally let him know that you were all here, but I sent you home to get some rest. I have to talk to him when he wakes up anyway."

Evie lets go of my hand that I have had a firm lock on, as she walks over to her brother. "Come on, Mattie. Let's go home like the doctor said and we will come back after we get some rest. We still have some things to discuss."

Mateo looks down at his sister and brings her to him in an embrace.

He kisses the top of her head as she rubs his back. "It's okay, Mattie. We are all here, bro, and we love you."

He nods and runs his hand over his face. His eyes are red-rimmed and tired. "Yeah, let's go home."

He walks away, and we all get up off our chairs and follow him out of the hospital.

The ride home is a blur. We decide to all head back to the condo to get some much needed sleep. Gus, Eli, and Philip all return to the safe house with Santi, where he and his daughter should be able to go home. Now that Mr. Martinez and his goons are dead, they don't have to worry about her assaulter returning or the threat to comply with his irrational and demanding requests. That will be one hell of a cleanup, but the fire did help escalate it. All evidence was burned and covered up with the help of our families and Santi, who had his daughter to think about.

We each take a room at the condo. Mateo uses the room that was turned into what looked like a crime scene investigation as his sleeping quarters for the night. I pull Evie into one of the rooms and use the bag Eduardo left out for us to dispose of our clothing.

We must have looked like a Halloween horror show gone wrong with our blood-streaked tuxedos and skull-painted faces, but no one said a thing, and I know that we have Santi, the police chief, to thank for that.

I really hope his daughter finds the peace she needs to heal, and knowing that Oro is gone and won't hurt her anymore should be the start to that healing process.

I drag Evie into the shower, and we bathe with purpose to get all the night's activities off our skin. Pink-tinged water circles the drain until it finally runs clear after a couple of washes. The face paint requires more washes though.

I bring Evie to me and kiss her. "Sleep, baby. I will dispose of these clothes and hand them to Eduardo before I come to bed with you." I close the door behind me and see Eduardo coming out of the office and taking a bag from Mateo. I hand my bag to him, and he smiles.

"I'll take care of this, buddy. Go back to your girl."

I run a hand through my wet hair, exhaling loudly. "Yeah. Alright. See you in the morning?"

He nods and walks out of the condo with the trash bags. I have no idea what he's going to do with them, but he is used to this, and I trust him to do the job right.

I return to the room where Evie is fast asleep. I hear her light, easy breathing as I pull back the covers. I climb into bed with her for the first time in a week, and she shifts toward me like an invisible force drawing her closer. I can't help but to reach for her, bringing her body flush with mine. I nuzzle my nose into her hair and breathe in her smell. I sigh in contentment knowing this is the start of our life together. I just hope there are no more truths to be told, but I suspect that there may be one or two more that need to come to light. There always is.

I open my eyes to morning light streaming through the sheer curtains of the condo, along with the sound of beach waves. It reminds me of a time not long ago when Dax and I met Liv and Emma for the first time on Padre Island for spring break. Who would have thought I'd be in bed with her sister? I am totally in love with her twin.

I lean forward and reach for Evie, but I come up empty. My hand touches the rumpled sheets. Her side is cold, as if she hasn't been there in a while. I lift my head up and hear the sound of talking coming from the kitchen. I throw on some sweats and a hoodie, as I walk with purpose toward the voices.

I see my girlfriend, Eduardo, Emma, and Mateo around the kitchen island with steaming mugs of coffee. A box of Mexican sweet bread is placed in the center, and I see Evie eating her favorite hot-pink colored frosted cake. I walk toward her and kiss her quickly before grabbing my cup of much-needed caffeine.

"How's Ramón?" I ask, taking my full, steamy cup and walking back toward Evie. I sit beside her and pull myself closer to her, decreasing the space between us.

"He was awake and in a little pain but seems to be doing well. Provided everything goes okay, he should be able to come home this week. I will stay with him and help him get around, take him to his appointments, and do any other errands he needs."

Emma reaches for her brother. "If you need any help with Grandpa, let us know." Mateo quirks an eyebrow at her, and she laughs. "What? That's what he is to you, right?" she questions him, and Mateo nods.

"Yes, I suppose he is. It's just weird, you know?"

I speak up. "If you need anything, any one of us will be there to help." I grab Evie's hand, and Mateo tracks the motion.

"Nah, I'm good, but thanks for the offer. I think you all need some alone time."

Emma's face flushes red, and Eduardo laughs. Mateo pushes two envelopes toward Emma and Evie. "Ramón gave me these at the hospital today. One is for you, and the other is for me."

Evie drops my hand and reaches for them. "Do you not want to open yours?"

I look at her and think about the way she worded that. It's almost as if she knows he doesn't, but I wonder to myself why.

He shakes his head. "No, it's from your mom."

Emma cringes at his phrasing. Although she wasn't much of one, she is his mother, too.

"Do you want us to open them, Mateo?" She reaches for the envelopes and picks up one manilla envelope, sizing it up its weight in her hand. "This one seems heavy."

She rips the envelope and empties the contents on the kitchen countertop. The metal object bounces with a loud clatter as it hits the granite.

"What the..." Evie trails off as Emma's hands go to touch the slightly damaged ring.

"Oh, wow!" Emma exclaims.

"It's the ring you got me for my birthday." Evie jumps up off the barstool. She picks up the ring and turns it around, studying the object. "This ring saved me."

Mateo reaches for it, and Evie hands it over to him.

"Yeah, it did. Ramón told me that was how they knew it was you in the morgue where they had to identify the bodies. Nothing was recognizable, but they sure did recognize your ring," Evie huffs out.

"What assholes," Emma chimes in.

"You made me leave it there that night, Mattie."

His gaze is far away, as if relieving the night her parents died and she pretended to be dead. "Yes, I did," Mateo confirms. "Ramón took it off of that poor woman they thought was you and kept it for you. I don't know why he did it, but he said to give it to you. It might help you find the closure you need."

Emma and Evie exchange a look and then glance over at the other package.

"You knew what was in it?"

He nods, but Emma continues. "So what's in the other package?" she asks, and Mateo stares out the window, looking at the waves rolling onto the shore.

"More closure," he says softly, as if to himself.

CHAPTER FORTY

EVIE

"MARY ON A CROSS" BY GHOST

I pick up the envelope and open it. Mateo isn't looking at us, but I can feel his anxiety rise to the surface. I empty the envelope's contents, and a single letter falls out of the folder. It is addressed to my brother.

"Mattie, what is this?" I pick it up and try to hand it to him, since it has his name on it. He doesn't make an attempt to take it from me.

He sighs, his face pained. He looks at me, sadness in his eyes and his body slumped.

"It's from Mom."

I recoil at his use of the word 'Mom.' Again, he used it to identify the woman who raised Emma and me but abandoned her firstborn—our brother. He has gone through great lengths to be there for us and keep us safe. A boy who grew up into a man without a family of his own. His whole life, he lived with the feeling that no one wanted him.

My heart hurts for the boy he was and the man he has become because he did it alone. He might have had our uncle and cousin to talk to, but then he was sent away to boarding school. I could see how hurt he was when he found out Ramón was his grandfather. He had someone around who pretended to be his friend. Someone who wanted to spend time with him but got to know him through false pretenses. Who knows what is real anymore with all the lies our mother kept from us?

I frown, turning my attention back to the letter sitting there mockingly.

"Are you going to read it?" I ask, picking up the letter but not wanting to open it. I feel that Mom wanted him to read it first and then maybe share it with the rest of us. He should read it.

"I don't know if I want to open it." He takes the envelope from me, twirling it in his hand.

"We could burn it?" I arch an eyebrow upward, and Emma snorts.

"Yeah. That seems to be a common theme with us these days. Can we stay away from the fire for a bit?" She looks wearily at Eduardo for comfort. He kisses her forehead, and she beams at him approvingly.

"I'm just kidding." I roll my eyes at their seriousness when I was just trying to make light of a depressing situation. "Well, mostly kidding, but you know, bro, if you don't read it, you'll never know what she had to say. You can't ask her. She's dead. These may be the last words you get."

Emma snorts. "Way to be sensitive about it, Eves." She points to the letter, and Mateo picks it up and surprises us by opening it.

He begins to read it aloud—no hesitation—before he can back out.

My Dearest Son,

If you are reading this, things didn't turn out as planned.

If you are reading this, you probably hate me because I never had the chance to change the events in my life.

If you are reading this, at least I know that you are alive and my death was worth it.

When you were born, it was the best day of my life. The nurse handed you to me, and

you grabbed onto my finger as I held onto you. I never wanted to let you go. I never sent you to the nursery while I was there. I didn't want to because I secretly knew. I knew those precious moments with you might be the only ones I was offered in this life.

I had you all to myself for nine months before I had to let you go. The day I brought you home, my brother told me what I must do. I begged for one more day with you.

If he found out about you, he would have held you over me forever and kept me because he knew I could never leave you. You would never be free. He would have molded you into what he wanted, much like how his other son turned out. You wouldn't have been the kind man who takes care of his sisters and follows them around, protecting them from the evils of this world.

The day that I returned to Brownsville, married with twins, he lost it. He always had the suspicion you existed. I confided in Ramón when I learned about the pregnancy, and he promised to find you one day if something happened to me and give this to you. He promised to be the family that you deserve, and I hope you find the love you deserve because, my sweet boy, you are worthy of ALL the love. Maybe one day, if you have children of your own, you will understand the love I gave up so that you could find yours.

Love Always,

Mom

The room is quiet, and there isn't a dry eye in the kitchen amongst us. I walk over to my brother and hug him. "I don't know what Mom was thinking, Mattie, but I know that whatever she did, she thought she was doing what was best. I have to believe that."

Emma strides over and embraces our brother from the other side. "I love you, and am so thankful you are in my life. I may disagree with what Mom did, but if Mr. Martinez was anything like his son, Julian, then I can understand some of the abuse she underwent to have to make the difficult decisions to keep you away from that toxicity. I'd rather die than be married to Julian."

Mateo nods, taking it all in. "I can't imagine what would have happened, but I can't dwell on this anymore. This letter proves that in her own mind, she was validated in abandoning me. I'm so tired of living in the past. I want to put this all behind me and live in the present. I want to forgive and live for my future. I know what we have to do."

Arriving at the cemetery after visiting the liquor store and supermarket, we loaded up on all our favorite food and beverages. We followed each other in two vehicles, along with Phil, Eli, and Gus, who insisted on coming with us. We aren't entirely used to not having to watch our back because there is always a threat in this line of business. You learn to look over your shoulder and anticipate the unexpected, if that makes sense. Clear as mud, my father would say.

TWISTED TIDES

Last heard from Santi, he took his daughter to get some much-needed counseling to help her heal. He told us everything had been handled and not to worry.

After this weekend, we will be returning to Houston and to the lives we were living before this final act. What we are looking forward to the most is our future—being united and spending time with our family.

We unload the SUVs and bring out the table, chairs, and food. We get everything set up, and much like in our celebrations in Día de los Muertos, we have a brief reunion with our deceased relatives where they are forever laid to rest.

We all sit around drinking and getting to know one another. Emma and I told stories about growing up—our family traditions. We compared stories of being in Mexico with our uncle. We learned so much about our brother. What it was like growing up for him. It seems that he had a good life, and that after our grandparents weren't around to, our Uncle Andrés and tía gave him the love he needed growing up. They wanted him to learn the way of their world, so they sent him off to boarding school, which was more of a military-type training. He would be prepared to become one of my uncle's soldiers when he returned.

Our uncle told him about us and little did we know that he would have him be our protector as well. If he hadn't been there to save us all those years ago, we might not have fully recovered from that kind of mindfuck trauma that happens with abuse and assault.

As the day turns into evening, the shade of the live oak trees provides a large canopy with its branches overhead. Emma, Mateo, and I stand up from our seats and gather in front of our mother's grave. Emma and I place a kiss on our hands and put it on their father's headstone.

Eduardo stands and walks over to Emma, offering her his hand. I feel Jameson behind me. He doesn't come forward, unsure of his position at this moment, but I want him to understand he belongs with me as long as he'll have me. I lean into his strong, hard frame, as he wraps his arms around me. Eli, Gus, and Philip begin to pack up the items for us to take them to the vehicles, so that we can make it back to the condo before it gets too late.

I extend my hand out to my sister like we've done to each other our whole lives. I take out the silver ring she had made for me for a birthday present. I begin to talk to my mom and start our final goodbyes.

"This ring saved my life, Mom. I was supposed to have died in that fire the night you passed away. In a way, I feel that a part of me did. It wasn't until I met someone that I can finally let go and surrender myself to being loved. I need to fully feel all the emotions I have kept suppressed for so long. We were forged in fire and came out stronger on the other end after all."

I bend down and grab the little spade the guys left for me while they packed everything away. I dig a hole into the ground where their gravestone rests. Under their names, the inscription reads: *Forever forged in our hearts.'*

I place the ring into the hole, and Emma covers it with dirt. It rests between the two headstones of my parents. We hold hands, smiling at each other, and back away.

Mateo steps forward and bends down to my mother's grave, touching her name. "Whatever your reasons were, Mom, I just want you to know that I forgive you. I know that in your heart, you believed you were doing the right thing. Maybe if circumstances were different, you would have returned to being my mother, but that time was taken from us. All I can do is move on and heal. I have to forgive you to move on. Thank you for giving me my life, and I promise to do something with it to make you and my family proud, but most of all, I am going to live and love every day I have on this earth." He places a kiss on the stone and stands.

I smile at him through tear-stained eyes, and I don't have to look at Emma to know that she is doing the same thing.

Eduardo clears his throat. "I'd like to say something if I could."

Emma tenses, and Eduardo gives her hand a squeeze, reassuring her that it will be okay, like he does frequently.

"I just want you to know, Mr. and Mrs. Taylor, that I love your daughter. I have always loved her, and I am going to marry her. I forgive you for keeping us apart, but I hope you find peace in knowing that I would give my life to keep her safe and give up my own for hers."

Emma reaches up to Eduardo and kisses him.

"Marry me, Emma."

Emma pulls back to look up at him. "We are already engaged, Eduardo." She giggles, not understanding his words, but I know what he means.

The look in his eyes says he is done waiting.

"Marry me *now*, Emma."

It's not a question, even though he poses it as one. She looks at him, her head tilted. Assessing.

"When?" she asks.

"As soon as possible," he answers just as quickly.

She beams a full smile at him. "Yes, I'll marry you whenever you'd like me to."

He picks her up in one fluid motion and twirls her around. He places her back on the ground, kissing her. "Did you hear that, guys? We're getting married."

PART III

THE FUTURE

EPILOGUE

"NOTHING ELSE MATTERS" BY METALLICA
"DANCE MACABRE" BY GHOST

THE WEDDING

We are gathered in the church for Emma and Eduardo's wedding. He meant it when he said he wanted to get married right away. His manager at his gym, Helena, helped Emma organize everything. They both had similar tastes in music, so it wasn't hard to get contacts who could meet the requests of what I can only describe as a goth wedding. Eduardo didn't care what wedding he had as long as he was married to the love of his life. It's been a long time coming, and I can't deny him the opportunity to marry her right now. One thing our past has taught us is that life is short. Make the best of it while you can because, even though they were given a second chance, we know that is rare.

I look out to the crowd gathered here, and I think we did well. The band is the same one Eduardo used to replace the original band the night we were going to be sold off at Mr. Martinez's party. I love their style, and they eagerly agreed to the handsome fee Emma's soon-to-be husband offered them for the day.

I look in the mirror at my deep blood-red dress. It's gorgeous, but not as gorgeous as my sister's. I can't wait to see Eduardo's reaction to her as she walks down the aisle. Her friends made the trip up from Corpus to be here, and some are bridesmaids. Eduardo has Jameson, our brother, Gus, Eli, and Philip as his selected groomsmen. They are all in tuxedos, much like on the night of the party. The jacket has silk embroidered roses, and Eduardo is wearing a ridiculous top hat.

"Oh God, is that black eyeliner?" Emma laughs behind me. She looks nervous.

"Are you ready?" I ask her, and she smiles. She looks over to Ainsley, Val, and Piper who are also wearing blood-red dresses.

Liv comes up to her. "Hey, babe. How are you holding up?"

She shrugs. "Nervous, but excited." There is a twinkle in her eye that always leads to mischief. "I wish I had a drink."

I bring the champagne bottle over and pour us each a glass.

"Ah, my wonderful sister." She sings my praises.

I raise my glass to hers. "To amazing second chances."

She pouts. "Don't make me cry, Eves. It's too much black eyeliner."

We take our drinks and down the champagne. Liv puts hers down without a drop being taken from the glass. Emma raises an eyebrow, and Liv shrugs.

Emma laughs, tossing her head back. "I knew it." Her hands go flying up in the air for emphasis. She throws herself at Liv. "Love you, bestie."

Liv hugs her back. "Love you, Em."

Helena comes through the door at us. "It's almost time. Are you guys ready?"

We all line up in anticipation of the procession starting. She takes the bridesmaids and groomsmen and lines them up. We are ready to start when Helena, the promoted wedding planner, gives us the okay. I hear the band begin, and the song "Nothing Else Matters" by Metallica begins to play. Fucking perfection.

I'm paired up with Jameson, and Liv is paired up with our brother. They go out first, and we follow. The rest of the party starts down the aisle as we take our places by the makeshift altar. Eduardo waits patiently, but the nervous energy is palpable. He is ready to have his bride.

She walks down the aisle, escorted by our Uncle Andrés. She is utter perfection. If there was ever a more beautiful bride, I would call them a liar. She is in a white lace dress that bells out with a black lace bodice. There are black embroidered flowers on the bottom part of the dress. She has a black choker with diamond hearts and earrings to match. Her bouquet of roses is a deep red to match the bridesmaid's dresses. And her red-soled shoes.

As she walks to Eduardo, she sees tears in his eyes. He swipes them away, not caring if anyone sees him.

I steal a glance at Jameson, and he stares at me. I bite my lip, and he licks his lip in response. I can't wait to get him alone after the wedding. I've done nothing but wedding planning.

Eduardo removes his hat as Emma stands beside him, and our uncle gives her a kiss on the cheek before walking away to take his designated seat.

The officiant begins the wedding, and there isn't a dry eye in the place. As the ceremony concludes, Eduardo doesn't need to be told twice to kiss his bride. There is a roar of applause and whistles as he kisses her in the most inappropriate fashion in front of all that are gathered to celebrate this joyous day.

We walk out of the venue and into the planetarium where the reception will take place. Jameson and I are hand in hand, following the guests.

The night sky is illuminated with a big moon in the background. There are more lights lit along the walls of the room to offer more than the provided twinkling of the stars. There are also lights on each table. The band is set up on the stage, with a large dance floor in the middle. The cake is off in the distance, and the ghoulish character bride and groom are on top.

The band announces the bride and groom to the crowd, and there are cheers and whoops as Emma and Eduardo take their place for the first song as husband and wife.

The band breaks into the song by Emma's favorite band Ghost, "Dance Macabre." Eduardo holds her hand and leads her to the dance floor. He pulls her into his embrace, swings her out, and brings her back to him. She walks around him in a circle as he tracks her with his eyes in a suggestive move. She touches his cheek and, as if in a trance, brings her into him again and kisses her as they dance in one another's arms in a solid embrace.

We return to the table and see Mateo is talking to his grandfather who is in a wheelchair and is giving off pissy vibes at being wheeled around. I am trying to listen in on their conversation, but soon a lady walks in, and Mateo freezes mid-sentence. Ramón looks over at the two with amusement. He wheels himself over to the table as they stand there staring at one another.

I hit Jameson's shoulder. "Hey, who's that?"

He looks in the direction I am pointing, where Mateo is trying to talk to a woman who is trying her best to avoid him, then leaves him there talking mid-sentence. He calls after her, but she continues to walk off as he follows her out of the planetarium.

"Hm. That's interesting." Jameson laughs. "Yeah, that's Ramón's nurse from the agency that has been helping him get around."

"Why do I get the feeling that there is more to that story, Jameson?" I lift an eyebrow up to him in question.

He chuckles, bringing my chair closer to him. "Well, because with you guys, there always is?"

I go to protest, but my words are silenced with a kiss.

"Jameson, did you just shut me up with a kiss?" I ask jokingly.

He stands and brings me to my feet with him. He looks around. "Actually, I'd like to shut you up with my cock."

I laugh, then stop, rethinking that. "Let's go."

We take off to find a place where we can be alone, when we see Mateo and Ramón's nurse sneaking into a room of their own.

I look over to Jameson. "I think they have the same idea."

We walk into a hall and see a door open that leads to a room with books lining the walls on astronomy. The fireplace is lit for ambiance, creating a soft glow throughout the spacious interior. I take it all in, feeling the warmth as Jameson comes over to stand in front of me.

I look up at him, feeling the intensity of his stare. "So now that you have me here, Jameson, what will you do with me?" I rest my hand on his white dress shirt. His hard muscles flex under my hand involuntarily.

"I'm just glad that everything is all over." He exhales in relief. He brings me closer to him, and I look into his eyes, which are so full of love and adoration.

"Oh, Jameson," I reply. I grab the back of his neck, pulling him to me. "We've been over this." His lips hover over mine. "I have a feeling that this is just the beginning."

I can feel the smile ghost over his lips. He pulls me to him again and kisses me. He pulls back slightly, looking into my eyes. "Our new beginning."

THE END

THANK YOU FOR READING!!!

Did you enjoy reading *Twisted Tides*? If you did, I would be grateful if you could please consider taking a second to leave a review on one, or all of your choices below. Reviews help to make me a better writer, and I appreciate your words and constructive criticism!

Love you all,

L. Renee Richard

Want to see where it all began? Then enjoy
an excerpt from the book:
Liv and Dax's story.

"Waves of You" now available on Amazon
Paperback, E-book, and free on KU.
https://a.co/d/e2WJp5o

WAVES
OF
YOU

L. RENÉE RICHARD

Liv is tired of the uncertainty of their relationship.
She has a plan.
Meet Brodie at the beach.
Clarify their relationship.
What she doesn't plan on doing while working her shift in the ER is
meeting Dax, her swoon-worthy patient. They plan to meet up the next
day, celebrating the last days of spring break on Padre Island.
There's just one problem—Brodie, her childhood best friend and recent
ex-boyfriend. When she receives a video of him with another girl, she
knows that they are not getting back together.
One last day at the beach is the most memorable of her life—the
sparks between Liv and Dax are undeniable. The future held so many
possibilities. That is until they witness Brodie's traumatic accident.
Pulled in two directions, Liv must choose between her new feelings for
Dax, and Brodie, someone who had always been there for her.
She makes a choice, but is it the right one?

Good friends, oh good friends we have lost
Along the way
In this great future, you can't forget your past
So dry your tears, I say

-Bob Marley

PROLOGUE

I sit in the waiting room surrounded by my friends and Brodie's family, watching the hospital staff going in and out through the operating room doors, hoping for an update on what happened after Brodie was rushed into the OR.

Another patient is being moved down the hall on a hospital bed, an IV bag of fluids dripping in sync with the beeping monitor as he passes by. Every sound is intensified, every smell more potent.

Dax is by my side. His thumb rubs circles in a continuous soothing manner on the top of my hand. The rhythmic motion settles me as the weight of his calloused fingers offers me the stability my hand needs not to shake. The fact that he hasn't left my side speaks volumes about his character. The way he handled the situation at the beach. The authoritarian personality and calm with which he controlled the situation—the accident. If I weren't so shell-shocked, I would have been turned on. If it had not been Brodie there on the wet sand, limp and unconscious. If a million things were different.

Brodie's parents are here. It's a stressful time for all of us without dealing with the awkwardness of his parents' divorce and the bitterness between the two parties. His dad must have flown down the interstate to get here in record time.

Everyone sits in silence, waiting to hear the outcome of Brodie's surgery. Finally, after what seems like an eternity, a man wearing blue scrubs accompanied by a female in similar attire exits the operating room doors and asks for his family. His parents walk down the hall and stand within view to receive the much-awaited results. It's as if time stands still, and it's so silent you can hear a pin drop. Except for the steps on the freshly waxed, tiled floor, no other sound exists.

The surgeon speaks, and then Brodie's mom raises her hands to her mouth and a sob escapes, relinquishing a terrible cry of pain. Brodie's dad just shakes his hands around, asking spitfire questions, not allowing a moment's pause for an answer. The surgeon just shakes his head in acknowledgment. His dad puts his hands up to his eyes and lowers his head. The surgeon touches his shoulder and says something to them before walking back to our group. I rise from my chair as though I am being pulled toward this invisible force.

As I stand, the surgeon stops at our group and says, "Is there a Liv here?"

I stare, stunned and unable to speak. I feel a nudge from my side.

The surgeon begins to speak, and I don't hear what he says. He repeats, "Brodie is awake and was asking for you specifically. He wants to see you."

I gasp. A breath let out that I didn't realize I was holding as it rushes out. I feel Dax bring my hand to his lips and gently kiss it. The heat of his mouth makes me shudder. He releases my hand without saying a word, telling me to go. I follow the doctor without looking back. I know he won't be there when I return to the waiting room. This is goodbye.

CHAPTER ONE

LIV

Something about driving with the windows down while cruising over the causeway makes me smile. The second I lower the window, the familiar scent of saltwater washes through the car. The beach has always been my happy place, and I was damn lucky to find an apartment and job so close to it.

While I make my way down the highway toward work, I steal glances at the view. The waves, the people sunning themselves on the beach, the surfers in the water, and even the seagulls squawking overhead make me smile. I drink it all in for a moment... that is until the hot-as-fuck blast of steam assaults my face and I'm ripped back to reality.

God, it's hot as Hades today. I pull at my shirt as the sweat trickles down into my cleavage. I turn off on the next exit ramp and pull into the employee parking lot of the Bayside Hospital Emergency Department.

"Great," I mutter to myself. Quickly looking around, I see multiple ambulances parked in the designated bays. It's going to be a busy night.

"What else is new?" I breathe out on a long, exaggerated sigh.

This is the norm for the start of any weekend, but this isn't just any weekend. It's spring break on Padre Island—guaranteed to supply an endless amount of ER visits from sun-induced dehydration to broken bones to college kids who have one (or five) too many beers. Lucky me.

With my work bag slung over my shoulder and iced coffee in hand, I make my way to the front doors. I say a silent prayer and hope that if I hide my badge and don't make eye contact, then no one will stop and ask me anything. This is my reasoning, at least, to not be bothered with a million questions before I start my shift.

I walk past the triage desk in the emergency room and subtly scan the packed waiting room. It's already filled with patients. I head to my locker, throw my bag in and make a spot for my lunch in the fridge, gently squishing it into a packed space.

Geez, I hope my leftovers from dinner last night don't fall out because that would royally suck. I had blackened catfish the previous night, and I plan on reheating it later. Nothing worse than stinky fish in the lunchroom, I chuckle to myself. Besides, there are worse smells in this place.

I keep a firm hold on my iced coffee as I leave the break room. I wish I could shoot this stuff straight into my circulatory system to get one immediate, gratifying caffeine rush. Lord knows I need it this evening. Working the night shift can be challenging, but not even the white noise produced by my oscillating fan could put me in my usual death-like sleep. I blame the grounds crew mowing at my apartment complex for four hours straight for my lack of energy today.

Although I'd like to blame it all on that, it isn't the real reason I had shity sleep. I've had a ton of crap on my mind lately, namely the unpleasant subject of my current boyfriend, Brodie. Being in a perpetual state of limbo with this guy is just dragging me down. Our relationship status is something we decided to chat about this weekend. It shouldn't be this hard. We've known each other practically our whole lives.

Before I go too far down that rabbit hole, I shove these thoughts to the back of my mind.

First things first, I just have to get through this shift. I walk to the nurses' station, take one last swig of my highly caffeinated drink, and reluctantly place it in the cubby. It sits among countless other beverages, condensation pooling all around the surface.

The assignment board is already updated. I scan it quickly and begin my hunt for Emma. I need to get a report on her patients so she can get out of this place. At least one person will be having fun tonight. Why did I sign up for this shift? Oh yeah, I need the money.

I shift my gaze down one of the corridors and spot who I'm looking for. Blond hair piled on top of her head in a messy bun, Emma is not only a nurse that I happen to be relieving at shift change but also one of my best friends. As high energy as ever, I can hear her excitedly babbling to one of our attendings. Her hand gestures raised above her head are so fast that I think she may accidentally smack him in the face. There's a reason people refer to her as the Energizer Bunny.

We both took the sign-on bonus offered at the hospital after our nursing school graduation a couple of years ago. She took a job on the twelve-hour day shift, while I decided to take the opposite twelve-hour night shift. My decision to take the less-desirable shift allowed me to enroll in classes for my bachelor's degree. Classes during the day, work at night. Grueling schedule for sure, but it's getting me where I want to be, so I'm sucking it up and embracing the chaos. My social life has taken a hit between school and work, but I'll graduate with my BSN in a couple of months and then continue to Houston, where I've been accepted into nurse practitioner school. Soon I'll be leaving this town and moving on to bigger and better things.

Emma catches my eye, and I nod to let her know I'm here.

As I walk toward her, she flashes me a huge smile. "Thank God you're here. It's been hell today."

I can't help but stifle a laugh. "You say that every shift."

She carefully counts the remaining narcotics in the bin and enters the correct count before closing it. "I only say it because it's true." She giggles. "I hope your night is better, but looking at the stack of pending charts..." she trails off and gives me a sympathetic frown.

Ready to brave the shift, I chuckle and head toward the nurse's station. "Judging by the waiting room, I think I'm forever and eternally fucked tonight. Let's hope nothing memorable happens."

Emma gently squeezes my shoulder before shoving some charts into my hands. "Come on, Liv, I'll give you a report on my patients. Room ten has some pain meds ordered, and I'll give her those before I leave. Can you reassess her pain in a bit?"

Thank goodness for Emma. The woman looked extremely uncomfortable when I peeked in as we passed her room. I do not want her to wait for her pain medication until after our shift change.

"I'll be back in a few minutes to give you a report on the rest of my patients. The sooner I do, the sooner I can get my drink on tonight." With that, she turns on her heels and prances down the hall.

Ten minutes later, Emma pops back up by my elbow. I'm only half-listening as she gives me the sign-out on her patients.

"The labs on the patient in room eight just came back, and room two is..." She can tell by the look on my face that I'm in no mood for work. "You know we're all going to miss you tonight, right? It's the first time in a long while that we've all been able to get together."

I don't need the reminder. The fact that I am missing out on tonight is a bit of a sore spot. Our mutual high school friends are returning again for the continuous spring break beach party. The days at the beach, sea sculptures, and live entertainment are just some things that happen on the island during this carnivalesque time.

"You have no idea how jealous I am right now, Em."

She makes a melodramatic pouty face while holding both arms out for a hug.

I give her a quick squeeze, feeling utterly deflated. For a second, I consider telling my manager I'm not feeling well so I can go home. But my stupid conscience won't allow it. I will only call out from my shift if I'm dead or dealing with some other near-death experience. I'm not sure if even that wouldn't require a call-out. As tired (and jealous) as I am, missing work is not an option. I need every penny for graduate school; the move to Houston won't be cheap.

"I'll see them tomorrow, Em. Actually, in less than twenty-four hours, you know that." As positive as I try to sound on the outside, I'm internally cursing this shift. "Well, I want lots of pics tonight to make me feel like I am there with you guys."

"Of course," Emma quickly replies. "You know we will. I expect to meet up with the whole gang later tonight, and I will send pics of that. You better go straight to bed after your shift and get the best four hours of sleep because I am picking your ass up by noon, got it?"

I laugh. "I expect a large iced coffee and preferably a greasy breakfast burrito."

She laughs as she grabs her bags and heads toward the door. "Naturally, only the breakfast of champions for my bestie," she says over her shoulder. "I'll see you tomorrow!" And with that, she grabs her purse and giant water bottle and heads for the door.

I shuffle my feet in dramatic flair. Yup, I am definitely not ready for this shift.

As soon as she leaves, I spot Dr. Hall, the handsome thirty-eight-year-old ER physician with a reputation for flirting with the staff.

"Hi, Dr. Hall."

"Hey, Liv. Glad you're on tonight." He throws me a wink.

Typically, that little gesture would have perked me up, but even that doesn't help my mood. "Thanks," I reply. "I've got some updates. The labs are back on the patient in room eight, and the completed chart for review is queued first in line when you get a chance."

I am met with kind but tired eyes, almost reflecting my own. "Great," he mutters as he quickly goes to retrieve the chart.

I check on my other patients and quickly chart and update vital signs. Dr. Hall comes over and informs me that he printed out the discharge instructions for bay eight, and they can go. At least someone is getting out of here quickly tonight.

I gather all the instructions and check to see if she needs anything else before making my way over there. The drape is still closed, so I call out her name before I peek in.

Mrs. Shea replies, "Just a minute, dear. I am just pulling on my shirt."

I wait patiently for her to finish and help her to the waiting room. As I pass the discharge instructions to her, we see her husband pulling up in front of the entrance. As I watch her drive away, I can't help but think about what the next patient will bring.

I let the ED tech know that the bay is empty so they can clean up the room and prepare it for the next patient. Our department is certainly busy, but thank goodness it's efficient. I grab the following chart in the queue and look at the chief complaint—ankle pain, related to a surfing injury.

"Well, that's a total surprise," I mutter as I make my way to the waiting room and open the door. "Dax Johnson?" I call out.

No reply. I see two guys sitting in the chairs wearing board shorts, T-shirts, and flip-flops, chatting animatedly with each other. When they get up, I bet there will be sand all over the seats too.

A quick scan of them shows one has a bruised and swollen ankle. That has to be him. But as my eyes wander up from the ankle in question, I notice the rest of him. I feel myself start to zone out a bit as they continue their conversation, and my eyes drift from his ankle up to his legs and over his lean body. He must be the most attractive man I have ever seen. Around six foot four inches, toned, tan, and totally delicious. His long, muscular legs are streaked with blond hair. His T-shirt is tight against his chest and shows off his narrow waist. His shorts sit low on his hips, just low enough that I catch the shadow of a V pointing straight to where I'm trying *not* to look.

I realize both are still oblivious to my announcement and the fact that I've been so blatantly staring at them. I look away as my cheeks begin to heat. I notice a couple of patients smirking at my lack of subtlety. I give myself a mental slap and call the name again.

"Dax Johnson?" My voice comes out an octave too high, and I pray they overlooked that too.

I see the pair halt their conversation, and one raises his arm. "That's me, coming."

His deep voice pierces right through me and sends a wave of butterflies straight into my stomach. He tries to get up but stumbles almost immediately, trying to avoid putting weight on his ankle.

I go to grab a wheelchair just in case he needs it. When I return, I see he's made his way across the waiting room—holding on to his friend's arm for support. It's then I notice his arms. Thick, muscular arms with every nurse's dream of pipe veins running up his forearms. If a forearm porn show were a thing, he would be the star. I lift my vision to his face and catch him staring at me with amusement.

Was I that obvious? My face immediately flushes with embarrassment, and it becomes about a hundred degrees too hot in the room. My blood seems to have been rerouted and is collecting in my now scorching face.

Taking a deep breath, I try to regain an ounce of professionalism and look up. I'm instantly met with the most exquisite pair of penetrating blue eyes. Wow, is there anything wrong with him? Oh yeah, his ankle.

He stares at me with such intensity that I feel he can almost read my thoughts as his gaze also shoots to his ankle. I immediately look away in embarrassment because he knows what I was thinking.

"Do you need a wheelchair?" I ask in the most squeaky-sounding voice I have ever heard myself make to further my humiliation.

He looks at the wheelchair and then back at me, smiling. As if he couldn't make me feel any giddier, a dimple appears on his left cheek, and I feel a slight warmth spread between my legs.

I try to move forward but feel my feet locked in place. It's as if my shoes are cemented to the waiting room floor. Damn, can I be any more pathetic?

I clear my throat and try again. "Do you need a wheelchair?"

He shakes his head, and I feel his unwavering stare, but I avoid eye contact this time. "No thanks, I can walk," he says while grabbing on to his friend's arm for support.

I go to put the wheelchair back and hit the button for the automatic door.

He begins to walk, and I hear him say, "This might take me a minute."

I reply over my shoulder, "That's fine. You can take your time with me. I mean, umm, no need to rush." I immediately rush around the corner and smack my forehead. Someone just shoot me now and end my word vomit. "We don't have far to go," I add. "Just around the corner."

We make it to the empty bay, and I notice that his friend hasn't come with him. I grab a hospital gown from the cabinet and hand it to him. As he reaches out for the gown, his fingers brush my palm. The touch is soft but electric. The zap immediately shoots through my hand into my body, making me tingle all over. Jerking my hand away and wondering if he felt that too, I take a step back to close the curtain and give him privacy. But let's be honest, I just need some space to pull myself together.

"I'll let you change and be back in a bit to check on you."

Before I can leave, I hear that deep voice say, "Miss?"

I pop my head back through the curtain.

He glances at the hospital attire with a questioning look on his face. "Do I really need to put this on? I mean, it's just my ankle, and I am wearing shorts. I'll probably just need an x-ray, right? Quick wet read by the radiologist, and I'll be on my way." He flashes me that dimple again.

I stare at him dumbfounded. He's right, and I realize I've been on autopilot, distracted by his unyielding gaze and that damn dimple. "Um, yeah. You can stay in your clothes." I manage, fighting the urge to see more of his body.

His use of medical terminology and willingness to question instructions intrigue me. Most patients comply without a word. Is he in the medical field? I want to ask, but I'm too flustered, desperate to escape before my blushing face betrays me.

"Have a seat on the stretcher, and I'll get you a pillow to elevate your leg and an ice pack while you wait. My name is Liv, and I'll be your nurse this evening. You're right about the x-ray. I'll go throw the order in now, so you won't have to be here any longer than necessary. How is your pain right now?"

I'm surprised I could get out a couple of coherent sentences in a row. Autopilot phrases I commonly use seem to be taking over my thinking. He looks at me with those smoking blue eyes, and I then notice lusciously thick lashes surrounding them.

Staring fixedly at me, he says, "Not too bad."

Why do guys have such thick eyelashes while women have to pay for that stuff?

He slumps back onto the stretcher and brushes his hand through his hair, still not looking away. It makes my breath hitch, and I look down at his leg to hopefully break the tension in the room.

"Good, then I'll have one of the techs bring you that pillow and an ice pack."

As I begin turning away for the second time, he stops me by saying, "Liv, I thought *you* were going to bring me those items."

I glance up and see the amusement on his face. He knows that I find him attractive. Now he is just fucking with me. Cocky much? I need to get it together.

With as much disinterest as I can muster, I turn back around and say, "I'll try, but otherwise, someone will be back shortly. If I cannot make it back sooner, that is." Before I close the curtain, I add more sway to my ass. I might as well play this up.

I head straight for the nurse's station to grab a tech and ask them to bring the items over. I'd like to avoid further embarrassment if possible.

I pick up my iced coffee and take a few large gulps. My mouth is dry, and my heart is hammering in my chest. I wonder if he feels the same way. Maybe it's all in my head? Either way, it's going to be a long night.

ABOUT THE AUTHOR

L. Renee Richard is a Hispanic author who lives in rural New England with her family. She's a born and raised South Texan girl who implements BIPOC characters into her books imbued with her cherished Hispanic culture. She is an avid reader, complete with her never-ending TBR, and a romantic at heart who appreciates a strong female main character and a good book boyfriend in the books she reads or writes. She loves summers in New England, sitting on the beach with a book, driving with the windows down through rural roads on cool autumn nights, and iced matcha lattes. Her books promise angsty romance where the journey to a happily ever after isn't always easy, but it's worth the trip.

ACKNOWLEDGMENTS

To my readers–Thank you for taking a chance on my book. I know that you can read any book, but the fact that you took the time out of your busy lives to read my story means the world to me. The months I poured into writing Black Wave and then finishing the conclusion of the Forged Hearts Series with Twisted Tides–finally holding a copy of this book–was a journey worth taking. Your support and kind words helped to see it through.

To my family– Thank you for allowing me time to sit in my office and write. I looked ridiculous cheering at your games while talking into my headset. You're so proud of me and my accomplishment of completing another novel. I see how excited you got when I told you it was done. Instead of asking what we will do, you ask when I will finish the next one. You believe in me when I get discouraged and don't believe in myself. For that, I am so grateful for your love.

To my PA–Morgan Evans, you are by far the best, and I'd be lost without you. Your feedback, comments, and help with all author things is invaluable. I am so glad I found you and am lucky to have your reassuring words and solutions to problems that arise. I appreciate you so much.

To my close friends–my work buddies who know I write spicy books and ask me about it in hushed tones in the lounge. I am glad that I am the reason you began reading romance novels. I thoroughly enjoyed our books and giving you recs, like candy you devoured each one. My besties Jess, Kris, and Lauren: you are always around when I need you, and your support and love are unwavering. My spicy book club, The Crowned Jewels: I hope one day we can finish a book together, but I do love a good brunch punch to match our gossip and inappropriate commentary.

KEEP IN TOUCH WITH L. RENEE RICHARD

Follow me on my socials

Author page:
www.authorlreneerichard.com

Amazon:
http://www.amazon.com/author/lreneerichard

Facebook page:
https://www.facebook.com/Author-L-Renee-Richard-105887815914160

Instagram:
https://instagram.com/l.renee.richard?igshid=OGQ5ZDc2ODk2ZA==

TikTok:
TikTok @l.renee.richard

Join my hype team:
https://forms.gle/9cnsA4gSfbezY7a17

Sign up for my newsletter:
https://mailchi.mp/authorlreneerichard/signup